ECLIPSE
HEART

ECLIPSE HEART

BOOK 2
KUZNETZOV BRATVA DUET SERIES
MYA GREY

ASIN: B0DLNN58QT

ISBN: 9798312361933

Imprint: Independently published

I didn't realize you were mending my heart, piece by piece, until I could finally feel it beating again—for you.

Also by Mya Grey

Belov Bratva Series

Unholy Bound (Book 1)

Shadow Bound (Book 2)

Kuznetsov Bratva Series

Onyx Heart (Book 1)

Eclipse Heart (Book 2)

Bond by Morozov Bratva Series

Silken Chains (Book 1)

Velvet Chains (Book 2)

Ivankov Legacy (Standalone) Edition Series

The Oath of Seduce (Book 1)

The Thorns of Seduce (Book 2)

The Veils of Seduce (Book 3)

Ivankov Bratva Trilogy Series

Twisted Seduction (Book 1)

Tangled Seduction (Book 2)

Fateful Seduction (Book 3)

Brutal Kings Series

Series I

(Dario & Nikki)

Owned (Book 1)

Craved (Book 2)

Ruled (Book 3)

Possessed (Book 4)

Desired (Book 5)

OR

Brutal Kings, Series I

(Complete Boxset)

Series II

(Mateo & Andy)

Dazzle (Book 1)

Charm (Book 2)

Blaze (Book 3)

Flare (Book 4)

Glitter (Book 5)

OR

Brutal Kings, Series II

(Complete Boxset)

Series III

(Raoul & Emma)

Captive (Book 1)

Savage (Book 2)

Sinner (Book 3)

Crown (Book 4)

Vow (Book 5)

OR

Brutal Kings, Series III

(Complete Boxset)

The Broken Prince Series

Chased (Book 1)

Seduced (Book 2)

Claimed (Book 3)

Desired (Book 4)

Craved (Book 5)

Loved (Book 6)

OR

The Broken Prince Series Collection

(Complete Boxset)

Content Warning

This book contains mature themes and explicit content that may not be suitable for all readers. Please be advised that the following topics are depicted or discussed: graphic violence, self-harm, domestic abuse, sexual situations, emotional abuse, physical abuse, and sexual assault.

Reader discretion is strongly advised.

Glossary & Translations

Russian to English

Jebat' eto der'mo (Fuck this shitt)

Suka (Bitch)

Blyat (Fuck/Damn)

Mudaks (Assholes)

Chyort voz'mi (Damn it!)

Yob tvoyu mat (Fuck your mother)

Pakhan (Boss/Crime boss)

Devchonka (Girl)

Dedushka (Grandpa)

Tigritsa (Tigress)

Konspirativnaya kvartira (Safehouse)

Ya v etom pizdets kak uveren (I'm f***ing sure about this)

Krasotka/Kiska (Cutie/Kitten)

Krasavchik (Handsome guy)

Solnyshko (Sunshine)

Neukrotimaya kotyonok (Untamable kitten)

Moya (Mine)

Ty takoy chertovski uzkiy (You're so damn tight)

Pizda (Pissy)

Cyka blyad (Fucking bitch)

Ty konchayesh' so mnoy (You're coming with me)

Khachu uvidet' kak ty konchayesh' (I want to see you come)

Ty naprosivayesh'sya (You're asking for it)

Zadnitsa (Ass)

Da (Yes)

Kakogo chyorta (What the hell)

Syn (Son)

Svolochi/Svoloch (Bastards/Bastard)

Snizu (Below/Down)

Bozhe moy (My God)

Syn suki (Son of a bitch)

Zaebis' (Fucking awesome)

Myshka (Little mouse)

Kotik (Kitty)

Khuy (Dick)

Golodny (Hungry)

Myaso (Meat)

Kosti (Bones)

Chto (What)

Ty sdurél (Are you crazy?)

Govno (Shit/Crap)

Pizdets (Fucked up)

Chert (Damn/Devil)

Poshol na khuy (Fuck off)

Ahhooi (Hey! Rude tone)

Peedor (Faggot)

Japanese *to* English

Bakayarou (You idiot/You fool)

Kutabare (Go to hell/Drop dead)

Italian *to* English

Bella signora (Beautiful lady – Italian)

One

Leonid

M^{eow?}

M I toss my phone onto the desk, annoyed as hell. Why does it even matter that the kid called me like I'm a cat?

Suka, why am I even thinking about it?

He's what? Three? Four?

Pizda. Four?

I freeze, my mind grinding to a halt.

Four... That's... the time. That night. The one I've shoved deep into the back of my mind. Her. Red. Clara. *Govno.*

I can still feel how her body trembled as my cock moved inside her, her eyes filled with lust behind her mask. She eagerly licked her lips, craving more.

Yob tvoyu mat'.

I shake my head, trying to clear the memory, but it sticks to me like smoke.

No. *It can't be.*

It's impossible. I shouldn't care. I don't care.

But the timing. The way the kid looked at me. The way he looks like... Damn it. I can't even finish that thought.

I stand up, pacing. *Patience*—it's what I'm good at. It's how I survived this long. But when it comes to this? *Chyert*, I'm not used to this feeling. All questions, no answers. And I'm not the type who waits for answers to come on their own. *Fuck that.*

The door creaks open behind me. Dmitry's heavy boots barely make a sound as he walks in. "The kid's sleeping now," he says, voice low, quieter than usual. I glance up at him.

On the monitor, Clara is still out cold, lying on the bed, unmoving. The kid is curled up next to her, his small body pressed close against her, his little hand gripping her shirt like it's his lifeline. He's holding some toy—something weird-looking—but his fingers tremble, even in his sleep.

Dmitry's massive hand hovers over the screen, fingers twitching like he wants to reach out, but he doesn't. He just stands there, staring at the kid with something that looks too much like... *regret.*

Blyat'.

I grunt, trying to shake off the weight that's pressing down on my chest.

"Good," I mutter, though it doesn't feel good at all. Not with that kid lying there, clutching onto her like he's got no one else in the world.

Kayla's voice echoes down the hall, a mix of panic and Spanish curses. She's freaking out. I can picture her, eyes wide, pacing the kitchen. Dmitry scratches his head, looking at me. "Kayla's... not handling it well. When she saw the kid, her eyes were as big as the fucking full moon."

I huff out a breath, leaning on the desk.

Of course she's panicking.

My eyes flick to the clock—2 AM.

I didn't expect a fucking kid either, but here we are.

"Tell her to calm down," I mutter, waving it off. My jaw clenches. My fingers drum against the wooden table.

A kid. I didn't sign up for this.

But no one—*no one*—gets a free pass for trying to poison me. Not even Red.

Dmitry shifts his weight from one foot to the other, his gaze still fixed on the monitor. His shoulders relax just a fraction, as if the tension is bleeding out, but his eyes keep darting back to the kid. A flicker, too quick to catch, then he shrugs, turning to move toward the table. He doesn't say anything else, but he flicks a glance at me before refocusing on the kid.

I notice, but I don't say anything.

"Kayla's making something for them tomorrow," he says, his eyes lingering a little longer than usual. The words are there, but the space between them feels heavy.

The door swings open with a muted thud. This time, Maksim strolls in, holding a plate of something. His mouth is half-full, and he's chewing like he hasn't eaten in days. "This... *blin*, whatever Kayla made... it's good," he says, crumbs falling from his mouth as he speaks. "You should have some."

I take a deep breath, feeling the tightness in my chest. *Suka,* it's almost two in the fucking morning, and Maksim is sitting there like he's watching a damn comedy show—completely relaxed, legs stretched out, ass sunk deep into the leather chair. His chewing is slow, deliberate, as if he's savoring every bite.

I clench my jaw, fighting the urge to toss something at his head.

"So," Maksim begins, the last bit of food swallowed, "am I the only one... or does the kid look awfully familiar?"

I glance at him, annoyed, my hands gripping the edge of the desk. "You're the only one talking," I mutter, my jaw tight.

Maksim's smirk widens, a glint of mischief dancing in his eyes. "Come on, you've noticed it too. The little guy's got the same attitude as—"

"Shut up," I cut him off.

He doesn't know what he's poking at. No one does.

"Just saying." Maksim pushes the last bit of whatever the hell he's eating into his mouth, chewing like it's the best meal he's ever had. His eyes lock onto mine. "You may want to get a DNA check," he adds with a wink.

Before I even realize it, my hand twitches toward my gun.

Shoot this mudak in the head or the dick? Can't decide.

Maksim catches the look and bursts into laughter, nearly choking on his food. He leans back, completely unfazed.

"Relax, boss, I'm just messing with you."

Dmitry shifts his weight, the heavy soles of his boots scraping against the floor, pulling our attention.

He clears his throat, breaking the silence between us. "Elijah thinks you..." he hesitates, eyes flicking between Maksim and me, then looks straight at me, "look like one of the Pokémon."

I blink. *Elijah.* That's right. Clara—*Red*—called him that earlier.

My head tilts, confused. "The *Poke-what*?" I shoot him a bewildered look, not sure if I heard him right.

"It's a cartoon," Dmitry says, glancing toward the monitor, his hand sliding into his pocket as he checks if the boy is still asleep. "Kids' show. Pokémon."

I stare at him. "You're telling me the kid thinks I'm some cartoon character?"

Dmitry nods, his massive arms crossed, looking uncomfortable. "Yes, it's the villain."

I stare at him, my mind struggling to connect the dots. *A cartoon series? You must be fucking kidding. Me? Leonid Kuznetsov, a cartoon character?*

"Meowth," the big guy says, dead serious. "He's the villain. But... kinda dumb."

I narrow my eyes, incredulous. "And how the fuck do you know?"

Dmitry shifts, stuffing his hands into his pockets. He's quiet for a moment, long enough for Maksim to start chuckling again.

Dmitry finally speaks, his voice low. "My sister's kid... It *was* his favorite."

Sister? I didn't know Dmitry had a sister... There's more to this, but he won't say.

Dmitry doesn't look at me, doesn't say anything more. Just stands there, staring at the ground like he doesn't want to talk about it.

Mudak Maksim clears his throat, breaking the tension. "So, boss," he says, his eyes still glinting with amusement but more subdued now, "what are we gonna do with them?"

I glance at Dmitry, his eyes now back on me, waiting for my answer.

They both want to know the plan.

The fucking plan.

The one I thought I had, the one where Clara was just another piece on the board, another problem to solve.

But now?

Now I'm looking at a kid who wasn't supposed to exist, and I'm not sure how to play this hand.

Two

Clara

I wake up to the smell of... lavender?

What the hell?

My head throbs. It's like my brain is too big for my skull, pounding against it with every slow beat. *Fuck,* what did they drug me with this time? I blink, trying to focus, but everything's fuzzy. The light pouring into the room is too damn bright, making my eyes sting.

I scan from the ceiling down to the bed, then land on Elijah, sleeping next to me, curled up in the blankets. His little hand is clutching onto my shirt.

Thank God. Oh, my baby.

I gently pull him closer to my body, pressing my lips to the top of his head. The familiar smell of him, the warmth—it calms the panic clawing at my chest. He stirs a little, letting out a soft murmur, but doesn't wake up. His tiny fingers twitch against my shirt.

I need to move. I need to think. *I need a plan.* Slowly, I slide myself apart from Elijah, careful not to wake him.

My head spins, a wave of dizziness hitting me the second I sit up. I wince, pressing my palm to my forehead, trying to will the pounding to stop.

Focus, Clara.

There's a weird taste in my mouth—chemical, bitter. I try to swallow it down, but it sticks in the back of my throat like poison. *Shit.* I run my tongue over my teeth, but it doesn't help.

I glance at the door.

Closed.

Locked, no doubt.

I don't even need to try it to know. The room is bigger than the one they had me in before. Lighter, too. The pale walls are a soft cream color, like something out of a hotel.

My eyes flick to the wide window across the room. *Daylight.* I close my eyes for a second, trying to ground myself.

Breathe, Clara.

I slide out of the bed, feet hitting the wooden floor. The warmth from the sunlight contrasts sharply with the cold fear twisting in my gut. How long do I have? My eyes dart to the door, listening for footsteps. Silence. For now.

I pace to the window. My fingers twitch, wanting to yank it open to see if there's a way out. But, of course, it's locked tight. Figures. I lean my head against the cool glass and close my eyes. Trapped. Again.

Just as I turn back to the room, the door clicks. My whole body tenses, ready for whatever's coming. But it's not Leonid or one of his goons.

It's her.

Kayla. She'd helped me escape once.

She steps inside, a tray in her hands.

Food.

Her eyes scan the room quickly before landing on Elijah. She freezes, staring at him like she's seen a ghost. Her face tightens for a second—shock?

She doesn't say a word, just moves toward the small table in the corner, her steps slow, deliberate. She sets the tray down carefully, but I can see it. The way her hands tremble. She knows something. I can feel it in the air.

Her eyes flick back to Elijah again. He's stirring now, probably from the smell of food. Kayla's face softens, but there's sadness there, too, something that pulls at her features. She glances at me, then back at him. Her lips part like she wants to say something, but she doesn't. Instead, she picks up a plate, bringing it toward us.

"Eat," she says quietly, holding it out to me. Her voice is gentle, but there's something heavy in it. Like she's carrying a weight I can't see.

I don't take the plate. I stare at her. *Now's my chance.* If anyone's going to help me, it's *her.*

"You have to help us," I say, voice low but urgent. Elijah sits up now, rubbing his eyes. He looks at the food, then up at Kayla, but doesn't say anything.

My heart clenches.

He's hungry. I can see it in the way his gaze lingers on the plate, cautious but hopeful, like he's afraid to reach for something he might not be allowed to have. It's the kind of look no child should have.

Not mine. Not my boy.

I take a small, hesitant step toward Kayla, my eyes searching hers for any hint of sympathy.

Right now, I need to try to get out... even if I need to beg.

Kayla's eyes meet mine for a split second. There's a flicker of something—guilt, maybe—but then she looks away. She shakes her head, lips pressed into a thin line, before setting the plate on the table.

"No *puedo*," she whispers, shaking her head.

"*Sí, por favor,*" I blurt out. *Please.* I take a step toward her, my hand reaching out like I can pull her back to reason, back to helping us.

Just fucking help me.

But Kayla backpedals, her movements quick, almost panicked. Her face tightens with something unreadable as she turns toward the door. She doesn't look back. The door clicks shut before I can take another step.

I stand there, staring at the door, feeling the cold grip of reality closing in. The lock clicks from the outside. *Of course.* My chance slips away just as fast as it came.

Fucking useless.

"Mommy?" Elijah's small voice snaps me out of the anger building in my chest. I turn to see him staring at the plate of food, his lips pressed together in that way he does when he's too afraid to ask for something.

"I'm hungry." He looks up at me, eyes wide, a nervous wrinkle on his forehead as he glances at the plate, and it breaks something inside me.

Elijah finishes the last of his breakfast, crumbs on his fingers as he licks them clean.

He sits cross-legged on the bed, eyes wide, waiting for whatever comes next.

He doesn't get it yet. Not fully.

I put the empty plates back on the tray, stacking them slowly, trying to buy time. How do I explain this without scaring the hell out of him?

"Elijah..." I start, my voice low as I kneel in front of him, wiping a crumb from his cheek. He looks at me with those big, trusting eyes, and my stomach tightens.

I hate this.

"These people," I say, struggling to keep my voice calm. "They're dangerous. We're in a bad place, but you listen to me, okay?" I grip his hands tight, maybe a little too tight, but I can't help it. "No matter what, I'm not going to let anyone hurt you. Do you understand?"

Elijah nods, his little hand squeezing mine back, trying to match my strength.

"I'll protect you too, Mommy," he says, his voice so small but so damn determined.

I force a smile. "I know you will, baby."

But inside, I'm screaming.

How do I protect him from men like Leonid? From whatever the fuck this place is?

Before I can say anything else, a sound from outside the door makes my blood run cold.

Footsteps.

Heavy.

That's not Kayla.

I shoot up from the bed, yanking Elijah up with me. My heart slams against my ribs as I pull him toward the far corner of the room, putting my body between him and whatever's coming through that door. *Fuck.*

"Elijah, stay behind me," I whisper, my eyes locked on the door, my body tense, ready for a fight. My pulse pounds in my ears, drowning out everything else.

The footsteps stop.

I grip Elijah's arm tighter, his small body pressed against my leg.

Be ready. Be ready for anything.

The door swings open.

A figure fills the doorway—huge, broad-shouldered, casting a shadow that seems to swallow the whole damn room. It's not Leonid. It's the biggest one, the giant.

Fuck. I'm not someone who scares easily, not after all I've been through. But this man—*monster*—he's different. There's something about him—the way he carries himself, the sheer size of him—that twists something cold in my gut. He doesn't even have to say a word, and I can feel it—the danger rolling off him in waves.

Stay calm. Just fucking stay calm.

But my body isn't listening. My legs tremble, heart racing. He's too damn close, fear gripping my spine, paralyzing me. *Shit.* I want to fight, but right now, I'm trapped—by him and by my own fear.

I open my mouth, ready to shout, to demand that he back off. "Get... away from us," I hear myself say.

It's supposed to sound strong, threatening. Instead, it comes out small.

Pathetic.

Three

Clara

The giant doesn't even blink.

"Get away from my mommy, bad guy!" Elijah yells.

What? Wait.

Before I can process what's happening, Elijah bolts from behind me, zooming past like a damn bullet.

Shit.

"Elijah!" I shout, reaching out to grab him, but it's too late. He's already flying toward the giant like some fearless warrior, his tiny fists raised as if he's going to take down a fucking mountain.

My heart stops. *No, no, no.*

But the kid's determined. He lets out this battle cry—"AAAAAAAAhhhh!" A high-pitched yell—and before I know it, he's swinging at the giant's legs. *Fuck.*

The fucking giant doesn't flinch. Not even a blink. Just stands there, solid as a brick wall, his massive frame towering over Elijah. And then, without warning, his hand moves—fast but controlled—scooping Elijah up like he weighs nothing.

"Elijah!" I lunge forward, adrenaline flooding my veins. I don't think. I just move, trying to grab him back, trying to make this monster feel something, anything—but he doesn't budge. My fist connects with his arm again. He looks down, one eyebrow raised, lips curling into an infuriating smirk.

Fuck. I'm panting, trying to rip Elijah from his grip, but he is calm, unbothered. He just stares down at me, holding Elijah like he's holding a bag of groceries.

"Stop fighting," he rumbles, his voice low but not angry. "Or I won't let you go to the TV room."

I freeze mid-swing.

What the fuck did he just say?

TV room?

Elijah's still kicking, but his tiny fists are no match for this monster. He holds him easily, his grip firm but not cruel.

Elijah glares at him, face scrunched in fury. "Put me down! Pikachu's gonna shock you!"

The man's expression doesn't change. "No Pikachu shocks today," he says, deadpan. "But if you stop fighting, you can watch him."

Am I hearing this right?

My brain stutters, trying to catch up.

Did this giant just promise my kid Pikachu movies?

Elijah pauses, his fists mid-air, considering. He looks back at me, his eyes wide with confusion and maybe—just maybe—a little excitement. "Mommy... Pikachu?"

I blink, completely thrown off.

Is this real life?

I look up at the man, half expecting him to laugh, to drop the act, but he's dead serious.

"Mommy…" Elijah squirms in the giant's grip, but his little face is scrunched up in that way it gets when he's trying to solve a particularly tricky puzzle. "We can watch Pikachu?"

The giant nods and gives Elijah a wink.

"Elijah, baby, we can't—" I lunge forward, trying to pry my son from the giant's grasp. His arm doesn't budge. *Fuck.* "Don't you dare bribe him with Pikachu, you—" I start pounding on his bicep. *Ouch!* It's like hitting a brick wall. Pain shoots through my knuckles. "Son… of… a… *biscuit eater!*"

He tilts his head slightly, looking down at me as if I'm some kind of dumb animal.

Well. I feel stupid.

Before I can even process my next move, the door swings open, and in walks Joker—of course. He's got that permanent smirk plastered on his face like he's the star of some private comedy show that only he understands. He's munching on something, again, because of course he is.

My eyes dart to the door, half-expecting Leonid to walk in behind him. But no. Just Joker.

Joker saunters in, placing himself by the window, arms crossed casually, like he's inspecting a painting or something. His eyes finally land on me, and the smirk grows.

"Well, well, well. Looks like our guests are settling in nicely," he drawls, taking in the scene. "What's the matter, sweetheart? Dmitry's hospitality not up to your standards?"

Dmitry. I make a mental note, side-eyeing the giant still holding my son. So, that's his name.

I glance at Elijah. To my shock, the kid isn't squirming anymore. He's leaning against Dmitry's chest like it's the most comfortable thing in the world. His little hands are clutching onto the man's shirt, and there's this weird calmness in his face that wasn't there a minute ago.

What the fuck?

Joker follows my gaze, chuckling. "You sure you want to fight Dmitry?" His eyes glint with amusement, that annoying smirk never leaving his face. "I mean, look at him—doesn't seem like the worst babysitter, does he?"

I want to punch that smirk right off his face.

"Let him go," I snap, trying to sound threatening, but it's hard when Elijah looks like he's about to nap against this massive thug. My fists are still clenched, but deep down, I know it's pointless.

What am I gonna do? Take on two of them?

Joker leans against the wall, his hands sliding into his pockets, looking far too comfortable for my liking.

"Listen, sweetheart. You can keep fighting, but it's not gonna get you anywhere. You're here, and you're gonna stay here—might as well enjoy it." He shrugs, completely unbothered. "We're not gonna hurt the kid. In fact, I'd say Dmitry's got a soft spot for him already."

I glance back at Dmitry, who's still standing there, calm as ever, holding Elijah like he's a kitten. I can't decide if it's terrifying or just bizarre.

Joker's voice cuts through my thoughts. "So, what's it gonna be? You gonna be smart about this, or are we gonna keep playing this game?" He's not smirking now, and his tone—no, his look—tells me this is more than a joke.

I swallow, looking at Elijah again. He's not scared. In fact, he's looking at me like he's waiting for me to say yes to the Pikachu offer.

Fucking hell.

I exhale, throwing up an invisible white flag. "Fine," I mutter, the word tasting bitter. "But I'm not playing nice. And I sure as hell don't trust any of you."

Joker's grin returns in full force. "Oh, *Clara Caldwell*, I wouldn't dream of it."

There's something off about the way he's looking at me like he's piecing together something I'd rather keep hidden. He gives Elijah a quick, knowing glance, and then his gaze snaps back to mine.

He knows.

No. *Not everything.* My breath hitches, and before I can stop myself, I glance quickly at Elijah.

Dmitry finally puts Elijah down, and to my shock, my son doesn't run back to me. He stands there for a second, looking up at Dmitry, then back at me, like he's waiting for the next move.

"Mommy, Pikachu?" Elijah asks, his eyes big and hopeful.

I pinch the bridge of my nose because of course this is happening. "Sure, baby," I say, trying not to sound like I'm losing my grip on reality. "Let's go watch Pikachu."

Four

Leonid

B *lyat'.* This day's already a waste of my time.

I stalk into the restaurant, my presence announcing itself louder than any pompous décor ever could. *Pizda,* I don't give a shit about the expensive chandeliers or the perfect little table settings. My mind is still back home, where Clara Caldwell and her kid, Elijah, are.

I wonder if she's awake yet. Or still unconscious. *Suka.*

I should be there. *Not here.*

I shove my thoughts aside as the manager rushes forward, his sharp suit a clear sign that he knows exactly who I am.

"Mr. Kuznetsov," he greets, head dipping in a quick bow. His voice is smooth, but the way his eyes flick nervously to my face says everything. "Your table is ready."

I nod, not bothering with pleasantries, and follow him through the restaurant.

The lunch crowd hums around us—polished business executives in tailored suits, soft clinks of chopsticks on ceramic plates, and the murmur of conversations that stop when I pass by. Eyes dart toward me, some in curiosity, others in quiet recognition. No one dares to hold my gaze for long.

The scent of grilled fish and miso drifts through the air, mixing with the faint floral notes of the restaurant's decor, a blend of Japanese elegance and modern luxury. Low, soft lighting reflects off lacquered tables and pristine white walls, each design element calculated to impress, to make people feel like they're part of something exclusive. But all it does is irritate me further.

Aleksei. That's the reason I'm here.

The old man's a relic. Nine years since Papa's gone, and he still thinks his word carries weight. The last time he pulled me into one of his "important discussions," I nearly walked out. But I'm here now. Because he wouldn't stop calling—texting me with his same tired tricks, dropping Papa's name like that would change something.

"Leonid, Andrei, the *Pakhan* knew how to balance the business. You should come hear me out. The *Pakhan* would have wanted it." Always *Papa.* The guilt trip never changes. I clench my fists, jaw tight. *Blyat',* the old bastard still knows how to push my buttons.

"Your private room, sir," the manager says, stopping in front of a door at the far end of the hallway. It's different from the others—taller, darker wood, with intricate patterns carved into the frame. Not some basic corporate design but something traditional, almost ceremonial. A deep red lacquer, polished so smooth that the light from the ceiling glints off it.

Tap, tap.

The manager knocks twice softly and waits, eyes flicking toward me like he's wondering if I'm impressed by the theatrics.

I'm not.

He slides the door open with a smooth, practiced motion. The shoji screen door glides into the wall with hardly a sound, a small gesture that feels more dramatic than necessary. I catch the faint scent of incense, mixing with the sharp smell of soy sauce and something sweet.

I look around, scanning the room. High-pitched giggles hit my ears first—some arm candy at the far end of the table, leaning in close to whatever Aleksei's saying to the businessman beside him.

Suka! Looks like...

I catch the tail-end of whatever flowery bullshit Aleksei's saying to the businessman sitting beside him.

He hadn't told me much when he called earlier. Just that there was "a very important matter" to discuss.

Last time he said that, I ended up in a room full of aging mobsters trying to sell me on some idea about expanding into real estate. Waste of time then, and I have no doubt this is going to be just as painful.

I step inside and let the door slide shut behind me, my eyes narrowing on the setup.

This screams *one* thing—Aleksei is trying to rope me into another one of his grand schemes.

At the far end of the table, Aleksei is deep in conversation with a man whose body shape catches my attention—short and pudgy. I don't recognize him at first, but something about his posture, the way he hunches forward like he's trying too hard, pisses me off.

As I move closer, the recognition clicks. Fucking *Kensington*. He's the same guy whose company has been dancing on the edge of bankruptcy for years. The Feds have been sniffing around him, too—he's dirty but not smart enough to cover his tracks. The kind of trouble that attracts more trouble, not someone I want to deal with.

Aleksei turns his head slightly, catching my entrance.

"Ah, Leonid," Aleksei says, waving me over like this whole thing was my idea.

My blood boils at the thought of all the precious seconds being wasted on this bullshit.

"Come, sit. We were just getting to the important part." His smile doesn't quite reach his eyes.

I don't sit. I stand there, towering over the table.

Kensington beams at me like I've just walked on water. "Mr. Kuznetsov," he says, rising halfway out of his seat, hand extended. "It's an absolute pleasure. I've heard nothing but incredible things about you. Your reputation, your... discerning taste."

I glance at his hand but don't bother taking it.

Discerning taste?

A soft giggle breaks through my thoughts. I blink, my eyes flicking toward the sound, and realize the two women sitting beside Kensington are whispering to each other. Their heads are close together, eyes darting toward me like I'm some exhibit they're dying to see up close.

Zaebis'. Now I know what this is. A fucking match-making session. Kensington isn't alone.

The two women sitting beside him are both angled toward me like they're the main event at this circus. The younger one, maybe early twenties, is wide-eyed like she's just seen a rockstar. Her makeup is layered thick, trying too hard to look older, but there's still that fresh-faced cluelessness about her. The other one is late twenties, and it shows. There's something sharp about her features, but it's buried under the layers of fake tan, too much filler, and more Botox than any human should have. Her lips, over-plumped, curl into what I assume is supposed to be a sultry smile, but all I see is desperation.

Aleksei motions again for me to sit.

Poshol na khuy.

If Aleksei hadn't been in the Bratva for as long as I've been breathing, I'd put a hole through his skull right now for wasting my time like this.

I clench my jaw so hard I'm surprised my teeth don't crack, but I finally give in, dropping into the chair across from them. It's not respect—it's obligation. Aleksei was loyal to my father, Andrei. And while that loyalty keeps him alive, it doesn't mean I won't make him pay for this later.

Kensington, the sweaty little pig, shifts in his seat like a child trying to impress a strict teacher. His fat fingers smooth over his silk tie—probably sweating through that, too—and he flashes a nervous smile. His skin is pale, but his forehead shines with an oily sheen, the kind that makes me want to slap the grease right off him.

"Mr. Kuznetsov," he starts again, his words spilling out too fast, "I've been following your ventures for years. Such discerning taste, in art, in business, in... everything."

More lies.

I stare at him, patience wearing thin.

This fool has no idea who I am. Or maybe he does, and he's just that desperate. I can see the sweat pooling at the edges of his temples, dripping down his neck. He's trying too hard to keep his cool, and it's pathetic. Every word out of his mouth is another lie, another ploy to get me on his side.

I lean back in my chair, eyes narrowing at Aleksei. The corner of Aleksei's mouth twitches upward as he savors his sashimi, his eyes half-closed in appreciation. A drop of soy sauce clings to his bottom lip, and he dabs it away with his napkin, taking his time.

His grin remains steady, even as I grit my teeth, the slow chew of his food almost mocking. He knows I'm about two seconds away from walking out.

"Leonid," he says smoothly, "You're well past the age for marriage. It's time to start considering alliances that benefit both business and... personal life."

I glance at Kensington, who's now beaming like a sweaty fool. The two women exchange glances, and I catch the older one giving me a once-over, her eyes trailing from my face down to my chest, lingering before they drop lower, not even bothering to hide it.

I'm seeing red.

"You've got to be fucking kidding me," I growl, my voice low. My eyes flick back to Aleksei. "This is why I'm here? To be paraded around like some prize bull for sale?"

Aleksei's smirk tightens. "You're past thirty-five, Leonid. It's time to settle down with someone... influential." He motions to the older woman like she's the prize he's dangling in front of me.

Kensington clears his throat, leaning forward, trying to salvage whatever this disaster is. "My daughters are well-versed in business, Mr. Kuznetsov," he says, his voice still too eager. "They've traveled extensively—Europe, Asia... You'll find their connections to be quite... valuable."

I don't even look at the women. "Valuable?" I shoot back, my voice dripping with sarcasm. "Is that what you call this?"

The older one—too much plastic in her face to even read a proper reaction—tries to lean in, flashing that overstuffed smile again. "I've always admired men of power," she says, her voice thick with fake charm. "Daddy's told me all about you."

I raise an eyebrow, my patience gone. "Did Daddy tell you that this isn't a fucking dating service?"

Aleksei, sensing my growing temper, shifts in his seat. "This is an opportunity, Leonid. Kensington's connections—his daughters—are exactly the kind of alliance you need to strengthen our position."

My fist tightens around the edge of the table, and for a second, I think about flipping it and walking out. But no. I sit, glaring at Aleksei; the only thing holding me back is the years he served under my father.

"If I wanted an alliance," I say slowly, "I wouldn't need... this." I glance at the women, making sure they understand that whatever this is, it's a joke.

The younger one blushes, her eyes flicking between me and her father. The older one just smiles wider, completely unfazed, as if she still thinks she's winning me over.

I turn back to Aleksei, cold. "This better be the last time you pull this shit, Aleksei. Or next time, I'll show you just how little patience I have left."

Aleksei's grin falters, but he nods, leaning back as if he's won something.

Kensington shifts again, his nervous smile returning. "Mr. Kuznetsov, I assure you—this arrangement would bring you more than you can imagine."

I lean forward, meeting his eyes with a glare. "I don't need anything you're selling, Kensington."

His face pales, the sweat building up again. But the older daughter, still thinking she's got a shot, leans closer, her breath catching slightly as her eyes roam over me again.

Aleksei's eyes flicker between us like he's waiting for me to fold.

But I won't. I've already made up my mind.

All I can think about now is *Clara Caldwell*.

Five

Clara

This isn't a TV room. It's a goddamn IMAX theater. Plush, red velvet seats stretch out in perfect rows, the kind of setup you'd expect in a high-end theater. The dim lighting hums low, making the giant screen in front of me glow even more, the edges blurred like something out of a surreal dream. Pikachu's face—cheerful, obnoxiously yellow—fills the screen, the high-pitched voice echoing in this oversized underground room.

"Mommy, look!" Elijah's voice chirps from the seat next to me. His little legs are swinging wildly, bouncing with excitement as his eyes are glued to the screen. He's practically buzzing, his fists clenching and unclenching with every flash of action. Pikachu's mid-battle and Elijah is living for it, his whole body moving like he's right there, dodging attacks alongside his favorite character.

"Yes, baby," I mumble, ruffling his curls. He grins, his legs kicking faster, bouncing off the edge of the plush chair like he's gearing up to jump into the screen.

An hour. That's all it's been. But it feels longer. I straighten my back and glance over quickly at Dmitry sitting a few seats away. The giant is still as a statue, his eyes flicking toward Elijah every now and then like he's keeping watch. It's unsettling seeing someone his size so... relaxed.

Holding onto Elijah, I sink back into the seat, trying to focus. The sound system is insane. "Pikaaaaaa!!"

Mother of a... banana hammock-wearing, titty twister!

It's like Pikachu is about to zap me personally; the booming audio makes my ears ring with each attack.

I shift in my seat, sinking deeper into the leather cushions that feel like they're trying to swallow me whole.

Why aren't they interrogating me? Tying me up?

Hell, at this point, I half-expected a blindfold, maybe some threats. But *no*—here I am, sitting in a luxury cinema, watching Pikachu zap Team Rocket, while the two Bratva thugs who dragged me here sit close by, relaxed as if we're just one big happy family.

Tilting my head slightly, I run a quick eye over the room, trying to focus on something besides the absurdity of my current situation. My brain's on overdrive, calculating every damn detail: *the way we were led down here in an elevator, the lack of windows, the plush carpets.*

One thing's for sure, this has to be an underground room, some sort of private space that Leonid—or whoever the fuck planned this—built to be out of sight. Out of reach. It's modern, sleek. Like they had more money than sense when they built this place.

But how far down are we? How deep? The exits? None that I can see.

Straightening my posture, I subtly shift my body to get a better view of the room, pretending I'm stretching while my eyes dart toward the door. It's far enough away that even if I tried to make a move, Dmitry or Joker would catch me before I reached it.

Then I feel it.

The weight of Joker's stare, and I slowly turn to meet his gaze. He's lounging a few rows back, his legs stretched out, arms crossed over his chest, watching me like I'm the real entertainment, not the damn Pikachu marathon. His eyes glint with something, amusement maybe, or that creepy sense of knowing he seems to carry around like a fucking badge.

I tear my gaze away from him for a second, trying to ignore the feeling that I'm being studied like prey. But then I sense it—something shifting behind me. A shadow.

How the hell did he move so fast?

"Finding your way out?" His voice cuts through the noise of the movie, low and taunting.

I clench my jaw, refusing to show how much he just startled me. My eyes narrow as I turn to face him, keeping my expression as tight as possible.

"Fuck off," I tell him.

He chuckles, leaning forward, resting his elbows on his knees, like this conversation is the highlight of his day.

"Or maybe you're wondering why we haven't strung you up somewhere yet? Why we haven't started with the blindfolds and the threats?"

Oh, this motherfucker is really digging in.

I stare at him, my mind half on escape routes, half wondering why I'm not already in some torture chamber.

"Yeah, why not?" I challenge. I'm not afraid of this asshole. Not in the way I *should* be.

He winks, the smirk never leaving his face. "Relax, Clara. We're not monsters."

He glances at Dmitry, who's still seated near Elijah, his huge body looking out of place in this plush, luxurious setting.

"Well, most of us aren't."

I picture myself punching Joker square in the jaw. It's a brief fantasy but satisfying enough that I clench my fist without thinking. My gaze hardens.

"You're Ravens. You're murderers."

My stomach twists as Jake's face flashes in my mind. Jake, my brother, the reason I'm in this situation in the first place. I'll never forget what the Ravens did to him. To us.

Joker stretches, kicking his feet up onto the seat in front of him, "Yes, we are." He shrugs. "But right now? I'm just entertained by someone as interesting as you."

Interesting?

My blood boils, and my nails dig into the armrest, but I force myself to glance at Elijah. He's still lost in Pikachu's world, completely unaware of the tension crackling around us. I bite down on the frustration building in my chest. "I'm not playing this game." I hiss through clenched teeth.

Joker's smirk widens as he reaches forward and ruffles Elijah's hair.

"Oh, you're already playing, Clara," he says, his tone like he's talking to a stubborn kid who doesn't get the rules.

SMACK!

I don't even process what happens until my hand is stinging and Joker's face is frozen in surprise. Both of us blink. That... *wasn't* exactly planned. Elijah turns toward the commotion, his eyes wide, confusion etched on his face.

Joker rubs his jaw, his expression turning to something between amusement and disbelief.

"Ouch," he says, loud enough for Elijah to hear, his voice dripping with mock sincerity. "Your mommy's so... strong."

Elijah giggles, and Joker turns to me, that grin creeping back across his face.

"No wonder our boss has a thing for you." He leans in slightly, his voice lowering to a conspiratorial whisper. "Though, I've got to hand it to you—I'm still amazed you're alive after trying to poison the *Pakhan*."

My body tenses.

Joker's eyes gleam as he watches my reaction, his smirk widening even more. "But you know... you're not the first. Just the first to get this far."

Six

Leonid

I shouldn't be thinking about the captive woman and her kid so much.

I also shouldn't be wondering who she's been with or where the fuck the father of the kid is.

I should be focusing on the fact that Aleksei's trying to marry me off like some Russian Jane Austen novel. Instead, I'm wondering if Clara's managed to break any of Dmitry's fingers yet.

Pizdets. That old man's gotten way ahead of himself. Thinks he can run my life like Papa's still alive, like I'm some teenager.

I make a left turn, leaving behind the fancy-ass restaurant district. The city around me is gray and worn, buildings leaning with age, the occasional flash of graffiti in the corners.

I push the gas; the road ahead stretches, cracked asphalt and faded yellow lines disappearing beneath the Brabus.

Traffic catches me at the next light.

Some asshole in a Prius is taking his sweet time, probably composing a tweet about saving the planet. I drum my fingers on the steering wheel, glancing up. The sky's hanging low, heavy clouds the color of wet cement. Noon and the sun can't even be bothered to show up properly.

Typical October.

My hand reaches for the radio, needing something to drown out my thoughts of Red's voice still echoing in my head.

Before I can hit the button, my phone buzzes on the seat next to me.

I snatch it up, one eye still on the road.

Maksim:

> **Watching Pikachu with the fam, boss. Kid says you look like Meowth. Mean and scratchy.**

I snort, tossing the phone onto the passenger seat. I shake my head.

Part of me is surprised Maksim managed to get them settled without having to tie Clara to the fucking couch. That woman's more feral than any street fighter I've dealt with. And here she is, apparently watching cartoons like this is some normal Sunday afternoon.

Most people—most sane people—do one or two things when they get kidnapped: They fucking cry, beg, or shit themselves.

And then there's Clara Caldwell and her kid Elijah.

Sitting in my TV room, enjoying whatever hell they're watching.

Chyert, she's way too confident. The Caldwell family is rotting six feet under, yet here she is, acting like she owns the place.

Makes no fucking sense.

The Irish have held New Orleans in their grip since before I was born—old money, old blood, old grudges. But they're bleeding cash faster than a gunshot wound these days. Their empire's crumbling like a cheap cookie, and here's Clara, starting a war she can't afford.

What's her fucking angle?

Even with generations of mob ties behind her, what makes her think she can take on the Bratva alone?

Unless she's not alone.

Suddenly, something flickers in my rearview. Black Audi, three cars back.

Could be nothing.

Could be *something*. It's been hanging back for a while now, maybe two or three turns. I check the mirror again. It's subtle, but I know when someone's trying to stay out of sight.

Could be Ludis being a pain in my ass again. My twin's got a habit of showing up when I least want him to.

I take a right turn, cutting off a minivan. The Audi follows.

Interesting.

My convoy's back at the compound, which means either I'm getting paranoid or someone's got balls the size of Russia. Nobody fucks with the *Pakhan* of the Kuznetsov Bratva. Nobody with a functioning survival instinct, anyway.

The light ahead turns yellow. I gun it, shooting through just as it hits red. The Audi runs it completely, earning a symphony of horns.

Definitely *not* Ludis. He's an asshole, but he's not sloppy. If Ludis wanted me tailed, I wouldn't see it coming.

This is too obvious.

I catch a glimpse of the driver in my mirror. Single occupant, male. Nasty scar running from his left eye to his jaw like someone tried to fillet his face.

Who the fuck is this guy?

The traffic thins out. *Perfect.*

I downshift, the Brabus responding like it can read my mind. Time to see what our friend in the Audi is really after.

Two more rights, then a sharp left. The Audi stays with me, getting closer now. Amateur. You don't get closer unless you're ready to make your move.

My phone buzzes again.

Maksim:

> **Now watching 'Cars.' Kid says you'd be the angry red one.**

I smile. At least someone's having fun.

The Audi's right on my ass now. Through the mirror, I can see Scarface gripping his steering wheel like he's trying to strangle it.

Enough playing around.

I slam on the brakes. The Audi swerves, nearly kissing a streetlight. I floor it, watching him scramble to catch up.

Suka, this is actually kind of fun.

We dance through the streets, my Brabus against his Audi. He's good, but not good enough. Not Bratva good.

So, who the fuck is he?

Everyone knows that trying to clip my wings is a death sentence.

I glance in the rearview, catching a better look. His face is twisted with frustration, jaw clenched, white knuckles gripping the wheel. Desperation, maybe. But who the hell is desperate enough to follow me alone?

Unless...

Unless they don't know who they're dealing with.

Now that's an interesting thought.

I check my mirror again. Scarface is sweating now, his face twisted in concentration.

Time to end this.

I take a hard left onto Canal Street, then immediately cut right into an alley. The Brabus barely fits, but that's the point. The Audi's wider, heavier.

The sound of scraping metal tells me I was right.

I burst out onto the next street, leaving Scarface wedged in the alley like a fat cat in a drainpipe.

Pulling into a spot behind the dollar store, I grab my phone.

Me:

> **Got a rat trapped on Canal and Bourbon.
> Send cleanup crew.**

Maksim replies instantly:

> **On it, boss.**

Blyat.

I check my Glock, sliding it back into its holster. The street's mostly empty—just a couple of tourists too drunk to notice it's barely noon. Perfect.

Adjusting my sunglasses, I step out into the weak October sun. My shoes crunch on broken glass as I approach the alley. The Audi's wedged tight, black paint scraped raw against both walls. But Scarface? He's just sitting there, hands on the wheel at ten and two, like he's waiting for a fucking driving test.

Something's off.

Most people panic when they're caught.

This *suka*? He's just sitting there, staring at me through the windshield. Then, without breaking eye contact, he reclines his seat all the way back.

What the fuck?

In one fluid motion, he kicks up both legs, smashing through the windshield. Glass rains down as he pulls himself through the opening like some spider crawling out of its hole. Not a single wasted movement. Not a sound of pain.

Yobany urod. Either this guy's professional or completely unhinged. Maybe both.

He stands, brushing glass from his jacket like he's dusting off after a pleasant stroll. Blood trickles down his hands, but he doesn't seem to notice.

I rest my hand on my Glock. "Hands where I can see them."

He raises them slowly, and that's when I notice the Celtic cross tattooed on his right palm. Irish work, old school.

The scar on his face isn't just a scar—it's a statement. Raw, twisted flesh cutting from eye to jaw like someone carved a road map of hell into his skin. But it's his eyes that make my skin crawl. Gray as nuclear winter, empty as a killing field. The kind of eyes you see in old photos of war criminals—men who stopped being human long ago.

I've seen men like this before.

The ones who've crossed so far over the edge, they've forgotten what it's like to be human.

He takes a step forward. *Blyat,* that right leg—it drags behind him like dead weight, hip jerking sideways with each move. The kind of fucked-up walk you only get when a hollow point tears through bone, and they can't put you back together right.

My Glock's steady at his chest, but this *suka* doesn't even look at it. Just keeps coming, blood dripping from his sliced-up hands, marking his path on the asphalt like some twisted breadcrumb trail.

"Where's she?" Another broken step. "Where's Clara?"

Seven

Clara

"Sit."

I look up at Dmitry. And up. And up.

"*Please*." I stare straight into his eyes before throwing a wink at Elijah.

My son—bless his tiny dictator heart—nods firmly. "You need to say please if you want something from someone. It's polite."

A vein pulses in Dmitry's neck. His jaw works like he's chewing glass.

"Please." The word comes out rough, like he's been chain-smoking for days.

Elijah beams, clearly satisfied with himself. "Good job," he says, patting Dmitry's arm as if he's just trained the biggest man in the room.

I hold his stare.

I pull out the chair. I sit.

My choice. Not his.

Dmitry grunts. His huge hands hover over Elijah's chair, adjusting it with the kind of care you'd use handling explosives. My son scrambles up, and Dmitry steadies him with a gentleness that makes my brain short-circuit.

I exhale. Slowly. The fact that he's not torturing us is a relief.

The giant shuffles toward what I assume is another kitchen behind those swinging doors. Because one massive kitchen isn't enough in a house like this.

I snicker quietly, glancing around.

This kitchen is something else.

It stretches out like an HGTV fever dream. White marble everywhere. Steel appliances that belong in a restaurant. Floor-to-ceiling windows framing a garden that would make Martha Stewart weep.

It took us a minute to get here—lift up from the TV room, past a couple of heavy doors, down a hallway that just kept going. This house is too big for its own good, but somehow everything feels bare.

Cold.

Like Leonid had enough money to fill it with furniture, but decided to keep things as minimal as possible.

Elijah's humming now, fork in hand, tapping it against the edge of his plate like it's a drumstick. His legs swing happily under the table.

"Mommy, this place is nicer than our kitchen."

I huff out a laugh. "Yes, baby, it is."

Movement catches my eye. Two guards patrol the garden, guns visible on their hips. I scan the corners of the ceiling. One, two, three—yep, cameras. Because of course there are cameras.

Left alone in an unlocked kitchen? Sure. They're watching us from somewhere, probably betting on what we'll try first.

"Mommy, Mommy." Elijah tugs gently on my neck, his small arm pulling me closer until I have to hunch down a bit so he can whisper into my ear. His breath tickles as he presses his face to mine. "Are they bad guys?"

For a second, a sharp sting hits my chest. He's too young for this. Too innocent to be stuck in a world where bad guys surround us. I swallow the lump forming in my throat.

"Yes," I admit quietly, bracing myself for the fear I expect to see in his eyes. Instead, Elijah leans in closer, his tiny hand still holding onto my neck for balance. He whispers with all the confidence in the world, "Don't worry, we'll train them to be good guys again, like Ash does."

I blink, and then a chuckle slips out. God, I love this kid. He's completely unfazed, convinced that with enough determination, he can flip an entire mafia operation like he's turning Pikachu into a superhero.

Just then, Dmitry pushes the door open and steps through. A wave of garlic and butter hits us, and suddenly, I'm starving.

Elijah's whole body perks up like a meerkat. "Smells so good!" His little butt lifts off the chair, nose in the air.

"Food's coming." Dmitry materializes beside us, two glasses in his hands. He puts one in front of Elijah, then places the other in front of me.

He stalks to the fridge, back muscles rippling under his black shirt like steel cables. Returns with a glass jar of orange juice that looks tiny in his grip.

He fills one glass, movements precise like he's handling nitroglycerin instead of Tropicana.

Elijah's eyes go from the juice to Dmitry, then to me.

Dmitry stands there, eyes flitting between the two of us.

I nod, aiming at Elijah. "Yes, you can drink it."

"YEAH! Orange juice!" Elijah bounces in his seat. "Thank you! See? You're getting better at being nice already!"

The corner of Dmitry's mouth twitches. Something shifts in his face. The hard lines soften, just a fraction, as he watches my son demolish his orange juice. It's the same look I've seen on guard dogs when they find a kitten to protect.

Unsettling. That's what this is.

The door swings open. I expect one of Leonid's plastic-perfect bots. Like the ones from The Aerie that night I slipped poison into his whiskey. All bedroom eyes and dead smiles.

Instead, Kayla bustles through with a tray that makes my stomach growl embarrassingly loud.

"My God, this smells incredible!" I say it out too loud.

Kayla beams, but her eyes keep drifting to Elijah. Just as quickly as I catch it, she's already looking away.

"Lunch is ready," she says as she drops the tray in front of us.

Oh. My. God.

Grilled cheese, but not like any I've made. Golden-brown sourdough, some fancy cheese melting out the sides, and what looks like caramelized onions peeking through. A bowl of tomato soup that's definitely never seen the inside of a Campbell's can sits beside it.

Kayla stands to the side, her eyes moving to Elijah again. She's staring at him like she's trying to solve a puzzle, her expression awkward, maybe even a little nervous.

My stomach growls again, but my throat tightens. Rich people poison, right? That's a thing. Especially rich people whose whiskey you've tried to spike.

Elijah looks up at me, sandwich already halfway to his mouth. Those big eyes full of trust.

I press my lips together. Take a breath.

A chair scrapes. Dmitry materializes across from us—how does someone that huge move so quietly?—and digs into his sandwich like he's got three minutes to live.

Right. If they wanted us dead, we'd be dead. No need for fancy cheese poison.

I nod at Elijah.

He takes one bite, and his whole face lights up. "Mommy! This is the best food ever!"

His right. I take a bite.

The food is... fuck. It's good. *Too good.* The cheese is sharp and nutty, the bread perfectly crispy, and there's some kind of herb situation happening that makes me want to cry.

I'm only halfway through when Dmitry's plate is suddenly empty. How did he even—did he unhinge his jaw like a snake?

His phone buzzes.

"Maksim." His voice goes flat.

Dmitry's eyes flit to mine, and for a split second, I feel something ominous, something more than just hostility.

What the fuck? It's heavy, dark, something to do with me.

I keep chewing, but every muscle in my body tightens, waiting for what he'll say next. I shove more food into my mouth, pretending I don't feel the weight of whatever the hell is happening.

"Okay, I'll be ready." He stands, chair scraping against marble.

The look he gives Elijah before turning away makes my blood run cold.

Not like a guard dog finding a kitten.

Like a guard dog who's just been ordered to hunt.

Eight

Leonid

*P*op. *Pop. Pop.*

"Boss, I think this is a horrible plan." Maksim blows another bubble with his gum. *Pop.*

"*Blyat*. One more pop, and I'll make you eat that gum wrapper." I lean against the wall, keeping my distance from the ring.

"Just saying. Three hours and still nothing." *Pop.* "Guy's got more lives than my ex-wife's cat."

Blood drips onto the canvas. The old man in the ring spits out a tooth, adds it to the growing collection by the corner post. His gray hair is matted red, right eye swollen shut. Still stands.

I built this ring myself. Not for training. Not for sport. Every man deserves one last chance to fight back, to die with honor.

Even my enemies.

Especially my enemies.

The old bastard earned that much.

Dmitry circles him, knuckles split and bruised. For once, the Siberian Slaughterer isn't smiling.

"Who sent you?" Dmitry's fist connects with the old man's ribs. A wet crack echoes through the basement.

The old man crumples, wheezing. Pushes himself up on shaking arms.

"Where's Clara?"

Same fucking question. Always the same.

"Getting creative with retirement homes, boss?" Maksim pulls out his phone, snaps a picture. "Thought we had an age limit on sparring partners."

"Shut up."

The old man's good eye fixes on me. There's something in that stare.

"You," his voice scrapes out. "You took her."

I look over at Dmitry, who's cracking his knuckles like he's warming up for another round. This guy doesn't know who the fuck he's dealing with. Either that, or he's too broken to care.

Maksim's bouncing on his toes now, amused. "You think he's had enough? Or should we let him keep asking dumb questions until he bleeds out?"

I shoot him a glance, but the truth is, Maksim's right. The man's barely holding on, his limbs trembling as he tries to stay upright. The ring reeks of sweat, blood, and defeat.

But that *look*. I've seen it before. In the mirror, five years ago, when Ludis appeared. The *look* of pure, unfiltered hatred. The kind that lives in your bones.

His good leg scrapes against the canvas. One step. Another. Blood trails behind him like breadcrumbs as he drags himself toward me, that dead-eyed stare never wavering.

"Where is CLARA!"

Dmitry's boot comes down on his knee. Another crack.

The old man doesn't scream. Doesn't blink.

Dmitry takes a step forward, but I stop him.

"Wait." I step closer to the ring. "Dmitry."

"Boss?"

"Look at his hands."

Maksim stops chewing. Moves in for a better look.

The old man's fingers. Shamrock tattoo wrapped around his ring finger, edges faded to blue. Old school Irish mark. The kind they gave their most loyal.

"*Der'mo.*" Maksim whistles. "No wonder gramps won't stay down."

The old man spits blood. Tries to stand again.

"Clara." His voice is stronger now. "Where is my—"

Dmitry's fist cuts off the question. The old man finally drops.

"Dmitry." I fix him with a hard glare.

Dmitry just shrugs, his expression blank, as if he didn't just knock out a man twice his age. "He wasn't going to say anything useful. You know it."

I exhale, pinching the bridge of my nose, trying to shake the strange feeling creeping up my spine. This guy's no ordinary captive. The way he keeps getting up, the way he keeps asking about Clara—it's bizarre. And it's starting to piss me off.

Maksim stretches, cracking his neck like he's just woken up from a nap. "So, what now, boss? Want me to drag him out back, or you wanna keep him around for another round of Q&A?"

"Fuck." I run a hand through my hair. "Check his prints. All databases. I want to know who the hell survived the purge."

"On it." Maksim's already typing. "Hey, boss?"

"What?"

"Think the cleaning crew accepts senior citizen discount?"

I grab his gum pack, throw it across the room.

"Hey..." Maksim stares at his gum pack in the corner. "I just got those."

"Get him to medical." I nod at Dmitry. The old man's chest rises and falls, shallow but steady.

"Boss?" Dmitry's knuckles crack as he flexes his hands.

"Clean him up. Fix what's broken." I step to the edge of the ring. "I want him coherent."

"Since when do we run a fucking retirement home?" Maksim's already on his phone, thumbs flying. "*Der'mo.* Boss, you need to see this."

I grab his phone. The screen shows an old file—IRA connections, marked classified. A younger version of our guest stares back. Same dead eyes.

Mitchell Colgrave. Age: 61 Former IRA connections. Explosives expert. Rumored enforcer for the Caldwell family, personal bodyguard to Jake Caldwell.

Jake Caldwell?

I pause, the name tugging at a memory.

A rumor that had floated around after Jake's death—people whispered that I, The Raven, had killed the heir of the Caldwell family.

I remember laughing at the time, thinking how convenient it was to let that rumor run wild. I never touched Jake Caldwell, but I never denied it. *Why should I?* Let them think the boogeyman did their dirty work. Good for business, good for fear.

Now, staring at Mitch's file, it makes sense. This old bastard spent decades guarding Jake Caldwell. And now, after Jake's gone, he's what?

Trying to protect Clara?

"Well?" Maksim leans over my shoulder. "Interesting reading material, no?"

"Get Yuri." I shove the phone back at him. "Tell him to bring his kit."

"The doctor?" Maksim's eyebrows shoot up. "Thought we only called him for—"

"Just do it."

Dmitry hauls the old man up, slinging him over one shoulder. Blood drips onto his shirt.

"And Maksim?"

"Yeah, boss?"

"Buy better gum. That cheap shit's giving me a headache."

He grins, already dialing. "Only the best for you, *Pakhan*."

I watch Dmitry carry our guest out. Too many questions. No fucking answers.

Time to pay Clara Caldwell a visit.

Maybe she'll be more talkative than her watchdog.

Nine

Clara

"Buddy," I plant a kiss on Elijah's cheek, "time to sleep."

We're sprawled across the king-sized bed, white sheets tangled around us. Elijah's head rests on my arm, his Batman pajamas—courtesy of Kayla's shopping spree—still stiff with newness.

The bathroom door stands ajar, steam still escaping from our bubble bath adventure. Elijah had gasped when he saw the marble tub. "Mommy, it's like a swimming pool!"

He wasn't wrong.

I peek at the floor-to-ceiling windows. More guards patrol the grounds now than during daylight. Four... *no,* five men circle the perimeter, their black suits stark against the manicured lawn.

"Can we have another bubble bath tomorrow?" Elijah's voice pulls me back. His damp hair tickles my chin.

"Sure, buddy." I run my fingers through his curls. "Did you count the bubbles this time?"

"Too many!" He giggles. "And the shower has rain, Mommy. Real rain!"

I squeeze him closer. For a moment, I *almost* forget where we are.

Almost forget that Kayla had locked us in after dinner, her only words being, "We need to go back to room." And *almost* forget that we're trapped on the top floor with three other mysterious doors that remain sealed shut.

Almost.

"Mommy." Elijah's small hand touches my cheek. His brown eyes, so like *his*, are heavy with sleep. "I miss Pikachu."

My throat tightens. His favorite plush toy, left behind in our hasty... departure. "I know, baby." I stroke his cheek. "We'll get Pikachu back once we're out of here."

He considers this, nose scrunching up like it does when he's thinking hard. "Yes, we'll train these bad guys, Mommy."

A snort escapes me. He's still on about this. Only my kid would think about rehabilitating the Russian mob.

"We'll train them to be good guys."

My hands slide down to Elijah's shoulders, patting him gently. My jaw tightens.

Sure, right after I figure out how to get us out of here alive. Right after I deal with Leonid fucking Kuznetsov. The man in the Raven mask. Jake's killer.

But something nags at the back of my mind. Those eyes. Leonid's eyes are brown, not blue like the ones I saw that day. The ones that haunted my nightmares for years.

The pieces of the puzzle won't fit together, no matter how hard I try.

I'm too tired to think now, so I tug Elijah closer, breathing in his baby smell. The one that still makes me soft, even after all these years.

"Yes, baby." I press my lips to his forehead. "We can try. Now sleep."

His breathing evens out almost immediately. My own eyelids grow heavy, but I force them open, counting the guards one more time. Six now. They've added another.

Elijah shifts in his sleep, clutching my T-shirt. Before him, I would've already tried to fight my way out. Would've done something stupid and reckless.

But he changed everything.

My eyes drift shut. The lavender-sandalwood scent from the diffuser fills my lungs. It's too nice, too peaceful for a prison.

That's what makes it dangerous.

That's what makes *him* dangerous.

My last thought before sleep takes me is that I need to stay alert. Need to stay sharp.

But Elijah's steady breathing and the ridiculously comfortable bed pull me under, anyway.

My eyes snap open to darkness.

Something's wrong.

Red drops hit my face. Warm. Wet.

Blood splashes across my face.

"Jake!"

My feet pound against wet concrete. The alley stretches endlessly, getting darker with each step. Jake's always just ahead, just out of reach.

"Stop! Please!"

Jake turns. His chest blooms red, the stain spreading like spilled wine. Those final moments replaying like a broken record.

"Run, Clara." His voice echoes. "Run."

The Raven steps out from the shadows. Black mask gleaming, those blue eyes burning through me. Fifteen years old again, paralyzed, watching my brother fall.

But this time, it's different.

"Mommy?"

My heart stops.

Elijah stands beside Jake, small hand reaching for his uncle.

No. No, no, no.

"Baby, come here!" I surge forward. My legs won't move. Concrete turns to quicksand. "Elijah, don't!"

The Raven extends his hand. That fucking mask tilts, considering my son like a predator eyeing its prey.

"You can't have him!" I thrash against invisible restraints. "Jake, don't let him—"

Jake crumples. Blood pools around his body. Elijah steps closer to The Raven.

"Look at me, baby. Look at Mommy!"

Elijah turns. His brown eyes meet mine—Leonid's eyes. The eyes he got from... him.

"It's okay, Mommy. We're training the bad guys, remember?"

The Raven's hand closes around Elijah's shoulder.

"NO!"

My scream tears through my throat. I fight harder. Muscles burning, straining. Concrete hardens around my feet.

A door materializes behind them. Steel and ancient, radiating heat. Hell's gate.

The Raven's mask catches the red light. Blue eyes pierce through me as he guides my son forward.

"Give him back!" My voice breaks. "Take me instead. Please. PLEASE!"

The door creaks open. Fire spills out.

Jake's body drags across the ground, pulled by unseen forces. Elijah follows, small steps willing. Trusting.

"Baby, stop! ELIJAH!"

The Raven's mask turns one last time.

Those blue eyes...

Something warm touches my cheek. Everything vanishes. Black swallows the door, the fire, my son.

I sob, the sound barely a whimper in the void. My heart squeezes so tight I can't breathe.

But I can't move. My body won't respond.

It's too heavy.

Like being buried alive.

"Shhhh," a deep voice cuts through the nightmare. Not Jake's. Not The Raven's.

"Sleep, Clara. Everything's okay."

The warmth spreads. Gentle. Almost... tender.

My eyelids fight to open. Just a sliver.

A massive shadow moves across our room. Moonlight catches on broad shoulders.

The door opens without a sound.

Something tugs at my consciousness. Important.

Those eyes in the nightmare were blue, but the shadow...

The door clicks shut.

I sink back into darkness.

Ten

Leonid

A few moments ago

If I hold my breath any longer, I'll be six feet under.

I stand at the door, my hand gripping the handle tighter than necessary.

Poshel na khuy! What the hell are you being such a wuss for? She's your prisoner, for fuck's sake. Quit screwing around and get in there!

I turn the lock on the outside of the door, and the heavy bolt slides back with a click.

But my feet freeze just outside the threshold of the door.

What the hell's wrong with me? I'm here for her, to remind her who's in charge.

I've spent the last hour planning exactly how to break this *suka*. The plan was simple: grab her, threaten her, make her play by my fucking rules.

But when I push the door open, every fucking thought evaporates.

Clara had turned off all the lights except for a dim lamp in the corner. Moonlight streams through the floor-to-ceiling windows, bathing the king-sized bed in silver. And there she is.

Chyert.

My feet root to the wooden floor. The hellcat who took down three of my men, who'd rather die than show fear, lies curled around her son like a protective tigress. Her dark hair spills across white sheets, features soft in sleep. The moonlight catches her face, and for a moment, I forget how to breathe.

God, she's fucking gorgeous.

This would be easier if she were trying to claw my eyes out. At least then I'd know what to do with the heat coursing through my veins.

I take a step forward, my gaze lowers, and my breath catches. She's wearing an oversized T-shirt that has ridden up, exposing a tantalizing stretch of thigh that makes my mouth go dry and my cock throb with desire.

Get it together, you pathetic mudak.

I'm not here to fuck her, but my primal instincts tell me otherwise. She's gorgeous, sleeping like an angel, unaware of the predator watching over her.

My cock clearly hasn't gotten the memo about her being the enemy. Traitor's been doing most of my thinking when it comes to this woman. First at that club, now here—

I drag a hand down my face, forcing my eyes away from those legs that go on for fucking days...

I'm the fucking Pakhan of the Kuznetsov Bratva, I remind myself again, *not some dick-driven piece of shit who can't control himself around a pretty face.*

Even if that face belongs to the most infuriating, beautiful *suka* I've ever—

Ostanovis'. Stop.

I force myself to breathe, my muscles tensing as I try to pull myself out of whatever spell she's casting.

Instead, I find myself counting her breaths.

The kid shifts in his sleep, and my eyes snap to him. Little fingers clutch her hand like it's a lifeline. Something twists in my gut at the sight. Those curls... *Der'mo*, they're just like my mother's photos of me at that age.

"No..." Her whisper slices through my thoughts. "Jake, don't..."

Her face contorts, body twitching beneath the sheets. Tears leak from beneath those long lashes, and *fuck* if that doesn't do something strange to my chest.

"Baby, please..." Raw desperation rips through her voice. "Look at Mommy..."

My hand moves before my brain catches up. *Stupid.* But I can't stop watching her face. The fierce little *tigritsa* who'd sooner shoot me than show weakness, now fighting shadows in her sleep.

This is perfect, the *Pakhan* in me whispers. *Wake her now. Use the boy. Break her.*

But my fingers hover over her tear-stained cheek. The mighty Clara reduced to pleading in her dreams. It feels... wrong. Like watching something I shouldn't see. Something private.

"ELIJAH!"

Her scream jolts through me. The boy doesn't stir—too used to his mother's demons. More tears track down her face, and before I can stop myself—

"Shhhh." The sound escapes like a betrayal. My thumb catches a tear. "Sleep, Clara. Everything's okay."

She settles under my touch, and *blyat*, her skin is soft. Warm. Her breathing evens out, but then those eyes flutter open—just a sliver of brown in the moonlight.

I yank my hand back like her skin burns. Which it fucking does. Burns straight through my flesh, into places I thought were long dead.

What the fuck am I doing?

Stalking toward the door, I try to shake off her warmth. Her scent. The way her body curves protectively around her son. The sight burns into my brain like a brand.

The door shuts. The walls seem to shrink as Dmitry strides down the corridor.

"Boss?" Dmitry steps aside, that knowing look in his eyes.

"Double the guard." The words come out gravel-rough. "No one enters without my permission."

"And the boy's Pikachu?" He holds up a ratty yellow thing.

My fingers curl into fists. The toy's dead eyes mock my weakness. "Leave it outside. What do I look like, a fucking babysitter?"

But as I stride down the hallway, that image burns behind my eyes. Clara fighting her nightmares. That familiar face on her boy. The way one tear felt against my thumb.

Sentimental piece of shit, I snarl at myself. Tomorrow, I'll remember who I am. Tomorrow, I'll make her talk.

Tonight... Tonight, I need a bottle of the good vodka. Maybe two.

The vodka burns like acid, but it's not enough to erase her tears from my mind. *Blyat.*

I slam the crystal tumbler down on my desk, watching the liquid ripple. The massive screens covering my office walls paint everything in an eerie blue glow—satellite feeds, security cameras, stock tickers, crypto movements. Power at my fingertips.

But I can't stop seeing her face.

The holographic display flickers as I swipe through files. There—Jake Caldwell. Every piece of intel I've gathered on the Caldwell family sits in my secure server. Know your enemy. Know their weaknesses.

"System, display file 2847-B."

The crime scene photos materialize in the air before me. Blood soaking into forest dirt. Summer leaves scattered with red. And there she is—15-year-old Clara, covered in it, screaming as three officers try to pry her off her brother's body. Her fingers leaving crimson streaks on Jake's shirt.

My jaw clenches. That summer, I was halfway around the world cleaning up my father's mess in Moscow. Some upstart thought he could take over our weapons pipeline while the old man was dying. Poor fuck learned the hard way why they called me The Raven.

I take another shot, memories of that bloody summer mixing with the image of Clara's tears tonight. Everyone blamed The Raven for Jake's death. Convenient. But I didn't give the order. And I never kill children.

"Cross-reference location data, summer 2010."

A ghost of a laugh escapes me. So that's her game.

My fingers drum against the desk, an old tell I thought I'd killed years ago. She thinks The Raven killed her brother. That I killed her brother.

Fifteen years old, covered in his blood, and someone fed her my name.

The Raven's reputation has served me well—kept rivals in check, territories secure. I never bothered clearing my name when shit went sideways. Let them fear the boogeyman.

But this...

I stand abruptly, the chair rolling back to hit the wall. Jake Caldwell's death file hangs in the air, his sister's screams somehow echoing in the pixels. Some *mudak* used my name, used The Raven, to destroy a little girl's life.

And now she wants me dead.

My jaw clenches as I watch the footage loop. Fifteen-year-old Clara, screaming over her brother's body. Today's Clara, with murder in her eyes and poison in her pocket.

Both of them bleeding for a crime I didn't commit.

Maybe it's the vodka making me philosophical. Maybe it's the memory of her tears on my thumb. Or maybe it's because, for the first time in years, I actually give a fuck about clearing my name.

A strange twist of pain tugs at my chest, something foreign, almost unwelcome, as the young girl's anguish claws at me. It's like a punch I wasn't ready for—sharp, deep, and settling uncomfortably under my ribs.

What the fuck is this? Guilt? Regret?

No... something worse. An ache that only gets worse with every scream that loops on screen, a hollow pain as if her suffering carved something out of me without permission.

Blyat. My fist tightens, but the feeling doesn't leave.

A knock interrupts my thoughts. "Enter."

Dmitry's massive frame fills the doorway. His eyes catch on the floating images, but he knows better than to comment.

"Mitch is conscious."

I lean back, studying the clear liquid in my glass. "And?"

"Not a word."

"Make him talk."

"*Da*, boss." He hesitates. Something's eating at him. "What... what's your plan for Elijah?"

The question hits like a bullet. My grip tightens on the glass. "What's it to you?"

"The boy is innocent in all this."

"You think I don't know that?" The words come out like ice. "He's leverage."

Dmitry's face hardens. "Children shouldn't be leverage."

I'm on my feet before I realize it. "Watch yourself."

He shifts—unusual for the killer I know him to be. His eyes drift to another screen showing the feed from Clara's room. Elijah clutches onto his mother.

"The boy..." Dmitry's voice roughens. "He reminds me of Sasha."

The name hangs heavy in the air. Dmitry's nephew. Dead at six from leukemia.

"Your point?"

"Just... the way he holds that Pikachu. Sasha had the same one. Wouldn't let it go, even in the hospital, when—" He cuts himself off, jaw tight.

I study my most loyal soldier, the man who's killed without hesitation. Now undone by a stuffed fucking toy.

"The boy isn't Sasha." My voice comes out harder than intended. Because that kid's face—those curls—hit too close to home.

"No." Dmitry straightens. "But maybe that's why she fights so hard. Like Katya did, trying to save Sasha."

His dead sister. The unspoken weight of family—lost, broken, stolen—fills the room.

I grab the decanter. Pour two shots. The routine of it steadies my fucking hands. Dmitry downs his without flinching.

Good. Back to business.

I turn the security feeds off with a sharp gesture. Enough of this sentimental *der'mo.* "Get creative with Mitch. I want answers."

The screens fade to black. Better. Cleaner.

"And Dmitry?" The vodka burns, but my voice comes out frozen. "Don't let feelings cloud your judgment. They're a liability we can't afford."

Like you haven't spent the last hour staring at her tears, mudak?

"Boss—"

"Feelings get you killed." My knuckles whiten around the glass. "Or worse—they make you wish you were."

Dmitry's jaw locks. His chair scrapes back.

I don't watch him leave. Instead, I pull up the weapons shipment data from 2017. Work. Death. Power. This is what matters.

Not some dead kid's sister.

Not some living kid's tears.

The door shuts with a soft click.

Eleven

Clara

S NRKKK-PFFFTTT

What the—?

My eyes snap open, mortified by the foghorn that just erupted from my face.

Good job, Clara. Real femme fatale material right here.

Nothing says "deadly assassin" like snoring loudly enough to wake yourself up.

Wait.

I blink at the ceiling, mind fuzzy. This isn't my ceiling. Too many fancy-ass crown moldings. Too much... everything.

The events of last night crash back like a hangover.

Kidnapped. Check.

Enemy's house. Check.

Probably drooled on thousand-thread-count pillowcases. Double check.

Something's not right, though. The room's too quiet, missing that soft little whistle-snore that usually—

My heart stutters.

"Elijah?"

Silence answers. Not even a rustle of sheets.

I bolt upright, head spinning. The massive bed stretches beside me, empty except for a squished Pikachu plushie. No tiny limbs sprawled everywhere. No kid-sized blanket cocoon.

No son.

My heart slams against my ribs. I throw the covers off, bare feet hitting cold wood. "Elijah!"

The walk-in closet's empty. Just rows of *his* designer clothes.

Why can't he hang his clothes in his room like a normal person?

The bathroom door's wide open, no tiny figure brushing his teeth or playing with the fancy soap dispenser.

Under the bed. *Nothing.*

Fuck, fuck, fuck.

My eyes drift to the bedroom door. No way. No *fucking* way Elijah would just...

But he's 4. And curious. And has zero sense of stranger danger because I've sheltered him too much and—

I press my palm against my chest, trying to cage the panic.

Okay. Think.

The door's probably locked, anyway. These are professional criminals. They wouldn't be stupid enough to—

My bare feet whisper across the polished hardwood. One step. Two. Like approaching a bomb that might go off.

My fingers hover over the handle. Just check. It'll be locked, and I'll feel like an idiot, and Elijah's probably just hiding in the closet again because he thinks he's a ninja and—

The handle turns.

Just... turns.

Like this isn't a kidnapping. Like we're guests at some fucked up B&B run by the Russian mob.

"You have got to be kidding me," I breathe, staring at the open doorway like it's personally offended me.

These absolute *morons* didn't even lock us in.

I step into the hallway, the smooth wood giving way to plush carpet.

"Elijah?" My whisper echoes off the high ceiling. Three other doors mock me from across the hall, all firmly shut.

I try each handle. Locked. Of-fucking-course.

"Baby?" My voice gets a little louder, a little more desperate. "This isn't funny, buddy."

The elevator at the end of the hall hums softly. Down is the only option unless my 4-year-old suddenly learned to pick locks or sprout wings.

My finger hovers over the button. I'm half-naked, trapped in a mobster's house, and my son is missing. This is fine. Everything is fine.

The elevator arrives with a soft *ding* that makes me jump. Empty. Thank God.

I step in, wrapping my arms around myself. The oversized white T-shirt I snagged from the closet keeps sliding off one shoulder. My reflection in the mirrored walls shows exactly what I am—a hot mess in borrowed clothes, barefoot and pissed off.

Mother of the Year.

The numbers tick down: 3... 2... 1...

A child's giggle floats up from somewhere below.

His giggle.

I'm out of the elevator before the doors fully open, bare feet silent on the marble floor.

More laughter. Adult voices. The clinking of plates.

I break into a run, T-shirt barely covering my ass, no bra, no dignity, no—

I skid to a stop in the doorway.

What. The. Actual. Fuck?

My son—my innocent 4-year-old—is perched on a marble counter like he owns it. Dmitry towers behind him, guiding his tiny hands over a spatula.

"Gentle, *mladshiy*. Like this—" Dmitry's gruff voice goes soft as they flip a perfectly round pancake together.

"Look! I did it!" Elijah bounces, Pikachu clutched under one arm.

"Mommy!" Elijah spots me, face lighting up like Christmas. "The bad guys are nice now! Uncle Dmitry showed me how to make circles! Way better than your squares!"

This kid. Way to throw me under the bus.

Wait, what? Uncle. Dmitry.

"Buddy..." I force my lips into something resembling a smile, every instinct screaming as I edge into the kitchen.

What kind of twilight zone bullshit is this?

"Well, well." Maksim's eyes drift down my bare legs. "Look who finally joined our little breakfast party."

My fingers itch for a weapon. Any weapon.

Movement draws my eye to the far corner. Sunlight streams through tall windows, catching on a familiar broad-shouldered silhouette. Leonid. Looking like some dark god in a perfectly tailored black shirt, sleeves rolled to expose corded forearms.

Fuck me.

No. No fucking way. Not going there.

His eyes drag from my bare feet, up my exposed legs, lingering on where his stolen T-shirt barely covers my ass. When they finally meet mine, they're dark. Dangerous.

Like I've personally offended him by not wearing pants.

Good.

"Uncle Dmitry says I can help cook every morning!" Elijah announces, completely oblivious to the tension crackling through the air. "Can we stay forever?"

My heart stops.

"Uh..." My brain short-circuits.

Stay forever? In the house of the man I'm supposed to kill?

Sure, why not? We can have pancakes every morning with the Russian mob. Maybe learn how to garrote someone over orange juice.

"Sure... I guess." The words tumble out before I can stop them. I pinch the bridge of my nose, glancing ceiling-ward.

Hey, God, if you're up there—what the actual fuck?

I watch Elijah beam at Dmitry, all gap-toothed innocence.

Okay. Play it cool, Clara. Just casually make your way to the—

"Want to see my pancake flip, Mommy?"

"Coming, buddy." I inch toward the counter. Nothing suspicious here. Just a mother showing interest in her son's culinary adventures. Who happens to be drifting closer to that lovely knife block with the really sharp— A wall of heat appears behind me.

Christ, how does someone so big move so quietly?

"Sit." Leonid's breath brushes my ear. His hand spans my lower back, fingertips burning through the thin cotton.

God, he's so... fucking *big.*

Was he always this *big*? This... everywhere.

My body betrays me, leaning into his touch for a fraction of a second before my brain catches up. What the hell, hormones? That's the enemy. The very hot, very touchable—

No. Enemy. Focus.

"I don't take orders from—"

His fingers flex against my spine, guiding me toward a chair. Not pushing. Not forcing. Just... suggesting. Firmly.

Joker watches the whole thing, mouth twitching. Asshole.

I sit. Not because Leonid told me to. Because I want to. Because it's a tactical advantage to... to...

Fuck, he smells good.

Fuck, stop it.

"Pancakes!" Elijah chirps, completely demolishing my murderous momentum. "Mommy, look! Dmitry made mine look like a star!"

Dmitry. The Siberian Slaughterer. Making my kid star-shaped pancakes.

I drop my forehead to the marble counter with a *thunk*.

"Coffee?" Leonid's voice rumbles above me, way too amused.

"Poison?" I mumble into the marble.

"Maybe later."

I lift my head to glare at him, but he's already moving away, the ghost of a smirk playing at the corners of his mouth. His very kissable mouth—

No. No, no, no.

I bang my head on the counter again.

"Mommy's weird in the morning," Elijah stage-whispers to Dmitry.

Thanks, kid. Keep spilling all my secrets to the mob.

"More chocolate sauce!" he demands, and Dmitry—may God strike me dead—actually complies.

So, this is my life now. Sitting at a mobster's breakfast table, half-dressed, watching trained killers spoil my son rotten while plotting ways to murder their boss.

Who, by the way, just set a steaming cup of coffee in front of me. Black, two sugars.

Exactly how I like it.

Bastard.

Twelve

Leonid

Four hours earlier

This morning has gone completely off plan.

I didn't sleep much, but at least I slept. Barely enough to keep me from losing it.

I'm used to quiet.

Dead silence. But instead, I wake up to the sound of a kid's voice over the CC TV screen.

Singing. Off-key and cheerful.

Der'mo.

I scrub a hand over my face, pushing the irritation away. I've dealt with cartel bosses, corrupt politicians, and worse, yet here I am, rattled by a 4-year-old's morning song.

Fuck.

The camera shows their room, and there he is—Elijah, wide awake and entertaining himself with some children's song while his mother sleeps.

Why the hell is he awake so early? Damn kid can't even sleep in like a normal human being.

I should turn off the fucking feed.

That's what a normal person would do—not sit here at six in the morning, watching some kid's solo concert through security cameras like a creep.

Instead, I drag myself to the shower, cranking the water hot enough to scald. Let it pummel my muscles, trying to wash away twelve hours of surveillance footage. Of watching her sleep. Of wondering if she dreams about killing me.

My head spins with plans, deals, loose ends that need tying. Mitch still needs breaking. Three shipments need routing. The Italians want answers.

But it keeps drifting back to her. To Clara.

And her *kid*.

Clenching my jaw, I shake it off and finish the shower. I dry off quickly, tossing on a black shirt and cargo pants. Practical. Time to handle this.

Walking out of my room, I head down the hallway, footsteps muffled by the plush carpet. Reaching their door, I twist the handle and unlock it. It swings open smoothly.

"Hi."

I nearly jump out of my skin. The soft little voice catches me so off guard that my hand jerks back from the door like I touched a live wire. Elijah's head pops out, curls sticking in every direction, eyes bright and wide—*too damn similar to mine.* Those deep brown eyes. *My eyes.*

No. Stop it. There's no fucking way.

I force myself to swallow down the thought, to ignore the resemblance gnawing at my gut like a goddamn parasite.

"Uh..." I grunt, trying to remember what the hell I was supposed to say. *This is Clara's kid.* The brat. But right now, he's standing there looking at me like I'm *not* the bad guy keeping them prisoner. Like I'm just... someone he trusts.

Then, without hesitation, his hand reaches out, fingers brushing against mine before curling around my palm. The contact jolts me, like I've been hit by something I didn't see coming. His hand is so small, soft, and fragile, like something I could crush with barely any pressure.

I freeze.

How can something this tiny fit in my palm and shock me like this?

My throat tightens.

For a second, I just stare down at where our hands are joined, his trust weighing heavier than anything I've ever held. It's unsettling. Foreign. But he's looking at me like it's the most natural thing in the world.

Before I can react, Elijah lets go, darting down the hallway with a burst of energy. I follow his gaze, and there, lying against the wall just outside the door is the ugly yellow toy plush thing.

"Pikachu!"

The kid's eyes light up like it's Christmas. His little feet move faster than I can register, and in an instant, he's scooping up the plush, hugging it like it's a damn treasure.

"Pikachu! You found him!" Elijah turns to me with pure joy, running back toward me.

I stare down at the yellow toy, and for a split second, my brain goes blank.

Then he looks up at me.

"Thank you!" He beams, assuming I'm the one responsible. And then it happens.

The kid hugs me.

Full-on, arms-wrapped, face-pressed-into-my-leg hug.

I freeze.

What the hell?

The warmth of his small body presses against me for a moment too long, and I stand there like a statue, unsure of what the fuck I'm supposed to do with this. Hug him back? Shove him off?

Instead, he pulls away, clutching Pikachu to his chest, beaming like I'm some kind of hero.

"Did you bring him back for me, Bad Guy Meowth?" Elijah looks up at me, all innocent trust. His fingers clutch the stuffed toy as if it's a trophy.

I frown. *Meowth?*

I narrow my eyes, "I'm not... Meowth." I rub a hand over my face again. "And I sure as hell didn't bring back your toy."

Elijah tilts his head as if that little detail doesn't even matter and just grabs my hand with his other free hand.

"I'm hungry," he says, like this is the most normal thing in the world. Like he hasn't been locked in a room all night. Like I didn't kidnap him and his mother.

I stare down at the tiny fingers wrapped around mine.

Something shifts, like a crack in armor I didn't know I had. Damn kid. Not the reaction I should be having. Definitely not.

"Let's go," I mutter, mostly to myself, and start walking down the hallway, dragging the kid with me.

He skips alongside me, no fear, no hesitation.

Current

Her face stops me cold first.

Flushed from sleep, a strand of hair sticking to her cheek. *She looks different.* Younger, like all the fight's drained out of her, leaving something raw behind.

Govno.

I didn't expect this; didn't expect to see her like this—so exposed. My eyes trace the curve of her jaw, the way her lashes flutter as she stirs.

Raw. Real. And fucking gorgeous.

Enough. My grip tightens around the cup before I push the coffee across the marble counter.

Clara peels her face off the counter, hair a wild mess around her shoulders.

No makeup.

No weapons.

Just her, stripped bare of everything except that oversized shirt that keeps slipping off one shoulder.

My shirt. *Suka blyad'.*

She takes the coffee without looking at me, and there's something so carelessly intimate about the way she wraps both hands around the mug like we do this every morning. Like I'm not the man she came to kill.

A yawn catches her off guard, and when she notices me staring, she doesn't blush or look away like most would. Instead, her lips curl into that familiar fuck-you smirk. Even half-asleep, she's ready for war.

"Take a picture, Kuznetsov. It'll last longer."

My jaw clenches.

Who would have thought I'd have *Red*—Clara Caldwell—sitting in my kitchen, head tilted sideways on the counter like she's given up all pretense? The hellcat who took down three of my men, now watching her son make pancakes with the Siberian Slaughterer.

She catches Maksim's lingering gaze on her bare legs, and something dark twists in my gut. Before I can stop myself, I step closer, deliberately crowding her space. *Mine.* The thought comes unbidden, unwanted.

"You always let your victims get this close?" she murmurs, not bothering to move away. Her breath catches when my hand finds the small of her back again.

"Only the ones I plan to keep."

The words slip out before I can catch them. Her eyes snap to mine, and for a moment, the air between us crackles with something that has nothing to do with hatred.

"Dmitry! Can I flip another one?" Elijah's voice breaks whatever spell is building.

Clara's attention shifts to her son, and I watch the transformation. The softness that creeps into her eyes. The way her fingers relax around the mug. Even the slight upturn of her lips—a real smile, not the sharp ones she saves for me.

It's like watching a tiger turn into a house cat. Except I know better. The tiger's still there, just waiting.

"This is temporary," she says quietly, but her eyes stay on Elijah. "Whatever game you're playing."

"Is it?" I lean closer, letting my breath stir the hair by her ear. She shivers. "Tell me something, Clara. When you dream about killing me, is it always with a knife? Or do you get creative?"

She turns her head slightly, and suddenly, we're breathing the same air. Too close. Her lips curve into something wicked. "Wouldn't you like to know?"

Maksim's low whistle cuts through the moment. His eyes are still on Clara's legs, and something in me snaps.

I grab her elbow, gentle but firm. "Time for you to change."

"I'm not done with my coffee," she protests, but I'm already pulling her to her feet.

"You are now."

"Mommy?" Elijah calls out.

"Just getting dressed, baby!" She manages to sound perfectly calm despite my grip on her arm. "Keep making those awesome pancakes!"

I guide her toward the elevator, very aware of the warm skin under my palm, the way she has to quicken her steps to match my stride.

"Possessive much?" she mutters as the doors slide closed.

I turn her to face me, backing her against the mirrored wall. "You have no idea."

The elevator starts to rise, and I watch her pulse jump in her throat. Not from fear—never fear with her. Something else. Something that makes this game we're playing far more dangerous than simple revenge.

"I hate you," she whispers, but her pupils are blown wide, and she's not pulling away.

"Good." I lean closer, letting her feel every inch of height I have on her. "Hate's honest. Hate, I can work with."

The elevator dings for our floor, and I step back, releasing her. She stays frozen for a moment, chest rising and falling rapidly.

"Change," I order, voice rough. "And Clara?"

She pauses in the doorway, that damn shirt still sliding off her shoulder.

"Next time you want to wander around my house half-naked..." I let my eyes drag over her bare legs one last time. "Remember who you're dealing with."

Her laugh is all smoke and promises. "Or what, Kuznetsov?"

The doors close before I can answer, but it doesn't matter.

We both know this isn't over.

Thirteen

Clara

"Who the fuck does he think he is?"

My back hits the bedroom door, waiting for the click of a lock that never comes.

"Controlling piece of shit," I mutter, stalking toward the walk closet. "Self-righteous, arrogant—"

The words bounce off the walk-in closet's mirrors, and— Oh.

Well, shit.

My reflection tells me exactly who he thinks he is: the guy whose white shirt is currently doing a piss-poor job of covering anything important. The fabric is so thin that I might as well be wearing nothing. And speaking of nothing, the lack of a bra is making things... obvious.

My nipples are hard under his shirt, poking through the thin fabric like they're begging for attention. The shirt's slipped off one shoulder, and my hair's a wild mess, making me look like I've been thoroughly fucked instead of... kidnapped.

Biting down my lips, I roll my shoulders back, trying to shake off the rising tension crawling up my neck.

"Shit."

I hate that he's right.

Hate even more that I liked watching his jaw tick when Joker checked me out.

Fuck, girl, you're only reacting like this because you haven't had a man for the past five years.

Sucking in a breath, my nostrils flare as my gaze catches on a section I missed last night—a hidden panel sliding open to reveal rows of casual wear. Because of course the perfectionist Russian would have a secret compartment for his fucking sweatpants.

The closet is a testament to expensive taste and control issues—everything arranged by color, texture, season. Probably alphabetized, too. I run my fingers along a row of identical black suits.

"Let's see how you like someone messing up your perfect system, Kuznetsov."

I grab the first pair of joggers I find—charcoal cashmere because of course they are—and yank them on. They slip past my hips immediately. Great. I cinch the drawstring as tight as it'll go, bunching the fabric until I look like I'm wearing a garbage bag. A very expensive garbage bag.

Next comes the hoodie hunt. I pick the bulkiest one I can find, dark blue with some Cyrillic text I can't read. It smells like him—cedar and something darker, dangerous. I absolutely do not inhale deeper as I pull it over my head.

The end result in the mirror is ridiculous. I'm drowning in fabric, looking like a kid playing dress-up in Daddy's clothes. The thought makes me snort. Leonid would hate being called *Daddy*.

Unless...

No. Not going there.

I roll up the sleeves eight times before my hands appear. The pants are a lost cause, pooling around my feet like I'm standing in a fabric puddle. But at least nothing's showing through anymore.

"Take that, you controlling bastard," I mutter, then immediately remember the cameras he probably has everywhere. "And yes, I'm talking to you, creep."

I flip off the nearest corner of the ceiling for good measure.

The hoodie keeps slipping off one shoulder no matter how many times I adjust it. Between that and the way I have to keep hitching up the pants, I look like a drunk trying to get dressed in the dark.

But it's better than giving his men another show. And if Leonid has a problem with me ransacking his closet... Well, he shouldn't have kidnapped someone with such excellent taste in revenge-wear.

I'm about to leave when I spot them—a row of perfectly aligned silk ties. Black, navy, charcoal, repeat. The temptation is too strong.

Five minutes later, I've used one as a belt (it matches the joggers; I'm not a complete heathen), stuffed another in my pocket for later because who knows when you might need to tie someone up, and deliberately rearranged the rest in rainbow order.

Take that, you obsessive-compulsive mobster.

I do one final check in the mirror. Still drowning in fabric, still looking absolutely ridiculous, but at least now I'm decent. And if the outfit happens to smell like him... Well, that's his fault for not providing proper clothes.

"Alright, Kuznetsov," I say to my reflection, practicing my best fuck-you smile. "Let's see how you like this look."

The smile turns real when I imagine his face. After all, he did say to change.

He just never specified how.

The bedroom door creaks open, and I nearly faceplant into a wall of hard muscle.

Leonid.

He fills the doorway, one shoulder propped against the frame, arms crossed over his chest. His double-take would be comical if it wasn't so satisfying—the almighty Bratva boss, staring at me like I'm some alien creature that crawled out of his closet.

Which, technically, I did.

"What the fuck are you wearing?"

"Your spring collection." I strike a pose, one hand on my hip, careful not to step on the pools of fabric around my feet. The garbage bag of cashmere joggers shifts dangerously low despite the silk tie holding them up.

"I'm thinking of calling it *'Kidnapped Chic.'*"

His eye twitches. Actually twitches.

His gaze travels from the rolled-up sleeves that took five minutes to arrange down to where his thousand-dollar pants puddle around my ankles like expensive drapes.

"Those are Brunello Cucinelli."

"Really?" I hitch them up for the hundredth time. "They look more like a potato sack to me. Very slimming, though."

The muscle in his jaw jumps as his eyes catch on the silk tie around my waist. "Is that my Hermès?"

"Oh, this old thing?" I give a little twirl, nearly tripping over the pants legs. "I had to improvise. But don't worry, I color-coordinated. And I took the liberty of reorganizing your tie collection. Rainbow order really brightens up the space."

His face does something complicated—like he's trying to decide between strangling me or laughing.

"Kayla left clothes for you on the bed."

"Did she? Must have missed them while I was redecorating your closet."

The look he gives me could freeze hell twice over.

"Put on something else."

"No thanks." I start down the hallway, the pants swooshing with each step like some demented symphony. "I'm quite comfortable. Though your taste in sweats is a bit pretentious. Would it kill you to own something from Target?"

His hand wraps around my elbow, and suddenly, I'm facing him again. "You're doing this to provoke me."

"Is it working?" I bat my eyelashes, even as my pulse kicks up at his proximity. The hoodie slips off one shoulder again, and his eyes track the movement like a predator.

"Everything about you is provoking." His thumb brushes my exposed collarbone, and I absolutely do not shiver. "The clothes. The closet. That smart mouth of yours."

"Funny, I don't remember asking for your opinion." I try to step back, but the pants tangle around my feet. His arm shoots out, steadying me before I can fall.

Great. Perfect. Just what I needed—his hands on my waist, his chest against mine, that cedar-and-danger scent making my head spin.

"Let go."

"Why?" His breath fans across my cheek. "So you can fall on your ass in my twelve-hundred-dollar joggers?"

"Twelve-hundred—?" I sputter. "Who pays that much for glorified pajamas?"

"Says the woman who used a five-hundred-dollar tie as a belt."

"It's called fashion, asshole. Look it up." I manage to untangle my feet and break away, heading for the elevator. "Now, if you'll excuse me, I need to go check on my son."

"Elijah's with Dmitry in the garden."

The tie slips from my waist as I yank it free. "You left my son with the Siberian Slaughterer?"

His eyes track the silk sliding through my fingers. "Planning something?"

"*Maybe.*" The pants slip lower without their makeshift belt. "Want to find out?"

I snap the tie taut between my hands. His lips curve—and then I'm swinging. The silk whistles through the air, but he's already moving. His fingers catch the tie, using my momentum to pull me forward.

The joggers hit the floor, leaving me rocking the no-pants revolution in his hoodie like it's a high-fashion statement.

I release one end, letting it slide through his grip as I duck under his arm.

The move brings me behind him. *Perfect.* I jump, wrapping my arm around his neck—but he's ready. His hands grip my thighs, and the world spins. My back slams into the wall, knocking the breath from my lungs.

"Amateur." His body presses me harder against the wall, his hand slides up the side of my neck, fingers curling just enough to remind me who's in control.

"Get off me." The words come out breathless. Angry. Definitely angry, not—

His teeth graze my neck. "Make me."

I buck against him, trying to break free. Bad idea. The friction sends heat pooling low in my stomach, and his grip on my neck tightens enough to bruise.

"I know you're angry, Clara Caldwell." His lips brush my thundering pulse. "So angry at the person who killed Jake Caldwell."

My vision blurs.

Everything goes red.

"Do not speak *his* name." The words rip from my throat. Grinding down my teeth, I try to headbutt him, but his hand tangles in my hair, holding me still. "Fuck. You."

"Such fire, *krasotka*." He drags his mouth up to my ear, and I hate how my body arches into him. Hate how his heat bleeds through the thin shirt, making my skin burn.

"But I'm not the killer you're looking for..."

I blink rapidly, trying to clear my mind, to make sense of his words.

Wait. What?

What the fuck did he just say?

Fourteen

Clara

"What... did you just say?" The words barely come out.

Fuck. They don't even sound like mine.

My chest heaves, and I hate that I'm still pinned between him and the wall, body betraying my mind.

Too close. It feels too fucking *good*.

NO.

"I didn't kill him." His voice is steady, but it feels like a sledgehammer to my brain.

I blink, my mind stalling.

No. He's lying. He has to be.

This doesn't make sense.

His hand tangles in my hair, holding me still. Trapping me against the wall while his breath fans across my skin.

"Clara, I didn't kill Jake."

The words hit like smoke—everywhere and nowhere, impossible to grasp. My brain shorts out, caught between his body pressing closer and the ground crumbling under everything I've believed.

"Stop." It comes out broken. Desperate.

I *need* my anger.

Without it, there's just... *him*. The mint-coffee heat of his breath. The grip that's more promise than threat.

His thumb traces my throat, and something molten pools low in my stomach.

"I didn't kill him." His lips ghost along my jaw, each word a brand against my skin. "Listen! I. Didn't. Kill. Jake."

Everything narrows to points of contact—his chest against mine, fingers controlling my head, the dangerous brush of his mouth.

Wrong. This is wrong.

My hands betray me, pressing against his stupid hard chest—whether to shove him off or pull him closer. I don't even fucking know anymore. Hard muscle beneath expensive fabric; his heartbeat thuds under my palms like it's calling out a challenge. Mine picks up pace, falling into rhythm with his, our bodies synced in ways I don't want to understand.

I never thought this is how I would feel.

Relief, confusion, more anger... when my brain snaps back to me thirty seconds later.

"Liar," I hiss in a whisper.

His teeth catch my earlobe. "Am I?"

Not the killer.

Not the killer.

Not. The. Killer.

Fourteen years of hating him. Fourteen fucking years of seeing The Raven's face every time I think about Jake.

If he's telling the truth... My head spins.

What if it's all been—? *No.* He has to be lying. Has to be.

I look into his eyes again, but those eyes—rich, dark brown, like freshly brewed coffee, deep enough to drown in. *Fuck.* My stomach twists.

No. The killer had blue eyes. *Blue.*

But what if...? *What if I'm wrong?* What if it wasn't blue? What if it was brown?

Shit, what if I've been wrong this whole time?

The memory flickers, hazy at the edges now, and doubt creeps in like a poison.

No. *I saw it.* But the more I look into his eyes, the harder it is to hold on to that certainty. Everything's starting to blur, and I hate it.

His hands are still on me, one in my hair, the other resting on my neck. It's looser now, not strangling, but... holding me. *I should be paying attention.* I should be pushing him off, but my head is spinning like I've been yanked underwater.

When the fuck did the hallway start tilting?

"Breathe, *krasotka.*"

"Don't." The word scrapes my throat. "Don't call me that. Don't touch me. Don't—"

Everything tilts sideways. Left becomes down. Up becomes wherever the fuck my stomach went. The only solid thing is his chest against mine, and I hate that I'm grabbing his shirt to stay upright.

"Let go of me." But my fingers won't unlock from the fabric.

Hallway walls blur past. Or maybe I'm the one moving. Following? Being led? The world's gone fuzzy at the edges, like someone dumped static in my brain.

If he didn't kill Jake, then who—

The ding of the elevator pulls me back.

Where the hell am I?

Before I can process my thoughts, my body is already reacting. I feel the warmth of his hand on my back, gently prodding me forward.

When did we leave the third floor?

I take a hesitant step, then another, my feet moving of their own accord. It's as if my body has taken over, leading me away from the crumbling truth.

Each step echoes with questions I can't process yet.

A door opens.

Sunlight hits my face, and the air changes—thicker, warmer, alive with the smell of wet earth and growing things. Glass walls stretch overhead, green shadows dancing across Leonid's face as he... says something? His lips are moving, but the words don't compute.

Fourteen years of wrong.

Fourteen years of lies.

Fourteen years of—

"Mommy!" Elijah's voice slices through the chaos. My head snaps up, vision finally focusing on—

What the actual fuck?

Dmitry is holding my son. No, not holding—my 4-year-old is perched on his massive shoulders like the world's most dangerous piggyback ride. And in front of them...

I close my eyes for a second, then open them again

"Is that a... peacock?"

Joker, lounging on a stone bench like he owns it—barks out a laugh.

"She speaks! Thought we lost you there for a minute, *printsessa*. You were doing this whole zombie walk thing—"

"Shut up, Maksim." Leonid's hand settles on my lower back, steadying me. When did I start swaying?

Maksim. So that's Joker's real name. Add it to the growing pile of weird shit going on here. Like the peacock strutting past my feet, dragging its tail like royal robes. The marble fountains everywhere like some kinda ancient palace. Like Leonid not being—

I suck in a breath. Count to three with my eyes shut.

No. Can't go there yet. Focus on the bird. The ridiculous, impossible bird that my son is trying to...

"Elijah, don't pull his feathers!"

"It's fine," the mountain holding my child says. "Pavel likes the attention."

"Pavel," I repeat numbly. "The peacock has a name."

"They all do, yes." Kayla appears from behind a massive fern, carrying what looks like a tray of food. Because of course she does. Of course there are multiple named peacocks in this glass castle where nothing makes sense anymore.

I press my fingers to my temples. "How many?"

"Seven!" Elijah's voice bounces off the glass ceiling. "Uncle Bear says they're all named after dead people who made pretty music!"

Uncle Bear now. The monster has a nickname. And peacocks named after composers. And my son on his shoulders.

A peacock—Pavel? Igor? Fucking whatever—waddles between my feet, and I have to grip the nearest plant stand to stay upright. The metal digs into my palm, grounding me just enough to notice Leonid and Maksim having some silent conversation over my head.

"Mama, look!" Elijah's standing barefoot in the grass, tiny hands full of seeds, tossing them out like confetti. Completely unfazed by all this insanity. "Pavel does a dance when you feed him!"

"That's... great, baby." The words come out automatic. Mechanical. Like I'm running on backup power while my brain's still processing the nuclear bomb Leonid dropped upstairs.

Leonid Kuznetsov *not* Jake's killer.

All these years of wrong. And now *peacocks*.

The space starts spinning again.

Fifteen

Clara

"You need proper clothes."

Leonid's voice is a low rumble, rolling through the air like a heavyweight boxer stepping into the ring. And if that wasn't disorienting enough, a whiff of his cologne hits me—a blend of Cedar and testosterone that's somehow designed to make me forget my own damn name.

"Both of you."

"What?" I'm still staring at the fucking peacock parade, my brain short-circuiting between "he didn't kill Jake" and "why does the Russian mob have birds?"

A blur of iridescent blue and green feathers swoops past my face, and I duck, yanking myself down so fast my knees almost buckle.

"Shit—!" My heart pounds, and I twist sideways, arms flailing to keep myself upright. The damn bird clips me with its wing, throwing me off balance.

"Ahhh!"

I jolt like someone yanked the rug out from under me, letting out a squeal that could make a pig blush.

"AHHhhh!"

"AhHHhh!"

"Ahhh!" My voice echoes off the glass ceiling, and suddenly, two peacocks join in, squawking in startled harmony.

"REEE-yaaah! REEE-yaaah!"

"REE-yaah!"

"REE-yaah!"

"Mother fu—*udgesicles*!" A swirl of green and blue swoops at my head. Again. Because apparently, one near-death experience isn't enough for these feathered demons.

I try to duck, but my feet tangle. The stone path rushes up to meet my face and—

A firm arm snakes around my waist, yanking me back against a solid chest.

"Careful," Leonid says from behind me, his voice low and way too close to my ear. My breath catches, every nerve in my body crackling with awareness. His grip is strong, steadying me as the chaos around us seems to fade for a moment.

Maksim coughs—the kind that sounds more like choking on laughter.

I spin away from Leonid's chest, twisting around to face him.

That fucking smirk.

"You scream like a—" His mouth quirks up. "*Girl.*"

"Oh, no! You didn't just—" The words die in my throat as the scent of bacon and maple syrup punch through the air. Fuck my traitorous stomach for growling right when I'm about to tell him exactly which body part he can choke on.

"Food's ready!" Kayla appears through one of the side doors, carrying a tray laden with plates of food. She moves gracefully, setting the tray down on the long wooden table that's been artfully placed in the middle of the glasshouse.

Like this is some family brunch instead of a hostage situation.

"Sit." Leonid's hand lands firmly on my lower back, guiding me to a chair. My legs give out before I can think twice.

This is fucked up. All of it.

Elijah scrambles into the chair next to me, face flushed with excitement.

"Mama, look. A colorful feather." He holds it out, and the iridescent greens and blues shimmer under the morning light, catching like tiny shards of precious stones.

I reach for it. "Baby, we shouldn't—" I open my mouth, about to tell him it's not nice to pluck feathers from the birds when Leonid sits down beside me.

Grabs a plate. Adds a pancake, dumps blueberries on top, shoves it in front of me.

"Eat," he says, then turns to Elijah. "You too."

"Okay, Meowth." He nods and stands on his chair, arms stretched high, trying to reach the pancake plate.

Leonid reaches over and helps him, guiding the plate closer. Elijah beams up at him.

"Thank you!" he chirps before sitting back down, clutching his fork with both hands to attack his pancakes.

"I'm not Meowth, kid," he mutters, suppressing a cough. "I'm Leonid."

"Or the *boss*," Maksim adds. I glare at him, feeling the heat rise in my cheeks. He keeps glancing between the three of us—Leonid, Elijah, and me—with an expression that makes my skin prickle, like he's savoring some inside joke at my expense.

The scene feels wrong, twisted, like I've stumbled into an alternate universe.

Fuck. This is too much like a family breakfast. A family that doesn't exist.

A family that can't exist.

Leonid doesn't know that the little boy sitting at the table is his son, and I intend to keep it that way.

Elijah, oblivious, shoves more syrup-soaked pancakes into his mouth, the mess spreading across his face.

"Mommy, look!" He waves a piece of pancake triumphantly before sliding down from his chair, too curious to stay seated. He runs toward the peacocks, laughter ringing through the glasshouse.

I tense, wanting to get up, to pull him back to safety. But Leonid's hand closes over mine, pinning me in place. His grip is strong, commanding, and I have to fight the urge to pull away.

"Stay," he orders, voice low, and my heart skips, even though I hate how he affects me. His hand stays on mine for a moment too long, and the touch sends unwanted sparks of awareness shooting up my arm.

I twist my head to glare at him, but his focus is already on Dmitry. The massive man rises, his eyes briefly meeting Leonid's before he makes his way to where Elijah is playing. My stomach twists. I don't trust any of them, no matter how gentle Dmitry acts around my son.

Leonid notices my reaction. "Elijah's safe," he says, and there's something unreadable in his gaze. "But Mitch..." His voice turns calculating, almost casual, and a sense of dread washes over me. "He's not as lucky."

The fork slips from my fingers, clattering onto the plate. The sound is too loud, slicing through the moment, and I can't hide the way my body stiffens.

Mitch.

"What about Mitch?" I hiss at him, but panic wells up in my throat. Leonid leans in.

"We have him." He grabs a blueberry. Pops it in his mouth. Crushes it.

He picks up another blueberry, rolling it between his fingers. "Behave, and I'll take you to him." The berry vanishes between his teeth with a soft crunch.

Sixteen

Leonid

I don't have to try hard to notice the way her olive skin loses color.

She looks like she's about to punch me or vomit. Either one would be entertaining.

I don't bother suppressing the smirk that curls on my lips.

I like this.

I like seeing her squirm, watching the anger and fear flicker across her face. It's better than that calm, unbreakable facade she usually hides behind.

Give me something real, Clara Caldwell.

It's real.

Her fists clench on her lap, fingers digging into her palms, and a spark of satisfaction lights up inside me.

Her eyes stay locked on mine, unblinking, but I know the anger is simmering.

Da, krasotka.

I shift a little closer, making sure she feels me right there. "Going pale doesn't suit you," I say, each word slow and deliberate. "Makes me think you're scared."

Her jaw sets, lips pressing into a thin line. "What about... Mitch?" she fires back.

Her eyes narrow, that fire flaring back up.

Yeah, that's more like it.

I lean in just a fraction. "Worried about your broken-down body-guard?" The taunt comes naturally. "He's not going anywhere, if that's what you're asking."

Her nostrils flare, and her gaze flicks toward the door down the hall.

I let her question hang in the air, savoring the tension. "That's for trying to poison me, *krasotka*," I say, leaning in just a bit closer.

She doesn't need to know I'm having too much fun right now, getting some sweet revenge.

Her lips part, and I catch the beginning of a curse. "You... bast—"

Before she can finish, Elijah's laughter echoes through the glasshouse, and he comes barreling toward her. He crashes into Clara, hugging her waist like he hasn't seen her in years. The way her entire demeanor softens for him...

It's almost endearing. Almost.

I side-eye Dmitry, giving a short nod. He steps forward, crouching down to Elijah's level.

"Want to see a snake?" he asks, that rare, almost paternal warmth sneaking into his eyes.

Elijah's face lights up. "Snake?" he repeats, already bouncing with excitement. Clara, on the other hand, stiffens beside me, her eyes darting from her son to Dmitry.

"Snake?" she echoes, her voice edged with panic. But before she can react, Dmitry has already scooped Elijah up, lifting him effortlessly. Elijah squeals with delight, grabbing at Dmitry's shirt.

"No!" Clara tries to move, but I grab her wrist, my grip firm enough to keep her planted in place. She twists to glare at me, fury blazing in her eyes.

"He's fine," I say, keeping my hold on her. "We're not going to hurt him."

Maksim strolls over, hands stuffed in his pockets. He's grinning because of course he finds this entertaining.

"He's just meeting Golubka," Maksim says. "Lazy bastard of a snake; sleeps for hours after eating." He shrugs. "Won't even move unless you bribe him with a rat."

Clara's face twists in a mix of anger and confusion. "What the fuck do you want from me?" she snaps, her voice shaking despite her best efforts to sound tough.

I release her wrist but stay close, my shadow still looming over her. "Reminding you who started this," I reply, a cruel edge slipping into my words.

She needs to understand.

But then the reminder hits me: She thinks *I* started this... by killing her brother.

Her eyes flash with something raw, and for a moment, I wonder if she'll launch herself at me. But she holds back, her breathing shallow.

"Come on," I say, breaking the moment. I stand and jerk my head toward the door. "Let's go meet Mitch."

Her entire body tenses, and I can practically hear the wheels turning in her head. She doesn't have a choice, and we both know it. As she stands, I lead her out of the glasshouse.

She walks like she's being led to her own execution.

Good.

Let her feel the dread. It's only fair.

Seventeen

Leonid

Maksim pulls the Rolls-Royce Phantom around to the front. The October morning sun catches in Clara's hair as she walks ahead of me, my hoodie skimming her thighs. *Blyat*. The sight of her ass and thighs makes me harder than a concrete wall.

She pauses at the rear door, those bare feet planted on the cobblestones like she owns the fucking place. Like she isn't standing half-naked on my property wearing my clothes.

I move before she can touch the handle. Not because I want to open her door like some fucking schoolboy with his prom date. But because I know Clara—know the way her mind works. Give her half a chance and she'll either run or try to knee me in the balls again.

"Such a gentleman," she drawls.

"Get in the car, *dorogaya*."

"I'd rather walk."

"It's a two-day walk to civilization from here, *krasotka*. In my hoodie. With no shoes." I let my gaze drag deliberately down her body. "Though watching you try might be entertaining."

She grunts out a curse, low and seething, and I don't hide the smirk that spreads across my face.

She's fuming. Good.

I step closer, crowding into her space, until her back nearly hits the edge of the car door.

"Watch your head." I push Clara forward, guiding her into the car with a hand on her back. It's supposed to be a shove, but somewhere between my brain and my body, it turns into something too gentle.

My palm stays there for a beat too long, and I make sure her head doesn't bump against the doorframe as she slides inside.

What the fuck am I doing?

I tug my hand away quickly, trying not to think about it.

She scrambles into the seat, the oversized sweatshirt—*my* sweatshirt—hiking up her thighs, revealing way too much bare skin. I pull the fabric back down, a possessive reflex I don't have time to analyze. My eyes flick to Maksim, catching him glancing in the rearview mirror, brows lifted. I glare at him, daring him to say something.

"Eyes on the road," I snap, sliding in beside Clara and slamming the door shut. He chuckles but turns back to the wheel, pulling us smoothly away from the compound. Clara shifts next to me, yanking at the hem of the sweatshirt like she's trying to cover herself, her lips pressing into a stubborn line.

Adorable, even when she's fuming.

"I can dress myself." She bats my hands away.

"Clearly not, since you're wearing my clothes."

"You're the one who—" She cuts off as I lean across her, reaching for the seatbelt. My chest brushes against hers, and her breath hitches. The sound goes straight to my groin.

I take my time with the belt, letting my knuckles graze her breast. Her teeth snap an inch from my ear.

"Try that again, and you'll lose fingers."

I pull back just enough to see her face.

"Making sure you don't go flying through the windshield, *dikaya koshka*."

Wildcat. Slowly, I let my gaze drop to her bare feet.

"Keep staring, and I'll dig your eyeballs out with my thumbs."

Maksim's laughter breaks the silence. He meets my eyes in the rearview mirror, the bastard clearly enjoying himself.

"You know, boss, there's a Four Seasons thirty minutes away. Just saying."

Clara snaps her head around, glaring at Maksim. "Or I could just shove your face into the nearest wall, *Joker*," she fires back.

He only laughs harder, clearly enjoying himself.

The road stretches on, lined with nothing but trees and land—*my* land. Clara shifts, restless, her fingers tightening around the seatbelt as she bites her lip. She stares out the window, taking in the expanse of property that belongs to me, every inch of it. No neighbors. No one to interfere. Just more and more land.

Her patience frays visibly when the scenery finally changes, turning into the sprawl of New Orleans. She taps her fingers against her thigh, bouncing one knee.

"Where's Mitch?" she demands, voice edged with anxiety.

I don't even look at her. "Breathing."

"If you hurt him—"

"You'll what?" I turn to her, my hand finding her jaw, tilting her face toward mine. Her pulse jumps under my thumb, and I can feel the heat of her anger. "Try to poison me again? That wasn't very nice, Clara."

Her eyes darken. "Neither was killing my brother."

The accusation hangs between us.

She stops, pressing her lips together, her gaze narrowing on mine like she's trying to decode a secret hidden in my eyes. Her brows pull together, almost touching, as if she's genuinely annoyed that she can't figure it out.

"You *still* think I killed your brother?"

She bites her lip, and I feel my cock twitch.

Those fucking lips that I want to bite until she moans, want to feel wrapped around my cock, want to taste until she forgets how to breathe.

"The evidence—"

"Is wrong," I finish for her.

She looks away. "I don't trust you," she mutters, shoulders tense.

I lean in, our noses almost touching. "Not asking you to."

Her eyes flash, and she hisses, "And if you harm Mitch... or Elijah..."

I grin, cocky and unbothered. "You don't have the upper hand here, *krasotka*. Remember that."

Her reaction is immediate. She jerks forward, headbutting me, and stars explode in my vision.

"Fuck. You," she spits.

I catch myself, eyes watering from the impact, but I can't help the laugh that slips out. I press my forehead to hers, my smile wide and infuriating. "Maybe later, *dorogaya*. We have errands first."

She headbutts me again.

The impact makes my eyes water, but all I can think is how fucking perfect she is like this—wild and furious and mine.

Wait. Not mine.

Enemy.

Right?

Blyat.

The city skyline finally appears through the windows. Clara's whole body coils tighter, like a spring about to snap. Her eyes dart between buildings, probably calculating escape routes.

Maksim pulls into the circular drive of Canal Place, and Clara's expression shifts from calculating to suspicious.

"A mall?"

"You can't wear my clothes forever." Though the sight of her in my hoodie does things to me. "Even if you want to."

"I'd rather wear a trash bag."

"That can be arranged." I nod to Maksim. "Wait here."

Clara's door opens before she can protest. I grab her wrist, tugging her out onto the sidewalk. She stumbles, bare feet hitting concrete, and crashes against my chest.

"Boss," Maksim calls through the window, grinning like the asshole he is. "Sure you don't want that hotel room first?"

"Drive," I growl, but Clara's already trying to wrench free. I tighten my grip, steering her toward the entrance. "Stop fighting me, or I'll carry you."

"You wouldn't dare."

I bend down, reaching for her legs. She jumps back.

"Fine! Jesus. I'll walk." She yanks at the hem of the hoodie. "But I'm not buying anything."

"No?" I guide her through the doors, into the cool air conditioning. "Then I guess you're keeping my clothes. Though they might get a bit... drafty."

Her elbow finds my ribs. Hard.

I laugh, steering her toward Saks. "Come on, *krasotka*. Let's find you something." Then it slips out, softer, almost under my breath, before I can catch it, "Something that covers those legs before I have to kill someone for looking."

Clara freezes mid-step. "What... what the fuck did you say?"

"Nothing." I push her forward, my hand spanning her lower back. But I catch her reflection in the store window—the slight parting of her lips, the flush creeping up her neck.

Blyat. I really am losing my mind.

Eighteen

Clara

The marble floors of Canal Place freeze my bare feet as I walk beside Leonid, his oversized hoodie barely covering what it needs to.

Security guards do double-takes. A woman clutches her Gucci purse tighter. And here I am, looking like I just escaped someone's basement.

Which, technically, I did.

"Walk faster." Leonid's hand presses against my back.

"Easy for you to say, *tyrant*. Try prancing around on this marble ice rink without shoes. My nipples could cut glass right now." I dig my heels in, literally, making him adjust his stride. "Oh wait, you wouldn't know what that's like, would you? Being all cozy in your thousand-dollar shoes while dragging half-naked women around like some discount Christian Grey—"

"Are you done?"

"I'm just getting started, actually. Would you like to hear about—?" The words die in my throat. Two women in matching Louboutins have stopped dead in their tracks, staring at Leonid like he's an all-you-can-eat buffet. One nudges the other, phone already raised.

"Oh, my God, isn't that Henry Cavill? The Superman guy?"

"No, you idiot, that's Chris Evans!"

"I thought Chris Evans was shorter—"

My body moves before my brain catches up. I step directly into their camera frame, spreading my arms wide.

"Ladies, hate to break it to you, but this is just a really tall Ukrainian accountant with a face symmetry problem."

Leonid's fingers dig into my hip. "Ukrainian?"

"Sorry, did I offend your Russian sensibilities?" I bat my eyelashes at him. "Should I tell them you're actually Jason Momoa's less attractive cousin instead?"

"Clara."

"What? I'm helping. Building your cover story. Unless you'd rather I tell them about your underground chess gambling ring—"

He yanks me sideways, practically carrying me now. My bare feet barely touch the ground.

"Put me down or lose that hand."

"Make me."

His fingers press into my skin, hot through the thick fabric. My body goes rigid—partly from anger, partly from something else I refuse to acknowledge.

He spins me to face him, one arm locked around my waist, the other hand sliding up my spine. I snap my teeth at his jaw, missing by inches.

"Bite me again, and I'll show you how I like to play, *malishka*." His lips brush my ear, voice dropping to gravel. "Though something tells me you already know exactly what you're doing."

Fuck. My skin burns everywhere he touches. I want to knee him in the balls. I want to— No. No, I don't want anything except to get away from him and his stupid hands and his stupid mouth and—

"I'd rather bite off my own tongue."

"Now, that would be a waste of a very talented muscle."

"Put. Me. Down."

"Be a good girl, and maybe I will." His grip tightens, fingers digging into soft flesh. "Though we both know you're anything but good."

I thrash against him, which only makes him chuckle. The sound vibrates through his chest and straight into places that have no business reacting to him.

"Fuck you."

"Promises, promises."

I twist my body, fingers finding the pressure point in his wrist that should make any normal man drop like a sack of potatoes. Should. Instead, he just looks amused. Great.

"Nice try, *malishka*." His grip tightens further. "But I've survived worse than your little parlor tricks."

I move my hand.

"Keep fighting me, and we'll take the scenic route to Mitch and Elijah."

That stops me cold. Bastard. He knows exactly where to hit.

"I hate you."

"So you keep saying." He finally sets me down, his hands lingering longer than necessary. "Yet here we are."

I turn, ready to launch another string of creative threats, when I catch the gleaming letters above: "Chanel."

My throat tightens. How many times had I walked through these doors, tossing thousand-dollar bills around like confetti? Back when my last name still meant something. Before Dad traded our family's legacy for empty promises and cheaper thrills.

"Move." Leonid's hand finds my lower back again.

I dig my heels in, just to be difficult. "What's wrong with Target?"

"Everything." He leans close, and I'm about to introduce his groin to my knee when the door slides open. A blast of Chanel No. 5 stops me mid-swing.

"Welcome to Chanel." The voice drips honey and commission dreams. I turn to find a blonde Amazon in four-inch pumps, her pencil skirt so tight it's a miracle she can breathe, let alone walk. Her name tag reads "Vivian," and she's looking at Leonid like he's her next meal ticket.

The urge to knee someone in the groin intensifies. Just a different target now.

"How can I help you today?" She bats lashes that definitely aren't real, twirling a perfect blonde curl. "We just got in the most amazing new collection—"

I jam my elbow into Leonid's ribs. "Yeah, got anything in 'kidnapping victim chic'?"

Vivian's perfect smile freezes. Her blue eyes dart between my bare feet and Leonid's hand still on my waist.

"Of course." Vivian's heels click against marble as she leads us deeper into the store. "We have some absolutely stunning pieces that would be perfect for—" she glances at my bare legs "—your *style*."

Leonid's hand slides from my waist to my hip. "Show us everything."

"Everything?" Vivian's eyes light up like she just won the commission lottery. "Well, let's start with our new collection. The dresses are simply—"

"Pants first." I yank the hem of Leonid's hoodie lower. "Unless you want the security cameras to get an even better show."

"Actually," Leonid's fingers trace my spine through the fabric, "let's start with lingerie."

I stomp on his foot. He doesn't even flinch.

Vivian's already moving toward a display of lace that probably costs more than my car. "We have this gorgeous matching set in black—"

"Red." Leonid's voice drops an octave. "Show us the red."

I spin to face him. "I am not your personal dress-up doll."

"No?" His thumb brushes the exposed skin of my thigh. "Then I guess we can take our time looking. Maybe try on everything in the store. I'm sure Mitch and Elijah won't mind waiting another few hours."

Bastard.

Vivian returns with something that's more string than fabric. "This is one of our most popular—"

I cut her off, a plan forming. My eyes scan the store. "Actually, bring me every piece of lingerie you have. In my size." I tap my chin, pretending to think. "No, make that a size up and down, too. Just to be safe."

Vivian blinks. "Every... piece?"

"Problem?" I mirror Leonid's earlier tone. Then spot a leather jacket that probably costs someone's kidney. "That, too. And that entire rack of sweaters. You know what?" I wave my hand at the whole section. "Just bring everything."

"Everything?" Her perfect smile trembles.

"Did I stutter?"

Her eyes dart to Leonid like a tennis match.

"You heard her." He doesn't even blink.

"Everything?" Vivian squeaks.

"You heard her," he repeats.

Vivian swallows hard, glancing at the growing pile.

"R-right away."

She's clicking away on her heels, barking orders at wide-eyed assistants, who start pulling items off racks like their lives depend on it.

As the counter starts piling up with everything from jackets to sweaters to shoes, something catches my eye—a hint of black lace in the chaos. It's a matching bra and panties, barely there, teasingly sheer.

I grab it before an assistant can whisk it away and dangle it between two fingers, raising an eyebrow at Leonid.

"Vivian," I say, holding up the lace. "Where's the fitting room?"

She blinks, caught mid-chaos, before pointing toward the back. "Just over there, ma'am."

"Perfect," I say, turning on my heel and walking toward it without waiting for her to lead.

I disappear into the fitting room and slip into the lace, the delicate black fabric hugging my body like it was made for me. The mirror confirms it—dangerous, bold, exactly what I need.

I step out, hoodie slung over my arm, and spot Leonid lounging by the counter, watching the chaos like it's his personal entertainment. His eyes flick to me, scanning from head to toe. Ignoring him, I walk toward the side of the counter.

"Shoes." I point to a wall of stilettos. "All of them."

"Feeling petty, *dorogaya*?"

"Me? Never." I grab a pair of red-bottomed heels. "Just making sure I get my money's worth. Oh, wait—it's not my money, is it?"

He steps closer, voice dropping. "You're playing a dangerous game."

"Good thing I like dangerous." I snag another jacket. "This, too."

Twenty minutes later, the counter is piled high with designer every-thing. Vivian's typing frantically into her register, mascara slightly smudged from stress-sweating.

Leonid just watches, looking amused. "Done?"

"Almost." I grab one last thing—a silk scarf that says *$2100* on it. "Now I'm done."

"The total is..." Vivian swallows hard.

"Card." Leonid doesn't even look at the number.

I feel a tiny stab of victory. Until his hand finds my waist again, pulling me close.

"Hope you enjoyed yourself, *malishka*." His lips brush my ear. "Because now you're going to model every single piece. Starting with that red lace."

My elbow's already cocked back for his ribs when I catch it: a flash of movement in my peripheral vision. A face in the mirror-lined wall that makes my blood freeze.

Same jaw. Same eyes—except it isn't him.

I whip my head back to Leonid, then to the mirror again. The face is gone...

Nineteen

Leonid

"Time to go," I growl.

Clara's body goes rigid under my hand, her usual smart mouth suddenly silent. I follow her gaze to the wall or mirrors, but there's nothing there except our reflection.

She whips her head around so fast I think she'll snap it; her mouth drops open. Then she looks at me like I've grown a second head.

"What?"

She blinks a few times, as if trying to convince herself of something.

"If you're admiring my face, *malishka*, we can stop and get a better look."

She blinks those big eyes at me, teeth catching her bottom lip. It's oddly... distracting.

"I thought I saw..." She shakes her head, curls dancing across her bare shoulders. "Nothing. It's nothing."

Blyat. Since when does Clara Caldwell pass up a chance to tell me I'm an asshole?

My phone buzzes. I fish it out without taking my eyes off her face, still catching those little glances she keeps throwing my way.

Maksim:

> *Need more alone time with your new toy, boss?*

Maksim:

> *Getting cozy in there.*

I type back:

> **Get the fucking car before I shove your dick up your ass.**

When I look up, Clara's attempting to juggle every shopping bag herself, stumbling slightly in her new Chanel heels. The sight would be adorable if it wasn't so fucking stupid.

"*Blyat*," I mutter, watching Clara struggling with the items like some sort of stubborn child. "Give me the bags."

"I'd rather dislocate both shoulders." She hitches them higher, nearly tripping. The sight would be amusing if half of Canal Place wasn't currently recording us on their phones.

I snatch three bags from her left hand. She responds by ramming her heel into my shoe.

"Such a sweet girl," I drawl, catching another bag as it slips. "Your mother must be so proud."

"Almost as proud as yours must be of your kidnapping habits." She flashes me a smile that's pure venom. "Speaking of which, how many other women have you forced to play Barbie?"

The question hits a nerve I didn't know existed. My fingers flex against the shopping bags. "You're the only one."

Clara stumbles mid-step. Her head snaps up, the smirk falters, and something unreadable flickers in her eyes.

"Am I now?" she drawls, arching an eyebrow.

Suka! Why did I say that? This woman is my prisoner, my enemy, and here I am, blurting out shit that could give her leverage.

I grab a few more bags, and we make our way outside. Maksim pulls up in the Rolls-Royce, rolling the window down with a smirk.

"Need help with the bags, boss?"

I toss a bag into the car. "Shut up, Maksim."

Clara shoves past me, sliding into the car with as much grace as someone in stilettos and an oversized hoodie can manage. I start to follow, but something catches my attention.

At the corner of my eye, there's a flash of movement across the street. A figure in a black SUV, parked too neatly along the curb, engine running. My instincts flare and I narrow my eyes. The driver's side window is slightly lowered, just enough for me to notice the glint of something metallic. A camera lens? A gun?

I turn back to Clara; she's eyeing me with suspicion as I pause. She notices my shift in demeanor, but before she can say anything, I nudge her fully into the car and slam the door, my mind racing.

Stay calm. Handle this.

I slide in beside her, closing the door with a deliberate click. Maksim pulls away from the curb, but I don't relax. My eyes flick to the side mirror, catching the black SUV pulling into traffic a few cars behind us.

Clara crosses her arms, trying to mask her unease, but I feel the tension rolling off her. I lean forward.

"Maksim," I say, my voice low, "take the scenic route."

He catches my meaning instantly, his smirk fading. "Understood."

Maksim's whistling. Some upbeat pop song that makes me want to shoot him. But my attention is fixed on the side mirror, watching the third black SUV merge into traffic behind us.

Clara shifts beside me, shopping bags rustling as she peers out the window. Her sixth sense for trouble must be tingling—she hasn't made a single smart comment since we left Canal Place.

"Maksim," I bark.

"Got it, boss." His hands grip the wheel tighter, and the Rolls lunges forward, slipping through a yellow light just before it turns red.

"Take the next turn left," I command, eyes flicking between the mirror and the street ahead.

His whistling stops, replaced by the hum of adrenaline buzzing through the car.

I narrow my eyes, every muscle in my face tense and focused, watching the black SUVs close in like vultures circling a dying animal.

Two motorcycles appear in my mirror, weaving through traffic. Their helmets and dark jackets scream, "Not here for a joyride." I don't need a fucking degree to know we're being chased.

"Seatbelt," I order Clara, eyes fixed on the chaos behind us.

She doesn't argue. The click of her buckle is immediate.

"Friends of yours?" she asks, voice steady despite the way her fingers grip the leather seat.

"Something like that." I catch her eye briefly before turning back to the mirror. The SUVs are closing in, spreading out across the lanes like they're trying to corral us. Sloppy. Stupid. "Maksim, take Chartres."

Maksim cuts across traffic, the Rolls sliding through gaps that shouldn't exist, drawing a chorus of blaring horns. Shopping bags spill onto the floor. Clara snatches a Chanel bag just in time, then ducks as the first bullet thuds into the back window.

"Bulletproof," I assure her, but I don't relax. "Stay down anyway."

"Because that makes me feel so much better." But she slouches lower in her seat, cursing under her breath as more shots ping off the car.

Maksim takes a hard right, sending the Chanel bags flying again. A black and white Chanel box ricochets off the passenger headrest, catching Maksim's ear.

"*Blyat!*" He swerves slightly. "Boss, we've got—"

"I see them." Two more SUVs up ahead, trying to box us in. They're getting bolder. Or more desperate.

Clara's watching me now, those sharp eyes catching every micro-expression. "This isn't random, is it? They knew where to find you."

"They knew where to find *us*." I meet her gaze. "My brother sends his regards."

Her face goes blank for a half-second before understanding hits. "*Brother?*"

A motorcycle pulls alongside us, the rider reaching for something at his waist. I grab Clara's neck, forcing her down into the seat just as the gunshot cracks through the air. The bullet hits the window with a sharp *ping*, leaving a spiderweb of cracks but nothing more. Bulletproof. Thank God.

"You never mentioned a brother," she says into my thigh, voice muffled and tight with anger.

"*Twin*, actually." I keep my hand on her neck, holding her down as Maksim swerves again. "Ludis always did have terrible timing."

She goes completely still under my palm. Then she turns her head, her cheek pressing against my thigh, her lips dangerously close to the growing bulge in my pants. *Great.* My cock reacts instinctively, despite the adrenaline coursing through my veins. *Blyat.*

"Twin brother. You have a *twin brother* who's trying to kill you?"

"We can discuss family drama later." Though knowing Clara, she's already fitting this new piece into whatever puzzle she's been building. "Maksim, lose them, or I'm cutting your pay."

"Like you pay me enough anyway," he mutters, but his next turn sends two of the SUVs crashing into each other.

Clara starts to sit up. I press her back down as something much bigger than a bullet hits the roof.

"I swear to God, Leonid, if we survive this—"

The rest of her threat is lost as the world tilts sideways. Maksim's taken us onto two wheels, scraping past a delivery truck with inches to spare. The move tears my hand from Clara's neck. She slams into my side, her head knocking against my jaw.

And that's when the first RPG hits the building ahead of us.

The explosion tears through concrete and steel, raining debris onto the street. Maksim curses, wrestling the wheel to keep us steady. Clara's hand fists in my shirt, and I can't tell if it's fear or fury, but she's breathing hard, her pulse racing against my skin.

"*Blyat.*"

I tighten my grip on Clara, determined to keep her safe.

But at this rate, none of us is making it out unscathed.

Twenty

Leonid

Six lanes of traffic, and somehow these *sukas* still find us. The black SUV edges closer, inch by fucking inch, until—

"*Blyat*," the word slips out before I can stop it.

Clara's head snaps up. "What?"

But she sees it too—my own face staring back at us through the tinted window. Ludis's lips curl into that familiar grin, the one that always meant blood was about to spill.

"You've got to be kidding me," Clara mutters.

The SUV edges closer. Ludis rolls down his window, silver Desert Eagle glinting in the sunlight. "Miss me, *brat*?"

"Maksim." One word. He knows what it means.

"On it, boss."

Clara's nails dig into my thigh as Maksim cuts across three lanes. Horns blare. Brakes screech. A semi swerves, its horn blasting like an air-raid siren.

"Pull over!" Ludis's voice carries over the chaos. "Or I'll make sure your pretty little *suka* gets a bullet first!"

I feel Clara's whole body go rigid. "*Pretty little—* Oh, I'm going to enjoy shooting him."

"Not if I shoot him first."

"You had your chance." She twists in her seat, eyes locked on the side mirror. "When were you planning to mention the evil twin?"

A bullet pings off the door. Clara doesn't flinch.

"Busy day." I grab her shoulder as Maksim swerves again. "Shopping. Car chase. Family drama."

"Cute." She shoves my hand off. "Your brother's a better shot than you."

Another bullet hits the window. The bulletproof glass holds, but spiderwebs crack across it.

"Takes practice," I tell her. "Shooting your own reflection."

She laughs. "Poor baby. Must be hard, having an evil twin trying to kill you." She pauses. "Though looking at your face, I get the urge."

"*Poshol na khuy!*" Maksim curses. Red and blue lights flash behind us. Perfect. Now we have cops to deal with.

"Options?" Clara asks, all business now.

"Working on it."

"Work faster." She points ahead. "They're setting up a roadblock."

Sure enough, police cars stretch across the highway like a metal wall. Ludis's SUV pulls even with us again, boxing us in.

"Maksim..."

"I see it, boss." His knuckles are white on the wheel. "Hold on to something."

Clara's hand finds my arm. I pretend not to notice.

Maksim hits the gas. The engine roars. We're doing ninety, ninety-five, the speedometer climbing as Ludis's laughter echoes across the gap between cars.

"Last chance, brother!"

"Maksim, now!"

Everything happens at once. Maksim cranks the wheel hard left. Metal screams against metal as we clip Ludis's SUV. The impact sends them spinning.

Right into the path of an eighteen-wheeler.

The crash is spectacular. But we're already gone, Maksim reaching the exit ramp at speeds that would kill us in any other car.

"Holy shit," Clara breathes. Her fingers are still digging into my arm. "Is he—?"

"Not dead." I catch one last glimpse of the wreckage in the mirror. "Takes more than that to kill a Kuznetsov."

"Noted." She finally lets go of my arm.

The smoke from the crash clears just enough for me to see Ludis kick out the crumpled door of his SUV. He drags one of his men out of a black Audi that stopped in the chaos, tossing the driver aside like garbage.

"*Blyat*." I watch him slide behind the wheel. "Stubborn *suka*."

"What?" Clara twists in her seat, then curses. "You've got to be kidding me."

The Audi's engine revs—that distinct sound that means Ludis just floored it.

Maksim takes the exit at ninety, tires screaming against asphalt. The sirens fade behind us—all except one persistent helicopter still circling overhead.

"Next tunnel's half a mile," Maksim calls back, still gripping the steering wheel like a lifeline. "Better make it count."

Clara's hand shoots out, grabbing my Glock from its holster before I can stop her. The metal looks wrong against her manicured fingers—until she checks the magazine with practiced ease.

"You're going to shoot me?" I should probably take the gun back. I don't.

She ejects the magazine, counts bullets. "If you survive this? I'm putting one right between your eyes." Her fingers slide the magazine back in with a click. "But first, we deal with your psychotic twin."

"So thoughtful of you to wait."

"Shut up and give me your spare clip." She holds out her hand without looking at me. "Do I have to do everything myself?"

The helicopter spotlight sweeps across us. Clara leans forward, squinting through the windshield. "Maksim, when we hit the tunnel, cut the lights. Hard right into the maintenance bay."

Maksim's eyes meet mine in the mirror. I nod once.

"How do you—?" I start.

"Because, unlike some people, I actually do my homework." She checks the spare clip I handed her. "Three maintenance bays in that tunnel. First one's twenty yards in. Your brother's men will expect us to take the second or third."

A bullet pings off the trunk. Clara doesn't flinch.

"If we live," I tell her, "we're discussing how you know the tunnel layout."

"If we live, you're explaining why you never mentioned having an evil twin." She shifts in her seat, angling toward the rear window. "Though the whole 'trying to kill you' thing tracks. You're not exactly lovable."

The tunnel mouth looms ahead. Maksim kills the lights. Darkness swallows us whole.

Three seconds of pitch black. Four. Five.

Maksim cranks the wheel. Inertia slams me against the door. Clara's shoulder digs into my ribs as she steadies the gun.

Light explodes behind us—headlights from Ludis's convoy hitting the tunnel. Clara's finger tightens on the trigger.

"Wait," I mutter.

The first SUV roars past our hiding spot. Then, the second.

Clara exhales. Squeezes.

The third SUV's back tire explodes. It fishtails, taking out the fourth car. Metal screams against concrete. The tunnel fills with smoke and chaos.

"*Blyat.*" I can't keep the appreciation out of my voice.

"Your Russian sounds better when you're impressed." She drops the gun in my lap, barrel still warm. "Now, get us out of here before your brother figures out where we are. I have a kid to get back to."

"You just shot up half a million dollars' worth of cars."

"Bill me." She slumps back in her seat. "Though technically, I just saved your life. So maybe we call it even?"

I shouldn't find this attractive. This woman has tried to kill me. She's probably planning attempt number two right now.

But watching her handle that gun... There's something wild in her, and fuck me, I like it.

"Mitch and Elijah," she says suddenly. "That's the only reason I didn't put that bullet in your skull instead." She gives me a sexy side glance. "Remember that."

I catch her wrist before she can pull away. "I don't expect anything less from you, *malishka.*"

Blyat. The way she threatens to kill me shouldn't make my cock this hard.

Twenty-One

Clara

*W*hat the fuck is up with today?

All I want is to see Mitch. But instead, I've gone Chanel shopping, endured a car chase that would put "Fast & Furious" to shame, and almost got blasted off a bridge.

The Rolls-Royce crawls through its fifth loop around empty streets. My bare feet are propped on scattered shopping bags, designer dresses spilling out between Chanel boxes. One lonely stiletto peeks out from under silk and lace. The other's probably decorating some highway by now.

"Is Mitch actually here, or are we just enjoying the scenic route?"

Maksim catches my eye in the rearview. "What? You don't trust us?"

"I don't trust anyone who needs three hours to park a car."

He chuckles.

Asshole.

The Rolls finally stops in front of a building that's seen better days. Probably around the time dinosaurs roamed the earth. A flickering "ByteCare IT Solutions" sign hangs crooked above boarded windows.

Perfect place to hide a secret medical facility. Nobody would look twice at this dump.

Empty lots stretch on both sides. Across the street, a coffee shop that hasn't seen a customer since 1985 sits next to a bookstore with newspapers from last month still in the window.

"Ditch the car." Leonid scans the empty street before reaching for his door. "And get these back to the house." He kicks at a cascade of silk and lace that's threatening to spill out.

I grab the handle. Locked.

"Maksim," I hiss.

"Following orders, ma'am."

"I will stab you with this last stiletto heel."

Leonid opens my door. "Ladies first."

"Fuck you very much."

Leonid cocks one of his eyebrows; the corner of his mouth curves into a crooked grin before he drags me out of the car faster than I intend to.

The sidewalk's cold under my feet.

"Such a fucking gentleman," I mutter.

"Just. Follow. Me." He strides ahead.

I trail behind, half-rolling my eyes and trying not to feel like a stray being pulled along. A bell chimes as we enter—because apparently, every shitty tech shop needs a bell. Two guys look up from ancient computers. One's got tattoos crawling up his neck like ivy. The other's sporting a beard that could house small wildlife.

"Boss." Beard-guy scrambles up, nearly knocking over his energy drink. He hurries to a shelf packed with dusty hard drives and punches something into a hidden panel.

The shelf slides sideways.

"You've got to be shitting me."

"Problem?" Leonid's hand finds my lower back.

"Other than this being the most cliché secret entrance ever? Nope."

"Would you prefer a trap door?"

"I'd prefer my other shoe."

Tattoo-neck and Beard-guy disappear behind their screens as Leonid guides me through the entrance.

And holy shit.

The shelf slides shut behind us with a click that sounds way too final. Darkness swallows everything except a strip of blue light stretching into forever.

Perfect murder spot. No witnesses, no body, just another dumb broad who trusted the wrong Russian.

I frown at the endless tunnel. "Are you serious?"

"Having second thoughts?" Leonid's breath hits my ear.

I spin around; my nose wrinkles. "About following a murderous mob boss into a dark tunnel? Never."

His hands land on my waist, turning me back around and pressing me forward. The heat of his chest burns through his clothes, and fuck, he smells like gunpowder and expensive cologne.

My body betrays me, leaning back against hard muscle.

I clench my jaw.

Get your shit together, Clara.

"Move." His grip tightens, thumbs pressing into my hip bones.

My lips curl into a sneer, even though he can't see it. "Bossy." But I step forward, trying not to let my apprehension show.

His hands don't leave my waist. I let him be.

The tunnel stretches forever. Blue lights pulse along the floor like something out of "Resident Evil." My bare feet slap against steel grating—because apparently, carpet is too mainstream for secret mob tunnels.

"How deep does this go?" My voice bounces off metal walls.

"Worried?"

"About being trapped underground with you? Yes."

Another thirty steps. Fifty. A hundred. The tech shop might as well be in another zip code.

"Wait." Leonid's arm shoots out, blocking my path. A red laser grid sweeps across the floor ahead of us. Because of course it does.

"Seriously?"

"Security measures."

"No shit."

The grid disappears. A section of wall slides open—I'm starting to sense a theme here. Behind it is a glass chamber big enough for maybe three people.

"Ladies first?" Leonid's got that smirk again.

"After you, princess."

He steps in. I follow, trying not to think about all the ways this could go wrong. The chamber seals with a hiss.

"Identification required," a robotic voice fills the space. Blue light scans us from head to toe.

"You guys really committed to the whole evil lair aesthetic, huh?"

"Says the woman who just spent ten grand on shoes."

"Nine and a half. And at least I can walk in them."

The chamber descends. My stomach lurches—we're moving fast. The walls around us turn transparent, revealing...

"Holy fuck."

We're dropping through the center of what looks like a massive silo. Except, instead of missiles, there's floor after floor of medical tech that probably costs more than the GDP of several small countries. Operating rooms with robots. Labs full of equipment I can't even name. People in hazmat suits moving between steel tables.

"This is how you're hiding from the feds? An underground hospital?"

"Among other things."

The chamber slows. Through the glass, I can see a long corridor lined with doors. Each one's got a keypad, a retinal scanner, and probably a blood sample requirement.

"I'm starting to think you guys have trust issues."

Leonid's hand lands on my back as the chamber doors open. "You're one to talk."

A doctor in scrubs hurries past, tablet in hand. His footsteps echo off steel walls. Everything smells like antiseptic and money.

"This way." Leonid steers me left. "Try not to touch anything."

"Why? Afraid I'll steal your secret formulas?"

"Afraid you'll set off another alarm. The last one gave me a headache."

Three more security checkpoints. Two more sliding doors. Each one needs Leonid's fingerprints, retinal scan, or firstborn child to open.

Finally, he stops in front of a door marked "High-Security Wing B."

"Ready?"

"To see Mitch? No. To get out of this sci-fi nightmare? Hell, yes."

The door slides open with a hydraulic hiss.

My feet freeze on the threshold. Every muscle locks up.

This isn't a medical wing. This is fucking "Star Trek."

Pristine white walls curve overhead into a dome of glass panels. Holographic screens float in mid-air, displaying vital signs in 3D. Doctors in what look like hazmat suits made of liquid metal glide between beds that hover—actually hover—three feet off the ground.

"What the actual fuck?"

A robot rolls past, carrying a tray of instruments that probably cost more than my house. The air smells like nothing—too clean, too pure, like even germs are too poor to exist here.

And at the far end...

"No way." The word comes out half-laugh, half-disbelief.

Mitch is propped up in what looks like a floating cloud of light, wrapped in monitors that pulse with his heartbeat. He's wearing what seem to be silk pajamas, watching something on a screen that's literally floating in front of his face.

And he's eating caviar. Actual fucking caviar.

"Welcome to the future," Leonid murmurs behind me.

Twenty-Two

Clara

Barefoot, dirty, and dragging the remnants of my dignity, I make my way over to Mitch.

I shake my head, not quite believing it. "Mitch, you've got to be kidding me."

He glances up, caviar fork frozen mid-air, his eyes sweeping over me like I'm some kind of ghost.

"Clara?" His voice drags slightly, like the words are fighting their way through molasses. He's staring. At my bare feet. At the mess that used to be me about five car chases ago.

One eyebrow arches lazily, almost comically slow. "What... happened... to you?"

"You know I was kidnapped by Kuznetsov, right?"

He blinks, his gaze wandering like he's trying to process the sentence, then lazily shovels another spoonful of caviar into his mouth. He chews deliberately, the sound almost cartoonishly loud in the silence.

"Yes," he finally says, dragging the word out like he's still piecing together the conversation.

"And you're just... eating caviar?"

"This is good," he says, lips curling into a slow, lopsided smile that feels all kinds of wrong.

Holy shit, Mitch is smiling.

There's a gap where his front tooth should be, which is new. In the decade I've known him, I've never seen him crack more than a grimace.

Not since Jake died.

"Well, in his defense, we had to pump him full of ketamine to get him to stay put." A doctor appears beside Mitch's bed, gray hair cropped military-short against his skull, wire-rim glasses perched on a nose that's been broken at least twice. "He tried to escape. Twice."

"Three times," Mitch corrects, spearing another bite of caviar.

"Three times," the doctor agrees. "Last time with an IV pole as a weapon."

Something hits my feet. I look down to find Leonid crouched there, hospital slippers in hand. He doesn't ask, just lifts my foot and slides one on.

What the actual fuck?

My brain short-circuits. The fearsome Raven, terror of the Russian underworld, is putting Cinderella slippers on my dirty feet.

I should move. Say something. Do anything except stand here like an idiot while he slides the second slipper on with the same efficiency that he probably uses to hide bodies.

"Your feet were cold." He stands up, hands in his pockets like he didn't just break my brain.

"I wasn't—"

"Yes, you were. Your toes were turning blue."

Mitch snorts into his caviar. The doctor busies himself with a floating screen, shoulders shaking.

I open my mouth. Close it. What exactly is the protocol when your sworn enemy starts playing fairy godmother?

"The ketamine explains a lot," I manage finally, desperate to focus on anything else. "Like why Mitch is eating fancy fish eggs instead of trying to murder everyone."

"Oh, he did try." The doctor taps his broken nose. "Hence the ketamine."

"God, Mitch..." My fingers find the bruises mapping his arms, spreading up his neck.

Leonid drops into a chair beside the bed. "Would you believe this man crawled through a broken windshield, bleeding, just to find you?"

"What?"

"Shot up my Audi on Canal Street." Leonid's mouth twitches. "Dragged that bad leg of his through glass and metal. Didn't even flinch. Just kept asking where you were."

The bruises make more sense now. "And you let him fight Dmitry?"

"Let him?" Leonid scoffs. "Your guardian psychopath here wouldn't stop until someone told him where you were. Dmitry just happened to be closest."

I grip Mitch's hand. His knuckles are split, glass cuts still visible.

"You shouldn't have—"

"He is a soldier," Leonid interrupts. "One of the old ones. The kind that dies standing. I'm merely honoring his choice."

"By drugging him into submission?"

"By saving his life." The words hit harder than they should. Mitch blinks at his plate, head tilting like he's trying to remember something.

"Caviar pairs well with cheese. And watercress. Did you know watercress grows in water?" He squints. "Like fish."

My chest tightens.

Even high as a kite, he's still trying to protect me. His hand suddenly clamps around mine. "Clara." His voice breaks. "I'm sorry. About Jake. About letting things slip—"

"Slip?" Something cold slides down my spine. "What slipped, Mitch?" He shakes his head, fighting through the ketamine haze.

"Should've seen it. The signs were there, but I was watching the wrong shadows. Looking east when I should've been looking—" His words slur, eyes unfocusing.

"Mitch?" I squeeze his hand. "What shadows? What signs?"

My eyes dart between Leonid and Mitch. Something's off. Leonid's too calm, watching Mitch like he already knows what's coming.

Tears streak down Mitch's weathered face. "Jake wouldn't want..." He swallows hard. "Wouldn't want to see you sad because of him."

Fuck that.

"Shut up." I turn away, but Leonid's there, those eyes burning into me. I snap my gaze back to the floor. Rage builds in my chest, hot and familiar.

My head snaps up. "He killed Jake." The words taste like blood in my mouth. My fingers dig into Mitch's bed rail.

I point at Leonid, hand shaking. "He killed Jake. The Raven killed my brother."

"No." Mitch's voice slurs, his head rolling side to side. "No, no, no, Clara..."

No?

The word hits like a punch to the gut. Relief floods in where anger used to be, and what the fuck is that about?

"No." Mitch coughs, struggling to focus. "Leonid Kuznetsov, the real Raven—"

Leonid nods, tapping his chest. Claiming the title.

"Was in Moscow," Mitch's words tumble out, fighting the drugs. "When the fucking fake Raven... they... they killed Jake."

The room tilts. Fourteen years of hatred crack down the middle.

If Leonid was in Moscow...

If The Raven wasn't The Raven...

If Jake knew something...

Black spots dance at the edges of my vision. The last thing I see is Leonid lunging forward, those damn eyes of his full of something that looks too much like concern.

Bastard. Even his eyes are lying to me.

Aren't they?

"Well, well." A familiar voice drags me back to consciousness. "The great Clara Caldwell is human, after all."

My eyes crack open to find Leonid in a chair beside me, jacket off, sleeves rolled up. He looks hot. Hotter than his usual *hot*.

"Fuck off." My throat feels like sandpaper.

"The doctor says it's exhaustion. Shock. Low blood sugar." He ticks them off on his fingers. "And something about stubborn idiots who don't eat between car chases."

I try to sit up. Bad idea. The room spins.

"Stay down before you face-plant again." His hand catches my shoulder. "Once was entertaining enough."

"Glad I could provide the day's entertainment." I squint at him. "Where's Mitch?"

"Sleeping off enough ketamine to drop a horse." His thumb traces circles on my shoulder. "He'll be fine. You, on the other hand..."

"Elijah?" My heart jumps. "Where's—"

He pulls out his phone, flicking through it before holding up a picture. My son sprawled on what looks like the world's most expensive couch, fast asleep with a massive German Shepherd curled around him. Pizza crusts are scattered nearby.

"He's fine. Demolished three slices of pizza, made friends with every animal I own, and passed out with Kayla." His lips twitch. "She hasn't left his side."

Something in my chest loosens. "You have a dog?"

"I have several. Though they seem to be his dogs now."

I stare at the picture longer than I should. At my son's peaceful face. At the way the massive dog wraps around him like a shield. At the casual evidence that the feared Raven keeps pets and feeds kids pizza.

Fourteen years of painting him as a monster, and here he is, letting our son turn his guard dogs into puppies.

Our son.

The thought hits like a sucker punch. I drop the phone like it burns.

"What? Going to drug me too?" I quip, hoping to change the topic in my own head.

"Tempting." His voice drops lower. "But I have better ideas."

Before I can tell him exactly where to shove his ideas, he leans in and kisses me.

Not like before. Not that angry clash of teeth and spite. This is slow, deliberate, like he's trying to tell me something his words can't.

I should push him away. Should remember fourteen years of hatred. *Should—*

Fuck should.

Deep down, I've always known. Known it wasn't him who killed Jake. The timing was wrong. The details didn't add up. But hatred is easier than uncertainty. Easier than admitting there's still a monster out there, one without a face or a name.

One I can't find.

Can't fight.

Can't kill.

Until today. Until I saw *him* in the auction. The truth I've been running from.

Leonid isn't my brother's killer.

He's just the face I gave my nightmares.

And God help me, but I'm glad. Glad it's not him. Glad I don't have to— My fingers curl into his shirt, pulling him closer. He tastes like coffee and danger and things I shouldn't want.

When he finally pulls back, those eyes of his are dark. "Still want to kill me?"

"Yes." I drag him back down. "But not until I find out who killed Jake."

Twenty-Three

Leonid

I shouldn't be kissing her.

Blyat. My self-control, built over decades of running the Bratva? Gone the moment she parts those lips.

The rational part of my brain—the one that's kept me alive through three wars and countless assassination attempts—is screaming to back away. To remember she's probably plotting fifty different ways to kill me right now.

But my dick's doing the thinking, and that treacherous bastard has always had a death wish when it comes to Clara Caldwell.

Yebat.

The things I want to do to this woman should be illegal in every country. Actually, they probably are.

Her body sinks into the king-sized medical bed—the same one I had specially installed in this private suite. Three cameras watch from discreet corners, their red lights blinking. Let my security team watch. Let them see who their *Pakhan* belongs to.

Sukin syn. I really need to stop thinking with my cock.

But her mouth opens under mine, and fuck—she tastes like fury and sin. Her tits press against my chest, soft and full against the Egyptian cotton sheets. My hands ache to rip that flimsy hospital gown off her.

"Don't," she whispers, but her thighs part wider on that massive bed, making room for me between them.

"Lies." I suck hard on her pulse point, right where the hospital gown's slipped down. Her whole body arches off the mattress. "Your cunt's probably soaked through these sheets already."

"Fuck you." But her legs wrap around my waist, the bed's hydraulics whirring as she grinds against me.

"That's exactly what I'm going to do to you." My hands slide under her, gripping that perfect ass. "Right here, with every camera recording how well you take my cock."

Her eyes flash with wicked amusement. "Oh, you like an audience?" she purrs, rolling her hips against my hardness. "Want your men to see how wet I am for you?"

Blyat. The thought of anyone else seeing her like this—spread out, desperate, *mine*—makes my vision go red.

"Never." I grab her wrists, pinning them above her head. "No one sees this pussy but me."

"Possessive, aren't we?" She lifts her hips, rubbing herself shamelessly against my cock. "What if I want them to watch? What if I want them to see how their big, bad *Pakhan* loses control?"

A growl rips from my throat. "You're playing with fire, *myshka*."

"Maybe I like getting burned." She arches, letting that damn gown slip further down. "Maybe I want everyone to see what you do to me."

My free hand wraps around her throat—gentle, just enough pressure to make her pupils blow wide. "The only one who gets to see you come is me."

"Prove it." Her tongue darts out, wetting those fucking perfect lips. "Show me who I belong to."

Chyert. The things this woman does to my self-control should be classified as chemical warfare.

I release her throat, pushing off the bed in one fluid motion. The hunter becoming the hunted. Let her feel what it's like when the predator steps back.

"Where are you—?" She props herself up on her elbows, hospital gown slipping dangerously low.

"Nowhere." I tug my wrinkled Henley back into place, not missing how her eyes track the movement of my muscles under the thin fabric. Standing at the foot of the bed, I drink in the sight of her—flushed, frustrated, legs still spread like an invitation to sin.

"You're seriously walking away?" Her voice holds a note of disbelief.

"Not walking away." I tap the nearest camera. "Just giving you what you want. An audience."

Her eyes narrow. "Coward."

"Patient." I roll up my sleeves, exposing the tattoos she was tracing with her tongue moments ago. "I can wait until you admit that this—" I gesture to her body, splayed out on my sheets "—is for my eyes only."

GRRRRROWWWWWL

The sound echoes through the room like a pissed-off bear. Clara's face goes from seductive to mortified in record time.

"Was that—?"

"Shut up."

"Your stomach just cockblocked me." I lean against the doorframe, lips twitching. "That's a first."

"Well, sorry my digestive system isn't operating on your sexual schedule." She yanks the sheet up to her chin. "At least it wasn't a fart."

Blyat. The laugh bursts out before I can stop it.

Then she starts laughing too, and fuck—her whole face transforms. A dimple appears on her left cheek, tiny and perfect, something I've never noticed before.

Her eyes crinkle at the corners, and those killer's hands clutch her stomach as she doubles over.

Dangerous. This is more dangerous than any weapon she's ever pulled on me.

"Five car chases and two explosions later," she wheezes between laughs, "and my stomach decides now is the time to demand breakfast?"

"Lunch," I correct. "It's past noon."

"Whatever." She wipes her eyes, still grinning. "My energy's gone. Need food. And," she plucks at the hospital gown, "real clothes would be nice."

I grab my spare hoodie from the duffel by the door. Black. Well-worn. It'll swallow her whole.

"Here." I toss it at her face. "Only option."

She catches it one-handed, then reaches for the ties of her hospital gown. Right here. In front of me. In front of the cameras.

Yob tvoyu mat.

Before she can flash my entire security team, I'm across the room. One arm under her knees, one behind her back, and she's airborne.

"What the—?"

I kick the bathroom door open, deposit her inside, and throw the hoodie after her.

"Change." I slam the door shut, leaning against it. "Unless you want my men starting a bidding war for that security footage."

"Aw." Her voice carries through the door. "Worried someone else might see what's yours?"

My forehead thunks against the wood. "Just put on the fucking hoodie."

Fabric rustles. "Or what? You'll punish me?"

Christ. I need to stop imagining her naked on the other side of this door. But the images flood in, anyway—*her bent over my desk, that smart mouth finally shut as I spank her ass red. Her wrists bound to my headboard while I edge her for hours until she's begging for my cock. Her perfect throat wrapped in my favorite tie while I—*

Blyat. When I finally punish her, it won't be quick. Won't be gentle.

Twenty-Four

Clara

Thirty minutes later, my thighs grip leather and metal, chest pressed against a back that's harder than the Ducati's chassis. The bike purrs between my legs, but that's not what's making me dizzy.

"Hands around my waist." His voice vibrates through his back into my chest.

Ah-huh, you've gone mad, Clara.

Indeed, because I slide my hands lower instead.

Much lower.

His abs tense under my fingers as they drift south. Rock-hard muscle jumps under my touch.

The traffic light ahead flashes yellow. He guns it, the bike's engine screaming as we thread between two SUVs. My fingers slip lower, tracing the edge of his belt. His thighs flex against mine as he maneuvers the bike, and I take advantage of the movement to press my palm flat against him.

My turn to feel him tense.

Not slowing the bike, he tilts his head to the right just a little. "Testing your luck, Caldwell?"

"Just improving my grip." I lean closer, "Safety first."

A sound rumbles through his chest—deep, primal. But he doesn't push my hands away. I let them stay there, pressed against the growing hardness beneath his pants. His back expands with each breath, solid and wide against my chest. When did he get so... massive? I didn't notice it the last time we fought.

The thought snags—

Ice-blue eyes behind black feathers.

No.

Jake's blood, hot and sticky between my fingers.

Stop.

"Run, Clara. Don't look back—"

Fuck. Focus on now. The solid wall of Leonid's back. *Real* things. *Here* things. Like how the bike suddenly growls like a goddamn beast, and the pulsing vibrations between my thighs are like a fucking invitation to go wild.

My stomach drops as we accelerate, wind whipping by. *Bastard.* But I'm not about to let him hold all the cards. I trace circles dangerously close to his zipper, feeling him grow harder under my touch.

The bike swerves slightly.

"Careful there." I keep my voice light. "Someone might think you're losing your edge."

His only response is to take the next corner faster, forcing me to press tighter against him. The city blurs past—all chrome and glass catching the late afternoon sun.

When was the last time I felt this... free?

Before Elijah. Before everything went to hell.

The thought sobers me.

What am I doing? Playing motorcycle chicken with a mob boss while my son...

No. Not now. I refuse to let guilt poison this moment. For once, I'm not Caldwell. Not a mother with impossible choices. Just a woman on a bike, tormenting the most dangerous man in the city.

He cuts through traffic like it's a game of Frogger, the streets his own version of Mario Kart. He dodges cars, weaves between lanes, and accelerates with a reckless abandon that would make even the most hardened stuntman cringe. I'm not sure if I should be terrified or impressed, but adrenaline is coursing through my veins, and all I can do is... enjoy the ride.

"Your mind's wandering."

"Noticed that, did you?"

"Hard not to when your hands get polite."

I resume my torment, tracing the inseam of his pants. "Better?"

His growl gets lost in the engine noise, but I feel it rumble through his chest. The bike accelerates again, weaving through traffic like a missile seeking its target.

His right hand leaves the handlebar, catches both my wrists, and yanks them up to his chest. Pins them there against hard muscle.

I should fight it. Should hate how easily he controls me.

Through my gloves, his heartbeat pounds steady and strong against my palms. My helmet rests between his shoulder blades, the visor fogging slightly with each breath. Safe. The word should make me laugh. Nothing about this man is safe.

And yet...

I close my eyes inside the helmet, feeling the wind whip past us. His body blocks the worst of it, like a wall between me and everything else. Everything I've been running from. *God*, I'm glad it wasn't him behind that mask. Glad the monster who took Jake wears a different face.

My stomach growls, loud enough to hear over the engine's roar. Perfect timing. For once, food actually sounds good.

I lift my head, catching our reflection in his side mirror. Two riders in black, my helmet pressed against his back. His head turns slightly—checking the traffic behind us. No, not the traffic. The black SUV that's been three cars back since we left the clinic. His shoulders tense under my hands.

"Company?" I squeeze his chest once.

He taps my fingers once. *No.*

Just being careful, then. Old habits. When you've got as many enemies as he does—as we do—paranoia keeps you breathing.

Five minutes later, we pull up to a faded brick building with a glowing sign that reads "Katerina's Hearth." Before I can swing my leg off the bike, his hand catches my wrist.

"When we're done here…" The promise in his voice makes my skin prickle. "You're going to regret being such a tease."

I lean in, letting my breasts press against his back one last time.

"I can't wait."

The helmet comes off, leaving my hair standing on end. Leonid's already scanning—left, right, rooflines, parked cars.

He yanks off his helmet with a satisfying snap, his hair tousled in that just-fucked way that makes my fingers itch to mess it up more. Meanwhile, I'm gaping at his back like I've never seen a man before.

My eyes devouring the way that damn Henley stretches over his shoulders, clinging to his chest like a second skin. It's unfair, really—he's just standing there, looking like every dangerous thing I shouldn't want.

Jeez, if he can set my hormones on fire just by standing there, I'm in deep trouble.

I swallow and take a breath.

Why don't you just drool on his boots while you're at it?

I shift my weight, the hospital slipper making an embarrassing squeak against the pavement. Christ. Nothing says "sexy" like paper-thin foam between your feet, and God knows what's on this street. At least the other one hasn't fallen apart yet.

"Where are we?" I ask, finally snapping out of my trance, and realize I've never been to this part of town before.

I glance around. This isn't what I expected. No sleek lines, no fancy valet out front. Just a crumbling brick building with faded red paint and old-style signage. There's a bunch of worn storefronts nearby and a few older folks chatting on benches, eyeing us like they're half-suspicious, half-bored. Not exactly a five-star spot. More like the kind of place you go if you don't want to be found.

"What're you looking at, *kiska*?"

His voice slides down my spine like warm honey, and I realize I'm still clutching the helmet like it's a life preserver. His fingers brush mine as he takes it, deliberate, lingering. That damn smirk appears—the one that makes me want to climb him like a tree or punch him in the throat. Maybe both.

My toes curl in the flimsy slippers, and I catch his eyes dropping to my feet. The slight twitch of his lips makes heat flood my cheeks.

"Not a word about the footwear," I warn, but it comes out breathier than intended when he steps closer, his body heat making my skin prickle despite the afternoon sun.

His eyes darken, that familiar molten brown that Elijah gets when he's spotted the last cookie and won't take no for an answer—

No. Stop that train of thought right fucking now.

He reaches the door first, those broad shoulders blocking most of my view as he does another security sweep.

"After you," he rumbles, holding the door. The gesture would almost be gentlemanly if his eyes weren't promising all sorts of filthy things. His gaze drops to where his hoodie hits mid-thigh on me, and suddenly, the air feels too thick to breathe.

The bells chime overhead as I brush past him—too close, not close enough. His heat radiates like a furnace, and fuck me if I don't lean into it just a little. The slight inhale behind me says he noticed.

Bad Clara. Very bad Clara.

But then the smells hit me, and holy mother of... The aroma wraps around me like a warm blanket—rich beef stroganoff that's been simmering for hours, mushrooms drowning in butter and herbs, something that might be *pirozhki* fresh from the oven.

My stomach growls shamelessly.

"Hungry?" His breath tickles my ear, and when did he get so close? His chest nearly touches my back, and I can feel the vibration of his words.

"For food," I clarify, "Just. Food."

For now.

His low chuckle makes things clench that have no business clenching in public. "Of course, *kiska*. Just food."

Twenty-Five

Clara

My eyebrows lift as I take in the scene.

I blink, adjusting to the dim interior. Dark wooden tables dot the room, each covered with embroidered cloths in deep reds and golds. Along the walls, cushioned benches stretch beneath rows of framed photographs—faces that could be anyone's grandmother or grandfather back in their motherland. A long counter dominates the right, its surface scattered with tin tea glasses in traditional ornate style, made from materials like silver.

A deep male voice croons in Russian from hidden speakers, the melody somehow both melancholic and warm. Behind the counter, a massive brass samovar commands attention like a throne, steam rising from its spout. The air is thick with the smell of dill and sour cream.

Three couples by the window freeze, forks suspended over plates of stroganoff. In the corner, a chess game sits forgotten, the players too busy staring at us to notice their timer's still running. Lace curtains filter the afternoon sun, and the whole place smells of the rich warmth of slow-cooked meat.

"Lyonya!"

A silver-haired woman materializes from behind the counter, moving faster than anyone her age has any right to. She's tiny—barely reaching Leonid's chest—but the way she barrels toward him with open arms makes me think of those nature documentaries where mama bears charge at things three times their size.

Leonid actually *softens*.

Holy shit. His shoulders drop a fraction, and that murder-strut loosens into something almost human. The woman reaches up, patting his cheeks like he's six instead of... whatever terrifying age dangerous men with criminal empires turn.

"Still too skinny," she scolds in accented English, and I nearly choke. The Henley stretching across his chest begs to differ.

I can't help but stare. The most feared man in the city stands here with his hands awkwardly at his sides, like he can't decide whether to hug her or run. The way he ducks his head when she reaches up to straighten his collar—Christ, he's practically shrinking to let her fuss. His usual prowling grace is replaced by something almost boyish, something that makes my chest do weird things. It's like watching a tiger turn into a housecat under grandma's scratches.

Note to self: *Cute is dangerous on him. Very, very dangerous.*

Movement behind the counter catches my eye—another figure emerging from the kitchen's steam. Before I can focus on him, the tiny woman's gaze locks onto me like a heat-seeking missile.

"And who is this?"

"I'm..."

"*Tyo-tya* Galina—" Leonid starts, a warning note in his voice that she completely ignores.

"A... pretty girl." Galina's gaze sweeps over me; those eyes might be warm, but they miss nothing. Slow and deliberate, from the top of my head to my toes. She arches an eyebrow, her lips twitching like she's fighting a smirk.

"But those slippers!" She points at my feet like they've personally offended her. "Lyonya, you bring her here dressed like a hospital patient?"

I bite back a laugh. "Actually—"

"Sit, sit!" She waves us toward a corner booth. "Ivan! Bring the good vodka!"

A tall man behind the counter—probably Ivan—just nods, already pulling out a frosted bottle. The familiarity of it hits me—they know exactly which vodka is *his* vodka.

"I don't need—" Leonid tries again.

"Nonsense. Growing boy needs feeding." She pats his cheek once more. "Still remember when you were this high, stealing *pirozhki* from my kitchen window."

Oh, really? I sink into the heavy wooden chair he pulls out, tucking this little nugget away. Baby criminal Leonid, climbing through windows for pastries? That's... surprisingly adorable.

"*Tyo-tya* Galina." His voice carries that don't-fuck-with-me tone that makes grown men wet themselves. She just tsks and pats his arm.

"You sound just like your papa when you do that. Same scowl, same growl." Her eyes soften. "But you have your mama's heart. She would be proud—"

"*Enough, Tyo-tya* Galina!" Leonid drops his head into his hands, and holy shit, is that a blush creeping up his neck?

The word cracks like a whip. I flinch, but Galina doesn't even blink. She just gives him a look that somehow manages to be both loving and deeply unimpressed.

WHACK.

My jaw drops as Galina's hand connects with the back of Leonid's head.

"You use that Bratva tone with me, I tell everyone about the time you cried because Ivan's cat wouldn't let you pet her."

Leonid's eyes go wide. Actually wide. I press my lips together so hard they might bruise, but a snort escapes anyway. His head snaps toward me, those dark brown eyes promising delicious murder, but Galina's already running her fingers through his hair, smoothing down the spot she just smacked.

"*Sorry, Tyo-tya*," he mutters. I clamp my hand over my mouth, fingernails digging into my cheek.

Stop finding this endearing, Clara. Adorable mob bosses are definitely NOT a thing.

"Now, sit!"

The wooden chair scrapes against the floor as Leonid pulls it out. He exhales—long and heavy—before lowering himself beside me. His fingers rake through his hair, and he won't look at me. The chess players have completely given up pretending to play their game.

"Stop it," he mutters.

"Stop what?"

He turns his head slowly, his eyes meeting mine. His jaw clenches, unclenches. I press my lips together, fighting the laugh bubbling up my throat. My shoulders shake with the effort to keep it in as I blink at him, all innocence.

Sudden movement makes me stiffen—Galina's behind me, her fingers working through my tangled mess of hair.

"And what is your name, *dorogaya*?"

I tilt my head back, meeting Galina's eyes. Even upside down, I can see traces of what must have been a remarkable beauty in her younger days—those high cheekbones, the graceful arch of her brows, the way she carries herself like a queen, even in a simple apron.

"Clara."

Her hands pause. Something flickers in her expression before she turns my face toward hers, studying me like I'm a puzzle she's trying to solve.

"Clara," she repeats, her fingers still in my hair. "Such a pretty name. Now tell me, what's a nice girl like you doing with this troublemaker?"

I lean back in my chair, flicking a loose thread on Leonid's oversized hoodie. "Oh, he kidnapped me and my son."

The restaurant freezes. A woman's spoon hovers halfway to her mouth, soup dripping back into her bowl. The chess players' heads swivel toward our table in sync, like they're watching a tennis match.

"She tried to poison me first," Leonid cuts in, both hands now flat on the table. The muscle in his jaw ticks.

The woman's soup spoon finally drops with a splash. The chess players lean forward so far they're practically lying on their table. Even the steam from the samovar seems to pause, hanging in the air.

Well," I fold my arms across my chest, "I thought he *killed* my brother."

A fork hits a plate with a sharp ping, spinning once, twice, before rolling off the edge. It hits the floor in the dead silence, the clatter echoing off the walls. One of the chess players reaches for his water glass, misses completely, and knocks over his king instead.

The silence stretches for exactly three seconds before Galina throws her head back and laughs. Not a polite chuckle—a full-bodied, shoulder-shaking laugh that makes the chess pieces rattle.

When she finally stops, wiping her eyes, her gaze lands back on me, sharper now, cutting through the humor.

"And where is your husband, Clara? Do you have a—*husband*?"

"No..." I say with a shrug, my eyes drifting to the side. "He's... *dead*."

"Are you taking care of your son alone? Without his father?" she asks, her voice sugary sweet, like she's offering condolences at a funeral she planned herself.

I manage a small nod. "Yes."

Galina's lips part into an exaggerated "aaah," her expression shifting to something almost... *pleased*. She shifts her attention to Leonid, her mouth curving like she's holding back a laugh, before turning back to me.

"Oh. I'm sorry to hear that," she says, though it sounds anything but sincere. "It must be tough, raising him alone."

I glance at Leonid, but he's staring down, his thumb tracing the edge of his glass like it's the only thing tethering him.

I square my shoulders, refusing to let the awkwardness settle on me. "It's not as bad as it sounds," I reply, my voice steady. "Elijah's a great kid. Smart, funny, and full of energy. Honestly, he makes it easier than you'd think."

Galina's smile widens, and there's something triumphant in the way she tilts her head, as if my answer was exactly what she wanted to hear.

"How lucky for you." Her eyes dart toward Leonid, almost daring him to respond.

"Sorry for the wait."

The interruption pulls me out of the silent tug-of-war.

I glance up at the tall figure beside our table. Ivan. A bowl of what looks like pickled vegetables in one hand, a bottle of Beluga Gold Line in the other. His smile is pleasant enough, but his eyes stay cold.

He places the bottle and bowl down. Those hands catch my attention. Rough, scarred across the knuckles.

Ivan catches me staring. I meet his eyes and give a slow nod. He returns it with that same pleasant smile that doesn't quite fit his face.

"Thank you, love." Galina reaches for his hand.

Ivan bends to kiss Galina's cheek, and I almost buy it—just a sweet old man in an apron.

"Just like the old days," he says softly to Galina. I cock my head, studying their shared look. Whatever those "old days" were, they definitely involved more than serving *borscht*.

I track his eyes. Never still. Door. Windows. The guys in the corner who've been here too long. I cross my arms, recognizing that stance.

But I'm too hungry by now, leaning forward, trying to identify the colorful array of pickled things.

Are those mushrooms? Maybe carrots?

Whatever that purple one is, it's calling my name. My stomach makes its opinion known loudly.

Ivan's eyebrows shoot up, and Leonid's lips twitch.

Great.

"When's the last time you fed her, *Lyonya*?" Suddenly, Galina slaps Leonid's shoulder—hard.

The crack echoes across the room.

Twenty-Six

Leonid

I di na khuy, Leonid. Two mistakes in less than twenty-four hours. A fucking record.

First, I kissed her. Stupid. Reckless.

Now, all I can think about is getting those sweet, supple lips wrapped around my cock, sucking and licking like she was born to please me.

Second, I brought her here. Even dumber. Bringing her into my territory, where everyone—and everything—wants to take a bite out of her. Myself included.

And yet, the only thing I can't stop replaying in my head is her saying, "He's dead." No husband. No one waiting for her. No one who gets to claim her, protect her, keep her from me. *Blyat*, the relief I felt when she said it—like something uncoiled in my chest.

The slap from Galina stings, sure, but it's nothing compared to the look Clara's giving me. She's got this defiant glint in her eye like she knows exactly what she's doing, and my pulse tightens. She's here, in *my* world, stirring things up with those soft curves and that mouth that seems to speak only in defiance. Cute. Dangerous, too. More dangerous than I'd like to admit.

I sigh, meeting Galina's eyes again. She folds her arms, unimpressed. Ivan stands beside her, as solid and unreadable as ever, the old soldier of the Bratva. Back in the day, he was one of my father's lieutenants, one of the deadliest enforcers. Now, he's the soft-spoken man who fell in love with Galina and turned his back on that life. My father let him go without losing a finger or a tongue—more than anyone else got. Because Ivan saved him once. Galina—well, back in Ukraine, she was a legend. They say she could handle a blade better than anyone, slipping in and out of places no one else could. Yet here she is, apron tied, scolding me like I'm some brat swiping cookies.

"So, uh…" I try to steer the attention off us, scrambling for something—anything—to distract from the way she makes my focus slip. "Well, she had pancakes."

"Hah!" Her lips twitch, and I want to reach across the table and silence her smug little mouth with mine. "Hardly," she huffs, feigning insult, but those eyes say she's enjoying every second of this. "He threatened me—with my child, my… bodyguard."

I narrow my eyes, hoping to communicate what words won't cover: *Keep pushing, and we'll see how far you'll go.*

She cocks her head ever so slightly, one eyebrow arching, a small, amused smile tugging at her lips. Like she wants to see what'll happen if I snap.

She turns to Ivan and Galina, as sweet as an angel, with that soft, rounded mouth of hers that's done more damage to my control than anything else.

"Can I… look at the menu, please?" Her tone's all innocence, but her eyes find mine for just a second, playful, almost wicked.

Hell. This woman's a menace. Sitting there with that look like she's made of sugar—and I'm the idiot letting her.

Galina's delighted. "Oh! Yes, yes!" she says, beaming. Ivan steps away to fetch a menu, handing it to Clara as if she's some prized guest. Meanwhile, I'm wrestling with myself, each second a reminder that I've brought her too close. Too close to *me*.

Galina doesn't go back to the counter, though. She drags over a chair, sits down, and leans in, folding her arms on the table like she's here for storytime.

"So..." She props her chin on her hand, her gaze soft yet piercing. "And your little one—how old?"

I clear my throat, trying to keep my cool, but I can feel my patience fraying. I don't bring women here. *Ever*. I barely even bring *me* here.

Carla's eyes dart up, meeting mine for half a second, wide and sharp, before narrowing. Her lips press into a thin line, like she's swallowing something bitter.

"He's... 4. Turning 5 soon."

Four. The word takes the breath from my lungs.

Something sharp coils inside me, snapping tight. Once again, I'm trying not to put two and two together too fast, but my mind's already there.

No, no. it can't be.

My hands clasp together on the table, fingers flexing tight, almost painfully, as I grit my teeth. "*Tyo-tya* Galina, she's not here as a guest. You don't need to..."

Galina doesn't spare me a glance. It's like I'm some third wheel nobody invited.

"What's his name?" she asks, her whole focus on Clara, leaning in just a little, her attention so intent it's like she's pulling every word out of her.

"Elijah." Clara's face brightens like the sun cutting through clouds just for her. And, *chyert*, I find myself smiling along with her. Damn it, *stop*. I press down hard on the flicker of warmth in my chest.

Ivan strides over with the menu and an extra chair, setting everything down with that infuriating calm he always has. Like this isn't a complete disaster of an idea, like this is all part of some quiet ceremony. *Chyert.* I thought this would be some kind of quick early lunch-dinner shit, in and out, but now I'm stuck in what feels like a family reunion gone rogue.

Before Clara can even pick up the menu, I'm already leaning forward. "*Pelmeni* with mushroom sauce, *borscht*, and a side of *kholodets.*"

"Hey... I can order my own food," Clara protests. Her eyebrows arch, her lips pinching tight.

Just as I settle back, thinking we can wrap this up fast, Galina slaps my hand away and takes the menu from Ivan's grasp.

"Let your girl order on her own!" she snaps in Russian.

"She's not my girl!" I mutter in English, pinching the bridge of my nose to keep from saying something I'll regret.

Ivan's hand lands heavily on my shoulder, that familiar, silent message to shut up. He doesn't say a word, but it's enough. I bite my tongue, nearly choking on the words I want to say. Fine. He wins. *She* wins.

I've fucked up. Badly. Obviously.

Katerina's Hearth isn't just some hole-in-the-wall Russian joint. It's my blind spot. My weakness. The one place where there aren't any security cameras, where my men aren't lurking in the shadows. Where I'm just *Lyonya*, the kid who used to climb through windows for *pirozhki*.

Clara's smiling now, leaning over the table with her fingers tracing the menu as if she's deciphering a damn code. I watch as her eyes narrow, focused, and her lips move silently, trying to sound out the words. Her mouth twitches, almost like she's mumbling something, before she flips the menu over, searching for a translation. Instead, she's met with a garish illustration of some Soviet relic—a cartoon bear wielding a balalaika and a bottle of vodka. Her brow furrows, and she flips the menu back, looking up at me with a half-frustrated, half-amused look.

"What's good here?" she asks, tilting her head.

I repeat the dishes I'd already ordered before they all started giving me shit about it, almost growling. "*Pelmeni* with mushroom sauce, *borscht*, and a side of *kholodets.*"

She flashes that smile, her eyes a brilliant, electric blue, like a lightning strike, lighting up with a spark that I feel right in my chest.

"Yes! Can we have two of those, *please?*"

"Sure, dear!" Ivan stands up immediately, pushing his chair back with a scrape and heading toward the kitchen.

Galina, already lifting the vodka, pours three shots. Quick. Clean. She slides one toward me, pins me with that look. The kind that makes you sit up straighter whether you want to or not.

"You need a wife," she says in Russian. "This one. She's good."

Govno.

Twenty-Seven

Clara

I catch every word they say in Russian, but I keep my face blank.

I push the menu aside, drum my fingers on the table. Smile back at Galina like I'm just another clueless American who can't understand shit. *Wife?* Over my dead body—which, considering who's sitting across from me, isn't exactly off the table.

Galina slides the bowl between us. "*Zakuska*, for the vodka." Pickles glisten in the brine.

"*Na zdorovie!*" Galina lifts her shot glass. I mirror her, playing follow-the-leader. Next to me, Leonid's fingers curl around his glass, his thigh a line of heat against mine. Three shots, three killers—though only one of us wears it on her sleeve.

I watch Galina smile without showing her teeth. No one moves that fast at her age unless they've spent a lifetime dodging bullets. Her eyes give it away—too sharp, too quick.

Her eyes tell a tale of violence and survival, a story I know all too well. Just like mine, once upon a time.

"Drink!" Steel under sugar. She watches me over her glass, probably counting the ways I could fuck up her precious Leonid. Like throwing me at him will fix whatever's broken inside him.

The first shot burns, but I don't flinch. Neither does he. Our eyes lock over the rims of our glasses, and for a second—just a second—I see something shift in that cold stare.

The vodka glass clinks against my teeth. His dark eyes bore into mine, unblinking, like a predator sizing up prey. I break first, focusing on the pickle bowl instead. Anything to escape that stare.

"So, Clara," Galina's eyes twinkle like she's about to share state secrets, "what do you think of our Leonid?"

I stab a pickle, waving it in his direction.

"He's a dick," I say flatly, and then bite into it—only to realize, too late, it's a carrot. The unexpected sweetness hits my tongue, and I suppress a grimace. I chew, swallowing quickly.

Leonid leans back, a lazy smirk tugging at his mouth. "Says the woman who's been stalking me for fourteen years," he drawls. "I must be growing on you."

I roll my eyes but can't ignore the spark flickering in his gaze. "Hah, you wish." This time, I spear an actual pickle and lift it slowly to eye level. Without breaking his stare, I part my lips and slide it between them, the crunch echoing in the sudden quiet. Sour floods my mouth, sharp enough to make my jaw clench.

Leonid watches me swallow, his lips twitching just enough to shift his face—softer, younger. Almost... happy.

Why the hell would he look happy?

But then, as if realizing he's let something slip, his jaw tightens, and the hint of a smile vanishes. He glances away first, inspecting his empty glass like it holds state secrets.

"Ah!" Galina's already pouring another round. "You two remind me of my good old days!"

"Your... good old days?" I arch a brow, leaning back.

"*Da!*" She sets the vodka bottle down with a decisive thunk. "When I met my Ivan in Moscow. I was supposed to kill him, you know. Instead..." She wiggles her eyebrows like she's about to launch into a steamy, spy-thriller romance.

Leonid groans. "*Tyo-tya* Galina, *please.*" He's leaning back in his chair, but his thigh stays pressed against mine. Thick, solid muscle, too warm against my bare skin, like he doesn't even notice—or maybe he does.

But damn, it's... distracting. I sneak a glance, side-eyeing him in disbelief. Is that a thigh or a steel beam? A log, maybe? For the love of all things sane, no one's leg should be built like that.

I don't move. I refuse to give him the satisfaction of reacting. But the moment he shifts away, I let out a quiet breath I hadn't even realized I was holding.

That's when the scent hits me. Rich, savory—garlic, onions, and something roasted, spilling out from the kitchen like Ivan's trying to lure us in with pure temptation. My stomach growls, the vodka sinking heavier with each breath. I'm hungry, lightheaded, and the sharp tang of alcohol has started to buzz in my veins. It makes the room tilt, just for a second, like the whole place is holding its breath.

Galina tugs at the knot of her apron, adjusting it as if she's settling in for something serious. Her fingers brush Leonid's hand, small against his, but he doesn't move.

I glance at his hand, then quickly look away, only to glance back again. Damn it. I swallow a lump of... saliva. Must be the vodka, but suddenly, I'm noticing things I shouldn't. Like how big his hand actually is.

It's not just big—it's strong. Broad, with long fingers that flex slightly, veins running along the back like a roadmap.

He shifts, rolling up his sleeve, and I swear the air in the room changes. Thick forearm, corded with muscle, the veins more prominent now. It's the kind of hand that could wrap around a glass—or my entire neck—with ease.

I grab my glass and take a quick sip as if that'll drown out the ridiculous thoughts bubbling in my head.

"Did you know our little *Lyonya* loves animals? Such a soft heart, that boy." Galina's face lights up, beaming with pride. Her eyes crinkle at the corners as she clasps her hands together like she's just announced her grandson won a Nobel Prize. "He's the sweetest!"

I blink, caught off guard. "What, now?"

Placing my glass down, I make the mistake of glancing at his hand again. Stupid, sexy man hand—big, broad, and entirely too distracting. My gaze drifts up, tracing the veins that disappear under his rolled-up sleeve, and I cock my head at Leonid.

His jaw tightens, a muscle ticking like he's fighting to keep control. "This conversation is over..."

But Galina leans in, conspiratorial. "He wanted to be a veterinarian." Her voice drops like she's revealing classified intel. "Can you imagine?"

That explains the peacocks. And the snakes. What's next—penguins?

A laugh bursts out of me, sharp and involuntary. "A vet?" I glance at Leonid, catching the briefest flicker of irritation—or maybe embarrassment.

"Until his father decided killing was more important than healing—"

"*Bozhe moy.* Not another word," Leonid hisses. He sets the vodka glass down with a quiet, deliberate clink.

The silence between them stretches.

Leonid reaches for the vodka once more, his fingers wrapping around the glass, but he doesn't drink. Galina's hand comes down lightly on his shoulder, her palm brushing the fabric before she gives him a soft pat. He stiffens, but only for a moment.

"You've carried enough, *Lyonya*," she says.

His hand shifts to the bottle, turning it just slightly, the glass base scraping against the table. He doesn't look at her.

"You know," I say, jabbing my fork at him, the pickle skewered like it's backing me up, "I always thought you wanted to be the mafia boss. The power, the throne, an endless supply of vodka—it's got your name written all over it."

Leonid rubs the back of his neck, fingers lingering there for a moment as though grounding himself. He shifts back in his chair, rolling his shoulders like he's shaking off a thought.

"Not everything's about power," he says, his hand finally letting go of the glass.

Galina glances at me, then back to him, her fingers brushing over the edge of his sleeve.

"Your father," she starts softly, pausing as if picking her words carefully, "he wanted you to lead, Leonid. Even after your mother..." She trails off, glancing down, her mouth tightening.

Leonid's Adam's apple dips, slow and deliberate, as a nerve flicks along his neck. "He wanted me to survive."

I lean back, crunching into the pickle, the sharp tang giving me something to focus on.

"So," I say, trying to lighten the mood... not because I need to know him better or anything. "What's this thing about your twin trying to kill you? Not enough room on the throne?"

The moment stretches taut again, Leonid's gaze snapping to me. His neck shifts, veins rising subtly as he swallows hard. His hand hovers over the vodka glass for a second too long before he picks it up and takes a slow drink. "You don't need to know."

"Actually, I do," I counter, my voice tight despite the sarcasm. "Enlighten me—since apparently almost killing me earlier wasn't enough to make your point."

Galina sighs, her hand still on his shoulder. "I promised your father I wouldn't tell you," she murmurs, the apology hanging between them like smoke. Her hand squeezes gently before pulling away. "But maybe I should have. It was... for your protection."

Leonid shakes his head once, sharply. "Enough, Galina."

But I'm not letting it go. "You're not the only one with daddy issues," I mutter, the words escaping before I can stop them. Both their eyes snap to me, and I suddenly feel the weight of their attention like a spotlight.

I push the empty pickle plate aside and settle into my seat, resting my elbows on the table.

"I didn't know anything about my father or my brother running the New Orleans crime scene," I say. "Not until the day Jake and I were hunted down. Not until the... *fake* Raven put a bullet in him."

The fucking memory weighs down on me like an anchor; I clench my jaw, fix my gaze on the table, and let the silence turn to a fucking funeral dirge.

"You can't change the past," Galina says finally. "Focus on the present. And on your son."

"You think I don't?" The words come out angrier than I intended, but I don't apologize. "I'm going to find out who killed Jake. End of story."

"Then what?" Leonid asks. His gaze is steady—no hint of teasing. Just something raw. "What happens after?"

"At least your brother's still alive," I snap, locking eyes with his. "Mine's dead."

Something shifts in his expression. His brow softens, eyes warming with what looks too much like understanding. Like fucking pity.

No.

My throat closes up, vision blurring. *Goddammit, not now.* I jerk my head away, blinking hard. He doesn't get to see this. Doesn't get to watch me crack like some broken thing that needs fixing.

Weak. Pathetic. Jake would've—

In my head, I see it clear as day—like I have every night for fourteen years. A bullet through the killer's head, then another through his heart. Simple. Clean. The way Jake's death wasn't. The way I've planned since I was fifteen, screaming myself hoarse in the woods.

Suddenly, all I see is red.

I thought having Elijah would soften the edges. Dull the pain. Maybe even give me something new to hold on to. *It does.* But right now, with their eyes on me, it feels like I'm back in that moment—raw, bleeding, and ready to destroy everything in my path.

That day in the woods, I stopped being a kid. Started being a weapon. Now all I've got left is this—find out who took the only person who ever loved me.

Twenty-Eight

Leonid

A few hours later

T he empty vodka bottles mock me.

Three... no, five of them stand like guilty witnesses to this disaster of an evening. The street lamps outside cast long shadows through Katerina's windows, and somewhere, a clock chimes. Almost midnight.

I watch Clara from across the room. That raw hurt from earlier—gone. Buried beneath steel and vodka and sharp edges that could cut a man open. Always the survivor, this one. Makes me want to—

No. Focus.

The chessboard in the corner sits abandoned, pieces scattered like the men playing earlier bolted mid-game. Chairs pushed in neatly as if to say, "No thanks, we've had enough insanity for one night."

My eyes drop to the scarred wood as Galina's wild, vodka-soaked laugh echoes off the walls. Ivan watches her with that same quiet look he's had for forty years, even as she wipes tears from her face with trembling fingers. Empty bottles crowd the table like casualties, plates shoved aside to make room for more.

"And then—" she wheezes, clutching her stomach, "little *Lyonya*, he just... he just..." Her words dissolve into more laughter, her face going red.

Clara isn't much better. One leg is folded beneath her, the other swinging lazily off the side of her chair, the hem of her hoodie riding higher with each swing. Too high. A sliver of black lace catches the light, and my jaw tightens.

"Don't," the warning rumbles from my chest, but it's about as effective as threatening a hurricane.

"Shhhh!" Clara slurs, her body lurching toward me. Before I can stop her, she presses a finger against my lips. "No more scary mafia voice. You shhh now."

I grab her wrist, pulling her hand away, but not before she sways even closer, practically planting herself in my lap. Her face is flushed, her hair a mess. But fuck, she looks sexy in all fucked up ways.

"Please," she begs Galina, "please tell me what happened next."

"He shit himself!" Galina explodes in another fit of laughter. "Right there in front of the entire Bratva meeting! His father was negotiating with the Ukrainians and—" She slaps the table, vodka glasses rattling. "He just—stands up, face all serious, and announces: 'Papa, I made *kaka*!'"

I drag a hand down my face.

"I was two," I growl, but Clara's already gone, collapsed against the table, shoulders shaking. Her laugh—it's not the controlled, polite thing most women do around me. It's raw, real, snorting occasionally like she can't contain it. Tears streak her cheeks.

"The—the entire Bratva—" Clara gasps for air, "the most dangerous men in Russia—"

"And my *Lyonya*," Galina adds, wiping her eyes, "he just stands there, proud as anything—"

"Enough." I slam my hand on the table, making the bottles jump. But Clara just laughs harder, if that's even possible. Her head falls back, and my cock hardens instantly at the sight of her throat, that olive skin I want to mark until she can't hide who she belongs to. The vodka's making my blood run hot, but I'm not nearly as wasted as she is.

She runs her fingers through her hair, and my hoodie slips, baring one shoulder. *Fuck.* My fingers crack the glass I'm gripping, imagining how that skin would bruise under my hands, how she'd gasp when I bite down on that spot where her neck meets her shoulder. The little sounds she'd make when I—

No. I drag my eyes away, but my dick's already hard enough to hurt, straining against my boxers. *Blyat.* The vodka's made me stupid.

Just as I'm about to stand up and put some fucking distance between us, Clara's hand lands on my thigh. Hot. Heavy. And sliding up. My muscles lock as her fingers drift higher, dangerously close to where my cock's already straining against fabric.

"Mmm," she hums, her body swaying until she's practically sprawled across my thigh. In the split second it takes to register, her hand dives into my sweatpants pocket, her chest pressing against my arm.

"What the fuck—?" I grab her hand, yanking it out along with my phone. Her skin's so soft under my fingers that I have to force myself not to squeeze harder.

"Need t'call Elijah." The words slur together as her head dips forward, dark hair spilling over my chest. "Oh, God... 'm such a bad mother."

"You can barely hold the phone," I growl, but her fingers are already trying to pry it from my grip.

"Please," she whispers, looking up through those fucking lashes. "Need to check on my baby."

Suka. Fine. I check the time—21:07—and dial Kayla.

"Hello, boss," Kayla's voice comes through in a whisper." The *pequeño angelito* just fell asleep."

I turn to tell Clara, but the words stick in my throat. Her face is way too close, her lips look tempting as fuck, and I'm finding it hard to think straight.

"Ngh, lemme talk to Eli'jah," she slurs, her words sloshing together like a badly mixed drink. Moving closer, her face is inches from my face, those full lips parted, breath hot against my mouth. She smells like vodka and something sweet—fuck—makes my already hard dick ache like a bitch, straining against my pants. *Blyat,* I want to bury myself balls-deep in her right fucking now.

A pointed cough makes me snap my head up. Galina and Ivan are watching us like we're some fucking soap opera—she's grinning like a cat that got the cream, and Ivan's got that knowing look that makes me want to punch something. I shoot them both a glare that would make most men piss themselves.

Galina just winks.

Before I can tell them both to go to hell, Clara lunges for the phone like a woman possessed.

"*Blyat.*" The curse slips out as my reflexes kick in. Two fingers land squarely on her forehead, holding her back just as she nearly crashes face-first into my crotch.

She freezes for half a second, her eyes darting up to mine with a mixture of outrage and disbelief. "Seriously?"

"Do you *seriously* want to headbutt my dick?" I counter, keeping my fingers firmly in place like I'm holding back a particularly stubborn goat.

She's squirming, pressing the phone to her ear, and every movement drags her body against mine in ways that make me want to bend her over this fucking table.

"Hellooo?" Her ass shifts in my lap, and I have to grit my teeth to keep from groaning. "You sure he's actually sleepin'? Cause my baby can't sleep without his—his special song and..."

She mashes the phone against her ear, swaying in my lap. "Hello? Hello? I can't—" She pulls the phone away, squinting at it like it's personally offending her, then nearly drops it. My hand shoots out to steady hers just as a message pops up.

A photo fills the screen: Elijah curled up in bed, Pikachu tucked under one arm, mouth slightly open in peaceful sleep. Clara leans in so close her nose nearly touches the glass, going cross-eyed as she tries to zoom in. Her finger keeps missing the button, jabbing random spots on the screen until she makes a frustrated little sound in the back of her throat.

"Why's it so... so tiny?" She pouts, trying to spread the image with clumsy fingers. The movement makes her shift in my lap, and I have to bite back a groan. If she keeps squirming like this—

"Here," I mutter through clenched teeth, enlarging it for her before she can torture me further. The grateful smile she flashes up at me does nothing to help my situation.

She fumbles with the phone, accidentally hitting the speaker button.

Kayla's voice fills the quiet restaurant: "He had so much fun today! Boss, he play with peacocks and feed snakes with Dmitry! Even pet tiger cub—very careful, I promise!" Her accented voice bounces off the walls. "Then we watch movie, and—" She switches to rapid Spanish before catching herself. "Oh! And he help make food in kitchen!"

"Fun?" Clara's voice hitches. "My baby had... fun?"

"*¡Sí, sí!* No worry, *Mamacita.*" The speaker crackles as Kayla's voice gets closer to her phone. "I sleep in his room tonight. He try make *pirozhki* but..." She giggles. "Look like potato more than food."

Clara suddenly stands, the phone tumbling from her fingers to clatter on the table. "I should—" Her legs give out, and I catch her before she hits the floor. Her ass lands right against my cock, the soft curves of her breasts pressing into my chest. My hands grip her waist automatically, and she melts against me like she belongs there, head lolling back on my shoulder.

Yebat. For years, I've run the Bratva without losing control once. Now I've got an armful of drunk, squirming woman who's going to make me come in my pants like a teenager.

I look up to find Galina and Ivan already on their feet. Ivan silently stacks empty bottles while Galina jabs a finger at the stairs behind the counter.

"Room three," she announces in Russian, tossing a key that I catch one-handed. "Clean sheets, thick walls." She winks. "*Spokoinoi nochi, Lyonya.* Try not to break the bed."

Twenty-Nine

Leonid

"*Tch*, whatever," I mutter, shrugging off Galina's orders with a roll of my eyes. Arguing isn't worth the hassle. Because there's just no point.

Because I know that they know—I want to fuck this woman until she screams my name, until she can't remember why she ever hated me. But *not* like this. Not with vodka clouding those blue eyes, not when she can't tell her ass from her elbow.

Besides, the way she's swaying, she's more likely to puke on me than suck me off.

Clara makes it three steps from her chair before nearly taking out a table. Ivan moves faster than a man his age should, sliding furniture out of her path like he's clearing a minefield. She giggles, stumbling sideways, and I catch her around the waist before she can face-plant into the checkered floor.

"*Spasibo*," I tell Ivan with a slight bow of my head. Some things are sacred in our world—respect for our elders, even when they're being nosy bastards, is one of them.

The wooden stairs creak under our weight, each step worn smooth from decades of use. Faded photos line the wall—snapshots of old Russia, black and white memories of Katerina's glory days. Clara stumbles, catching herself on a dusty frame of Lenin giving some speech or other, and I have to grip her waist tighter to keep her upright.

"Oops!" She giggles, dragging her fingers over my knuckles like a goddamn tease. The sound echoes up the stairwell, and I grip her tighter. If these walls could talk, they'd tell stories of blood and betrayal.

But, tonight, they're getting front-row seats to me playing fucking babysitter to a woman who can't walk straight.

"You're so..." her hand finds my abs, fingers splaying wide, "... hard."

"Stairs," I growl. "Focus on the stairs."

She ignores me, as usual. "Ever'where hard." Her other hand joins the first, mapping my stomach like she's reading fucking braille. "Like, here..." She pokes my chest. "An' here..." Her hand drifts lower, and I catch her wrist before she can make this situation worse than it already is.

"*Blyat.* You want to fall and crack your skull open?"

She snorts. "You'd catch me." Then she wiggles her ass against me. "Like you caught me b'fore. When we..." She tries to turn, stumbling. "Remember that night? When you bent me over and—"

"*Zatknis.*" Shut up. Because if she keeps talking about that night, I really will bend her over. Right here on these stairs.

Third floor. Only two doors up here, and I know the other one's empty—Galina keeps it that way when I'm around. Old habits. The hallway's dim, just one yellow bulb casting shadows on the floral wallpaper that's peeling at the corners. Soviet-era charm at its finest.

Clara trips again, this time falling back against my chest. Her head tips back, and *blyat*—the way she's looking up at me makes my cock throb harder.

"Are we going... home?" she mumbles, trying to turn in my grip and nearly taking us both down.

Home? The word hits harder than any bullet. But this drunk woman slurring that one fucking word makes my throat tight.

I step closer, positioning myself a step below her so she won't tumble down like a fucking *yebuchiy* Humpty Dumpty.

Bad move.

Now her ass is perfectly aligned with my cock, and every tiny sway of her body has her pressing back against me. One wrong move and—

"*Nyet.*" I steady her with both hands on her waist now. I glide one hand lower, tracing the curve of her spine, trying to get that perfect ass away from my cock and up the stairs where it belongs.

"No?" The word barely leaves her mouth before she's grabbing for the railing, the drunk little menace trying to prove she can handle stairs. Instead, she falls back and grinds her ass right against my cock. Fuck. My dick jumps, and so does she—like she's just discovered a loaded weapon.

She spins around, tits pressing against my chest through my hoodie, and nearly brains herself on the railing. I grab her just in time. Her face is so close I can taste the vodka on her breath, those fuck-me blue eyes trying to focus as she sways.

"Uhhh..." she smirks, tapping that finger against my chest. "You're... hard down there." Her finger trails lower, tracing a path that makes my cock jump.

Her tongue swipes across her lips, eyes glazed but hungry. "God, you were so big I couldn't even—" She hiccups, then giggles.

"*Blyat*," I curse. I know that look—the same one she gave me that night before dropping to her knees.

Nyet. Not happening.

Before those sinful lips can reach mine, I've got her over my shoulder like a sack of trouble.

"*Suka*," I growl, because now her ass is right by my face, my hoodie riding up to show black lace that barely counts as underwear. My hand slides up her thigh, dangerously close to where I can feel her heat.

"Hey..." Her bare feet dangle by my chest, dirty from the floor but somehow making my dick harder. Everything about her is fucking filthy perfect—raw and real and making me want to mark every inch of her skin.

I tear my eyes away, juggling this squirming handful of trouble while fighting with Galina's ancient fucking key. Clara shifts again, and I feel wetness through that thin lace. *Yebat.* The key nearly slips from my sweating hand.

"Leonid," she moans, and Christ, the way she says my name—like she's already coming.

I shift my grip, palm full of her ass, to keep her from somersaulting over my shoulder.

"Stop squirming," I growl, but she just wiggles harder, making these little sounds that go straight to my cock. The shirt's ridden up to her waist now, giving me a front-row view of that black lace barely covering her ass. Fuck me, it's the kind that disappears between her cheeks, leaving exactly nothing to my imagination.

"Make me," she purrs. Her position over my shoulder has my hand splayed dangerously close to where that thin lace is already damp. Every time she moves, my fingers slide a fraction higher up her inner thigh, and I know one more inch will have me touching that wet cunt.

Focus!

The key finally catches, and I shoulder the door open, flinging it wide as we burst in. Clara's head lolls against my back, her words slurring into my shirt.

"Where're you takin' me, Bratva man?" Her hands hang limply, swaying with each step. "Better be somewhere fun... 'cause your shoulder's not very comfy."

"*Suka*," I mutter, trying to focus on getting us to the bed without dropping her.

I'm two steps from throwing her on that iron-frame bed when she goes completely still. "Leonid?" Her voice is small, different.

"What?" My voice comes out rougher than I mean it to.

"I don't..." She swallows hard—I can feel it against my back. "I don't feel so..."

Blyat. I know that tone.

I spin toward the tiny bathroom, but I'm not fast enough. She makes this little hiccup sound, then—

"Sorry," she chokes, and I feel something wet hit the back of my sweatpants.

Yebat menya.

The most dangerous woman in my world just puked down my ass.

Thirty

Clara

"Sorry," I mumble into his shirt, my cheek pressed against the hard plane of his back. The world spins as he moves, fast and precise. My stomach rolls again.

Oh, God.

Another hiccup escapes, and Leonid curses.

The bathroom light flickers as Leonid practically kicks the door open, nearly taking it off its ancient hinges.

The white porcelain swims in my vision, cracked tiles pressing cold against my knees. Another gag wracks my body, but nothing comes up except the ghost of vodka and *pelmeni*. The mushroom sauce and *borscht* dance at the back of my throat, threatening but never delivering.

My stomach clenches. Heaves. Empty.

The *kholodets* was a mistake. Who the fuck eats meat jelly before doing shots?

I do, apparently.

"*Blyat*," Leonid mutters above me, his calloused fingers surprisingly gentle as they gather my hair back. His ruined hoodie shifts against my skin—God, I can feel the damp spot where it clings to my chest. The same spot where his pants probably need to be burned.

The tiny bathroom spins, black-and-white tiles blurring like a checkerboard kaleidoscope. A broken shower head dangles sadly above a rust-stained tub. Water drips.

Tap. Tap. Tap.

"M'sorry about your pants," I groan between heaves. His grunt is the only response as he reaches around me to run the faucet.

"Arms up," he orders, and I comply without thinking. The hoodie lifts away, leaving me in just— Oh. Right. That scrap of black lace that's trying to masquerade as lingerie. The cool air hits my skin, and I shiver.

"It wasn't that... bad," I manage. Half-digested *pelmeni* and vodka. Could've been worse—at least I made it to the toilet.

"You done?" His hand stays between my shoulder blades, ready to aim me back at the toilet if needed. "Or is there more *pelmeni* looking for revenge?"

My stomach rolls experimentally. "Maybe?" The matching black lace bra suddenly feels like overkill for someone hugging a Soviet-era toilet. "Gimme a minit," I slur, my tongue tripping over the syllables like it's drunker than I am.

The nausea rolls again. Nothing comes up, but the taste of vodka lingers, mixing with the sour reminder of everything I tried to prove tonight. His fingers brush my neck as he gathers a few escaped strands of hair.

"Ugh..." I lift my head slowly, wiping my mouth with the back of my hand. My hair tumbles free as Leonid's fingers slip away, strands falling around my face like I'm starring in the world's most pathetic shampoo commercial.

I turn—carefully, because my head feels like it's stuffed with cotton and vodka—one hand white-knuckling the toilet bowl rim like it's my only friend in this spinning room. The porcelain groans as I use it to pivot, my other hand sliding on the wet tile until my ass lands with a graceless thump. And suddenly, I come face-to-face with...

Jesus Christ.

My eyes cross slightly, trying to focus on what's right at my eye level.

The gray sweatpants do absolutely nothing to hide what's underneath, and drunk or not, I know exactly what that bulge means.

I lick my lips. Heat floods my cheeks as I force my gaze upward, past where that black Henley stretches across his body like it's painted on, outlining every ridge of those abs that could grate cheese, past a chest so defined I can see each muscle straining against the fabric, all the way up to his face.

Leonid looks like thunder and sex had a baby. A very angry, very hot Russian baby.

"About your, um..." I can't help the giggle that escapes. "Your ass." My head tilts sideways, hair falling across my face like a curtain. The movement throws off what little balance I have, and I slump sideways, sagging into a heap. "Son of a bitch!"

A hiss of steam draws my attention to the shower, where water sprays in three different directions from the ancient showerhead like a drunk sprinkler. When I look back, Leonid's stepping away, his hands going to the waistband of those ruined sweats.

Oh.

Oh fuck.

He peels them down with the kind of efficiency that should not be this hot.

But it is.

It really, really is.

Every movement reveals another stretch of muscle, another patch of skin that makes my mouth water for reasons that have nothing to do with nausea.

"I'm sorry," I blurt again because apparently, drunk-me is both horny and polite. "About the... you know." I wave vaguely at his legs, which is a mistake because it draws my eyes right back to... everything.

The black Henley joins the sweats on the floor. I'm pretty sure I whimper. He's just... everywhere. All muscle, tattoos, scars, and danger wrapped in skin that I want to lick like a fucking ice cream cone.

"Fuck... me." The words slip out in a whisper before I can catch them.

His head snaps down, eyes locking with mine. The shower steam curls around him like some kind of pagan god of violence and sex, and the way he's looking at me...

I swallow hard. Maybe I'm not as done with that toilet as I thought.

His jaw clenches—I can see the muscle jumping there from my spot on the cold tile floor, where my ass is probably going numb. He hooks his thumbs into the waistband of his boxers, and I forget how to breathe. One smooth motion and they're gone and—

Holy mother of...

I actually gasp. My drunk brain tries to reconcile what I'm seeing with what I remember from that night, but this, his cock is... Bigger. Harder. My mouth goes dry despite the steam filling the tiny bathroom.

"Up," he growls, and suddenly, his hands are under my arms, lifting me like I weigh nothing. The room spins—or maybe that's just me—as my back hits the cool tile wall.

His fingers find the clasp of my bra, and I arch instinctively, pressing against him as he works the delicate hooks. The lace peels away from my skin, and the cooler air makes my nipples harden instantly. When I fall back against his chest, they drag against his hot skin, sending sparks straight between my legs.

"*Blyat,*" he mutters, and his cock is right there, hard and heavy between us. My back's against the cold tile, but everything in front of me is burning hot—all muscle and scars and that thick length pressing against my stomach. I sway slightly, and his hands grip my hips harder, pinning me in place.

"Stay still," he orders, but his voice has dropped an octave, dangerous. Even through the steam, I can see how his pupils have blown wide; his eyes are the color of aged rum, dark and potent, like a shot of liquid sin ready to corrupt me.

His fingers hook under the thin lace. One sharp tug and the panties tear like paper.

"You smell like a fucking distillery," he growls.

I open my mouth to protest the destruction of perfectly good lingerie, but what comes out instead is— "*hic.*"

Thirty-One

Clara

*T*his is probably not what they meant by "take his breath away."

I press my lips together, cheeks puffing out like a demented chipmunk as I try to hold back another hiccup. My eyes cross with the effort, and I can feel my nose scrunching. The hiccup builds anyway, making my whole body jerk against him.

"*HIC!*"

His hardness throbs against my belly, and a sound rips from his chest—somewhere between a growl and a curse.

Sexy? Yeah, 'cause hiccups are a total turn-on.

"You're impossible," he grits out, but his hands tighten on my hips.

"I *hic* know," I manage, trying not to giggle as his jaw clenches. Even drunk, I know that look. The same heated look that got me into trouble five years ago. The look that gave me Elijah.

A smirk plays at his lips as he reaches past me, grabbing something from behind. When his hand comes back, there's a toothbrush. "Open."

I giggle—actually giggle—as he squeezes paste onto it. "You gonna brush my teeth for me, too, *boss*?"

His cock twitches against my stomach at the word "boss," but his face stays stern. "You're not putting those vodka-soaked lips anywhere near me."

I take the toothbrush, but my drunk hands make it more challenging than it should be. Minty foam dribbles down my chin. His thumbs stroke my hipbones as I brush, and I can't tell if he's steadying me or torturing me.

"You missed a spot," he murmurs, eyes fixed on my mouth.

"Cree-*hic*-py," I manage around the toothbrush, but my nipples tighten under his stare.

We're standing toe-to-toe, almost brushing against each other. His eyes are locked on mine, dark and wicked.

There's a first time for everything. The thought bubbles up from nowhere as I watch him watching me brush my teeth. The great Leonid Kuznetsov, feared Bratva boss, making sure I don't choke on toothpaste. A laugh threatens to bubble up with my next hiccup.

I turn to the sink, needing a moment away from that intense stare. Mint and vodka swirl down the drain as I rinse. In the steam-clouded mirror, his reflection looms behind me, all scarred muscle and dangerous intent. His eyes meet mine in the glass, and my knees wobble. Could be the vodka. Could be the way his gaze is devouring every inch of bare skin, like he's memorizing where he plans to put his mouth next.

His hand slides up my ribs, and my spine arches instinctively. "*Myshka,*" he growls against my neck, "I'll fuck you in the shower."

"*Hic*" is my eloquent response because it seems my body's forgotten how to form actual words. Though, to be fair, it's hard to be articulate when you're naked and pressed against two hundred pounds of angry Russian sex god. The shower curtain scrapes against its rusty rod as he maneuvers us inside; water hits tile, changing rhythm as his body blocks the spray. I risk a glance all over him—

Oh, sweet baby Jesus on a motorcycle.

Water sluices down the valleys of his chest muscles, following paths between tattoos and scars that look like they were carved by something meaner than knives. One droplet catches my attention as it slides past his navel, down that thick length that is still pressed hot and hard against my stomach. I make a sound that's somewhere between a hiccup and a moan.

"It's hard for you, *krasotka*," he growls, but his cock jumps against me. "Suck it."

"You're not my boss," I slur.

"*Nyet*," he agrees, and I hear the smile in his voice—the dangerous one. "I'm much worse."

I try to stand, I really do. But my legs apparently took a vacation to Drunktown without leaving a forwarding address. I sway, and his other hand catches my hip. My hands work on autopilot, reaching down to grab his throbbing cock. It feels hot and heavy in my grip, the heat from his arousal burning into my palms. Oh, fuck. It's been so long. Too long. My clit pulsates in desperate hunger, my pussy practically drooling at the thought of being filled.

"Don't worry about standing," he whispers.

He pushes me down to my knees, a wicked grin on his face. I'm face-to-face with his monster cock, all glistening and veiny.

"Mmm..." My lips part, my tongue swirling around the head, tasting the salty pre-cum that's already dripping from the tip. Oh God, I need him inside me. I start licking, sucking, devouring him like a goddamn nympho, swirling my tongue along the shaft, taking as much as I can into my mouth.

His hands tangle in my hair, pulling me closer, urging me to take more. Instead of giving in to his commands, I tease him, moving my mouth lower to his balls. I trace circles around each one with my tongue, taking one into my mouth and gently sucking on it, twirling my tongue in lazy circles. My hand strokes his cock, my fingers circling around the tip, spreading his pre-cum over his shaft like a slick lubricant.

"Fuck, *krasotka*," he groans, his hips bucking forward, trying to get me to take him back into my mouth. But I'm in control, and I'm not about to let him call the shots just yet.

I stand up, our bodies pressing against each other, our breathing ragged and eager. With my free hand, I grab his wrist and push it down to my pussy, letting his fingers graze against my wet, throbbing lips.

My eyes lock onto his, my lips curving into a devilish smirk. "I *hic* want your fingers in me, deep and rough. Fuck me with your hand until I come all over it."

The corners of his lips curve into a devilish smirk. But his eyes, smoldering with desire and dark with lust, fix on me as I stroke his throbbing cock from tip to base, slow and tantalizing.

"*Blyat*," he curses, his breath hissing out in a guttural groan.

His fingers slide between my folds, coating themselves in my slick juices. I grind against his hand, my body begging for more. He slips a finger inside me, teasing me, rubbing against my G-spot.

"Leonid," I gasp, the sound of my own cunt juices mingling with the running water in a filthy symphony. "Oh fuck, *hic*, I'm about to fuckin' explode if you don't— *Hic*." I can't finish my sentence, my words swallowed up by a moan as his fingers piston into me relentlessly.

He leans in, his breath hot against my ear. "I know what you need, *krasotka*," he growls, his grip on my hips tightening to make sure I stand still, his fingers leaving bruises.

"You need to be fucked. Hard. Rough. Until you scream my name like a goddamn prayer." His words are interspersed with my deep, guttural moans as his fingers work my sensitive clit.

"Jesus, you feel so fuckin' good, Leonid," I pant, my legs shaking as my orgasm builds, aching for release. Water droplets cling to his chiseled chest and roll down his shoulders, his muscles popping like a goddamn road map of sexiness.

"Make me cum," I moan, my breath stuttering with a hiccup as he pushes me to the edge of ecstasy. My nails dig into his shoulder, another girlish hiccup slipping past my lips as I hang on to the last shreds of control. "Please... make me fuckin' scream," I beg.

He leans into me, the hardness of his cock digging into my stomach as I stroke him. *Fuck, he is even harder now.* I grasp his shoulder to steady myself.

"Fuuuuck," I groan, my voice breathless and needy, my hips bucking against his hand. "Yes, Leonid... just like that."

He responds, fingers driving deep into my pussy, pushing hard, then retreating, then pounding deep again in a relentless rhythm that has me begging for more.

"Harder, Leonid," I moan, my back arching against him, my nails digging into his skin.

"You like that, *krasotka?*" he growls, his fucking voice driving me wild.

The world is spinning, my brain short-circuiting from the relentless waves of pleasure crashing over me. Whatever sense, logic, or even sanity I possessed before is gone, blown away by the hurricane of lust swirling around us.

"Fuuck, yes."

His fingers plunge hard and slow, fucking me with a relentless rhythm that pushes me over the edge.

"Yes, yes!" I cry out, my voice echoing off the tiled walls as my cunt clenches around his fingers. The water splashes against the tub as my orgasm ripples through me, my body shaking with the force of it.

He doesn't let up, his fingers pumping into my greedy cunt like pistons.

"Your tight cunt is fucking gripping my fingers like it never wants to let go," he growls, a wicked smile playing on his lips. "Fuck, you're insatiable."

I'm a writhing mass of pleasure, my body vibrating with the force of his touch. I arch my head back, whimpers escaping my lips, my hair cascading down my back. Leonid takes advantage of my exposed neck, his lips pressing against my skin, his hot breath sending shivers down my spine.

His tongue traces a slow, sinuous path down my neck, and I whimper again, this time with a note of desperation.

"Fuck me. More, Leonid," I plead, my voice breathy and weak. "I need more."

"*Krasotka*, I can't wait to feel that pussy wrapped around my cock."

He keeps thrusting, my moans rising in pitch as my body trembles with the aftershocks of my second orgasm.

Thirty-Two

Leonid

The third fucking mistake?

More like the best goddamn decision I ever made. She's a wildcat, a fucking temptress, and I'm a goddamn junkie, hooked on her pussy like it's pure adrenaline.

But it's not just about fucking her. It's about how much I want to keep fucking her over and over.

Blyat, she's fucking insane.

She's cumming again, her body spasming, her cunt squeezing my fingers like a goddamn vise.

I pull my fingers out, her pussy still pulsating, and I bring my hand to her neck, pressing it against her skin, my fingers curling into a fist. I kiss it, suck it, and bite it, my teeth sinking into her flesh just hard enough to make her gasp.

"Mmm..." Her moan is like music to my ears, the vibrations of her voice traveling through my hand on her neck, down to my cock, which aches with need. The warm water pummels my back, and I know I can't hold back any longer.

Instead of spinning her around to face the shower wall so I can fuck her so hard from the back, my lips crash against hers, rough, ravenous, devouring her mouth like a starved beast. Our tongues wrestle, a heated battle of lust, our moans and gasps blending into one carnal chorus. We're fucking with our mouths, my lips dominating hers, her tongue hungrily seeking more of me.

I grind my rock-hard cock against the seam of her pussy and against her clit, my fingers pinching and twisting her hard, sensitive nipples.

I pull her closer, backing her under the hot spray of the shower, her body slick with water and desire.

"Fuck me," she gasps.

"Say please, *krasotka*," I hiss, leaning in close to her ear, my voice dark and commanding. I tug at her nipple, flicking it with a sadistic glee that makes her cry out. "Say it."

She gasps, her body writhing with need. "Please, Leonid," she begs, her voice a desperate plea, "Please, fuck me. I need to feel you inside me. Please."

I smirk, my cock pulsing with desire.

"I'm going to fuck you raw, *krasotka*," I growl, the hot water sluicing over my shoulder like a baptism of lust. I turn her and push her against the wall, her hands splayed against the cold tile, her ass arched up and presented to me like a goddamn offering.

"Yes," she moans, pressing her hips back, her wet, swollen pussy glistening with desire. "Please, fuck me. I need you inside me, Leonid."

I clench my jaw, veins popping in my neck as she begs and writhes for me.

"I'll fuck you until you can't walk straight, *krasotka*," I growl. With one hand gripping her hip, I slide inside her wetness slowly but forcefully.

I bottom out in her tightness, my cock stretching her walls, a low growl rumbling from my chest.

"Fuck, you're so big," she gasps, her body trembling with pleasure. I grip her hip, my other hand tangling in her hair as I begin to move, my hips a rhythmic piston, pumping into her with a steady force that's merciless, relentless, and goddamn savage.

She turns, our eyes locking, my cock still buried deep in her pussy. She licks her lips, her chest heaving with each breath, her body taut and tensing around me. I'm lost in the heat of her, in the wetness of her, in the sheer fucking power of this moment.

"Blyat, kotenok," I growl, my hand slipping below her, my thumb finding her swollen clit. I rub it in slow, maddening circles, my hips hammering into her with relentless precision.

"Fuuck, *yes,*" she gasps, her body shuddering, her pussy walls clenching around my cock. But I'm not done with her, not even close. I slow my pace, the thrusts becoming deliberate, measured, each stroke designed to draw out her pleasure, to prolong her ecstasy.

"Not yet," I whisper, my voice a low, dangerous hum.

Not until I've had my fill of you.

"Harder!" she demands, her face flushed with heat, her eyes wild with lust.

SMACK! My hand connects with her ass, the sound echoing through the tiny space like a gunshot. Her cheeks bounce, jiggling with the impact, the skin reddening with each slap. She gasps, her face a mask of anger, but before she can react, I thrust into her hard and fast, my cock pounding into her tight, wet heat.

"Fuck, yes," she moans, her eyes rolling back in her head.

I'm riding the edge of ecstasy, my body burning with the effort of holding back, but I'm determined to keep going. I want to feel her, taste her, consume her, but my body has other plans. With a growl of frustration, I pull out, leaving her empty and panting.

She turns, her eyes blazing, her mouth opening to protest, but I silence her with a searing kiss, my tongue tangling with hers.

Her words are hot against my lips, a hiss of protest as our tongues continue to battle. "What the hell?" she demands, her body tensing, her voice strained with frustration. "I was so fucking close!"

I pull back, my gaze intense, my lips curving into a wicked grin. "And that's exactly why I stopped, *kotenok*. You're not allowed to come yet. Not until I say so," I whisper.

With the shower shut off, the air in the room is thick with steam, droplets of water beading on her glistening skin. She stands before me, a goddess of lust, her hair damp and clinging to her body, her face radiant.

"You look like a goddamn nymph, *kotenok*," I rumble, my voice low and hungry. "So fucking beautiful, it hurts."

She squeezes her eyes shut, that smart-ass smirk playing at her lips. "You... think I'm... beautiful?" She's still riding the high of orgasms and vodka.

"*Blyat*, of course I think so," I growl, tugging her toward the bed. "You're fucking irresistible, *kotenok*, and I'm not finished with you yet."

Thirty-Three

Leonid

Sleep? Pah. Sleep is for the weak. And I, Leonid Kuznetsov, am not weak.

I pull out of her, my cock still throbbing, and spill my seed onto her stomach. It's the fourth time tonight, the fourth time I've fucked her senseless, and she still wants more.

"Blyat, kotenok," I groan, my body limp, my muscles spent. "I think you may have sucked the life out of me." I flop down next to her, my body hitting the bed with a groan of squeaking springs. The mattress creaks beneath my weight, the protest of worn-out coils the perfect soundtrack to my satisfaction.

She wipes herself down with a tissue, the rustle of paper barely audible over the steady hum of the AC. The room is thick with the scent of sex, our bodies still simmering with heat.

"At least my hiccups are gone," She rolls over, her eyes meeting mine with a mischievous glint.

I raise an eyebrow, my grin lazy and self-satisfied. "Glad I could be of service, *kotenok.*"

She makes this soft noise, half-purr, half-yawn, then she wriggles closer, molding herself against my side like she's done it a thousand times before. Like we're actual lovers instead of... whatever the fuck this is. Her curves fit perfectly into the hard angles of my body, soft skin sliding against mine, one arm draping possessively across my chest. The gesture is so natural, so *intimate*, it steals my breath.

I stare at the ceiling, counting the shadows cast by headlights passing outside. My body is satisfied, but my mind... my mind is in chaos. No woman has ever made me feel this...

Needy.

As if hearing my thoughts, Clara shifts closer, nuzzling into my chest like a cat seeking warmth. Just yesterday, she wanted me dead, that delicious fire in her blue eyes promising creative ways to end me. Now, here she is in my bed, in my *arms*—

The irony hits me with the subtlety of a Bratva initiation.

Blyat.

My hand smacks against my forehead, loud enough to startle my own demons awake.

Clara jolts up. "Who?" she mumbles, head popping up like a drowsy meerkat. Her hair is a magnificent disaster, one side flattened where she'd been pressed against me, the other side staging its own revolution. There's an imprint of my collarbone branded pink across her cheek.

Something unfamiliar claws its way up my throat—a laugh. Not the cold sound I use to watch men squirm, but something genuine that feels like it's been locked away since before I learned to hold a gun.

You're getting soft, Leonid. Like a fucking teenager with his first crush. The Bratva don who brings women home to cuddle? Pathetic.

But I'm already pulling her back down, my traitorous hands gentle as they guide her head to rest over my heart. She settles instantly, her breathing evening out as sleep reclaims her.

She melts into me, her weight pressing against my chest as I keep my eyes on the ceiling. Just for today, I'll let this happen.

Tomorrow, I'll remember who I am and why I can't have this.

Thirty-Four

Clara

Someone's gone full Martha Stewart on my closet while we were at Katerina's. Every fancy-ass Chanel piece is lined up like soldiers. Kayla's work—had to be. Woman probably irons Leonid's underwear.

I pull a towel tighter around myself, water dripping from my hair as I stand in front of the closet. The shower was quick, barely enough to scrub away the mess of vodka, sweat, and regret clinging to me, but now I'm here, staring at rows of silk, lace, and buttons that scream discomfort.

I flick through the hangers, my fingers pausing on a black cashmere sweater before moving on. Today's underwear—red lace—itches against my hip, a choice I instantly regret. Why didn't I grab something sensible during that Chanel spree?

Oh, right—because I was too busy grabbing red-bottom heels and leather jackets, acting like a petty diva. One second, I'm playing dress-up, the next, we're peeling out of the parking lot like something out of an action movie. Now, all I've got is skimpy, lacy, and nowhere near comfy. Perfect for a fancy hostage situation, not so much for surviving Leonid's unpredictable moods.

I sign, grabbing a white silk dress. Simple. Basic. Unlike the clusterfuck that was last night. Unlike the three hours it took me to get from Katerina's to here, trying to ignore the way Leonid wouldn't even look at me. He shoved the helmet at me without a word, kept his visor down the whole ride, like last night hadn't happened. Like he hadn't whispered *"beautiful"* against my skin hours before.

Instead, he was distant. Silent. And I'd spent the entire ride with the taste of vodka and remorse in my mouth, trying to forget the way his hands felt on me.

I yank the dress off the hanger, shaking my head.

Christ, Clara. What happened to "I'm going to kill him"? Instead, you were begging him to—

"Mommy! Mommy! Holy cow, there's a Charizard in your room!"

Elijah crashes in like a tiny tornado, iPad practically glued to his face. Kid's acting like I didn't disappear last night, too busy with his shiny new toy. His hair's still wet—someone gave him a bath and dressed him in a Pokémon T-shirt and tiny Burberry joggers.

"Look what Dmitry showed me!" He shoves the iPad in my face, bouncing like he's mainlined sugar. "Pokémon GO! They're *everywhere*, Mommy! I got three Pikachus already!"

I drape the dress over my arm, dropping to one knee. "That's really cool, baby." I stand, running my fingers through his damp curls.

Turning to the full-length mirror, I wince. That fancy-ass massage shower with its eighteen different settings might've worked out the kinks in my muscles, but it did jack shit for my dignity. My skin's still flushed, marked up like a goddamn road map of last night's mistakes.

Here I am, a shitty-ass mother and a shittier revenge-seeker, still tasting vodka, still feeling the goddamn throbbing ghost of Leonid's delicious cock and the throbbing vein in that perfect "V" spot. But hey, at least my kid's living his best life hunting digital monsters in our... what? Prison? Sanctuary?

"Mommy! Mommy! Did you see that?" Elijah's fingers mash the iPad screen like he's cracking a secret code. He bounces on his toes, eyes glued to the screen. "I caught it! I caught it!"

"That's awesome, buddy," I say, forcing a smile as I drape the white silk dress over the bed. The fabric gleams under the light, sleek and understated, its fitted waist giving way to a subtle flare at the hem. Not exactly my style, but it's the least complicated thing in this ridiculous closet.

Elijah doesn't even glance up, too busy muttering about Charizards and Pikachus. "Dmitry says I'm so good, I can beat anyone!"

"Sounds like you've got it all figured out." I drop the towel from my body and tug the dress over my head. The silk feels cool against my skin, a sharp contrast to the flush still lingering on my cheeks. Just as I smooth the hem, two sharp knocks sound at the door.

"Come in," I call, glancing over my shoulder as Kayla steps inside.

She moves with her usual quiet efficiency, her silver-streaked bun neat as ever. Her warm, slightly formal smile softens the edges of her sharp features. "*Señorita* Clara, lunch is ready downstairs. Will you and Elijah be joining us?"

"How's everything been here?" I ask, hesitating for a beat before adding, "I'm sorry I wasn't here last night. Was everything... okay with Elijah?"

Kayla's hands smooth the apron tied around her waist. "Elijah was fine, *Señorita*. Dmitry kept him entertained. He's quite good with children."

A flicker of guilt tightens my chest, but I nod. "And Dmiry and Maksim... and Leonid." I press my lips down, speaking his name. "Are they here... now?"

Kayla's crow's feet deepen slightly. "*Señor* Leonid and the others had... business." She smooths her apron yet again—a tell I'm starting to recognize. "They'll return for dinner."

Business. Oh, that's a cute way to describe the kind that involves polished suits, offshore accounts, and people who disappear without a trace.

Kayla's eyes shift to Elijah, now pacing in circles with the iPad clutched tightly, mumbling something about "catching the next one." His small sneakers scuff faintly against the rug as he focuses on the screen, brows furrowed in a concentrated frown. Kayla watches him for a moment, her lips pressing together, her expression softening. But only slightly. Then, as if deciding she's lingered too long, her gaze flicks back to me, sharp again.

She adjusts her apron and begins to turn but halts mid-step when I speak. "Kayla, how long have you been with Leonid?"

She freezes for half a second before turning to face me fully.

Her dark eyes meet mine. "Fifteen years, *Señorita*," she says, her tone steady but quieter now, as if she's choosing her words carefully.

"Fifteen years..." I repeat, nodding slowly. "That's a long time."

Elijah breaks his pacing routine, walking directly into my legs. The soft thud jolts me. I steady him with a hand on his shoulder, shaking my head at the oblivious look he gives me before returning to his game.

"Careful, buddy," I murmur, my fingers brushing his curls briefly.

Note to self: screen time is for special occasions only—like surviving mornings like this.

I glance back at Kayla and offer her a small smile. "Thank you... for taking care of him."

She hesitates for a beat as if unsure how to respond, then her expression softens. "No, *Señorita*," she replies, her voice warming slightly. "Thank you."

Something about the way she says it makes me pause. There's weight behind her words, a meaning I can't quite place. "Why do you say that?" I ask, tilting my head.

Her hands smooth her apron for the umpteenth time, her fingers twitching like they need something to hold. "*Señor* Leonid," she starts, her voice softer now, almost hesitant. "He looks... happy."

She presses her lips together, perhaps realizing she's said too much. Her gaze darts briefly to the door before settling back on me.

Happy? My heart tightens at the word. Why? What's changed? Questions churn in my mind, but before I can voice them, Elijah pipes up from his spot near the rug.

"Mommy! I caught another one!" He beams at me, holding up the iPad like a trophy. His eyes finally drift to Kayla, lighting up with excitement. "*Tía* Kayla!"

Kayla's face softens instantly. She crouches down, her hands automatically smoothing Elijah's shirt. "*Sí, pequeño.* Did you catch the big one?"

"*Tía*, did you make those special cookies again? The ones shaped like stars?" Elijah asks, bouncing slightly on his toes.

Her lips curl into a faint smile, the kind that comes from someone who's worked hard to hide her warmth but can't help letting it slip. "*Sí, pequeño*," she replies. "With extra chocolate chips."

I watch them, something twisting uncomfortably in my chest. Two days ago, we were prisoners. Now my son's running in circles over Pokémon, getting star-shaped cookies, and wearing little designer joggers like we've been here all along. The bedroom door's been unlocked since breakfast. No guards. No threats. No cages. Just an illusion of freedom.

What's your game, Leonid?

Kayla rises, her attention still half on Elijah as she pulls something from her apron pocket. It's a photo, the edges creased and worn. She hesitates before holding it out to me. Her eyes shift between the picture and Elijah, who's already back to rambling about his Pokémon stats.

"He is very much..." she begins, her thumb brushing the photo's edge. "The way he tilts his head when he concentrates. Just like *Señor* Leonid."

My fingers freeze on the strap of my dress as I take the picture. It's old—Leonid, much younger, bent over paperwork with the same intense focus Elijah gets when he's drawing. The resemblance punches me in the gut.

Shit.

"The eyes, too," she adds quietly.

I glance at Elijah, who's oblivious, still rambling about Pikachu. My fingers tighten on the edges of the photo as the room feels suddenly too small.

"Do you think so?" the words slip out before I can swallow them back. It's the only thing I can manage.

Fuck. Fuck. Fuck.

Thirty-Five

Clara

Ten minutes later, I'm looking at the way the entire kitchen glows under the noon sun. The air smells of fresh basil and marinara with the faintest undertone of lavender soap.

Elijah swings his legs under the table, barely tall enough to keep his plate steady as he digs into another forkful of spaghetti. His red mustache—watermelon juice this time—stretches wide as he grins at me.

The peacefulness is almost offensive.

I glance at Kayla. She's wiping the counter, but her gaze keeps flicking to Elijah, lingering just a second too long.

Oh, shit.

I feel this icy chill creep over me, like I just realized I've been walking around with my tits out in public.

We need to leave. Soon.

Before **EVERYONE** connects the dots.

"Mommy, can I have more juice? Pleeease?" His puppy-dog eyes are in full effect, but I see right through him.

"You've had two glasses already," I say, picking up the jug. "Do you think you'll grow taller if you drink more?"

He gasps, nodding furiously. "Yes! Uncle Bear said it makes you strong like him—'cause he's a big bear!"

I snort, pouring a small amount into his glass. "Did he now? That explains so much."

Kayla chuckles softly, her hands steady as she stands at the counter, slicing more fruit with practiced precision. "*Señor* Dmitry is quite the influence on him."

"Oh, he's a role model," I say dryly, brushing a strand of hair behind my ear. "Next, he'll be telling him to skip naps because 'real men don't need rest.'"

Elijah giggles, kicking his legs. "Uncle Bear said I can beat anyone if I eat spaghetti every day!"

"Did he?" I raise an eyebrow, leaning closer. "Well, did he also tell you that spaghetti turns little boys into silly noodles?"

"No, it doesn't!" Elijah protests, laughing so hard that his fork clatters onto the plate.

"REEE-yaaah!"

"REEE-yaaah!"

I jump so hard that the plate in my hand jolts, sending a splash of marinara onto my dress. Right on my left tit.

"For f—uuuudge sake, Pavel!" I hiss, grabbing a napkin to dab at the stain.

The peacock freezes mid-strut, turning his head slowly to level me with the kind of side-eye that belongs to ex-boyfriends who "accidentally" show up at your favorite café. His feathers shimmer as he straightens, his beady eyes practically screaming, "How dare you?"

"Mommy said the *F* word!" Elijah sings, giggling through a mouthful of pasta. Red sauce now decorates his Burberry pants like an abstract art project.

Great. Hopefully, someone's stocked more clothes for him.

"No, baby, Mommy said *fudge*. Fudge starts with F." I shoot Kayla a sheepish glance as her eyebrow arches slightly. "Because Pavel is being a little sh—" Her brow lifts higher, and I course-correct mid-word. "—show-off."

Elijah laughs harder, his tiny legs kicking under the table as more sauce makes its way from plate to pants. "Pavel's silly! Like a dancing chicken!"

"Elijah," I say, crouching slightly to meet his eye level. My tone is firmer now, though I soften it with a smile. "Sit still, buddy. We don't kick the table, and we definitely don't eat pasta like it's a mud fight, okay?"

His giggles slow, and he blinks at me, tilting his head like he's deciding whether to listen. "But I'm eating!" he protests, waving his fork in the air like a tiny conductor leading an orchestra of spaghetti.

"Yes, and you can eat without wearing half the plate." I pluck the fork from his sticky fingers and demonstrate. "See? Scoop, twirl, and—bam—clean bite. Now you try."

He frowns, grabbing the fork back and mimicking my movements with exaggerated precision. It's awkward but effective—mostly. A single noodle dangles from his lips like a comedic mustache, but at least it's progress.

"Good job," I say, ruffling his curls as he grins proudly. "Now, keep practicing."

"REEE-yaaah!" Pavel's piercing call draws all our attention back to the garden. He flicks his tail, clearly feeling himself, and pauses by the fountain to admire his reflection. Then, as if on cue, he starts flexing—stretching his wings out like he's auditioning for a bird fitness ad.

This is what rock bottom looks like—watching a peacock practice self-love while my revenge plot crumbles.

The silk of my dress twists in my grip. Stephan's probably at the office right now, running what's left of our operation, while Dad drowns in his fancy whiskey. What would Stephan say if he knew? That Leonid—the man we've been gunning for, the reason he's been keeping our family's empire from crumbling—didn't kill Jake, after all.

I exhale sharply.

Even Mitch confirmed it.

Fourteen years of vendetta. Fourteen years of Stephan picking up Dad's pieces, training me to take over while Dad talked to Jake's ghost in his study.

All that hate. All that planning. Wrong target.

Chop. Chop. Chop.

The rhythmic sound of the knife on the cutting board jolts me back to reality, snapping me out of my own mind.

"You're a good mom, *Señorita Clara*," Kayla says. She doesn't look up from her slicing, but the words catch me off guard.

I glance at her, and my laugh comes out too quick, too forced. "Yeah, well... thanks." I shrug like it's no big deal.

Kayla glances up. Her eyes catch mine over Elijah's head—soft, knowing. Like she sees me in a way I'm not used to being seen. And for a moment, I wonder if this is what it feels like—to have a mom. Someone who'll be in your corner when you're barely holding it together.

My throat tightens, and I quickly turn my attention to Elijah, trying to wipe his hands as an excuse to keep myself from unraveling.

Because how do you explain to someone that you don't know how to be nurtured? That you never had a mom who looked at you like that, with pride and affection, like you were enough?

"*Tía* Kayla!" Elijah bounces in his chair, his hands sticky from watermelon juice and cheese crumbs. "Pavel's doing the dancing thing again!"

Kayla, ever composed, approaches with a fresh tray of watermelon slices and a subtle smile. "*Sí, pequeño*. Perhaps he is lonely."

"Or overcompensating," I mutter, picking up Elijah's discarded fork and placing it back in his hand. The absurdity of it all—this massive estate, the sun-dappled garden, the damn peacocks—isn't lost on me.

Two mountains of designer suits suddenly fill the kitchen doorway. My brow twitches upward as I glance at them, the corner of my mouth tightening before I can stop it. Dmitry looks like a bodyguard auditioning for a Bond villain role, his pristine Armani suit somehow making him even bigger. Meanwhile, Maksim's rocking that "tech billionaire at a Met Gala afterparty" vibe—broad shoulders, effortless confidence, and just the right amount of scruff to make him look annoyingly perfect.

"It's too early for a hostile takeover in the kitchen, isn't it?" I drawl, dabbing at another splash of marinara on Elijah's chin. "Or did someone declare war?"

Neither of them answers. Dmitry grunts, already looking unimpressed, while Maksim leans against the doorframe, his smirk as sharp as ever. My eyes flick between them before sliding to the space behind them.

Empty.

My chest tightens, just for a second—a quick, stupid squeeze I shove down before it shows. Of course he's not here. Why would he be?

Why would I care?

But my fingers tighten on the napkin, twisting it into a mangled knot.

It was just sex. Casual. Nothing.

What did I think—hope?—that he'd suddenly appear? Stupid.

Urgh!

A low chuckle pulls my gaze back. Maksim's watching me, his smirk curling into something meaner, sharper, like he's caught me red-handed. My stomach clenches. He doesn't say a word, just quirks an eyebrow, the unspoken *"Looking for someone?"* hanging in the air.

My lips press into a tight line as I force my attention back to Elijah.

"Uncle Bear!" Elijah squeals, pasta forgotten, as he launches himself at Dmitry. The huge Russian catches him with practiced ease, seemingly unbothered by the red sauce now decorating his pristine suit.

"Little warrior!" Dmitry's voice booms through the kitchen. "Growing strong with spaghetti, yes?"

Kayla sets a fresh bowl of fruit on the counter and picks up her knife, the soft *thunk* of each slice breaking the quiet.

"*Señora,* no need for dinner preparations tonight." Maksim leans against the doorframe, his smirk making my teeth itch. "We have that charity gala at the Astoria."

Kayla's knife pauses mid-slice, her chin lifting slightly. "*Sí, señor.*"

My fingers go still on Elijah's napkin. I catch Maksim's reflection in the window—he's watching me, waiting. I don't ask. I won't ask.

"Ah, yes," he continues, his smirk widening as our eyes meet in the glass. "Boss left early. Something about picking up Fiona Blackwood."

He pauses, savoring each word like expensive wine. "That pretty little young blonde."

Kayla looks up from her chopping, brow furrowed. "No, *señor*. I do not know this Miss Blackwood."

"Oh, Kayla, Kayla." Maksim's voice drips with fake sympathy. "You should see her. All legs and designer dresses. And the way she looks at the boss..." He fans himself dramatically. "So passionate. They might not make it to the gala at all."

"*Señor* Maksim." Kayla gathers her fruit platter with precise movements. "I do not care for gossip." She catches my eye as she heads to the fridge, her slight eye-roll making me bite back a smile.

Dmitry mutters something that sounds suspiciously like "idiot" in Russian.

"Come, little warrior. Let's clean that pasta face, yes?" He turns to Elijah, who's still wielding his fork like a tiny conductor's baton.

The napkin shreds between my fingers.

Nice try, Joker. But I don't play jealous ex-lover in your little theater.

Dmitry picks Elijah up in one smooth motion, muttering something in Russian under his breath. He spares Maksim a quick glance that practically screams, "Are you retarded?"

I stack plates with enough force to make Pavel screech his judgment from the garden. The sound perfectly matches the laugh I'm choking back because, really? *This* is his play?

Fiona, huh. I don't care. Not a fuck given.

The plate in my hand wobbles, my grip tightening until my knuckles ache.

Not. One. Fuck.

Thirty-Six

Leonid

I'm supposed to be focusing on this goddamn gala, but all I can think about is her.

Blyat. Every time I take a breath, I'm reminded of just how badly I want her again.

Her taste. Her smell. The way she moaned, like she couldn't decide if she wanted to scream or bite. It's fucking with my head.

She's like a goddamn itch I can't scratch, and every time I close my eyes, I see her again—sprawled across the bed, her nails digging into my shoulders, that smart mouth of hers silenced for once.

It was supposed to be once. One time to get her out of my system. Instead, it was four. And now, I can't stop thinking about how she looked when I woke up this morning next to me—wrapped in my sheets, her hair a mess, her lips still swollen.

Clara.

I clench my jaw, letting the weight of her name settle in the back of my mind like an ache I can't shake. It's why I came early, why I'm standing here now under the massive oak tree at the center of the event hall. Its branches are wrapped in twinkling white lights, ornaments glinting like scattered stars. Strands of evergreen garland spiral up the trunk, transforming it into a towering, indoor Christmas spectacle. I need space, distance—anything to clear my head.

Besides, this deal with Fiona is too big to screw up.

Fifty billion big.

Gold has been the best bet for years, and if everything goes smoothly tonight, it'll seal an empire-level profit. Enough to keep my Bratva untouchable for years.

I grit my teeth and scan the room, searching for Maksim. He was supposed to be here, keeping an eye on things, but he's nowhere in sight.

The hall hums with quiet power— but not the kind that inspires. No, this is the kind that makes you check for knives in your back.

Charity. A joke, really.

These people wouldn't donate a ruble unless it came with a contract. Men in suits that scream "money laundering" and women draped in diamonds they probably stole from their third husbands. Every handshake hides a deal, every smile a sharpened blade.

The jazz quartet plays soft, seductive nonsense in the corner, but no one's listening. They're too busy pretending to care about saving the world while they carve it up behind crystal champagne flutes.

Idi na khui. Hypocrites, the lot of them.

And me? I'm no better. I'm here to make my cut.

I nod at a passing waitress, her black dress cut high at the hem but low enough at the neck to guarantee tips. A glittering brooch—a cheap nod to the night's jewelry theme—pins her name tag in place. Her tray balances a row of champagne flutes alongside a pair of vodka shots that look more like an afterthought.

"*Spasibo,*" I mutter, plucking one of the shots from the tray. The liquor burns clean, sharp, and familiar as it slides down my throat. I set the empty glass back with a faint clink, catching her startled glance before she moves on.

Better. A little vodka sharpens the edges. Enough to keep my focus on what matters tonight.

The room is quiet, not crowded yet. Waitresses move between tables with trays of champagne, and a few guards linger near the exits, their eyes scanning without urgency.

I'm early, which is deliberate. Time to assess the crowd before it thickens. The gala is a stage, and I've got my role. Black shawl-collar blazer, crisp white shirt, everything tailored to perfection. Minimalist but sharp—exactly the opposite of the woman bearing down on me, dripping in enough gold to blind a man.

"Leonid!"

And here we go. Fiona Blackwood barrels into view, her laugh loud enough to drown out the jazz ensemble in the corner. She's decked out in emerald green, her gown squeezing every inch of her as if it's barely holding her together. The sheer weight of her jewelry could sink a ship. Her lips—recently inflated beyond reason—shine like she's dipped them in oil.

"Fiona." I meet her halfway, leaning in to kiss each cheek.

"Oh, Leonid," she purrs, her lips smacking audibly as she releases me. "It's been far too long. What's it been—two weeks? Three?"

"Three," I reply smoothly. "You look... younger." The word sticks in my throat, but it's better than telling her she looks like she lost a fight with a Botox needle.

Her lips twitch, and for a second, I wonder if she can tell I'm lying. "You charmer! I knew you'd notice. It's the lips, isn't it? I told my doctor to give me something unforgettable. What do you think?" She puckers dramatically, the sound like suction peeling off glass.

Unforgettable is one word for it.

"You always stand out, Fiona," I say, scanning the room for an escape. "I hear the evening's shaping up to be... lucrative."

She beams, taking that as a compliment. "Lucrative? Darling, it's monumental. If this goes smoothly, we're looking at fifty billion. Gold is a sure winner right now, especially with Switzerland tightening its grip on alternative assets."

Fifty billion reasons to tolerate her for a few hours. I glance at her bodyguards—massive men stationed like chess pieces around her. She waves at one of them.

"Silver! Get me another champagne." The man obeys without a word, and Fiona turns back to me, fluttering her eyelashes, which I swear are weighed down by gemstones.

"You must be dying to have a drink with me," she says, sliding a hand—cold, thanks to her bracelets—up my bicep. "Or are you on one of those dreadful 'cleanses'? You look so... tight." She gives my arm a squeeze. "And firm. Do you live at the gym, or were you just born this way?"

I smirk. "Born this way."

"I knew it!" She smacks my chest lightly, her bangles clinking. "A true masterpiece. And speaking of masterpieces, when are you going to let me spoil you? I just got a shipment of vintage watches. One of them screams *you*."

"Generous as always," I reply, prying her hand off my arm and stepping back. "But you're spoiling me enough with this deal. Let's focus on that."

Her lips curl into a pout—or at least they try. "Always so serious, Leonid. When are you going to let me have some fun with you?"

"Tonight's about business." My tone hardens just enough to send a message, but she laughs like I've told a joke.

"Oh, fine. But don't think I'll stop trying." She winks. "You should loosen up, Leonid. Life's too short to be all work and no play."

I let a thin smile form. "And yet, work keeps me alive, Fiona."

Blatant truth.

Suka, I force my focus back to the deal, the numbers, the logistics. Anything but Clara and that I can't keep her there forever. She'll need to go home... eventually.

Fiona is watching me. Her lashes flutter so hard I'm half afraid one of them might take flight—or worse, a chunk might come off entirely. She slaps my chest lightly again, her hand lingering there on purpose, her rings cool through the fabric of my blazer.

"Oh, Leonid, darling," she purrs, "you're no fun at all." She bites her swollen lower lip, and for a second, I wonder if it's about to pop like an overfilled balloon.

I puff my chest out, just the way she likes it, and her delighted giggle bubbles up, loud and shamelessly.

I lean in next to her ear. "Fiona," I say, my voice smooth but firm, "why don't we focus on the business?"

She tilts her head, clearly pleased with herself. "Oh, Leonid, you're going to love this."

I give her a sidelong glance, cautious. "Love what, Fiona?"

She winks, tugging me gently forward. "You'll see. Don't you want to know what happened to your little gold bars? Or have you forgotten already?"

Forgotten? *Blyat.* As if I could. That shipment alone is worth more than most of these hypocrites combined.

But Fiona's not like the rest of them. She's dangerous in her own way—an empire-builder who doesn't need blood or bullets to conquer. I have to give it to her. She's a fucking genius when it comes to business. Those gold bars? She had them melted down, turned into bracelets, necklaces, earrings—carefully designed and scattered across her hundred stores in the U.S., sold as "exclusive collections." Every piece washed clean, profits sky-high.

No one launders better than Fiona.

"Gold doesn't disappear," I mutter, walking alongside her. "You had it melted. The jewelry is ready."

"Leonid," she says smoothly, gesturing toward a server carrying a tray of crystal tumblers filled with amber liquid. She plucks one, swirling the drink with practiced ease before holding it out to me. "Relax. You'll get your answers. But first, enjoy the moment. This isn't some second-rate deal we're closing here. It's a legacy."

I take the glass, the scent of aged scotch cutting through the tension in the air. Probably something rare and absurdly expensive. Fiona doesn't do cheap.

She clinks her own glass lightly against mine, her gaze steady. "To partnerships," she says, her voice rich and commanding. "And to staying untouchable."

I down the scotch in one go, the burn sharp and clean. She smiles approvingly, sipping hers more leisurely.

"Better?" she asks, arching an eyebrow.

"No," I reply flatly, setting the glass back on a passing tray. "The goods, Fiona. Now."

Her lips curl, not in offense, but in amusement. She tilts her head slightly, her gold earrings sway. "You're lucky I like you, Leonid. Anyone else would already be out the door for talking to me like that."

"That's what we're talking about," I tease, the corner of my mouth tugging up just enough. "You know you're sexy when you talk business."

She lets out a low, throaty laugh, rolling her eyes as her fingers trail slowly up to her collarbone, tapping lightly in a rhythm that matches her smirk. "Ah, Leonid. Always so serious, even when you're trying to charm me. But I like that about you."

She steps closer, her voice dropping into something just above a whisper. "This isn't just about the jewelry anymore." There's a glint in her eye, sharp and conspiratorial. "Trust me—you'll want to see what's behind door number two."

I don't trust anyone who says "trust me."

She turns sharply, motioning for me to follow. I take a last glance around the room. The low murmurs of the not-yet-crowded gala hum in the background, but something feels... off. Still no Maksim.

Suka! Where the fuck is he?

Thirty-Seven

Leonid

I let Fiona lead the way, her gown trailing like a ripple through still water.

The room seems to react to her, not the other way around, as conversations drop an octave when her bodyguards fall into line behind us. A wall of black suits and stony expressions, they move with military precision, their presence as natural as a shadow and twice as menacing.

I follow her toward the quieter corners of the gala, my mind half on her and half scanning the room one last time. Still no Maksim.

Idi na khui, Maksim. This isn't the time to disappear.

She glances back once, her red lips curving into a smile as she catches me watching.

"Don't look so tense, Leonid," she purrs. "This is the fun part."

"Fun isn't what I came for," I mutter, adjusting my cufflink as I keep pace with her.

She stops in front of a set of tall, ornate doors near the far end of the hall, gilded with gold that's almost too on the nose for a jewelry-themed gala. The kind of detail that screams *money* and whispers *danger.*

I let Fiona step back to stand beside me, her hand slipping under my arm smoothly.

From the shadows of her bodyguards emerges her right-hand man, a stocky figure with a military-cut salt-and-pepper buzz, his thick neck bulging slightly above his tailored black suit. A jagged scar curves down from his right temple to the edge of his cheekbone.

Without hesitation, he steps forward and punches in a series of digits on the keypad embedded in the gilded door. The screen flickers, requiring his eye scan. He leans in, his scar catching the light, and a soft beep unlocks the ornate panels.

"Now, Leonid," Fiona purrs again, her voice a mix of indulgence and amusement as she tilts her head to glance at me, "you'll see. Trust me, darling. Surprises are what keep life interesting."

"I don't like surprises," I mutter, my tone flat. My fingers twitch at my side, a reflex I don't bother suppressing. Hidden under the fabric of my suit jacket, the weight of my gun presses reassuringly against my ribs. A second blade is strapped to my ankle—small, discreet, sharp enough to get the job done if it comes to that.

The doors swing open with a soft hiss, revealing a space that feels worlds away from the grandeur of the gala outside. Dim lighting casts shadows across the room, the air cooler, carrying a faint hum of machinery. Her bodyguards fan out behind us, silent as sentinels.

Fiona strides in, her hand still loosely linked through my arm. The room is vast but designed to intimidate, not impress. Glass display cases line the walls, showcasing pieces that scream exclusivity: diamond necklaces that would bankrupt small nations, rare stones that gleam with an otherworldly hue, and custom sets that practically radiate untouchability. The center of the room is dominated by a long table, empty but polished to a mirror-like sheen.

She pauses mid-step, turning her head toward me with a sly smile. "Do you realize how long we've been working together, Leonid?"

"Ten years, eleven months," I reply automatically, my gaze moving over the room. My unease itches at the back of my neck, but I don't let it show.

"That's why I like you so much! You remember every detail..." She squeezes my arm harder, her rings pressing into my suit. "Oh my, so strong..." Her tongue darts out to wet those ridiculous lips.

The door clicks shut behind us, the lock engaging with a faint metallic thud. I glance back. Two guards have taken position, their stances firm, hands close to their holstered weapons. Military-trained, no question.

Govno, something's up.

Fiona steps away from me. I turn my attention back to her standing at the center of the room, her emerald gown catching the faint glow of the overhead lights. She watches me, her red lips curling with amusement.

A long display table stretches across the center, lined with velvet cushions cradling the gold. Necklaces, bracelets, rings—all glittering under precise, cold lighting.

Fiona walks toward the table, her fingers gliding over a bold gold necklace studded with diamonds.

"Your shipment," she says simply. "Melted down, repurposed, and polished to perfection."

I step closer, my eyes narrowing as I inspect a necklace. The craftsmanship is flawless; bold, without being gaudy. Fiona's people know their work. This isn't just jewelry—it's power, wealth, the kind of pieces that can't be questioned in her world of elite clientele.

"You've outdone yourself," I say, my tone neutral but edged with approval.

Her smile sharpens, her gaze meeting mine. "It's what I do, darling. You bring me the gold; I make it into something irresistible. You wouldn't believe how fast this collection will sell out."

But something doesn't sit right. I glance around again, the itch in my instincts growing.

"And the rest?" I ask, my voice calm but sharp. "Where's the remainder of the shipment?"

"Oh, darling, don't rush me," she chides, waving a perfectly manicured finger. "There's more. But you'll have to come a little further for the full show."

She steps in closer, her fingers lightly brushing the edge of the table as she leans forward just enough to close the space between us. Her lips curve into a slow, knowing smile, the kind that makes promises she has no intention of keeping.

"And this is just the beginning," she says, her words soft but deliberate. "Imagine what we could do with a little more... cooperation."

I tilt my head, narrowing my eyes. "What kind of cooperation?"

Before she can answer, the door behind us opens. Heavy footsteps echo through the room, breaking the tense quiet.

I turn sharply, my hand brushing the inside of my jacket where my gun rests.

A voice cuts through the air. "Hello, *brat*."

And there he is. Ludis, stepping out of the shadows, his bruised face a glaring contrast to the crisp lines of his tailored suit. A cigar smolders between his fingers, smoke curling lazily upward as he takes a slow, deliberate drag.

His grin widens. "Miss me?"

Thirty-Eight

Clara

The greenhouse smells like soil and citrus, the air thick and warm like a jungle. I roll up my sleeves, feeling the faint stickiness on my skin from the humidity. Elijah runs ahead, his little sneakers squeaking on the polished stone floor. His giggles echo, too loud for the stillness, but I can't bring myself to shush him.

"Come on, Mommy! You have to see this!" His voice bounces off the glass panels, too loud in the serene space.

"Inside voice, little man," I attempt to whisper, but the words tumble out in that parent-whisper way that's about as subtle as a foghorn.

But he's already running further into the greenhouse, the soles of his shoes too loud on the damp stone floor. I shake my head and glance at my watch—five hours since lunch. I swipe a bead of sweat from my forehead, feeling the dampness cling to my skin.

Leonid's still not back. Probably off charming his diamond-draped blonde. Maksim's smug words about "Fiona" replay in my head like a bad song on repeat.

Damn it. Or maybe something more colorful: *Fuck Maksim. Fuck Fiona. Fuck Leonid, too, while I'm at it.*

I exhale sharply, tugging my hair off my neck, like the heat—or the irritation—might evaporate if I just try hard enough. But I'm not thinking about that. Not now.

The path narrows ahead, forcing me to duck slightly under the sprawling leaves of something huge and waxy. The plant is so green it almost looks fake, its massive leaves brushing against my arms as I pass. Another step, and I have to squat a little to avoid the low-hanging branches of a tree covered in bright, unfamiliar blooms. It smells faintly of lemons and something sweeter, a sharp contrast to the damp, earthy air.

"Mommy, come on!" Elijah's voice carries from up ahead, and when I straighten, I spot him near the far end of the greenhouse, standing in front of a tall metal door.

He bounces on his toes, his excitement practically vibrating off him as he turns to me. "He's here, Mommy!"

The door looks like it belongs in a vault, the steel polished to a dull shine, and I glance around instinctively. No guards in sight, no one watching us. It's strange, but then again, I'm not running. Not with Mitch still in their clinic. Not when Elijah's smiling like this. It feels more like an open cage than a hostage situation, but the bars are still there.

"Who's 'he,' buddy?" I ask, moving toward the door.

"You'll see!" Elijah chirps, turning back toward the metal door. His excitement pulls me forward, but a soft crunch of gravel under heavy footsteps makes me freeze.

I glance over my shoulder, my pulse ticking up for a split second. A man steps out from the back of the greenhouse, his bulk impossible to miss. He's massive—barrel-chested, with broad shoulders stretching the seams of his black T-shirt. His beard is thick and reddish, streaked with gray, and his sharp gray eyes take us in with a calm, practiced ease.

The sleeves of his shirt are rolled up, revealing forearms covered in faded ink. A coiled serpent winds up one arm, a grinning skull leers from the other. He carries himself with that relaxed confidence you only see in men who know exactly how strong they are.

He bows slightly, just enough to mess Elijah's hair with a big, calloused hand.

"Elijah," he says, his voice low and gravelly, thick with a Russian accent. His lips quirk into a small, polite smile as his eyes meet mine.

"*Dobry vecher*," he says, inclining his head toward me.

Elijah beams, dimples flashing as he points at the man like he's just introduced a celebrity.

"Mommy, this is Adrian! He's so cool. He knows *everything* about snakes."

Adrian straightens, his sharp gray eyes still on me. "You brought your mama, huh?" He grins, a little sharper now, as his gaze flicks back to Elijah. "Good. She'll love this."

I raise a brow, watching as Adrian casually taps the door behind him, his movements smooth and unhurried. Elijah is bouncing on his toes again, vibrating with excitement.

I fight the urge to laugh under my breath. Of course, Elijah's making friends.

Adrian pulls a key from his pocket, the metallic jingle breaking the quiet hum of the greenhouse. He slides it into the lock, the door groaning softly as it swings open. A waft of cool, stale air seeps out, faintly metallic and earthy, like wet stone and steel.

Elijah grabs my hand instinctively, his fingers warm and small against mine.

"It's dark in there, Mommy," he whispers, half-excited, half-wary.

The door creaks open, and the first thing that hits me is the cool, sterile scent of the room—a mix of glass cleaner and something faintly metallic. I step inside, and my breath catches.

The enclosure is enormous, stretching from floor to ceiling, made of reinforced glass so clear it feels like there's nothing separating us from what's inside.

"Holy—" I clamp my mouth shut before I finish, swallowing the word.

A yellow Burmese python moves sinuously, her golden-yellow scales shimmering under the specialized lighting. She's enormous, at least fifteen feet long, coiled loosely around a thick branch and a smooth rock slab. Her head lifts slightly, her black eyes sharp and watchful as her tongue flickers in and out.

"She's so big!" Elijah squeals, his voice bouncing off the glass.

"She's fat," I mutter under my breath, stepping closer despite myself.

"She's perfect," Adrian corrects, a hint of pride in his voice. "And very well-fed. That's why she's so... substantial."

I snort at the word, unable to help myself. Substantial. Right. The snake looks like she ate a small dog for breakfast.

Elijah presses closer to the glass, his face glowing with fascination. "What's her name again?"

"Golubka," Adrian says, his tone softening as he crouches near the edge of the enclosure. "It means 'little dove.'"

I raise an eyebrow, shooting him a sidelong glance. "Little dove? Seems ironic."

Adrian chuckles, shrugging one broad shoulder. "She's gentle... when she's not eating."

Golubka shifts slightly, her massive coils gleaming like polished gold under the lights. Elijah presses his face closer to the glass, his breath fogging the surface as he stares, transfixed.

"What's your story, Leonid?" I murmur under my breath, not expecting an answer.

As if reading my mind, Adrian straightens, moving to the side of the enclosure. His boots make a soft *thunk* against the concrete as he crouches by a cabinet tucked neatly against the wall.

"You know," he begins, his voice low and conversational, "this girl wasn't always so lucky."

I glance at him, intrigued despite myself. "Lucky? She's a fifteen-foot python in a luxury enclosure. That doesn't exactly scream 'hard luck.'"

Adrian chuckles, shaking his head as he opens the cabinet door with a faint creak. "Boss found her in some backwater dump a few years ago. Small-time gangsters were skinning snakes for leather goods. She was half-dead when he got her out."

I blink, surprised. "So, what? He rescues snakes now?"

Adrian pulls out a wooden box, its hinges squeaking. Inside comes another sound—sharp and high-pitched. Squeaking.

Elijah whirls around, his curiosity piqued. "What's he doing, Mommy? What's in the box?"

"Feed day," Adrian says simply, his tone almost cheerful as he grabs a pair of tongs. He glances at me, smirking. "And yeah, he saves the odd thing. Not people usually, though. This is... different."

Different. The word hangs in the air, and my mouth opens slightly, but no words come out.

Adrian continues as if the silence invites him to fill it. "Golubka's gentle now, but back then, she was a mess. He didn't have to save her.

Could've left her like the rest." He shrugs, then lifts the lid of the box, revealing a squirming white rat.

Elijah's eyes widen, his excitement bubbling over. "Can I help? Mommy, can I feed her? Please?"

I glance between Elijah's pleading eyes and Adrian's steady, amused gaze. "Uh, I don't think—"

"Safe as can be," Adrian cuts in smoothly, already lifting the rat with the tongs. "Golubka's well-behaved. You'll like this, kid. With your permission, of course."

I pinch the bridge of my nose. "Fine," I sigh, already regretting it. "But if you lose a finger, it's not my fault."

Adrian laughs, crouching to Elijah's level. He hands over the tongs, guiding Elijah's small hands with care. "Just hold it steady and close to the glass. She'll do the rest."

Elijah hesitates and then grins as he grips the tongs, his determination shining through. "I'm doing it, Mommy!"

"You're definitely doing something," I mutter, fighting back a laugh.

Golubka's head moves with deliberate slowness, her black eyes locking onto the rat. Her tongue flicks once, twice, and then—

With a sudden, smooth strike, she grabs the rat, coiling her body with a speed that belies her size. Elijah gasps, his mouth falling open in awe.

"That was awesome!" he shouts, his voice echoing off the glass.

Adrian straightens, brushing his hands off on his pants. "She's a queen," he says simply, his pride unmistakable.

I raise a brow, watching the snake work. "So, let me get this straight—Leonid rescues snakes from being skinned but skins his enemies without blinking?"

Adrian's laugh is deep, filling the small space. "Something like that." He leans casually against the glass, his dark eyes glinting. "But he doesn't bring women or kids here. Never seen it before. You guys must be... special."

Special. That word again.

I glance at Elijah, who's now pointing excitedly at Golubka's tail, oblivious to the weight of Adrian's words. My chest tightens as I force a smile.

"Special," I repeat softly, like saying it out loud might make it make sense.

Adrian shrugs, moving back toward the cabinet. "Boss doesn't save much," he says, his tone softer now. "But when he does..." He lets the thought hang, unfinished, as he locks the box away.

I exhale sharply, ruffling Elijah's hair. "You did great, buddy."

I watch Elijah beam at me, and all I can think is, *Damn, he's so much like him.*

Fucking hell, I wonder what Leonid's doing right now.

Thirty-Nine

Leonid

"*Suka blyad*!" My lips twist into a feral snarl, the cigar clenched between my teeth as I glare across the table. "What the fuck do you mean, splitting the profit between us?"

The room presses in, too goddamn small for this shit. Fiona's theatrics are all over it—velvet drapes, gold-trimmed chairs, an antique Persian rug with intricate patterns, and the marble-topped table, 18th-century French, flawless down to the hand-carved legs. *I'd know. I gave it to her.* A fucking calculated gift to buy her loyalty, to remind her where her fucking alliances should lie.

Yob tvoyu mat. And now?

She's pissing all over it, tearing everything apart with that smug look on her face like she's untouchable.

The smell of old wood and smoke hangs in the air—a mix of decadence and deceit. Her bodyguards stand like statues, dead-eyed and stiff, but it's Ludis across from me who burns through my focus.

Always Ludis. *My twin, my enemy.*

He leans back in his chair, eyeing me with smug satisfaction. Makes me think of snapping bone. Cuban smoke curls from his lips as he takes a long pull, the ember glowing brighter before he exhales slowly, letting the smoke curl upward like a fucking victory banner. A slow blink follows, his gaze steady, daring me to make the next move.

Mudak.

"Controlled violence breathing" doesn't help. Nothing helps when you're watching a dead man try to steal your empire.

Fiona claps her fat hands together. "Oh, Leonid," she coos, her voice pure venom disguised as silk. "Always so dramatic."

Dramatic?

Her lips stretch wide, the mole on her upper lip twitching as she grins like a cat about to eat a cornered rat. Like she's seconds away from giving Ludis and me each a dagger to finish this the old-fashioned way.

"Don't fucking toy with me, Fiona," I growl. My gaze flicks to Ludis, his face already smug. The bastard leans back in his chair like he's sitting on a throne, not across from the one person who'd shoot him without blinking.

"You don't like it? Then walk away," Ludis says, his tone light but his eyes dark as sin. "Oh, wait—you can't. You need this deal as much as I do, *brat*." He spits the word like it burns his tongue.

"The answer is a fucking NO, Fiona." My cigar snaps between my fingers, tobacco scattering across her precious marble.

Fiona lets out a dramatic sigh, resting her chin on one hand. Her other hand toys with the gaudy ring on her finger, turning it slowly.

"Oh, darling boy," she says, her voice a mix of amusement and exasperation. "Do you really think you have a choice? Because I assure you, Leonid, you don't."

I glare at her, my jaw tightening as I force myself to stay in my seat. The heat crawling up my neck demands violence, but I hold it back—for now.

"This is the difference," I say, "between the Bratva and these fuck-ing mongrel criminals you're so fond of surrounding yourself with, Fiona. We *don't* backstab. We *don't* play these dirty little games." I lean forward, the edge of the table pressing against my forearms. "We have a code. Rules. We protect our own and handle our business clean. No chaos. No loose ends."

Fiona tilts her head, an infuriating smirk playing on her lips. "If I didn't know better, I'd say you like this pissing contest. But let's not waste my time, shall we?"

"You're wasting mine," I snap, my gaze flicking back to her. "You think I'd work with this piece of shit? He's unstable, Fiona. A fucking wildcard with more bodies on his record than sense."

"Flatter me more, *brat*," Ludis interrupts, ashing his cigar onto the floor like he owns the place. "I might start to think you care."

Fiona's laugh bubbles up—that artificial, glass-breaking sound that makes my molars grind.

Suka blyad', I should have broken her neck the moment she led me down here.

"That's the thing about you, Leonid," Ludis says, crossing one leg over the other with the kind of precision that makes me itch for violence. "Always clinging to your precious *code*. Like it'll save you."

He takes another long drag from his cigar, exhaling a thick cloud of smoke that curls between us.

"You think rules make you better than me? You're just as dirty. The only difference is, I don't lie to myself about it."

My jaw tightens, the ache spreading down my neck. "The Bratva has survived for years because of those rules. Without them, you're nothing but a rabid dog waiting to be put down."

"Maybe." Ludis shrugs, flicking ash carelessly onto the rug beneath him again. "But rabid dogs get results. And right now, Fiona needs results, not your moral fucking high ground."

"Boys, boys, boys." She clicks her tongue and shakes her head, her face twisting into a sour, condescending smirk. As if we're children who just shit in our diapers and need changing. "You're giving me a headache. Leonid, I don't care about your *code*. Ludis may not follow rules, but he gets things done. And for what I'm planning, I need both of you."

Something snaps loose inside me. *Code.* Like it's some fucking joke. The cigar crushes in my grip as I surge forward, chair scraping back.

"My *code* is why your empire hasn't crumbled, you stupid bitch." My voice drops to a growl. "My *code* is why every shipment arrives pure. Why your precious jewelry business isn't drowning in blood. Why the Swiss still trust us."

Ludis snorts. "Such nobility from a glorified delivery boy."

I ignore him, eyes locked on Fiona. "You want to play? Fine. But the moment you let this rabid dog off his leash," I jab a finger at Ludis, "everything burns. The mines, the connections, the trust. All of it." I lean closer, close enough to see her pupils dilate. "You're not just making a mistake, Fiona. You're signing your own death warrant."

She drums her ringed fingers against the table—*tap, tap, tap*. "Let me be crystal clear. Leonid controls the mines. Pure, Swiss gold that makes my little empire," she twists one of her gaudy rings, "sparkle. And you, my dear Ludis, you have what I need to expand. Those underground routes, those dirty little secrets that make problems... disappear."

"And now you want more." I pull in a breath to steady myself. "Not satisfied with just turning my gold into your pretty trinkets anymore, are you, Fiona?"

"A girl's got to grow." Her lips curl. "Besides, imagine what we could do. Your glorious gold, Ludis' shadow network—"

"Fuck your imagination," I hiss. "Give me back my shipment, and we're done."

Her smile widens, all teeth. "Oh, that lovely little half-ton sitting in my vault? Pure. Swiss. Gold." Each word drops like a stone. "Would be a shame if something happened to it. Melted down, perhaps? Mixed with cheaper metals?" She taps her ring again. "Or maybe just... lost."

Ludis leans back, blowing smoke rings toward the ceiling. "Sounds expensive, brother. How much was it again? Fifty billion? Sixty?"

My jaw clenches so hard I taste blood. That gold was meant for the Chinese deal next week. Without it... "*Suka.*"

"Now you're getting it." Fiona's voice drips honey over steel. "So, let's try this again. Your mines, Ludis' routes, my... protection. Unless you'd rather explain to your Chinese friends why their investment is decorating my fingers?"

A muscle jumps in my jaw.

The ticking of the clock behind me—ornate and gilded, one of Fiona's unnecessary indulgences—beats like a slow drum, a reminder that every second here costs me more than time.

Forty

Leonid

*P*izda. The bitch has me cornered, and she knows it.

I press my palms flat against the table, the smooth surface cool under my skin. My eyes burn into Fiona.

"So, what the fuck do you want me to do now?" My voice crackles with fury—like a fucking blade pressed to a throat.

She thinks she's won? That she can toy with me like some fucking puppet? When this is done, she'll be nothing but a bloated corpse floating in the sea.

Her lips curl upward, her mole twitching with the motion. "Leonid, dear," she begins.

I don't answer; just tilt my head slightly... enough to let her know I'm not in the mood for her games.

"There's a deal I need brokered. Something delicate. Something requiring your... particular set of skills," she says, her voice turning coy. "I need you to fly to Zermatt."

"Zermatt?" The name grates on my nerves, "What's in Courchevel that requires me?"

"Oh, let's call it an opportunity." Her smirk deepens, "An arrangement that could benefit all of us—if handled correctly."

"And if I refuse?"

Her laugh is soft, barely a breath, but it cuts like glass. "I already told you. Refuse, and your precious gold might find itself... misplaced. Or worse, diluted. A little mix of base metals, a touch of carelessness—it would be such a shame, wouldn't it?" Her eyes glitter as she delivers the threat.

Bitch.

"And you need this handled now?"

"Tonight." She clasps her hands together like it's a done deal. "You can take my private plane. It's already fueled and waiting."

I let out a dry, humorless laugh. "No need. I have my own."

Her lips twitch in annoyance before she recovers. "Of course you do, darling. Well, I'm sure you'll make the most of it. I'm positively thrilled to see how this plays out."

She stands, smoothing the fabric of her glittering gown, "Now, if you'll excuse me, there's a gala waiting, and oh, so many people to meet. Do try to keep things... civil while I'm gone."

Her laughter echoes as she exits, her bodyguards following like shadows.

Ludis and I remain seated. Finally, he stands, slow and deliberate. My fingers twitch toward my side, the comforting presence of my gun calling to me as he steps closer.

"Relax, brother." He approaches, his steps lazy, "I'm not here to fight."

"Then keep your distance," I spit. My hand hovers near my hip, but Ludis just smirks. He stops just shy of invading my space, his head tilting slightly as if examining me for cracks.

"And, *brat*—" he says; his hand lands on my shoulder.

"I said fuck off." I shift my shoulders, brushing him off, but he doesn't back away. Instead, his hand lands on me; he brushes off invisible lint like this is his space to claim. His thumb and forefinger tug at my collar, as though he hasn't been one misstep away from death since the moment he walked in.

"Speaking of which—" he starts, his grip lingering just long enough to make it personal. His fingers smooth a wrinkle from my jacket like we're brothers sharing an inside joke. "Do look after your little fighter. Two of my men are still in intensive care because of her—*Clara Caldwell.*"

The name detonates between us, but I don't give him the satisfaction of a reaction. Not the kind he wants.

My body moves before the thought is finished. A step forward. Close enough to feel the heat radiating off him. My hand comes down on his, clamping it to my shoulder like a trap. I lean in, my face an inch from his.

"*Idi na hui,*" I spit out the words like a curse, each syllable laced with venom. "Touch a hair on her head, and I'll gut you like a fucking pig. You won't need intensive care; you'll need a goddamn body bag."

The corner of his mouth twitches, his muscles shifting like he's deciding whether to shove back or yield. He settles on the latter, his body going slack just enough to loosen my hold. Ludis steps back slowly, pulling his wrist free.

"You found a fun *toy.*" His tongue darts out, wetting his bottom lip. "One that I'd like to play with."

Suka blyad'. I'm halfway toward him when his guards materialize. Two mountains of muscle and Kevlar between us.

"Good luck in Zermatt," he says.

Blyat. I feel a vein throbbing in my neck like a goddamn drumbeat, fueled by the need to tear his throat out.

Fiona's voice drips honey from the stage, her words lost under the pounding in my skull. The crystal chandeliers throw shadows across faces I want to break, the evening crowd pressing in like cattle waiting for slaughter.

I spot them at the bar— The *mudak* Maksim slouched against polished mahogany like he's at a fucking beach resort, Dmitry rigid beside him, eyes scanning the crowd. Neither looks like they've spent the last two hours wondering if their boss was walking into an ambush.

The crowd parts for me. Smart fucking move.

"Having fun?" I stop inches from Maksim, close enough to smell the untouched whiskey in his glass.

He lifts his chin in greeting. "Boss. Still breathing, I see."

My hand shoots out, fingers wrapping around the glass. It shatters against the bar, whiskey and blood mixing on marble. The nearby chatter dies.

"Still breathing?" The words taste like ash. "That's what you have to say after leaving me alone with that *suka* and my brother?"

"Ludis was here?" Maksim quirks an eyebrow. Dmitry shifts his weight. Good. At least one of them remembers what fear feels like.

"Sorry, boss, we thought... The orders were clear." Maksim leans closer, voice dropping below Fiona's ongoing speech. "Her people said you were checking the gold shipment. Together."

"Checking the—" A laugh tears from my throat, sharp enough to draw looks. "And you believed that bullshit?"

"Didn't have much choice." His eyes flick to the balcony where three of Fiona's men stand watch. "They insisted. Strongly."

Dmitry clears his throat. "Boss, we stayed close—"

"Close?" I turn on him, watching him swallow. "Close enough to hear her threaten to melt down fifty billion in pure Swiss gold? Close enough to watch my brother plan my execution?"

The muscle in Dmitry's jaw jumps. At least he has the decency to look ashamed.

"Get the plane ready." I grab Maksim's collar, yanking him closer. "And next time someone tells you to stay put while I walk into a trap? Shoot them."

His lips twitch. "Any preference on where?"

"Surprise me." I release him, straightening his jacket with more force than necessary. "Wheels up in thirty. We're going to fucking Switzerland."

"Zermatt?" Dmitry's eyebrows rise. "In the middle of—"

"Are your ears as useless as your brain, or is this intentional stupidity?"

From the stage, Fiona's laughter rings out like breaking glass. I turn toward the exit, my men falling in step behind me.

"Oh, and Maksim?"

"Boss?"

"You're buying me a new bottle of whiskey. The expensive kind."

His quiet chuckle follows me out. "Consider it hazard pay."

Forty-One

Clara

The soft glow of the lamp in the corner is the only thing keeping our room from descending into complete darkness. It casts long shadows over the hardwood floor and the expensive, fussy crown moldings that seem to mock me with their perfect edges. The bed—king-sized, with sheets so soft they probably came from the hair of angels—feels far too big for the two of us, yet somehow, it's still too small to contain my restless thoughts.

Pathetic. The man kidnapped us, and here I am, wondering if he's having fun at his fancy gala with his bottle-blonde arm candy.

"She's been after the boss for years," Maksim had said, smirking like he knew exactly how much that would piss me off.

Well, congratulations, asshole. Mission accomplished.

I turn my head sharply toward the clock on the bedside table, the small motion making my hair catch on my bare shoulder. Midnight. Of course.

Fucking shit.

My jaw tightens as I grind my teeth against the frustration threatening to bubble over. He's still not back. He probably isn't coming back anytime soon. My nails dig into the edge of the bathrobe belt as I take a slow, deliberate breath. In. Out. Calm.

A soft, sleepy giggle bubbles out next to me— "Hehehe," light and breathy, the unmistakable sound of a child laughing in his dreams.

I freeze for a second, turning my head to look down at Elijah. He's curled up on his side, just inches away, one tiny hand still clutching his battered soft toy. A big, wide smile spreads across his face, so pure and happy it almost makes me forget the storm raging in my chest.

I scoff quietly, pressing a kiss to his chubby cheek. His skin is impossibly soft, baby powder warm, and it makes me want to wrap him in my arms and shield him from everything. Instead, I gently adjust the Pokémon toy in his hand to make sure it stays close to him.

"Sweet dreams, kiddo," I murmur under my breath.

Carefully, I ease back onto my side of the bed, sinking into the impossibly soft mattress.

Step one: Close your eyes.

Step two: Don't think about him.

Step three: Sleep. Easy. Logical. Just shut it all down like a computer.

My eyelids flutter shut.

Nothing.

I crack one eye open. Okay, step one isn't going so well. My gaze flickers toward the lamp, the soft light catching on the satin of my nightgown.

Ugh. The damn nightgown.

I snort softly to myself, shaking my head.

What kind of idiot buys this? Oh, wait, me. The idiot in question.

It had seemed like such a great idea at the Chanel store. A little retail therapy to shove in Leonid's face, grabbing every tiny, impractical piece I could find just to piss him off. But now? This white satin monstrosity is my penance. A size too small, it clings to me like shrink wrap, the hem barely clearing the curve of my ass. If I move wrong, I'll give the whole room a peep show.

I pull the bathrobe tighter around me, but not before running my fingers over the fabric again, the silk cool and smooth against my skin. Like his hands would be, probably. Those big, warm palms sliding over the satin, bunching it up as he—

Jesus Christ, Clara, get it together.

This is the same man who's probably letting *Fiona* drape herself all over him right now.

The same man who's keeping us here against our will. The same infuriating, arrogant, impossibly sexy—

Stop. It.

I flop back against the pillows, staring at the ceiling.

Step one: Close your eyes.

Step two: Don't think about him.

Step three— Fuck, coffee. Did I have coffee? I didn't have coffee. Why does it feel like I had coffee?

I press the heels of my hands to my eyes, groaning softly. Sleep isn't happening, and I know why. The knot in my stomach won't go away until I get answers. This isn't about petty grudges or satin nightgowns. It's about Elijah. It's about me.

Before I know it, I'm on my feet. The cool floor beneath my bare toes sends a small shiver up my spine, but I ignore it. I glance at the closet as I tie the robe tighter, half-tempted to throw on something more appropriate. But no. Let him see me like this if it bothers him. He deserves a little discomfort.

I'll just talk to him. That's all.

Just a conversation.

A polite, calm inquiry about when exactly he plans to let us out of this place.

Totally reasonable. Logical.

Nothing to do with the way my chest tightens at the thought of facing him or the way his voice lingers in my head like an unwelcome guest.

Yeah. Totally logical.

I step toward the door, my pulse quickening despite my best efforts to keep it steady. Whatever happens next, I'll get my answers.

One way or another.

The house is so quiet it feels like I'm walking into the pages of a ghost story. My pulse thrums in my ears, a metronome counting down to... What? Answers? Or more questions?

The hallway stretches in front of me, lit by soft, recessed lights along the ceiling. Plush carpet muffles my steps, but my robe swishes faintly around my thighs. I glance toward the elevator at the end of the hall, its doors gleaming like it belongs in some five-star hotel instead of Leonid's fortress of secrets.

I stop at the door across from mine.

Locked doors were a theme earlier this week, but this one opens when I twist the handle. The hinge gives a faint creak, and I freeze, holding my breath as though expecting someone to materialize from thin air.

Nothing. Just silence.

I step inside and pause, blinking at the sight in front of me.

A grand piano sits in the center of the room, black and polished to a mirror-like sheen. The top is propped open, revealing strings and hammers that catch the dim light like cobwebs spun from gold. A low chandelier hangs above it, simple but elegant, its crystals reflecting tiny rainbows onto the walls.

I approach slowly, the air suddenly feeling thicker, like stepping into another time. My gaze drifts to the far wall, where pictures hang in neat rows, their black frames stark against the creamy white paint. The faces in them make me stop short.

Little Leonid.

My chest tightens as I take it in—photo after photo of him as a boy, standing stiffly next to a man with a sharp jawline and a stare like stone. *Andrei Kuznetsov.* The two of them stand beside a massive fish, its tail almost grazing the ground, the boy's hands gripping a fishing rod too big for him. Another photo shows them in the woods, Leonid clutching a rifle that looks absurd against his small frame, the man behind him correcting his stance. In another, Leonid is shirtless in a boxing ring, his little fists raised and his mouth pressed into a grim line, like smiling wasn't part of the lesson.

And then it hits me.

Elijah looks eerily like Leonid did as a boy.

My breath catches as I glance between the pictures; the resemblance is undeniable. The same solemn eyes, the same high cheekbones and stubborn set to the jaw, even the wild hair that refuses to behave. It's as if I'm staring at my son in another life, one that's harder, colder, filled with expectations that weigh heavy enough to steal a childhood.

The thought twists something deep in my chest. Elijah's laugh, his warmth, his joy—all the things that make him who he is—would they survive in a life like Leonid's? The idea of Elijah standing stiffly in these photos, expressionless, a stranger to happiness, makes my stomach churn.

My fingers brush the edge of one frame, lingering on the boxing ring photo. Leonid can't be more than 8 or 9; he doesn't look like a boy learning to fight for fun. He looks like someone fighting because he has to.

There's something missing in every single one of them.

Joy.

My heart sinks. He looks so small, so serious, as if happiness wasn't something he was allowed to have.

I move toward a table tucked into the corner, its surface cluttered with scattered sheet music and a single photo in a gold frame. The sight of it stops me cold.

The woman in the picture is stunning, her smile radiant and soft all at once. Her hands rest protectively on her very pregnant belly, and her eyes—Leonid's eyes—seem to sparkle even through the photograph.

I reach out and pick up the frame, my fingers trembling slightly as I take it in. Leonid's mom, opposite to Andrei Kuznetsov, the warmth in her expression feels like it doesn't belong in this house. I place the photo back carefully, almost afraid of disturbing the moment frozen within it.

Turning back to the piano, I lift the fallboard and run my fingers lightly over the keys. They're worn, slightly yellowed, and faint scuffs mar the polished finish. It isn't the expensive showpiece I expected—it's old, well-loved, the kind of instrument that carries stories in its cracks and scratches.

I press a single key. A soft, tentative *ding* fills the room. The sound is delicate, almost hesitant, as if waiting to be judged.

Another key.

Ding.

The notes stir something inside me, a memory I haven't thought about in years. *Jake.* His hands on the keys, his lopsided grin as he played the same silly song over and over just to make me laugh.

"Twinkle, twinkle, little bug," he'd sing, dragging out the notes in the worst falsetto imaginable. His voice would crack on purpose as he added ridiculous lines, *"Climbed a tree and squashed a slug,"* before shooting me a mischievous look.

I'd collapse into giggles every single time, my cheeks aching from smiling so hard.

"You're awful," I'd manage between fits of laughter, but he'd just keep going, making the lyrics worse and worse until neither of us could breathe.

I press another key, softer this time, but the weight in my chest grows heavier. My vision blurs, and before I can stop myself, a tear slips down my cheek, landing on the edge of the piano with a soft splatter.

"Can't sleep?"

The voice is low, deep, and it sends a jolt through me like a livewire.

I whip around, and there he is, standing in the doorway like he owns the universe. Because he does.

Leonid Kuznetsov in a sharp black suit that looks painted on, the top buttons of his shirt undone just enough to hint at the hard lines of his chest. His hair is slightly mussed like he's run his fingers through it one too many times tonight, and his dark eyes burn as they sweep over me.

"What are you doing here?" His voice is quieter now but no less intense, like every word is a hook meant to drag me closer.

I open my mouth to answer, but nothing comes out. My pulse quickens, and the room suddenly feels too small, too hot.

Forty-Two

Clara

Well, shit. Of all the ways to get caught snooping—here I am with a tear-stained face. My finger is still stuck on middle C, like an idiot. Though really, if he didn't want people playing his secret piano, maybe he shouldn't leave doors unlocked. Just saying.

His eyes drag over me slowly, deliberately, from my bare feet to my definitely-not-tear-stained face, like he can see right through the silk robe to the barely-there nightgown underneath. The undone bow tie hanging around his neck should make him look disheveled. Instead, he looks like sin in a bespoke suit. Perfect. This is exactly how I wanted him to find me—crying over his piano while playing dress-up in his stolen clothes. Totally nailing this whole captive-spy thing.

I slowly lift my finger off the piano key, like maybe if I move carefully enough, he won't notice me standing here in his private room.

"I..."

The soft *click* of the door lock sliding into place has me freezing mid-movement.

"Care to explain this little performance?" His voice is rough, rumbling, like a diesel engine on a cold start.

My head snaps toward him, my pulse a staccato rhythm in my chest. "What?" I manage, my voice higher than I'd like.

Leonid takes a step forward, and the air in the room shifts, heavy with something I can't quite name. His dark eyes gleam, anger simmering just beneath the surface, but it's the heat in his gaze that leaves me breathless.

"Do you like snooping, Clara?" Another step, and I swear I can feel the heat of him despite the distance still between us. "Or was this about finding something to use against me?"

His words should sting, should make me defensive, but all I can focus on is how tightly his jaw is clenched, the way his hand flexes at his side like he's fighting the urge to reach for something—or someone.

"I wasn't..." My voice falters, and I hate the way he tilts his head just slightly like he's caught a weakness and plans to exploit it.

Oh, hell no.

Clara Caldwell doesn't stutter. She doesn't falter, and she sure as hell doesn't let men with God complexes and jawlines carved by Lucifer himself make her knees weak.

What is wrong with me?

He steps closer. Silent. Deliberate.

The space between us shrinks, and my breath hitches—too quick, too loud. I clench my jaw, but it doesn't stop the heat crawling up my neck. His hand skims the edge of the piano. His brown eyes look darker now, almost black in the dim light, like they're swallowing everything in their path. They're locked on me.

I shift my weight, willing my body to move, but it doesn't listen. Instead, my fingers curl tighter around the edge of the piano.

He looks like he's planning something, like he's already written the script. And my body... Jesus, my body is buying into it.

No. Not tonight. Get a grip, Caldwell. He's not the boss of...

Oh, God, he is sexier tonight...

He's too close now. Too controlled. My pulse spikes, a traitorous beat against the tension rolling off him. My shoulders square on instinct, defiance flaring, but it falters under his gaze.

Like he already knows what's going to happen.

Like I've already lost.

Leonid's hand moves faster than I expect, grabbing the edge of my robe. With one sharp tug, the knot comes undone, and the silk parts just enough to bare my shoulder, the curve of my collarbone.

My breath catches, sharp and involuntary. "Excuse you—"

"I asked you a question," he growls, his hand sliding to my waist and holding firm.

He leans in, his lips brushing dangerously close to my ear, his voice dropping to a hiss. "Do you like snooping around, *krasotka*?"

I try to take a step back, but the piano digs into my lower back, cold and unyielding. Before I can move, Leonid's hand slides to the edge of the piano beside me, his knuckles brushing against my waist as he grips the surface. His body shifts closer, his heat pressing into the space between us, leaving no room to breathe—no room to escape.

"Let go!" I bark, shoving at his chest with both hands, but it's like trying to move a fucking brick wall.

He's so fucking hard. He doesn't budge, just tugs me closer until I can feel the hard ridge of his cock straining against my hip.

This bastard. He thinks he can just manhandle me like this, make my body respond like it's a fucking marionette on strings.

Fuck, but why do I want him to tear into me like a savage beast?

He shoves his hips into me, and my body betrays me, nipples hardening like goddamn spikes.

"Fuck..." But the word gets swallowed up as his scent hits me, a fucking freight train of smoke, leather, and animal heat. My body arches into his without my consent, like a goddamn traitor.

I grit my teeth, trying to maintain control.

"I needed to talk to you." I glare up at him, refusing to let him see how much his touch affects me.

His brow arches slightly, a flicker of surprise breaking through the tension. "Talk?"

And then he moves in, inhaling deeply at my hair, his breath a hot caress against my skin. Goosebumps ripple down my arms, spreading to my thighs like wildfire.

I shove against his solid bulk once more. "Yes, damn it! But you need to listen!"

He chuckles again, the sound like a gravelly chuckle. "So, you decided to creep into my private room? At midnight? In this?" His gaze drags down, lingering where the robe gapes open, and I feel the heat of his eyes like a physical touch.

"Door's not locked," I spit out the words like a curse.

"It is now." He brushes aside the flimsy robe, and it falls to the floor in a pool of silk, his lips crashing against mine before I can say another word.

He kisses me with a violence that rivals my own, his mouth rough, demanding, and it sets my blood on fire. I kiss him back, but my ass slams onto the piano, the force of our kiss and the weight of my body creating a cacophony of discordant notes that reverberate through the room.

I gasp, my eyes flicking to the closed door. "Elijah's sleeping..."

But Leonid doesn't hear me, or if he does, he doesn't care. He's pissed at something. My breath catches. I've seen Leonid angry before, but this? It's different.

He spins me around, our bodies grinding like gears in a machine. He steers me toward the sofa, tossing me onto the cushions like a sack of meat. I let out a sharp breath, anticipation thrumming in my veins, ready to explode at the slightest touch.

"No, no, no," I whisper to myself, struggling against the raging tide of desire, the echo of my resistance already sounding hollow in my ears.

But it's too late.

Forty-Three

Clara

*G*oddammit. I'm not some weak, spineless bimbo.

But his hands—fuck. They're everywhere. Heat pours off him like a furnace, his grip searing into my waist as if branding me his. His body presses down, heavy and commanding.

The name "Fiona" flashes in my mind. The way Maksim smirked when he mentioned her. Anger and jealousy bubble up, boiling over into something molten, something reckless.

Rage and desire combine in a violent cocktail that propels me into action. I buck my hips, flipping Leonid over so I'm straddling him, my hands pressing him down into the cushions. I let out a feral growl, a challenge to his alpha status, as I loom over him, my eyes blazing like twin suns.

"Fuck you, Leonid," I spit out, my voice low and laced with venom. "I'm not some plaything for you to toy with."

Leonid's eyes widen, surprise flitting across his face, but he recovers quickly, a smirk curling his lips. He slides his hands down my hips, grasping me firmly. With a cruel twist of his hips, he grinds against my wet, throbbing heat, drawing a gasp from my lips despite my best efforts to stay silent.

"You're so fucking responsive, *krasotka*. So wet and warm, just like the dirty little slut you try so hard not to be."

His hand seizes my right tit, kneading it like he's making fucking dough, the satin doing fuck all to hide the hard nub of my nipple.

"Fuck!" I can't help but grind against him, my body betraying me like a goddamn snitch, my hips rocking against his granite-hard cock like I'm dancing to the beat of my own damn demise.

"See, there it is. Your pussy doesn't lie, Clara. You want it."

Oh... fuck no.

In one swift motion, I release my thighs from their grip around his cock and shimmy my body upward, clamping Leonid's torso between my knees. I press my arm across his neck like a guillotine blade and dig my hands into the cushions on either side of his shoulders, trapping him on the sofa.

"My pussy doesn't run me, Leonid," I snarl into his ear. "Don't forget who you're fucking with."

Leonid's face contorts with effort as he strains against my grip, but he can't budge an inch. He emits a low chuckle, his voice gruff and defiant.

"Is that so?" he taunts, his breath hot against my skin. "What makes you think I'm forgetting anything?"

With a sudden twist, Leonid flips me onto my back, pinning my wrists to the cushions above my head. The look in his eyes is feral, his body taut and ready to strike. "You're right, I shouldn't forget." He bares his teeth in a predatory grin. "I shouldn't forget that you're nothing but a wildcat who needs to be tamed."

His mouth slams down on mine, kissing me like he's trying to devour me. I bite down on his lip, drawing blood and a sharp hiss from his throat. He releases my wrists, rearing back, a trail of blood staining his mouth. I bare my teeth, my eyes blazing.

"Bite me, will you?" Leonid snarls, swiping the blood from his lip. "You're only digging yourself a deeper grave, *krasotka*."

Leonid's eyes narrow, his body tense as he considers his next move. I extend my leg, using it as a barrier between us.

"First, tell me," I demand, my voice a whipcrack in the silence. "Did you fuck *Fiona*?"

The words leave my mouth before I can think, my jealousy and anger simmering over like boiling acid.

Fuck. Fuck. I'm here to ask him when he's letting us go, not to have a pissing contest over some pretty blonde floozy.

I clench my teeth, willing myself to refocus.

Leonid stares at me like I'm Dave Chappelle, about to deliver the punchline of the century.

"*Fiona*?" The corner of his mouth twitches. "Are you asking me," he's practically vibrating with contained laughter, "if I *fucked* Fiona?"

He says her name like he just stepped in dog shit at the park. "Who told you about Fiona?"

I glare at him, the rage in my chest so hot it could melt steel. "No one told me about Fiona, Leonid," I seethe, the words hissing between my teeth.

Leonid pins me down with all that muscle mass I pretend not to notice, his stupid gorgeous face hovering above mine.

And he's... laughing? The bastard is actually laughing.

"What's so funny?" I try to sound threatening, but it comes out breathier than I'd like.

"Maksim..." He's still shaking with laughter, his face inches from mine. "He played you like a cheap violin. I'd rather cut off my own balls than put my cock anywhere near that woman."

The relief hits me first, then embarrassment. Of course Maksim would pull this shit. That sneaky little rat probably orchestrated this whole thing just to—

"Wait." Leonid's eyes gleam with something dangerous. "Were you *jealous?*"

"Please. Jealousy is only for real... *couples.*" I tilt my chin up defiantly, but my breath catches as his lips find that spot just below my ear.

"Is that so?" he murmurs against my skin, and damn him, he knows exactly what he's doing. His teeth graze my neck, and I hate how my body betrays me, arching into his touch.

"For real couples, huh?" His grip tightens on my wrists. "Then explain why the thought of me with another woman makes you want to tear something apart," Leonid murmurs, rolling his hips against mine. I feel the hard, unmistakable proof of his arousal against my thigh, and my traitorous body responds yet again, my breathing turning ragged.

I try to find a retort, but my words turn to dust as he shifts again, this time thrusting against my core. "Tell me again," he growls into my throat, his lips searing my skin, "how you don't care who I fuck."

"I don't care," I snarl back, but my words lack conviction, the power of his presence overwhelming my senses. "Fuck whoever you want. I don't give a shit."

But Leonid's smirk deepens, and he shifts again, grinding harder against my core. "Oh, I will fuck who I want," he murmurs, his lips grazing my neck. "And right now, that's you."

The pressure of his body, the heat of his breath—it's too much and not enough. I'm going to kill him for making me feel this way. Right after I let him do whatever he wants to me.

Still pinning my hands to the sofa, Leonid's fingers push my panties to the side, his skilled digits finding their mark. My clit pulses under his touch, sending a bolt of pleasure coursing through my veins.

"Fuck, *krasotka*," he grunts, "You're a wet mess. You're fucking aching for it. For my fingers, my cock."

I bite down on my lip, my hips betray me, rocking against his hand like a bitch in heat.

I moan, my body arching toward him, wanting more, wanting it all.

"Tell me... *krasotka*." He is circling my swollen clit with his thumb. "Tell me what you want me to do to you."

"I want... I need..." I stammer. "Please, fuck, make me cum." Leonid plunges his fingers into me, rough and relentless, filling me to the brink. My pussy is drenched, a clear sign of how much I crave him.

"Yes... Oh God, yes." My body is on fire, every nerve-ending sparking with pleasure as Leonid's fingers pump in and out of me, his thumb still circling my clit. I can feel my release building, aching to break free.

"Fuck, yes!" I scream as Leonid's hand rips off my nightgown, and my swollen breasts spill into view. He hungrily latches onto one nipple with his mouth, sucking, biting, sending jolts of pleasure through my body. His other hand relentlessly pumps in and out of me, his fingers finding every sweet spot inside me. And the sound... a wet, sticky symphony filling the room as our bodies collide and merge together. With his powerful legs, he spreads mine further apart.

"Fuuuuck!" I moan louder as he intensifies his assault on my body. "I want you to fuck me."

He grunts in response and picks up the pace, driving me toward the edge with every thrust of his fingers. I can feel myself getting closer and closer until, finally, it's too much, and I explode into a blinding climax.

But before I can even catch my breath, he murmurs into my ear, "We don't have time." In one swift move, Leonid flips me over and rips off my panties. I lean against the smooth leather sofa.

"What?" I manage to gasp out before he unzips his pants. "Time... for what?"

He ignores me and positions himself at my dripping entrance, and plunges deep inside of me. He grips my hair tightly with one hand while the other holds onto my hips, controlling every movement and thrust. Each powerful stroke brings me closer to the edge until I am completely lost in a haze of pleasure.

My mind is reeling with confusion and ecstasy as he takes full control of my body. He reaches down to pinch and tease one of my nipples while his other hand glides down to circle and flick at my swollen clit. I am so wet, so consumed by pleasure that I can't even remember my own name.

"Fuck! Fuck!" I cry out, unable to contain myself any longer. But just before I can reach my peak, Leonid slaps my left cheek hard, adding a new layer of sensation that pushes me over the edge.

Leonid growls, his fingers digging into my flesh as he rides out my orgasm.

"*Suka blyad*," he mutters, spitting out a string of Russian that I'm too lost in ecstasy to understand.

The warmth of his release fills me, the force of it sending a shockwave of pleasure through my body. He drops his head against my shoulder, his breathing ragged and hot against my neck. I lie beneath him, spent and shaking, when his fingers wrap around my throat—not squeezing, just... claiming.

"You're mine, *krasotka*." The words slither across my skin as he slowly pulls his cock out of me, making me feel every inch.

"You're my captive, my prisoner." His teeth graze my pulse point, and I feel his lips curve into that cruel smile I pretend not to crave. "You belong to me, Clara Caldwell."

Forty-Four

Leonid

The soft hum of the engines is the only consistent sound on the Gulfstream G700, but Maksim is about to change that. He slouches into the leather seat across from me, stretching out like he owns the damn plane.

"*Pakhan*," he starts, settling forward. He never calls me that unless he's dead serious. And Maksim is rarely serious—maybe five times in the entire time I've known him. Whatever this is, it's going to be good.

I glance up from the tablet in my hand, skimming through logistics reports about the mining operation. The screen reflects back a tired version of me—sharp brown eyes, tension etched into my forehead, and a jaw that hasn't unclenched since we left New Orleans.

"Don't do this *mudak*," I warn.

"Do what?" Maksim's grin is all teeth, the kind that makes people nervous if they don't know him well.

"The thing where you pretend you have a legitimate question, but really, you're about to waste my time."

He holds up his hands like I've caught him in the act. "Fine, but explain something to me, yeah? What exactly is the plan here? Because forgive me, but bringing your *devushka* and her little one along isn't exactly your style."

I don't answer. Not immediately.

I let him squirm under the silence, even as he shifts in his seat, the leather creaking slightly.

"I mean," he continues, undeterred, "we barely got her to leave her house. Had to dig out their passports from a drawer *exactly* where she said they'd be."

His eyes gleam with amusement, but it's the kind that irritates me.

"I don't need to explain myself to you, Maksim."

"Maybe not," he says, leaning back like he's settling in for a show. "But I've gotta say, watching you wrangle a woman and a kid like some kind of doting husband and father is not what I expected from our fearless leader."

The tablet slips from my hand onto the table with a muted thud. I fix him with a look that would shut most people up, but Maksim thrives on pushing limits.

"The plan..." I start, but the rest of the words hang there.

The plan wasn't to fuck her.

Wasn't to have her around for so long, either. Wasn't to sit here, wondering if Ludis will try something while I'm gone or if Fiona's already setting the chessboard for her next move. And it definitely wasn't to care about whether Clara's comfortable in my jet—or if she's glaring daggers at the door like she's imagining how best to jump out at 40,000 feet.

Which, to be fair, isn't entirely wrong.

Maksim leans forward, his eyebrow arching like he's challenging me to finish my sentence. "The plan is...?" he asks, dragging the words out like he's savoring them.

I don't answer right away. My gaze flicks to the tinted window, where dawn spills over the horizon, streaking the sky with pink and gold. The Swiss Alps are out there somewhere, waiting, but the weight in my chest makes them feel farther away than they should.

"The plan, *mudak*," I finally say, leaning back and reclining the seat slightly, "is to find out what the fuck Ludis and Fiona are doing behind my back. Their little games stop when I say they stop."

Maksim's grin widens, but I keep going before he can interrupt.

"We'll need more muscle, more loyalty, and more eyes on the ground. No one betrays me." *Suka*, my voice drops a notch as I tilt my head toward the door to the private sleeping quarters, where Clara and Elijah are tucked away. "And no one touches what's mine."

Maksim whistles low, shaking his head.

"Right. No one touches what's yours—meaning Clara." His tone is drenched in mock innocence, but his eyes gleam with mischief. "Because this is all about the Bratva and not about playing house with your woman and her kid. Totally makes sense."

I level him with a look that should shut him up, but Maksim only shrugs and grins wider, a man immune to threats—or too stupid to heed them.

"You're slipping, *Pakhan*," he adds, dragging the word out in that way he knows I hate. "Next thing I know, you'll be organizing play-dates."

"I should throw you off this plane," I mutter, but there's no heat in it.

"You'd miss me too much," Maksim quips, sprawling back in his seat like he doesn't have a care in the world.

I grab the edge of the table and push myself upright, brushing past him. "*Yob tvoyu mat*, get ready for a fight. If Ludis so much as sneezes wrong while I'm gone, I want his whole operation buried. And tell the men we might need reinforcements. No excuses."

Maksim's grin dims slightly, though the amusement doesn't leave his eyes. He nods, sitting up straighter.

"Consider it done. Dmitry's already on the trail, by the way. Digging into who really killed Jake Caldwell, finding the right threads to pull. If there's someone we can pin it on, he'll find them."

"Dmitry knows what he's doing," I say, but the thought of Jake Caldwell sets my jaw tight. Another loose end that refuses to stay buried.

Jake Caldwell wasn't a saint, but his death was more than business. This feels personal, and personal means unpredictable.

The cabin door creaks open, and a woman steps out from the cockpit—a flight attendant with crisp dark hair and an immaculate uniform.

"We're an hour away from landing at Sion Airport, Mr. Kuznetsov. Your car is ready on the tarmac," she says, her voice smooth and practiced. She pauses, glancing toward the sleeping quarters. "I'll have breakfast ready for... the guests," she finishes, her hesitation subtle but enough to pull Maksim's smirk back into place.

"Thank you," I say curtly, dismissing her. She nods and slips away, her heels muffled by the plush carpet.

Maksim watches her go, then swivels back to me, his expression sly. "Guests, huh? You going to ask if she's awake, or are you just going to pretend you don't care?"

I glare at him but keep my mouth shut. The truth is, I'd been tempted to ask the flight attendant if Clara was up, but I stopped myself. Caring too much is dangerous. Caring gets you killed.

Before Maksim can needle me again, the door to the sleeping quarters creaks open, and Elijah pads out, his hair sticking up in soft tufts, clutching a stuffed Pikachu in one hand. He rubs his eyes with the other, his face scrunching in that half-awake confusion that only kids can pull off.

"I need to pee," he announces. And then he looks straight at me.

I blink at him, my brain grinding to a halt.

Why is he looking at me? I don't have answers for this. I can't pee for him.

He looks around the cabin, his tiny brows furrowing as if he's already figured out something's off.

"Where's Uncle Bear?"

Maksim, of course, is the first to react.

"Uncle Bear had to go hunting," he says, deadpan, leaning back with a smirk that promises trouble.

Elijah squints at Maksim, clearly unconvinced, but he doesn't argue. Instead, he shifts from one foot to the other, his little knees knocking together.

"I really need to pee," he says, louder this time, his voice edging toward panic.

I stare at him, my thoughts whirling.

Where's Dmitry when you need him?

"You heard him, boss," Maksim says, his grin widening as he gestures lazily toward Elijah. "The boy's got needs."

I glare at Maksim, who looks entirely too entertained for someone sitting in my jet. Elijah fidgets more, tugging at the hem of his pajama top, his face scrunched in pure, childlike desperation.

"Where's the toilet?" Elijah asks, his eyes darting around the cabin like it might magically appear if he stares hard enough.

Maksim whistles low, shaking his head in mock disappointment. "You mean you didn't give him a tour of the jet? What kind of host are you?"

I ignore him and gesture toward the rear of the cabin. "Down that way," I say gruffly, hoping the kid will just figure it out.

But Maksim isn't done. "You realize he is four years old?" he points out, his tone dripping with sarcasm. "And good luck getting him to work the latch on the toilet. You might as well just—oh, I don't know—help him."

"I'm not doing that," I snap, but Elijah's wide, watery eyes cut through my resolve like a knife. He's staring at me like I'm his last hope, and damn it, I've faced down men twice my size without blinking, but this? This is different.

"Fine," I mutter under my breath, standing and crossing the cabin in a few long strides. "Come on."

Elijah brightens immediately, holding out his hand, which I don't take. Instead, I scoop him up under the arms like he's a bag of groceries, ignoring the way his little feet kick in surprise. He giggles, the sound bubbling out unexpectedly, and for a second, I'm too thrown off to react.

"Whoa! I'm flying!" he announces, holding his Pikachu aloft like it's some kind of flag. Maksim snorts behind me, but I don't turn around. If I look at him now, I'll throw him out the nearest emergency exit.

I carry Elijah toward the lavatory, his weight surprisingly light in my arms. "This is the toilet," I say, setting him down in front of the door.

He stares at it like it's some kind of puzzle box, his head tilted to one side. "How do I open it?"

Maksim's laugh echoes through the cabin. "This is gold. Pure gold."

I shoot him a glare over my shoulder before leaning down to push the latch. The door swings open, revealing the compact, marble-lined bathroom. Elijah steps inside, clutching Pikachu to his chest, and turns to me with a serious expression.

"Do I close the door?"

"Yes," I say firmly. "And don't touch anything you don't have to."

He nods solemnly, like I've handed him life-or-death instructions, and shuts the door. A few moments of rustling follow, then a flush. The door creaks open again, and Elijah steps out, his chest puffed out like he's just conquered the world.

"I did it!" he announces proudly.

"Great," I say, reaching out to ruffle his messy hair despite myself. He beams at me, his face glowing with triumph, and for a moment, the weight of everything waiting for me in Switzerland fades.

"Did you wash your hands?"

His expression falters for a second, twisting into something mischievous. "Nope!" he says, sticking his tongue out at me. Before I can stop him, he shoves Pikachu into my hands like it's a time bomb. "Hold this!"

"Wait—what?" I fumble with the stuffed toy, holding it awkwardly as though it might combust. "You're not serious."

He dashes back into the bathroom, and the door swings shut with a bang. A pause. Then, slowly, it creaks open again, and Elijah's head pops out.

"I... can't reach the sink," he says, his voice small but not even remotely embarrassed.

I roll my eyes hard enough to strain something. "Fine."

Setting Pikachu on the nearest seat, I stride toward the bathroom, muttering under my breath. The door opens wider as Elijah steps aside, looking up at me with wide-eyed expectation.

Inside, it's exactly what I feared—water on the counter, soap smears everywhere. The stool is pushed to the side, useless.

Without a word, I grab him under the arms and hoist him up. "Hold still," I grumble, angling him toward the faucet. He squirms just enough to make it difficult.

"You're heavy," I add, pressing the soap dispenser and lathering his hands for him.

"I'm not heavy," he retorts indignantly, wriggling in my grip.

"Then stop moving," I snap, rinsing his hands under the running water.

He falls still for a moment, long enough for me to finally focus. Through the mirror, his reflection catches mine. It's just a glance, but it's enough to make my chest tighten unexpectedly.

My heart stutters. His wide, brown eyes—curious, trusting, and far too familiar—meet mine. Something about the way they catch the light makes my grip falter slightly.

He looks way too...

I stop. A knot forms in my throat.

"There," I say gruffly, setting him back down and handing him a towel. "Now you're clean. Go."

Elijah grins up at me, his damp hands wiping on the towel haphazardly. "Thanks, Big Boss Bad Guy."

I stiffen. "I'm not—"

But he's already opening the door, strutting out like he's just brokered some major deal. I follow him, tossing the damp towel onto the counter as I step into the cabin.

Maksim looks up the second Elijah appears, and his grin widens like he's been waiting for this moment.

"This kid," he wheezes, wiping at his eyes. "He's got you trained already, *Pakhan*."

I meet Maksim's gaze, his laughter like a jab I refuse to dignify with a real response. My eyes narrow briefly, just enough to remind him of his place, and his smirk falters—slightly.

"Shut up," I mutter, cutting him off before he can needle me further. My attention shifts down to Pikachu, abandoned on the seat. Its round, glassy eyes stare up at me like it's mocking me, too.

Unbelievable.

"Now what?" Elijah's voice comes from across the cabin. He's perched on the edge of one of the leather seats, his stubby legs swinging as he looks between Maksim and me, his face full of expectation.

Before I can answer, the air hostess walks out, a tray in her hands that fills the cabin with the smell of eggs and something sweet. Elijah practically launches himself toward the scent.

"Now we eat!" he declares, tugging at the side of my pant leg, his little fingers curling into the fabric.

But I'm not looking at him anymore. My phone buzzes in my pocket—a single vibration, sharper than it should feel. I pull it out, tap the screen, and a message from Dmitry opens instantly.

It's an image.

It doesn't make sense. It shouldn't exist.

My grip tightens on the phone, the edges digging into my palm as my thoughts spiral. This isn't just unexpected—it's impossible. And yet, it's right in front of me.

I glance at Maksim. He's still smirking, oblivious to what's on my screen, like the world hasn't just shifted. He doesn't know yet.

But when he does, this flight will feel like the calm before the storm.

Forty-Five

Maksim

A moment ago

I watch Leonid haul the kid toward the lavatory like he's handling an armed bomb. My great *Pakhan* of the Bratva reduced to toilet duty. If I hadn't seen it myself, I wouldn't believe it.

Elijah is giggling like Leonid just pulled a rabbit out of a hat. That's not normal. Kids don't laugh around Leonid. Hell, *grown men* don't laugh around him unless it's nervously and they're signing their wills.

And yet, here we are. Him, ferrying a kid to the toilet, and me sitting here with a front-row seat to the strangest sight of my life.

But it's not the giggle that gets me. It's the way the kid looks. That unshakable confidence, and *blyat,* the more I stare at the kid, the more I can't ignore the feeling in my gut—the one whispering that this isn't a coincidence.

Elijah's got the same tilt to his head—the kind that screams, "You can't tell me shit." The same scowl when something doesn't go his way.

And those eyes?

I've seen them before. In a photo Leonid's father used to keep on his desk. The resemblance isn't close. It's exact.

I lean back in my seat, fingers drumming against the armrest. Five years ago, we went to The Viper's Nest. It wasn't supposed to be messy—just find out who the hell was running the place, figure out if they were laundering through it, and decide whether they needed to be crushed. Simple. Clean. Except Leonid didn't stick to the plan.

He disappeared the second he saw her. The woman in red. Clara Caldwell, though I didn't know her name at the time. She wasn't just some girl in the wrong place—someone tried to kill her that night. Leonid stepped in, and the entire operation went sideways. For hours, he was gone. With her. And when he showed up the next day? He acted like nothing happened. Like the night hadn't just gone to hell.

And now?

Now, there's this kid, looking like a carbon copy of my boss, clutching a stuffed Pikachu and turning Leonid into someone I don't recognize. Toilet runs. Small talk. Like he's some kind of father. If I hadn't seen it myself, I wouldn't believe it.

The timing, the features—it's not just coincidence. It can't be. And I don't need Leonid to tell me. Hell, I don't even need to ask him. I need proof.

A DNA test. Simple. Quick. Quiet. No one even has to know I'm doing it.

And if the results prove what my balls already know? *Pakhan* will probably gut me like a fish and use my intestines as Christmas decorations.

I smirk. But fuck it—some shit's worth dying for.

Forty-Six

Clara

U gh. I wake up to a soft hum that reminds me I'm not on Earth anymore—or at least not the Earth I grew up on.

My throat's dry, my body's sore in places that shouldn't even be sore, and there's a metallic tang of sex and regret clinging to the edges of my memory. Last night flashes in fragments—Leonid's hands, his mouth, the way he moved like he owned me. Like he'd carved his name somewhere deep inside, just to make sure I didn't forget.

And then the bastard pulled a gun on me.

No dramatic flourishes or action movie bullshit. Just cold steel aimed at my face because I had the audacity to say no.

"Get ready. You're coming with me."

Because apparently, in his world, a gun to the head counts as afterplay. Most women want to cuddle after sex—I get death threats. Same thing, right?

Fuck.

I fumble for the water bottle on the small table beside the bed and gulp it down, wincing at the chill in the cabin air. That's when I notice my surroundings—or remember them, really.

The bedding ruins me for normal sheets forever.

Thanks for that, bastard.

Switzerland. *Fucking Zermatt.*

Leonid's clipped voice from this morning echoes in my head, calm and matter-of-fact, like he wasn't kidnapping me across continents.

"We're flying to Zermatt."

No explanation, no discussion. Just a command wrapped in a geographic fact.

And because my life is a joke now, I'm surrounded by muted golds and deep navy like some floating five-star hotel suite—except this one cruises at 40,000 feet and comes with its own armed entourage.

My eyes drift over the room as I lower the bottle, and I catch myself staring. To my right, a built-in shelving unit gleams under soft ambient lighting. Crystal decanters of whiskey sit untouched next to a row of books I'm sure Leonid hasn't read. There's a chaise lounge near the window that practically screams, "I'm worth more than your dignity," and a touchscreen panel mounted discreetly into the wall, probably controlling everything from the lights to the jet's defensive countermeasures.

My eyes wander instinctively toward the other bed. The covers are pulled up tight, forming a small, rounded bulge near the center. Elijah. He's still curled up, sound asleep, just like he always does—knees tucked close, face buried in the pillow. My chest softens, the tension in my shoulders loosening ever so slightly.

I hold my breath, afraid even the sound of it might wake him. How many days has it been now? Too many. Not enough to get my bearings. Time has become shapeless, just like everything else since Leonid stormed back into my life.

My fingers twitch toward the blanket, but I pull back. Let him rest. He deserves at least that much.

I glance at the window instead, trying to steady my thoughts.

"Jesus," I breathe, staring out the window. "This is beautiful. Impossibly fucking beautiful."

Clouds drift lazily beneath us, faint shadows of mountains stretching toward the horizon. The Swiss Alps. Beautiful, impossible, and so far removed from the life I knew that it makes my stomach twist.

The view throws me off balance—it makes it hard to remember I'm supposed to be pissed off right now.

Fuck.

I can't tell what time it is now, like everything else in Leonid's little world. Like I don't know how long we are going to be Leonid's captives.

I glance at the bed again, at the lump that hasn't moved since I woke up. He's safe, at least. Warm. One of us should get some peace in this flying prison.

But then, from somewhere beyond the door, I hear it—a burst of giggles, light and unmistakable.

"Maksim! You cheat!"

My head snaps toward the sound.

What. The. Fuck?

I turn back to the bed. The lump under the covers doesn't move, but now my chest tightens with doubt.

That's not Elijah.

I yank back the covers. A fucking throw pillow. Of course.

The plush carpet floor is soft against my feet as I step into the main cabin. Whoever designed this Chanel sleepwear clearly never considered "kidnapped on a private jet" scenarios in their design planning. My nipples could cut glass right now.

"No, no—you gotta time the jump better!" Maksim's voice carries through the cabin. "See that platform? Wait for it... wait... No, you're jumping straight into lava—and now you're dead again."

I freeze in the doorway. Elijah is sitting next to Maksim, who has one arm slung casually around his little shoulders while showing him a game on a Nintendo Switch. Elijah's face is scrunched in concentration, his fingers furiously tapping the buttons as Maksim narrates.

"Maksim, it's too hard!" Elijah whines.

"Life's hard, kid. Welcome to Level Three."

And then there's Leonid.

He's sitting opposite them, one leg crossed over the other, radiating grumpiness so thick it's almost visible. His jaw is clenched, his dark eyes fixed on the window as though he's plotting to murder the clouds. Or maybe Maksim. Or maybe me.

"Elijah seems cozy," I mutter as I approach, gesturing to the scene.

Leonid doesn't look at me. "He's fine," he says flatly, his voice low and controlled.

Maksim grins up at me, all teeth and mischief. "You should join us, *devushka*. The kid's a natural. Better reflexes than Leonid."

"Better attitude, too," I mutter, earning a sharp glare from Leonid. Maksim chuckles, clearly enjoying himself.

I sink into one of the leather chairs, the chill still biting at my legs. Elijah looks up from his game long enough to wave at me.

"Mommy, look! I'm beating him!"

Maksim raises his hands in mock defeat. "He's ruthless, this one. Might take over the Bratva before his fifth birthday."

Leonid's jaw tightens even further, his hands clenching into fists on the armrests. I glance at him, half-expecting him to snap, but he doesn't.

Something shifts in the cabin's atmosphere. Literally. The jet dips slightly, making my stomach do that weird floating thing.

A crisp voice comes over the intercom, speaking rapid-fire Russian. Before I can even pretend to understand, Leonid cuts in: "We're landing."

"Thanks for the translation service," I say, but he's already moving, phone forgotten as he stands. His eyes rake over my barely covered body, and suddenly, I'm very aware of how much skin this sleepwear shows.

"Sit down and buckle up," he orders. "Unless you want to explain that outfit to Swiss Customs."

"What?" I snap, crossing my arms over my chest. "Never seen a woman freeze to death in Chanel before?"

He shrugs off his suit jacket in one fluid motion and drapes it over my shoulders before I can protest. The warmth of him still lingers in the fabric, along with something that makes my head spin—cedar and leather and pure male. Not that I'm going to tell him that.

His hands settle on my shoulders, steering me into the seat beside him. When he reaches across to grab my seatbelt, his cologne hits me again, and—*fuck*—my brain short-circuits for a second.

Maksim snorts from across the cabin, though he wisely keeps his head down, pretending to be fascinated by Elijah's game. My son scrambles into his own seat, Nintendo Switch still glued to his hands like it's a vital organ.

"At least someone in your family knows how to follow instructions," Leonid mutters, clicking my belt into place.

"Yeah, well, he didn't get his attitude from me," I shoot back.

Leonid's mouth twitches. "Obviously."

I roll my eyes and burrow deeper into his jacket, definitely not inhaling the scent of him like some lovesick teenager. He settles next to me, all coiled power and expensive cologne, his fingers drumming a restless beat on the armrest.

When he finally turns to look at me, his eyes are dark with something that isn't just annoyance.

"Tell me something, Clara." His voice drops low enough that only I can hear. "I expected Stephan Lombardi to come charging in by now."

My pulse jumps. Stephan. My father's right-hand man. My mentor. The one person who should've torn everything apart looking for me by now.

"What's it to you?" I keep my voice steady, but Leonid's already caught the flash of uncertainty in my eyes.

His mouth curves into something that might be a smile on anyone else. On him, it's a weapon.

"Strange, isn't it? Your father's most trusted man..." He lets the words hang there, heavy with implication. "And yet here we are, flying over the Alps and not a single rescue attempt."

His question slams into me like a goddamn freight train.

Where the fuck is Stephan?

That fucking question that's been eating away at me like a goddamn parasite is now thrust in my face by Leonid.

Forty-Seven

Leonid

The buzz of my phone pulls my attention from the frosted windowpane. The Matterhorn stares back at me, sharp and defiant against the brilliant sky. I glance at the screen—Maksim. A message flashes.

> **Boss. Running errands. Don't miss me too much. Be back before meeting.**

I exhale through my nose. *Running errands.*

That could mean anything from bribing a local official to flirting with some ski bunny. The man has all the discipline of a stray dog. My thumbs move over the screen with a bite of frustration.

> **Don't be late, suka.**

I hit "send" and shake my head, muttering *"mudak"* as I pocket the phone. Maksim's irresponsibility is a small stone in the mountain of betrayal and chaos crushing down on me lately. Fiona, Ludis, Dmitry's cryptic message—everything gnaws at my patience like a dull blade.

A sound pulls me from my thoughts, light and high-pitched. Laughter. I glance toward the floor-to-ceiling windows, my gaze drawn by the unexpected burst of joy. Below, on the terrace, Elijah is stomping in the snow, scattering powdery flurries into the cold, bright air.

"Mommy! Look, I'm making a snow volcano!"

Clara stands beside him, her hands tucked into a tailored white coat, the fur-lined hood framing her face. Her dark hair spills over her shoulders, catching the light as she leans down to fix Elijah's scarf. She's laughing too, her shoulders shaking slightly, the kind of unguarded moment that seems rare for her.

She's dressed better than I expected—thankfully. The coat is fitted perfectly, the slim cut showing her figure without trying too hard. Leather gloves cover her hands, sleek and practical, while knee-high boots crunch softly in the snow. I'd made sure my retail manager had their sizes before we left New Orleans. I'm not dragging them into the Alps just to watch them freeze to death.

"That's not a volcano, silly. That's a snow pancake. What kind of lava does a pancake have?"

"Chocolate lava!" Elijah crows, twirling in a clumsy circle, his arms stretched out for balance.

Clara laughs, a sound that doesn't belong in my world—light, unguarded, completely free of calculation. She kneels to adjust his knitted beanie, her gloved hands moving with care. "Chocolate lava it is," she says, her breath visible in the cold.

Blyat, she's... fitting in here in a way I didn't think she would. Classy, composed. Beautiful.

Galina's voice slithers into my head, uninvited, smug. *"The perfect wife, Leonid."*

"Perfect," I huff under my breath, the word heavy with derision. Galina always knew how to twist the knife, even from a distance. Perfect isn't real. Perfect gets you killed.

I catch myself. *Too long...* My eyes have lingered too damn long. My eyes have no damn business staying on her. She's my captive, not a fucking daydream. I scrub a hand through my hair.

There's too much shit piling up—Ludis's scheming, Fiona's betrayal, Dmitry chasing shadows. I don't have time for distractions. Certainly not one wrapped in a fur-lined coat, laughing in the snow like none of this touches her.

But I saw her face earlier. When I asked about Stephan. The way her jaw tightened, the flicker of something beneath the surface, gone before she thought I'd notice. The question bothers her, too—maybe even more than it should.

I step back from the window, running a hand through my hair as if I can shake off the thought.

The phone's cold weight anchors me, a tether to control in the midst of chaos. I dial Dmitry.

It rings twice before his gravelly voice breaks through. "Boss."

"Talk."

The line goes silent for two seconds, a hesitation heavy with meaning. In the background, faint clicking and clattering reach me. Keyboards. Dmitry is in the lab— our lair of wires, monitors, and shadows. The Kuznetsov Bratva's hidden nerve center, manned by tech savants who don't see daylight unless it's reflected off a screen.

"I don't have anything on the picture yet," Dmitry finally says. "But we're looking into it."

I clench my jaw. "That's not what I asked."

He exhales, sharp. "Boss, it's fresh. The text came in a few hours ago. No sender ID or IP. Anonymous."

"What do you mean, anonymous text?" I hiss; my own voice echoes slightly in the vaulted ceiling of the suite. Exposed beams and stone walls frame the room, the kind of rustic luxury people pay for when they want to feel connected to nature without leaving their comfort zone. "Anonymous isn't good enough. I need names."

"There's no metadata, Leonid," Dmitry says, his voice tightening with an edge of his own. "No IP, no location tag. It's scrubbed clean, like a ghost sent it."

I grip the phone tighter, staring at the grain of the wood floor. The faint hum of electricity from the suite's fixtures suddenly feels oppressive. "Then tell me about the photo."

Another pause. The tapping stops, replaced by muffled voices—someone in the lab murmuring something too low to catch. Dmitry mutters a quick curse in Russian, likely waving them off, and then he's back.

"We're digging," Dmitry says, his tone carefully neutral. "The team is pulling records. Accounts, family connections—hell, we're even checking their pets. But whoever sent those photos knew what they were doing. The metadata is clean. No trail."

"No such thing as clean. Keep looking. I want every detail of their lives since they were born. I don't care if it's a kindergarten report card; find it."

"Understood."

I pause, the image from the message flickering in my mind again. These two. What the fuck is happening here? How long has this been going on? *Yob tvoyu mat'.* The questions circle like vultures, feeding on the unknown.

A gruff chuckle crackles through the line; Dmitry's version of easing the tension. It doesn't work. I end the call without another word.

My watch catches the light as I check the time—Rolex Daytona, practical but unapologetically excessive. 1:04 PM. Montclair. In an hour, I'll be sitting across from the man who has a knack for making order out of chaos. Victorien Montclair isn't just a business partner;

he's the kind of ally who doesn't need theatrics to command respect. Swiss-born, raised in luxury, and a mastermind of both legitimate trade and black-market ingenuity. He's kept his family's empire clean on the surface, while its foundation runs deep with gold laundering, smuggling, and logistics that leave no trail. Trustworthy. Consistent.

He's everything Fiona isn't. That *suka blyad'.*

I walk to the balcony, pushing open the glass doors. The cold hits me immediately, but it's refreshing. The sound of Elijah's laughter reaches me again, a high, clear note that carries in the thin mountain air.

Clara stands now, brushing snow from Elijah's hat as he twirls in place. She glances up, almost instinctively, as if she can feel my gaze. Our eyes meet for a moment. She doesn't smile, but there's something in the tilt of her head, the way she doesn't look away, that stirs something I can't name.

Chyert. I force myself to look away, stepping back from the railing as if the distance could sever the pull. *Business trip,* I remind myself. Ludis is circling, waiting for weakness. That's why we're here. That's why I need to keep them close—Clara and Elijah. Not because she's standing there like she's already doing something to my fucking heart.

I turn back inside, letting the door close behind me with a muted click. I need to think. About Ludis. About the photos. About anything but her.

Forty-Eight

Clara

"I said no tomatoes," Elijah announces, holding up the offending slice like it's a declaration of war.

"Just take it off," I whisper back, leaning over to grab it before it hits the floor. The last thing I need is a scene. He huffs, watching me with a mix of suspicion and pride, like I'm finally proving my worth as his mommy.

He settles back into his seat, munching on a fry, and I glance at my own plate. The slow-braised short ribs look like something out of a food magazine—rich, tender, perfect—but I haven't touched them. My stomach's too tangled to care.

Elijah looks up, ketchup smeared across his cheek.

"Mommy, you don't like your food?" His words dig at me, soft but insistent.

"No— Oh, I mean, yes, I do," I stammer, grabbing a bite of the buttery polenta beneath the ribs. The flavor is as good as it looks, but I barely notice.

Elijah's already back to his fries, humming happily like the whole world's finally right again. "This is the best lunch ever!" he declares, kicking his legs under the table. "We should live here forever, Mommy. Bad guys make good food!"

I snort, nearly choking on the bite I just forced down. "What?"

"Yeah! We trained the bad guys to be good now!" He grins, holding up a fry like he's making a toast. His confidence is so pure, so unshakable, that I almost believe him.

I glance out the massive windows of the Alpine Aiguille Retreat, the view almost mocking in its perfection. Snow-covered peaks stretch endlessly, the Matterhorn standing tall and jagged against the cloudless blue sky. The restaurant is perched high enough that the world below feels impossibly far away, like nothing bad could ever touch us here.

"This place is fancy," I murmur under my breath, pushing at my food with my fork. A waiter glides by with the kind of effortless grace that makes me feel clumsy just for existing, balancing a tray with wine glasses that sparkle like diamonds in the afternoon light. Everything about the Kuznetsov's retreat screams wealth—sleek marble floors polished to a mirror finish, exposed beams that somehow manage to look rustic and expensive at the same time, and the faint scent of something floral lingering in the air.

Elijah doesn't notice any of it, too busy stacking fries into a tower. He beams at his creation before demolishing it with a loud crunch.

"Mommy, can we go to the snow play after this?" he asks, pointing a fry toward the activity center we'd passed earlier. "I wanna make a snowman bigger than this whole restaurant!"

"We'll see," I say, which he takes as a yes. His grin stretches wide, ketchup dotting the corner of his mouth like battle paint.

My thoughts drift as he chatters on, the food in front of me going cold. The penthouse we checked into earlier sits at the top of the retreat, complete with a hot tub I have no intention of using and heated floors that feel like a luxury I don't deserve. And, of course, it's next to Leonid's. Because of course it is.

Why? The question burns in my head.

Why put us so close together? It's not like I'm his wife—or anything else, for that matter. I don't even know how long we're supposed to be here. Judging from the clothes he brought for us—multiple suitcases filled with designer labels and enough winter gear to last a season—it might be months. The idea makes my head spin.

I shake my head, trying to clear the thought, but it doesn't help. His words from earlier echo in my mind.

"Don't do anything stupid."

What does he think I'm going to do? Run? As if I could. He has our passports, for one. And for another, if I was going to run, I'd have done it days ago. *No.* I'm here because he put a fucking gun to my head.

Then Stephan's name flits across my mind like a loose thread I can't stop tugging at. What did Leonid mean when he brought him up? Does he know something?

Something's up.

I squeeze my fork tightly, unknowingly. I poke it into the meat in front of me; my stomach twists as the thought digs deeper. A nagging pull tugs at the edges of my conscience. Stephan wouldn't abandon me—he's too careful for that. But it doesn't explain why no one has come to rescue me on his behalf... or why Leonid's question felt less like idle curiosity and more like a test.

"Mommy, you're doing that face again," Elijah says suddenly, frowning at me.

"What face?" I blink at him, startled.

"Like you're looking, but you're not *looking*," he says, tilting his head like he's solving a puzzle. His small hand waves in front of my face. "Do you wanna try my cheeseburger? It'll make you happy. It's the best ever!"

I laugh softly despite myself, reaching over to swipe the ketchup off his cheek with a napkin.

"I think I'll stick with mine, but thanks, baby."

I take another bite of the short ribs, the tender meat practically melting on my tongue.

Before I can stop myself, the thought slips out. "Where does this cow even come from?"

Elijah giggles, shaking his fry at me like it's a sword. "Maybe the cow lives here in the snow, Mommy! A snow cow!" His laugh is so loud it turns a couple of heads.

"Not quite," a voice cuts in, smooth and practiced.

I glance up to find a woman standing at our table, her bright smile wide enough to show perfect teeth that practically glow in the afternoon light. She's petite—shorter than me by a good margin—and slim, her tailored black uniform emphasizing her straight, angular frame. The gold accents catch the light as she shifts slightly, her blonde hair pulled back so neatly it's almost severe. The kind of person who looks polished to the point of perfection.

"This is A5-grade Kobe beef," she continues, folding her hands in front of her. "Imported from Japan. Mr. Kuznetsov spares no expense."

I stop mid-chew, my fork frozen halfway to my plate. The way she says "Mr. Kuznetsov"—so polished and familiar—sets my teeth on edge. Like she knows him better than I do... better than anyone should.

"Of course he does," I mutter, swallowing the bite with more effort than necessary.

"I'm Anya," she says, her tone pleasant, but her gaze flickers over me, landing briefly on Elijah before darting away again. She doesn't even spare him a proper look, like he's furniture in the background. "I'll be coordinating your activities for the day."

"Activities?" I echo, already wary.

"Yes," she replies with a smile that doesn't reach her eyes. "Mr. Kuznetsov wanted to ensure your stay was enjoyable. After lunch, you'll begin with private ski lessons on the north slope. It's perfect for beginners—safe, scenic, and exclusive."

"Ski lessons?" Elijah's face lights up like I just promised him a pony. "Mommy, we get to ski?"

I plaster on a smile for his sake, even as my stomach twists. "That sounds... great."

Anya's professional grin sharpens just slightly. "After skiing, there's an ice sculpting workshop for children in the activity center. They'll teach him how to create something magical with snow and ice." Her eyes flick to Elijah, though she still doesn't quite look at him. "He'll love it."

I nod stiffly, my grip tightening around my fork. "Uh-huh."

"And after that," she continues, either oblivious to my growing irritation or just enjoying herself too much to stop, "a hot choco-late-tasting by the outdoor fire pits. We've flown in specialty choco-lates from Switzerland, Belgium, and Ecuador for a truly global expe-rience."

Elijah bounces in his seat. "Hot chocolate! Mommy, we have to do that!"

"Of course," I say, my voice tight but steady. What else can I say?

"And lastly," Anya finishes, her tone light but calculated, "dinner this evening at our Skyview Terrace. Mr. Kuznetsov will be joining you, as well as Mr. Montclair and his family. It's the perfect way to end the day."

Dinner with Leonid, *and* who the fuck is Montclair? My jaw tightens, and I set my fork down carefully, afraid I'll snap it in half.

"Wow. That's... a lot."

"It's all been arranged," Anya replies smoothly, her smile unwavering. She takes a small step back, clearly preparing to turn and leave.

"Hang on a sec," I snap, my voice booming like a thunderclap, reminding everyone who's really in charge here.

Anya freezes mid-turn, her head tilting slightly as she looks back at me.

I don't rush. I spear another bite of meat, chew slowly, and swallow, letting the silence stretch. When I set my fork down, it's deliberate.

I glance at Elijah. "Go wash your mouth and hands before we leave, baby."

"Okay, Mommy!" Elijah hops out of his chair and bolts toward the bathroom without hesitation, weaving through the tables with all the grace of a caffeinated squirrel. A few high-end diners glance his way, their expressions somewhere between disapproval and disbelief, but I don't care. My focus is on Anya.

I stand, adjusting my posture as I move closer to her. Her polished smile flickers for half a second, just enough for me to notice. Good.

"Tell Mr. Kuznetsov," I whisper fiercely, my hand lands on her shoulder, my grip firm but measured; it's a silent signal of my authority, "that I need to see him. Now."

Anya's eyes widen briefly before she recovers, her professional mask snapping back into place. "Mr. Kuznetsov is currently unavailable—"

"That's not what I asked," I interrupt, stepping just a little closer. I'm taller than her, and I make sure she feels it. My gaze locks on hers, and I don't blink.

"Tell him. Now."

She hesitates, her perfect composure cracking as she takes a half-step back.

"I'll see what I can do," she murmurs, her voice quieter than before.

"Good," I reply, still holding her gaze as I step back. I give her just enough space to make her escape.

Anya doesn't waste a second, nodding stiffly before turning on her heel and walking off, her quickened pace betraying the calm she's trying so hard to project. I sit back down, exhaling slowly, the rush of adrenaline thrumming beneath my skin.

Before I can fully settle, Elijah comes barreling back, his hands slightly wet but not clean enough to pass inspection. He skids to a stop in front of me, grinning as he holds up his hands.

"All clean, Mommy!"

A nearby couple frowns, one of them muttering something about "manners." I catch the woman's glare and raise a brow, daring her to say it louder. She doesn't.

Elijah climbs back into his chair like nothing happened. "Can we go skiing now?" he asks, completely unaware of the tension still simmering in the air.

Not yet. Not until I get some answers.

Forty-Nine

Leonid

"Do you spend your life in the gym?" Vic asks, his blue-gray eyes flicking over me as I pour vodka into a crystal glass. He leans back in the leather chair across my desk, straightening the cuff of his perfectly tailored jacket.

"Or is this what happens when you avoid Swiss chocolate?"

I glance at him but don't take the bait. "Someone has to stay sharp."

Vic smirks, running a hand through his silver-streaked hair.

"Sharp, yes. But I've known you a long time, my friend. And this?" He gestures broadly around the room, the office bathed in golden light spilling through tall windows, clouds stretching out like an ocean below us. "This isn't like you. You don't just... appear. Not without a plan."

"That's because I have one." I take a sip, savoring the burn, and lean against the edge of my desk. The glass feels cool in my hand, grounding me. "You didn't think I'd let Fiona continue unchecked, did you?"

Vic's eyebrows lift, and he tilts his head, his expression somewhere between curiosity and approval.

"Fiona. Of course. The woman who thinks she can run both sides of the board without tipping it over." He taps a finger against the side of his chair. "She's getting greedy."

"Greedy doesn't even cover it," I say, setting my glass down with a deliberate clink. "She's using my gold to buy Ludis's connections. She wants expansion. Everywhere. But she doesn't realize she's playing with fire."

Vic leans forward, resting his elbows on his knees, his sharp features shadowed in the low light. "And you're here to remind her what happens when someone burns you. Yes?"

I don't answer immediately, but Vic knows. He always does. He adjusts the vintage Patek Philippe on his wrist, a subtle pause before he speaks, like he's calibrating his next move.

"You could freeze her out," he says casually, "Cut her routes. Make her deals dry up. But that's a slow burn. Effective, but slow."

"And your way?" I ask, meeting his calculating gaze.

He smiles faintly, a predator's smile. "Squeeze her. Use her greed against her. Offer her something she can't resist—more than she's already taken. But build in a choke point. A place where you can cut her off and make sure she knows it. If you do it right, you won't have to lift a finger. She'll destroy herself trying to grab it all."

I lean back, considering his words. It's a clean strategy and one that avoids a messy confrontation. But there's something about the way Vic shifts in his seat, his eyes glinting with subtle amusement, that makes me pause.

"You've used this before," I say.

Vic nods, adjusting his cufflinks. "With someone who thought they were untouchable. They weren't."

"Fiona's not as smart as she thinks," I say, a dark edge creeping into my voice. "But she's bold. Too bold."

"And boldness, my friend," Vic says, raising his glass, "is often the quickest path to ruin."

I watch him for a moment, the way he sits so damn calmly, like he's got the whole world already figured out. *Suka,* I think, the edge of a grin tugging at my mouth.

They don't know it yet but Vic's plan will bury them, and I'll gladly drive the shovel.

"How's the family?" I ask, pouring myself another drink. "Juliette still keeping busy with the foundation?"

Vic's smile softens. "She is. Keeps her busy, but you know Juliette—she wouldn't have it any other way." He pauses, swirling the vodka in his glass like he's contemplating the secrets of the universe in there.

I watch the liquid catch the light.

A family man. Who'd have thought? Twenty years in this business and he still manages to keep that wholesome Father-of-the-Year facade. The really annoying part is that it's not even a facade.

"Alix is getting too smart for her own good. Always asking questions about the business. I'm trying to keep her focused on school, but you know how daughters are."

"She's what, 16 now?"

Christ, when did I start caring about his kids' ages?

"Yes, 16 going on 30." Vic rubs his temple. "Mathis is the quieter one, more into his piano and chess than anything else. They balance each other out." His eyes lock onto mine. "You should meet them sometime. They'd surprise you."

"Maybe," I grunt and lean back, the leather chair creaking under my weight. The images bubble up anyway: morning kisses, school runs, bedtime stories—all while running an empire built on blood money.

"Family man Vic." The words taste bitter. "You built yourself a beautiful house of cards. One wrong move and—" I flick my fingers open, miming an explosion. "Everything burns. That's the risk I won't take."

Vic's eyebrow twitches. *Great. He caught that.* His glass stops halfway to his mouth before he sets it down, deliberate and slow.

"Risk?" He laughs. "My wife, my kids—they're not a weakness, Leonid. They're why I own this city."

I drain my glass. Worth the risk? Tell that to the three bullet holes in my jacket. Vic walks this tightrope like it's solid ground—devoted father, loving husband, ruthless leader.

Kakogo cherta.

Clara and Elijah's faces flash through my mind. I grip the glass harder. *Blyat.* Where did that come from?

"You make it sound easy." I lean back, studying him. "How do you keep it alive? You and Juliette."

Vic considers me silently for a moment. This isn't my kind of question—feelings, family. I wait for him to deflect, but his lips curve into that knowing smile I hate.

"Communication," he taps his glass, "and effort. You can't half-ass it, not with someone you want to keep."

I snort. "Communication? That's your secret?"

"It's not a secret, Leonid. It's work." He shrugs, the gesture almost insulting in its simplicity. "And you need to want it to work. Without that, the rest doesn't matter." Vic studies me for a beat longer than I'm comfortable with, his expression unreadable. "You're asking a lot of questions today, my friend. Makes me wonder."

"Don't wonder," I say flatly, setting my glass down with a firm thud. "I'm just curious."

A sharp knock cuts through the moment, and I glance at the door.

Maksim? Blyat, that mudak's an hour late.

My irritation flares as I stand, rolling my shoulders before stalking toward the door. But then it hits me—Maksim never knocks.

I grip the handle and yank it open, my annoyance already climbing. Anya stands there, looking far less polished than usual. Her face is pale, and her lips press into a tight line, as if she's holding something back. Her hand twitches, squeezing the edge of her uniform before smoothing it out again, a nervous tell I don't miss.

"What is it?" My tone is clipped, and her gaze flicks up to mine like she's bracing for impact.

"Ms. Caldwell..." She hesitates, and for a second, I think she might bolt. Then she clears her throat, her voice quieter than usual. "She wants to see you. Right now."

I arc an eyebrow. "And?"

She looks guilty, like she's the one who interrupted the meeting. Her lips part, but no words come out. Just silence.

From behind me, Vic's voice cuts in, smooth as ever. "I'd say this sounds urgent, my friend. Romantic entanglements often are."

"It's not romantic," I snap, turning just enough to glare at him. "It's... business." The words feel forced, even to me, but I keep my tone firm.

Vic's smirk deepens, his blue-gray eyes gleaming with amusement. "If you say so, Leonid."

My jaw tightens as I turn back to Anya. Her expression hasn't changed—still pale, still nervous—but I catch the faintest twitch at the corner of her mouth, as if she's trying to keep herself invisible.

I inhale slowly through my nose, forcing the anger to settle, even though it's crawling under my skin.

That woman.

"Fine," I say, the word sharp but contained. My gaze stays locked on Anya. "Take me to her."

Blyat. Whatever this is, I already hate it.

Fifty

Maksim

"*Yob tvoyu mat', suka blyat'.*" The string of curses slips out like a reflex. "I fucking knew it!" I laugh under my breath, shaking my head as I look at the paper in my hand. Of course, I was right. It's always funnier when you're right and no one else sees it coming.

The report feels heavier than it should, the words staring back at me with a kind of smugness that matches my mood.

DNA TEST RESULTS: 99.99% POSITIVE. The kid is Leonid's. No room for doubt. No room for error.

I let out a low whistle, shaking my head as a grin tugs at the corner of my mouth. It's not often you get to be right in a way that's this satisfying.

Yob tvoyu mat', Leonid. You've really outdone yourself this time.

I lean back against the cold steel counter, the sterile smell of the lab almost overpowering. The place isn't much to look at—white walls, gleaming equipment, and screens flashing more numbers and graphs than I care to decipher. But it's fast. Swiss efficiency at its peak. Anything you need tested—blood, hair, the mystery meat from

a bad dinner—three hours, tops. It's like a crime syndicate's version of
Amazon Prime.

"Fast, huh?" I say aloud, mostly to myself but loud enough for the
doctor to hear. "You people test everything this quick? Or do I get the
VIP package because I'm so charming?"

The lab doctor—no, lab technician? No, *geneticist,* that's the
word—doesn't even look up. A wiry man with glasses that slip halfway
down his nose and a face carved from stone. His lab coat is pristine,
not a wrinkle or stain, like he's afraid chaos might kill him.

"You paid for speed," he says flatly, tapping away at a keyboard.
"And crypto transferred instantly. That's all I care about." His voice
could put caffeine to sleep. Eyes glued to the screen. "VIP package," he
mutters under his breath, almost like he's amused. But I'm not sure.

I snort, folding the paper and slipping it into my jacket pocket. This
guy wouldn't be curious if I rolled a severed head in here.

"You ever wonder about the people behind these tests? Who they're
for?"

"Not once," he says, deadpan, not missing a beat. "You want wonder, try art school."

Smartass. I like him.

I push off the counter, glancing around one last time. The place
hums with quiet efficiency, a world of microscopes, centrifuges, and
machines I can't name. It's the kind of place where you could drop
a bombshell, and no one would flinch—as long as the crypto keeps
coming.

Just as I'm about to leave, my phone buzzes in my pocket. I fish it
out, Leonid's name flashing across the screen. I already know it's not
a friendly check-in.

The message pops up before I can answer.

Get back before I slide you and feed you to the dogs.

I bark out a laugh, tucking the phone back in my pocket. He'd do it, too, but not before I drop this little bombshell in his lap. The smirk spreads before I can stop it.

Speak of the devil.

As I walk out, my hand presses against the folded report like it's a secret only I know. Leonid's world is about to tilt on its axis, and I'll be there to see the exact second it happens.

Chyert, I might even savor it.

Fifty-One

Leonid

Anya walks a step ahead of me, her heels crunching faintly on the frosted path outside the restaurant. She's stiff, nervous, and not doing a good job of hiding it. Her hands keep fidgeting with the hem of her coat, and every so often, she glances over her shoulder like she expects me to bark at her.

I don't. Not yet.

My mind is too preoccupied with *why*. Why is Clara demanding to see me?

Blyat, this had better not be another one of her tests.

Anya stops abruptly, turning toward me. "They're just outside," she murmurs, her voice almost too low to hear as she opens the glass door leading to the balcony.

The cold hits immediately. I step out, and the world stretches in every direction—mountains blanketed in snow, the horizon endless and clear. It's the kind of view that makes people stop, stare, and feel small.

But I don't stop for the mountains.

I stop for her.

Clara is standing a few feet ahead, her back to me, arms crossed tightly against the cold. She's looking down at Elijah, who is crouched in the snow, his little hands working diligently to shape something. It's not a snowman—it's more of a lopsided lump, but he's completely engrossed, muttering to himself about "fixing it."

Something in my chest tightens as Clara's head tilts back, her face turning toward the sky. Her shoulders rise and fall with a breath that looks heavy enough to carry whatever weight she's trying to shed. The wind picks up, sending loose strands of her rich, chestnut brown hair dancing across her cheeks, and *blyat*, I shouldn't notice how the sunlight catches each strand, how it makes her look almost ethereal against the stark white landscape.

Yebat. I want to walk over and pull her against me. Feel her back against my chest. Press my face into her neck. The urge is so strong it pisses me off.

I cough, just enough to break whatever moment she's having with the sky. Her shoulders go rigid before she turns, and those blue eyes hit me like a physical force.

She's even more beautiful than I remembered, which is annoying as hell and puts me in an even worse mood.

Maybe it's the cold turning her cheeks pink. Maybe it's that stubborn set of her jaw. Maybe it's just that she's real, standing here, not just another memory keeping me up at night.

I walk closer. She smells like vanilla and winter, and my hands clench at my sides.

"Clara." I keep my voice flat.

Her eyes narrow. "Leonid." She spits my name out like it tastes bad.

I stop a few feet away, my gaze dropping briefly to the rise and fall of her chest, the flush in her cheeks. It's infuriating how much she gets under my skin.

Elijah's still playing in the snow behind her, talking to himself about whatever he's building. But all I can focus on is Clara and how much I want to kiss that anger right off her face. Which is exactly the kind of thought I need to shut down. Now.

"You wanted to see me," I remind her, watching her jaw clench tighter.

"Damn right I did," she snaps, her voice low enough not to reach Elijah.

"Remember, *kiska*, you're my captive," I whisper fiercely back at her. "And you—"

"Let us go home," she cuts me off before I can say *"you'll be safer here."*

"No."

"I want answers. And I want them now."

I arch a brow. "About?"

She throws her hands up in frustration. "Don't do that. Don't act like you don't know why I'm angry. Why are we here, Leonid? Why drag us across the world to... this?" She waves a hand vaguely at the pristine, snow-covered landscape as if it offends her.

I don't answer immediately, glancing over her shoulder at Elijah. "Nothing that concerns you."

She steps closer, close enough that I can see the tiny freckle near her right eye. "What do you know about Stephan?"

The name hits like ice water. I keep my face blank, but she catches something—she always does. Her eyes narrow into blue slits.

She steps closer still, her voice dropping to an icy hiss. "Don't give me that bullshit, Leonid."

"This isn't a discussion," I say firmly, my tone cutting.

"It damn well is," she fires back, her cheeks flushed with more than just the cold. "You dragged us here, uprooted everything—*for what?* To play puppet master? To keep me and Elijah in the dark?"

I straighten to my full height, my hands sliding out of my coat pockets as I square my shoulders. Her defiance sparks something in me—a fire I don't want to name, let alone feel. She's right in front of me now, her anger radiating, but I don't back away. Instead, I lean forward just enough to close the gap, meeting her glare head-on.

"You're not in charge here, Clara," I tell her, "You'll stay where I put you, and you'll do what I tell you to do. That's how this works."

Her breath catches, and I don't miss the flicker of fury in her eyes as my words sink in.

"And Stephan?" I continue, my tone colder now, slicing through the frost in the air. "He isn't your concern. Not anymore."

She stiffens, and for a second, I think she's going to shove me. Her lips press into a tight line, and for a moment, I think she's about to scream. But then a soft *thwack* interrupts her, and I glance down to see snow sliding off my coat.

"Elijah!" she gasps, her voice laced with shock. I look over her shoulder to see him standing with another snowball already in hand, his face red with a mix of cold and frustration.

"You're mean!" he shouts, glaring at me. "You're making Mommy upset!"

The sting of his words is sharper than the snow, and I stand there for a beat, frozen. He's right, and I hate how he looks at me.

I crouch slowly, my hand sinking into the snow. "Alright," I say, my tone softer now. "Let's see what you've got."

Elijah blinks, surprised, before his face breaks into a grin. He hurls the next snowball, but I'm ready this time, dodging it easily. Clara watches in stunned silence as I toss one back, deliberately aiming wide.

"Elijah," I call out, smirking. "You're gonna need to try harder than that."

Elijah squeals with laughter as I lob another snowball his way, deliberately missing by inches. He scrambles to gather more snow, his little hands barely able to pack it before he's throwing again. His joy is infectious, the kind that fills the cold air and chips away at the tension lingering between me and Clara.

I glance at her, expecting her to still be fuming, but something in her expression has softened. She watches Elijah, her arms still crossed, but her breathing slows, and I can almost see the fight draining out of her.

"Clara," I call out, my smirk widening as another snowball sails past me. "You're just going to stand there, or are you going to pick a side?"

Her brow arches, and she tilts her head, skeptical. "You're kidding."

"Does it look like I'm kidding?" I pack another snowball and let it fly, this one landing squarely near Elijah's boots. He squeals again, aiming his retaliation at my chest.

"You're insane," she mutters, but I catch the faintest twitch of her lips like she's trying not to smile.

"Mommy, come on!" Elijah yells, his grin so wide it's impossible to resist. He waves her over with one hand while clutching a lumpy snowball with the other. "You gotta help me get him!"

Clara sighs, letting out a visible breath in the cold air. She crouches, grabbing a handful of snow, her movements deliberate. Then, with a flick of her wrist, she throws it—right at me.

It hits my shoulder with a satisfying thud.

Elijah cheers like it's the winning move in a championship game, and Clara shrugs, her lips curving into a sly smile.

"Not bad," I say, brushing the snow off my coat. "But you're out of practice."

"Oh, really?" she quips, bending down to gather more snow. "Let's see you say that after this."

What follows is pure chaos. Snow flies in every direction—Elijah giggles uncontrollably as he tries to dodge and throw at the same time. Clara targets me with military precision, her throws fast and unrelenting, while I split my efforts between dodging her and giving Elijah a fighting chance.

At some point, I decide to shift tactics. "Elijah!" I call out, pointing toward Clara. "New target."

He stops mid-throw, his face lighting up with mischief. "Mommy?"

Clara freezes, her eyes narrowing. "Don't even think about it, Leonid."

I smirk. "Think fast, *Mommy*."

Before she can react, Elijah hurls his snowball at her. It hits her coat with a soft splat, and her mouth falls open in mock outrage.

"Oh, you're both dead," she declares, grabbing two handfuls of snow. She's laughing now, a sound I haven't heard from her in... forever, it feels like. The kind of laugh that makes me forget everything else for a moment.

From the corner of my eye, I catch movement near the far end of the balcony. Anya stands there, her mouth slightly open, her eyes wide as if she's just walked into an alternate reality. She looks between me, Clara, and Elijah, clutching her clipboard like it might anchor her to sanity. I ignore her, focusing instead on the snowball Clara just launched at my chest.

The war escalates quickly, with Elijah switching sides every thirty seconds and Clara surprising me with how ruthless she can be. My coat is soaked by the time I finally manage to dodge one of her throws and retaliate with a perfect hit to her arm.

"Truce!" she calls out, laughing as she raises her hands in mock surrender.

Elijah, however, is not finished. He runs toward her, throwing another handful of snow at her legs. She scoops him up mid-charge, tickling his sides until he's shrieking with laughter.

And for a moment, just a moment, it feels... real. Like this is normal. Like this is *mine*.

That thought hits me harder than any snowball. I freeze, watching them, my chest tightening in a way that's both unfamiliar and uncomfortable. *Blyat*. What the hell is happening to me?

Before I can dwell on it, a voice cuts through the air, dripping with sarcasm.

"Well, well, well... what a lovely happy family."

I turn sharply to see Maksim strolling up the path, his usual shit-eating grin plastered across his face. He's holding a white envelope in one hand, spinning it casually between his fingers. "Didn't know you were the snowball fight type, boss," he adds, his tone practically oozing smugness.

Maksim waves the envelope like it's a trophy. "Just thought you'd want to see this. But hey, don't let me interrupt your family fun."

"What's in it?"

He shrugs, his grin widening. "Oh, just a little something I thought might brighten your day. Or ruin it." His eyes flick to Clara, his expression turning almost gleeful. "Depends on your perspective, boss."

Fifty-Two

Clara

*T*ake *a deep breath, Clara, this is nothing. It's nothing.*

Fuck, I haven't done this since… Jake died.

The gondola creaks higher, swaying in the wind. "Shit." A nervous laugh escapes my lips. My stomach's doing that thing where it can't decide if this is excitement or pure stupidity.

I tighten my gloved hands on the safety bar. Below, Elijah's tiny red jacket bobs on the bunny slopes like a bright speck against the snow. He wobbles, catches himself, then throws his arms up like he just won Olympic gold. His instructor claps, and I can picture his gap-toothed grin from here.

That's my boy.

The wind whips against my face as I adjust my goggles. Jake would've loved this view. He used to drag me up slopes in Aspen when I was twelve, with me complaining the whole way while he went on and on about proper ski techniques.

"Come on, baby bug," he'd say, ruffling my hair through my hat. "You think I'm letting my little sister embarrass me on the bunny slopes forever?"

My throat tightens, the memory sharp and sudden, like the bite of the cold air. Back then, I'd hated his bossy older-brother energy, but now I'd give anything to hear his teasing again. To feel that effortless joy he carried, the way he made the world seem lighter just by being in it.

I shift my weight on my skis, glancing over my shoulder at the lodge far below. Leonid and Maksim are down at the lodge, locked in what I'm sure is some intense discussion about whatever envelope Maksim brought. Leonid's expression when Maksim handed it over earlier was unreadable. Frustratingly so. I shake off the thought, refusing to let it ruin this. Whatever's in that envelope can wait. Right now, I have snow, skis, and a sliver of freedom.

I unclip at the summit, pushing off with my poles. The first rush of speed hits, and everything else falls away. Wind hisses past my ears. My skis cut through fresh powder, each turn sending up a spray of white.

Freedom tastes like mountain air.

I lean into the next curve, muscle memory taking over despite the years. Left, right, left. The world narrows to just this—speed and snow and sky. No Leonid. No revenge. No dead brother haunting my dreams.

Just me and the mountain.

The snow sprays around me as I lean into a turn, the mountain opening up below like a canvas. Everything is vast, open, endless—a stark contrast to the walls that have been closing in around me lately. Jake's voice echoes in my head again, his laughter, his teasing, his stubborn belief that I could do anything if I just stopped overthinking.

"Respect the mountain," he'd said once, serious for a moment, standing with his hands on his hips as he surveyed the endless white. "It's big, sure. But it's not bigger than you."

I hit a stretch of powder so soft it feels like gliding through clouds, my chest tightening again—not from sadness this time, but from something brighter. I wish he were here to see this. To see me now.

As the slope levels out, I let myself slow, savoring the ache in my muscles and the warmth spreading through my body from the effort. Below, the lodge is a speck in the distance, and I know Elijah's lesson is probably wrapping up. But I can't stop yet. Not yet.

I glance at the lift and decide on one more run. Just one. A little longer to stay in this moment, this freedom. I head toward the next gondola, the snow crunching under my skis. But as I step into line, something catches my attention—two men standing off to the side, too far from the main area to be casual tourists.

"What the fuck?" I mutter through my mask.

They're dressed wrong for the mountain, in dark coats instead of ski gear, their stances stiff and deliberate. One of them scans the area, his eyes sharp and calculating. A chill runs through me, colder than the air around me.

I keep my pace steady, casual, pretending not to notice as I step into the gondola. But my stomach knots, my instincts humming with that familiar, unwelcome tension. Whatever they're here for, it's not skiing.

The gondola creaks shut, and I force myself to sit calmly, my poles resting across my lap like nothing's wrong. But when I peek through the small window, it's clear—they're not just heading to the lift, they're tracking me, every movement measured, every glance calculated. It's like their entire world has narrowed down to a single point, and that point is me.

My stomach churns.

These fuckers are not here to enjoy the mountain.

I tug at my gloves, feigning nonchalance, but every muscle in my body is tense.

Maybe it's just in my head, right?

Maybe they're just— Fuck no. I've been down this road before. I know when I'm being sized up, when people's eyes are picking me apart. And it's fucking clear to me now, these eyes, they're not friendly. They mean harm, and I'd be a goddamn idiot to ignore them.

The gondola lurches upward, and I glance out again. They're not waiting in line like normal skiers. They're bypassing the crowd, talking to a lift operator. One of them gestures toward my gondola. The operator hesitates but eventually nods.

"What the fuck?" I mutter again. My fingers tighten around the poles until they creak under the pressure.

The gondola sways, rising toward the summit, and I shift to look down. The slopes sprawl out below me, quiet and empty this late in the afternoon. Too empty. My chest tightens as I scan for an exit plan. By the time I reach the top, they'll be behind me.

I need to stay ahead.

Think, Clara.

The gondola bumps to a stop, and I don't waste a second. As soon as the doors open, I push off, my skis digging into the snow. The slope is steep here, a sharp drop before leveling out, and I lean into it, letting gravity do the work.

Wind tears at my face.

I can't shake the prickle at the back of my neck. Something feels off. I glance over my shoulder, and my stomach flips.

The two figures are getting off the gondola behind me, and this time, they're not empty-handed. Snowboards. Not tourist rentals—they're geared up, sleek and professional. Their movements scream one thing: pursuit.

"Shit," I mutter, bending lower to pick up speed. My poles dig into the snow as I swerve, cutting a sharp line across the slope. They're faster than I expected, closing the gap with every turn.

The snow sprays behind me as I cut another sharp turn, the path ahead narrowing through a grove of trees. I lean into it, legs burning with effort, but the wind in my ears carries more than just my breathing. The unmistakable sound of board edges carving through the snow—closer, gaining.

I push harder, my muscles screaming in protest. The world blurs as I carve a path between the trees, ducking low to avoid a branch that nearly catches my goggles. Another glance back—mistake. The first man is close now, too close. He raises an arm, a glint of metal catching the sun.

A gun.

"Fuck!" The curse rips out of me as I twist hard, my skis skidding against the snow. The first shot cracks through the air, splintering a tree inches from my shoulder. Splinters spray against my jacket, and I bite back a scream.

"Focus, Clara," I growl under my breath, cutting through a tight turn that nearly throws me off balance. Another shot rings out, and the snow beside me explodes in a spray of powder.

Motherfucker. Too close. Too damn close.

My breath comes in ragged bursts, the slope ahead opening into a steep drop. I don't think—I just take it, my body moving on instinct. My skis hit the incline, and the world tips forward as I rocket downward, the wind tearing at my face.

The sound of pursuit doesn't let up. They're riding the edge of control, fast and reckless. I glance back just as one of them lifts his weapon again. My foot catches on an unseen bump, and suddenly, I'm airborne, tumbling down the slope in a tangle of limbs and gear.

The impact rattles through me as I hit the snow hard, sliding on my side until I finally stop. Pain shoots through my ribs, my goggles askew, one pole missing. The mountain is spinning, the sound of board edges screeching above me.

I try to get up, but my legs don't cooperate. The first man slows to a stop a few feet away, gun raised and steady.

"This is it," I whisper, my breath fogging in the cold air. My hand scrambles for anything—my other pole, a rock—but I'm exposed, helpless. He takes aim.

The shot comes—but it's not his.

The man screams, clutching his leg as he collapses into the snow. A second shot follows, and his partner drops his weapon, falling with a grunt.

I blink, stunned, my ears ringing from the echoes. A figure emerges from the trees above, gun raised. Leonid.

He moves with the precision of a predator, his steps deliberate as he closes the distance. His face is a mask of cold fury, the gun in his hand still trained on the downed men. One of them reaches for something in his coat, but Leonid kicks him hard in the ribs, sending him sprawling.

Leonid's men appear from the shadows like wolves closing in on wounded prey. Three of them, dressed in black, their expressions as cold and unrelenting as the glacier. One yanks the gun from the crawling man's hand while another cuffs the second, pinning him to the ground.

Leonid spares them only a glance before speaking, his voice low and venomous. "*Pizda*. You are so dead."

The man groans under his boot, curling in on himself, and Leonid finally turns to me. His gaze sweeps over my crumpled form, his jaw tightening.

"You hurt?" he asks.

"I'm fine," I manage, though my ribs scream otherwise.

Leonid doesn't wait for clarification. He strides over, his arm sliding under mine with a firm, unyielding grip. He pulls me to my feet as though I weigh nothing, steadying me with a hand on my arm. The world spins briefly, but his hold anchors me.

"What about—?"

"Elijah's safe," Leonid cuts me off. "You shouldn't have been out here alone."

I don't argue. For once, I don't have the energy.

Fifty-Three

Clara

"Everything hurts," I mutter, wincing as the nurse presses a hand lightly against my shoulder. And I mean *everything*. My ribs scream when I breathe, and shifting in this oversized armchair sends needles of pain down my spine.

The nurse doesn't respond. She's tall, broad-shouldered, and built like she could take a ski slope down in one stride. Her scrubs, a pale green that does nothing for her complexion, fit like they're about to give up entirely. Her hair is scraped back in a tight bun so severe it makes me want to wince in sympathy.

"Ms. Caldwell, please hold still," the doctor interrupts. He's short, barely taller than the nurse, with sharp, dark eyes that flick between me and his tablet like he's already deciding how much effort I'm worth. His beard is neatly trimmed, and his white coat looks like it came straight from the dry cleaners.

He doesn't sit; just stands beside me, peering down. "Your ribs are bruised, not broken. Same for your shoulder—strained, not torn. You'll need to rest, ice, and avoid anything that aggravates it."

"Aggravates it?" I lift a brow. "Like breathing?" The nurse's lips twitch.

"Ouch." I bite back a hiss when he touches a particularly tender spot.

The oversized leather armchair feels like it's swallowing me whole in this ridiculous suite, all crystal chandeliers and gold-trimmed everything. I try to shift, to sweep my tangled hair from my face, but my shoulder screams in protest.

"Nothing's broken, yes?"

"Fortunately." He straightens, adjusting those glasses with one knuckle. "Though you'll need to ice it regularly. Nurse Heidi will show you how to wrap it."

"Mommy, look! Pikachu caught the bad guy!" Elijah waves his chocolate-smeared hand at the TV, oblivious to my grimace as Nurse Heidi helps me lift my white top. The fabric pulls tight across my chest as I sit up straighter, and the pain flares sharp and immediate. I glance down at the mottled bruise curling under my collarbone, the edges deepening to black and blue like an ink stain spreading under my skin. It's ugly, raw, but not as bad as it could've been. A reminder that things can always get worse.

"Mommy!"

I turn my head, biting back another wince. He's cross-legged on the couch.

"That's great, buddy," I call, forcing a smile. My ribs protest the effort. "He's the best, huh?"

Elijah beams, pride lighting up his little face. "Told you!" He turns back to the TV, completely absorbed, licking a smudge of chocolate off his fingers.

He doesn't know the truth. I told him I fell. I made it sound harmless. His little hand had pressed against my arm earlier, his face scrunched with worry.

"Be careful next time," he'd said, his voice so serious.

God, I don't deserve him.

The doctor clears his throat, drawing me back. "We'll leave detailed instructions with your security staff," he says. "Leonid's staff. Of course.

Because Leonid didn't come himself. Not to check on me. Not to say anything.

I press my lips together as the nurse hands me an ice pack, her gaze brisk and practical.

"Keep this on for fifteen minutes, then off for fifteen," she says. "Rotate like that."

I nod, but my head's already elsewhere. Leonid's silence rings louder than her voice.

What the hell is he so mad about? Because I skied alone? Because I didn't ask for his permission? Or does he know something I don't? Were those men Ludis's men? Fiona's? Someone else entirely?

"Call if you experience any worsening pain," the doctor says, already gathering his things. His voice fades into the background as my thoughts spiral.

The door clicks shut, and the silence is almost oppressive. I slump back in the chair. The ice pack pressed against my side is already losing its chill, and so am I.

Leonid didn't even look at me after the mountain—just turned away, cold and silent, like I wasn't worth the effort.

Goddamnit.

The door creaks open again, and my breath catches before I can stop it. For a split second, my chest flutters—

It's him.

Get a grip, Clara. You're not some lovesick idiot.

But it's not Leonid.

"Don't look so disappointed," Maksim drawls, strolling into the room with all the grace of an unwelcome guest. His smirk is cocky, the kind that tells you he's here for his own amusement as much as anything else.

"What do you want?"

Instead of answering, Maksim's attention shifts to the couch where Elijah is sprawled, giggling at the screen.

His smirk softens—just enough to catch me off guard—before he strides over and crouches beside my son.

"Hey, buddy," he says, his tone warmer than I've ever heard it. From his jacket, he pulls out a sleek Nintendo Switch, holding it out like an offering. "Got something new for you. Want to try it?"

Elijah's eyes light up, his grin spreading so wide it almost eclipses the chocolate smudged on his face. "For me?"

Maksim nods, his smile widening as he gestures toward the door to Leonid's room. "Leonid's got a nice setup in there. It's quieter, too—perfect for games. What do you think?"

Elijah hesitates, looking at me. I force a smile past the tight knot in my chest. "Go ahead, sweetheart. Just don't forget to say thank you."

"Thanks!" Elijah chirps, grabbing the device and darting to the connecting door. Maksim leans down, pushing it open just enough for him to slip through.

"Remember to save your progress," he calls after him, a teasing lilt in his voice.

The door falls halfway shut, muting the sounds of Elijah's cartoon and leaving me alone with Maksim.

He turns toward me.

I glare at him, my nails digging into the armrest. "What the hell do you think you're doing?"

Maksim takes his time settling into the chair beside me, one ankle resting on his knee. He glances around the room as if appraising the décor, then meets my stare with deliberate calm.

"So," he says, stretching out the word like it's a game. "Are you going to tell him about Elijah, or should I?"

The air feels like it's been sucked out of the room. My lungs seize. The ice pack in my hand is suddenly a vise, its chill biting into my skin, but I can't let it go. My mind races, clashing with the dead silence that follows.

"What the fuck are you talking about?" I whisper.

Maksim tilts his head, his expression sliding into something dangerously close to amusement.

"Oh, come on," he drawls, his tone so casual it makes my skin crawl. "Do I really need to spell it out for you, Clara?"

I shake my head, gripping the edge of the ice pack tighter, as though that might ground me, steady me, stop the floor from tilting beneath me.

"You're out of your goddamn mind."

Maksim leans forward, tipping his head slightly.

"No, I'm not. And neither are you. You've known it all along, haven't you?" He waits a beat, watching me, savoring the moment. "Elijah is the heir of the Kuznetsov Bratva."

Fifty-Four

Leonid

"Marcus Coburn." The name tastes like copper on my tongue as I read from the passport. My blood-stained fingers leave prints on the gold-embossed leather.

Fitting. A name destined for death.

Two naked men slump in metal chairs before me, skin mottled purple where the zip ties bite into their flesh. Their possessions rest on the steel table beside me—clothes folded with military precision, two 9mm Glocks, two burner phones. A condom. A stack of passports with different names but the same faces. The same mistake.

I roll up my sleeves, watching dried blood flake onto the pristine floor. Vic's basement has seen worse, but he watches me like I'm an artist painting outside the lines. His tech analyst stands a step behind him, hunched over a tablet. The screen's blue glow reflects off Vic's sharp features, lending him an eerie, aristocratic edge.

"Your employer invested in quality documentation." I trace the watermark on Coburn's passport, remembering how Clara's blood had looked similar on my hands hours ago. "But they made one critical error."

The larger one, Marcus, according to his papers, spits blood onto the floor. "We don't know who—"

I silence him with my fist. The familiar crunch of bone grounds me, keeps the rage from consuming everything. They touched her. They dared to touch what's mine.

"They sent you after Clara." Another hit. My knuckles split further. "After *my* Clara." I don't recognize my own voice anymore.

In my peripheral vision, Vic checks his Patek Philippe. Always precise, even now. His tech analyst whispers something and he tilts his head to listen.

"Leonid." Vic's Swiss accent sharpens my name. "The payment traced back to Caldwell Industries. Caribbean holdings."

The smaller one, James Wilson—probably another fake name—pisses himself. The acrid smell mixes with blood and sweat.

"Please... we didn't know she was a Caldwell. Just told to make it look like a robbery gone wrong."

I go still. My fingers find Wilson's burner phone. "Call your employer. Tell them it's done."

"What?"

"Tell. Them. She's. Dead." Each word feels like ice in my veins. "Or I'll ensure your actual death takes significantly longer than hers would have."

The phone rings three times. Static crackles.

Wilson croaks out the words, terror making him surprisingly convincing. "Job's done. The woman... she's taken care of."

A pause that stretches like a garotte wire. Then: "Good. Confirmation photo within the hour."

The line dies. The phone cracks in my grip.

I look at Vic. He nods—call traced. His tech team never fails.

"Thank you for your cooperation." My Glock feels heavy as I draw it. The weight of what's coming settles in my chest. "Unfortunately, I can't say the same for your employer."

His eyes widen. "No, wait—"

Two shots. Clean. Professional. More mercy than they deserve.

Vic's tech guy interrupts us, "Sir, the call we traced... it came from the same account we tracked earlier. Caldwell Industries. But—" He hesitates, clearing his throat. "There's another call on the same line, sir. I'm patching it through now."

Vic smirks, clearly enjoying himself. "Old school burner phones," he says, casually slipping his hands into his pockets. "They underestimated you, Leonid. Big mistake."

The recording fills the concrete room. An unfamiliar voice, deep and sleek as black ice: "Clara Caldwell's been taken care of."

A pause.

"What about the boy?" My stomach churns as the second voice takes its time.

"*Blyat*," I hiss. My father's most trusted man. Aleksei.

Just like the ones in the photo Dimitri sent to me.

Ice clinks against glass. A soft chuckle scrapes my nerves raw.

"Elijah is now orphaned. Leonid's done playing nice. No more leverage. No more loose ends. That boy is dead weight."

"Tsk, tsk." The sound crackles through the speaker, and for a moment, I'm back in Papa's study, watching Aleksei's thin lips curl as he whispered poison in Papa's ear.

"You're one cold *suka*, Stephan. Thought you had a soft spot for that bastard boy. All those times playing uncle."

"I should've put a bullet between her eyes when I took care of Jake. The stupid bitch doesn't even know it was me, standing right in front of her at his funeral. Then again, she never met dear Stephan until after I put five bullets into her brother dearest."

My knuckles crack as I clench my fists, the sound sharp as gunfire in the basement. For fourteen years. Fourteen fucking years Clara's been hunting the wrong killer, while this *svoloch* played family friend. I force myself to breathe, to listen. To memorize every detail of how I'll make him suffer.

"Remember when I sent her to The Viper's Nest?" Stephan continues.

"The place has been so lucrative for us." Aleksei chuckles from the other end.

"The whore was supposed to die that night, but the bitch got lucky. And wouldn't you know it—" Stephan's words slither through the speaker. "The slut ends up pregnant, couldn't even tell us who the father was."

My heart stops. The night at The Viper's Nest. The club where I first saw her, where I—

Blood rushes in my ears. My fingers leave dents in the steel table edge as the pieces click into place. *My son.* They tried to kill my son before he even drew breath.

"I told her to get rid of it. Even arranged the clinic. But no—"

The room seems to shrink, the walls pressing closer as Stephan's voice keeps coming. Vic's basement smells of copper and revenge, and all I can think of is Elijah's small hand in mine, how fragile his fingers felt. How close I came to losing him before I even knew he was mine.

"Clara fucking Caldwell had to play mother, acting all high and mighty about keeping some random bastard..."

I draw in a deep breath to center myself, but my lungs feel like they're filling with ice. Every muscle in my body coils tight, ready to snap. My son. The child I'd dismissed as another man's blood. The boy who has my mother's eyes—

Aleksei's laughter cuts off abruptly. "But what about Leonid? He's getting smarter with his business deals. The expansion into Europe, the new alliances. He's not the reckless boy we could easily manipulate anymore."

There's a pause as they both seem to consider this.

"*Suka blyad'*," Aleksei spits. "Always was an arrogant *mudak*. Just like his father. Andrei thought he was untouchable, and now his *syn suki* struts around like he owns everything."

The mention of my father strikes a nerve so deep it reverberates in my bones. My grip on the table shifts, fingers splayed, grounding myself.

"Patience," Stephan soothes. "Leonid and Ludis will do the job for us. They've been destined to destroy each other from the start. Andrei made sure of that."

"Remember how beautifully this worked last time? Your position in the family made it so easy. That suggestion to Andrei about separating the twins—masterful. Nothing like a mother's death to tear a family apart."

I ball my hands into fists. I want to tear these men apart, to rip their throats out with my teeth.

Jebat' eto der'mo.

"Six-month-old twins," Stephan muses through the static. "Should've been an easy job."

Aleksei's grunt crackles over the line. "Who would've thought Sofiya had it in her? Diving in front of those bullets, using her own body as a shield." His laugh scrapes like nails on concrete. "Both brats survived because of that stupid *suka*."

My vision blurs red.

"But it worked out better than we planned, didn't it?" Stephan's voice drips satisfaction. "Watching Andrei break, thinking his precious wife died protecting their sons from outside enemies..." A pause. "The fool never suspected the man he trusted the most ordered the hit."

"Love makes men weak. *Pizdets*." Aleksei chuckles. "The fool wasn't listening to me after he became a father. *Blyat*. He turned into a pussy. But convincing him to separate the twins? 'For their safety,' I said. The grieving father, so desperate to protect his remaining family, he'd do anything—even tear it apart."

"Time to finish what we started." Stephan's voice fades into static. "Send confirmation when it's done."

"*Da*." The line goes dead.

The steel table crumples under my grip.

Vic's hand on my shoulder stops me from crushing the speaker.

My jaw clenches so hard I taste blood. In the old days, traitors like these were fed to the dogs, piece by piece. But dogs are too quick, too merciful. I think of Elijah, Clara, of my mother, dying to protect her sons from a threat that came from within.

No. Dogs won't do. I'll take them apart myself, slowly, intimately. I'll make them experience every moment of fear they inflicted on my family. And when they beg for death, I'll remind them how they laughed about my son.

"Your move," Vic says quietly, but I'm already reaching for my phone. It's time to remind these *svolochi* exactly whose blood runs in Elijah's veins.

The *Vory v Zakone* has old rules about traitors. But for men who target children? We have special protocols. Ones that make the old punishments look like mercy.

Fifty-Five

Clara

"I'm not doing this," I say flatly, gripping the ice pack tighter against my ribs. The chair creaks as I shift, but it doesn't help. My ass is practically glued to the leather, the oversized armrests boxing me in. Maksim doesn't move from his perch, one ankle propped lazily over his knee, like he's settled in for a show.

"Not doing what?" He lounges deeper into the chair, one dark brow lifting as his teeth flash. "Telling Leonid the truth? Clarifying the little... mix-up about Elijah's last name?"

Shit, shit, shit! This is not good, not good at all. What the hell am I gonna do?

My fingers dig into the ice pack, the plastic biting into my skin. "There's nothing to tell."

"Hmm," Maksim murmurs, drawing the sound out like he's savoring it. "You're stubborn, I'll give you that. Reckless, too."

His eyes flick to the bruise curling under my collarbone, then back up, like he's ticking boxes on a mental checklist.

"But lying to him? That's bold, even for you."

"Fuck off," I snap, gripping the ice pack tighter as the plastic slips against my sweaty palms. My ribs ache with the effort, but I refuse to let it show.

Maksim doesn't back away. Instead, he leans forward, the air between us feels heavier. He tilts his head slightly, his gaze flicking to the ice pack I clutch and back up to my face.

"You think he won't find out?"

"I don't know what the fuck you're talking about." My eyes dart to the half-open door, to where Elijah's Nintendo music has faded to soft, sleepy beats.

Fucker's enjoying this.

"You're not just messing around, Clara. You're standing in the middle of a damn inferno." His thumb tapping against his knee.

Tap. Tap. Tap.

"Get out." I push him, my free hand shoving against his chest, but the movement sends a burst of pain ripping through my ribs. "Ah—damn it," I hiss, my body recoiling.

The ice pack slips from my grip, landing on the armrest with a soft thud.

Before Maksim can respond, the door creaks open abruptly; his head snaps up, his entire posture stiffening.

I don't need to look. The room shifts, the air heavier, and I already know who it is.

Leonid.

He steps in with an unhurried stride, but the tension in his shoulders is impossible to miss. His sleeves are rolled to his elbows, his forearms flexing slightly as his hands hang loosely at his sides. His eyes land on Maksim first, dark and steady, holding just enough menace to make the air feel colder.

Maksim starts to rise, hands up in what looks like surrender. "Boss—"

Leonid doesn't let him finish. He crosses the room in two steps and grabs the front of Maksim's shirt, yanking him halfway out of the chair. The force is enough to scrape the chair back against the floor.

"*Pizda*! What the fuck are you doing?"

"Relax, *Pakhan*," Maksim says quickly, his hands staying where they are. He flicks a glance in my direction. "Just trying to help her do the right thing."

"*Jebat' eto der'mo*, Maksim, I swear if you don't fuck off right now..." Leonid's voice is measured, low, the kind that makes the hairs on your neck stand up. He doesn't look at me; his focus is entirely on Maksim, who hasn't moved a muscle.

Maksim tilts his head slightly, his smirk still there but quieter now, like he's debating whether to press his luck. His eyes narrow, and for a beat, it feels like they're speaking without words—deciphering intentions in a way that only two people who've known each other for too long can. Maksim shifts his weight just a fraction, reading something in Leonid's stare.

"You know..." Maksim says finally.

What does he know?

My spine stiffens, my jaw clenched tight, and I force my expression to remain impassive, betraying none of the fear that courses through me.

He can't know the truth. I won't let him.

Leonid doesn't answer. His jaw tightens, and the way his arm flexes is enough to make Maksim take half a step back, his smirk twitching as if bracing for what comes next.

"*Blayt*," Leonid mutters, his voice heavy with frustration. His hand moves fast, planting firmly on Maksim's chest and shoving him back into the chair with enough force to scrape the legs against the floor. Maksim catches himself before he tips backward, muttering something under his breath, but Leonid's glare keeps him silent.

"Well, then," Maksim says, rising and smoothing the front of his shirt like it's all part of the show. "I'll take that as my cue." His smirk is back, full and deliberate, as he straightens his cuffs.

He takes a step toward the door, but he doesn't leave without turning over his shoulder to glance at me.

"Good luck, Clara," he says, the words laced with just enough weight to leave my stomach in knots.

The door shuts behind him with a quiet click, but the silence he leaves behind is suffocating. Leonid doesn't move, his back still to me, his hands opening and closing at his sides like he's trying to let the tension bleed out of him.

A twitch runs through my arm as I grip the chair tighter, my body's silent protest against the pain.

He finally turns, eyes zeroed in on mine like a hawk on its prey. His hard gaze softens for a brief moment, exposing a hint of vulnerability as he asks, "Where's Elijah?"

"In your room," I say. "Maksim gave him a Switch."

Leonid doesn't wait for more. He strides to the connecting door, yanks it open, and disappears inside. From where I'm stuck in the chair, I can hear the low timbre of his voice, followed by Elijah's sleepy response. A minute later, Leonid returns, his movements slower now as he closes the door with care.

"He's asleep," he says, but his eyes are already back on me, taking in every detail—the way I'm clutching the armrest,

"We need to talk." The same words, spoken at the same time.

I'm going to deny everything.

DNA doesn't make you his father.

Fifty-Six

Clara

Leonid's words hit me like bullets, one after another. My brain refuses to process them, short-circuiting with each revelation. Jake. Stephan. The lies.

No, this can't be...

I blink at him. He's on his haunches in front of me, but I'm not really seeing him anymore because my brain is stuck, snagged on the words I just heard. It's like someone flipped my life upside down and handed it back to me as a cruel parody. A joke. The punchline is mine, and it isn't funny.

"No..." I can't breathe. My ribs feel tighter, like someone's wrapped them in barbed wire.

"Clara, everything you thought you knew..." His voice changes, goes soft in a way that makes my stomach clench. "The story you've been carrying all these years..."

I lift my hand to push him away, but damn him – he catches my wrist. His touch burns through my skin, and I hate how fucking strong he is.

"Look at me."

I can't. Because the Leonid I know doesn't sound like this – gentle, careful, like he's handling something breakable. And I'm not breakable. I'm not.

His lips are moving, but my brain's stuck on replay.. All these years of Sunday dinners. Christmas presents. Birthday cards. Each memory twists like a knife, cutting deeper than the last. My hands won't stop shaking.

"Stephan...?" The name barely comes out, half-whisper, half-wheeze. It doesn't sound like my voice at all. My hands shake harder, my fingers flexing uselessly before they clench again.

The man who taught me how to drive. Who brought me soup when I had the flu at 17. Who stood beside me at Jake's funeral, his hand on my shoulder.

"We'll avenge Jake," he'd said with steely determination. "They'll pay for what they did; that's a promise."

The same hand that had pulled the trigger.

"Clara." Leonid's voice breaks through the static in my head. "Stay with me."

A laugh bubbles up – sharp, hysterical. "Stay with you?"

"That low-life wore the mask," Leonid says, his voice unnervingly calm, like he's stating a fact that doesn't rewrite the past fifteen years of my life. "He killed Jake. It was all planned—he and Aleksei wanted to destabilize your family and mine. And it worked."

I laugh again, a harsh, brittle sound that breaks into the room like shattered glass.

"Planned? No. No." My head jerks from side to side, my body moving of its own accord, trying to shake off the weight of his words.

"You're wrong. He wouldn't—he couldn't."

Leonid watches me. He doesn't argue, doesn't press, just waits, and that patience makes me want to scream.

"You're lying," I snap, my voice sharp and raw. "You're saying this to—what? To manipulate me? To break me down? Because that's not going to work." The words tumble out, quick and defensive, but they can't stop the tremor in my voice, the way my chest feels like it's caving in.

"I have no reason to lie to you, Clara." He says, but chaos spinning inside me.

My ears are ringing, every word hitting like a brick I'm not prepared to dodge.

"The bastard confessed everything when we hacked into their comms." Leonid says, his hands gripping my shoulders, holding me in place when I try to pull away, he doesn't let me. His eyes stay locked on mine.

"Stephan and Aleksei, were talking through the radio, bragging about how easily they manipulated both sides. They thought no one could hear them. They were wrong."

I blink at him. "Aleksei?" I shake my head. "Who the fuck is Aleksei?"

His jaw tightens. "Aleksei Sokolov. My father's enforcer. The one he trusted most." He pauses, and for a moment, his grip on my shoulders tightens before he catches himself, his fingers relaxing slightly.

I press my brows together. "What?"

The room feels colder, like all the air has been sucked out.

Leonid's jaw clenches as his hands curl into fists. "When Ludis and I were six months old, they came for us. For my mother." He exhales sharply, his shoulders stiff. "They made it look like an attack from one of my father's rivals. My mother—She..." He stops, his voice dropping to a low growl. "She threw herself in front of the bullets. Shielded us. Took every hit."

My breath catches in my throat. His words claw at something raw inside me. "Leonid..."

"They killed her, Clara," he says, his voice rising, the anger simmering just beneath the surface. "Aleksei ordered it. Stephan coordinated it. My father never knew. He thought it was an outside hit, but it was his own men, the ones he trusted the most. They tore my family apart."

I swallow hard, my chest tightening as his words crash over me. "But why? Why would they—?"

"For power." Leonid's voice cuts through the room, sharp and unforgiving. "They wanted control. They wanted to destabilize him. And they succeeded." He turns to face me again, his gaze like a blade, piercing and unyielding. "My father blamed himself. He thought he'd failed to protect us. So when Aleksei suggested separating Ludis and me 'for our safety,' he didn't hesitate. He sent us away. Ripped us apart."

My stomach twists as I imagine the scene—an infant Leonid, torn from his brother, his mother's blood still fresh in his father's mind.

But then I remember who Leonid is. He's manipulative, ruthless. He's the kind of man who twists the truth to his advantage. He could be lying. To split me from the one person I've always trusted.

"No." I hiss at him. My fists slam against the armrests, the sudden jolt sending a fresh wave of pain through my ribs. "No, no, no. Stephan wouldn't do that. He—he saved me. He took me in when I had nothing, no one. He was—"

"He was using you," he says.

"You were part of the plan, Clara. A distraction. A way to keep me blind while they moved to take control of everything."

I shake my head again, harder this time, even though it feels like it might snap my neck. My hands are trembling too much to grip anything now. "You don't know what you're talking about. You're wrong.

You're—" My voice cracks, and I bite down on it, hard, because I can feel the tears threatening to spill. I won't let them. Not in front of him. Not now.

"You're lying," I snap, pushing his body away harder now. But he won't fucking budge.

"Am I?" Leonid asks, "Or are you finally starting to see the truth?"

I can't answer. My chest feels like it's caving in, my breath is shallow and sharp as the weight of his words presses down on me. If Leonid's telling the truth...

"I've been – *God*, I've been having Sunday dinners with Jake's killer. He helped me pick out Elijah's first Christmas presents. He—"

The words choke off as bile rises in my throat. Leonid's hand tightens on my wrist, but I barely feel it. All I can see is Stephan at my college graduation, beaming with pride. Stephan helping me move into my first apartment. Stephan suggesting I visit The Viper's Nest that night.

Wait.

The Viper's Nest.

My head snaps up so fast that my vision blurs. "The Viper's Nest," I whisper, and Leonid goes very, very still beside me.

"Yes," he breathes, his stare hardening.

Oh my God.

His hand slid up my cheek, his fingers tracing my jawline, urging me to face him.

"The plan was to kill you that night."

Fifty-Seven

Leonid

"The plan was to kill me." She says again, like she's only just beginning to believe it herself.

"I'm so ... fucking stupid." Clara muttered under her breath.

I can see it in the way her body trembles, her chest heaving as she tries—and fails—to push me away. Her fury burns bright, a wildfire consuming everything in its path, but underneath it, I see the cracks. The pain. The betrayal.

Blayt. I hate it.

I hate the way my name sounds on her lips when she spits it like a curse. I hate the tears glistening in her eyes, the ones she refuses to let fall. But most of all, I hate the truth that I can't protect her from —not this time.

I've broken bones, slit throats, and spilled blood without a second thought, but none of that prepared me for this. For her. For the way she's looking at me now, like I'm the reason her world is collapsing. Like I'm the enemy.

She doesn't realize how much it kills me to see her like this. She looks at me with those blue eyes, raw and wet with unshed tears, it's like standing in the middle of a fire. I know I'm the one who lit it, but I'd still burn to ashes if it meant saving her.

"Why?" she chokes out, "Why are you telling me this?" Her eyes prick with tears, but she link them back,

Because I love you, Clara Caldwell. I almost say. But I bite it back.

I hold her arms firmly, keeping her from pulling away. When she flinches, her body jerking under my grip, I ease my hands just enough to stop myself from bruising her. The tension between us is electric, her chest rising and falling unevenly against the stillness of the room.

She doesn't try to hide the flicker of pain in her expression, and it guts me in a way I don't expect. My thumb brushes over her skin without thinking, stopping near the edge of a fading mark from the attack that almost took her from me. I remember the blood, the limp weight of her in my arms, and the way I'd promised myself this would never happen again. But here I am, holding her while she looks at me like I'm the one who pulled the trigger.

"Because you deserve the truth," I say. watching her closely. "Even if it destroys you."

"Destroy me?"

Clara shifts, her body drawing closer to mine as she yanks away from my grip. The movement accentuates the contours of her breasts beneath the white fabric of her shirt, their tantalizing bounce sending a hot rush of lust surging to my cock.

For fuck's sake, Leonid.

Why do I have to be such a *blin*? One look at Clara's curves and my cock is harder than a frozen Kalashnikov.

"You think I'm not already destroyed? You think this doesn't—?" She stops, her gaze darting to the next room where Elijah sleeps.

She squeezes her eyes shut, a pained groan escaping her lips. I don't move, even as she shifts closer until her breasts press against my chest. Her breath comes in short bursts against my neck.

"All these years..." Tears fall as she grips my shirt. Her body shakes against, fists pressed weakly against my chest. I don't let her go. One hand stays firm on her waist, the other cups the back of her head.

Clara's head snaps up, her glare sharp enough to cut through steel. "You think telling me this fixes anything? It doesn't."

"It just proves I can't trust anyone—not Stephan, not Jake, and definitely not you."

She looks at me like I'm the enemy. Like I'm the one who betrayed her, broke her trust, shattered her world. And maybe I am. Maybe I deserve every bit of it. But there's no way I'm walking away now.

"I'm not your enemy, Clara," I say quietly. She doesn't hear me. She's in her head now.

"You think I can come back from this?"

I want to tell her yes. That she's stronger than she knows, that I'll make sure she gets through this no matter what it costs me. I hold her tighter as she presses her face into my neck.

"You will."

Her body stiffens, her anger flaring again. "How?" she demands, shoving against my chest. Her fists connect with me, but I don't move. Her strength is nothing compared to the fire raging in her, and I'll take whatever she needs to give. "How the hell am I supposed to do that, Leonid? Tell me!"

Her fists pound against me again, harder this time, but I don't let go. I let her rage, let her scream into my chest. "I will protect what's mine."

The words hang between us. Clara's body goes still against mine, but I feel the tension coiling in her muscles. When she lifts her head, her eyes are blazing.

"Yours?" She's still fighting me, but her body betrays her. Each push against my chest brings her closer, until I can feel her heart hammering against mine. Her scent—vanilla and gunpowder—fills my lungs. *Blyat*, even broken, she's dangerous.

"Yes, *Krasotka*. Mine." I lean forward, brushing my lips against her ear. Her pulse races under my fingers, fast and frantic, and I let myself revel in it for a moment. "You've always been mine."

Clara's eyes dart to my room, her resolve still strong. "You're delusional," she murmurs, her lips parting slightly as she glances at my mouth. Then, just as quickly, she looks away, turning her face to the side.

I catch her wrists in one hand, pulling her closer until she's flush against me. I crush my mouth to hers, swallowing her gasp.

Seizing the opportunity of her stillness, I take her mouth with mine, parting her lips with my tongue and devouring her like a wolf on the hunt. As Clara's senses return, she claws at my chest, her fingers digging into my shirt like talons. I claim her lips, my mouth moving over hers with a hunger that can't be sated.

Her tongue matches my hunger, its desperation stirring me into a frenzy. I pull Clara's body against mine, her soft breasts crushing against my chest. My hand tangles in her beautiful hair, tugging her head back as I move my mouth down her throat.

Her scent, rich and intoxicating, dances across my tongue as I taste her warm skin. She moans, and the vibrations reverberate through my lips, shooting sparks straight to my cock.

Without hesitation, I cup her breast beneath the fabric of her shirt. Clara's arms encircled my neck, a tacit invitation that only fuel my desire. My thumb glides over the swell of her breast, tracing the hard peak of her nipple. My cock strained against my pants, begging for the chance to bury itself deep inside her.

Blyat! My cock aches at the mere thought of what I want to do to her. I want to suckle her nipple, to make her come with my fingers. The need to tear her clothes off and fuck her here on the chair hits me like a sledgehammer. Hard. Fast. Make her remember who she belongs to.

I want to make her scream my name, to remind her exactly who she belongs to, but my mind catches on one detail.

*My kid—our son—*sleeping right next door. *Poshol na khuy.*

Govno. I uncoil my arm from around her waist, my fingers brushing the fabric of her shirt as I release her. The cold absence of her body stings, but I step back, forcing the space between us.

"*Krasotka...* we'll have to wait." The words scrape their way out, jagged and unwelcome, but I mean them. For now.

"Wait?" Clara stares at me, wide-eyed, her lips parted, red and swollen from my kiss. Her chest heaves with every breath, her shirt clinging to her skin, and the dim light from the lamp nearby paints her in chaos. – Wild hair. Flushed cheeks. Eyes burning with defiance, with confusion, with heat.

She looks like she's about to claw me apart or beg me for more. I can't decide which would be better.

"Yes, wait." I drag a hand over my face, willing myself to ignore the hard ache straining against my pants. "Elijah—" I stop, catching her gaze, her pupils blown wide like a rabbit caught in headlights. "*Our son.* He's sleeping next door."

I watch her face go white. Her eyes widen.

"*Our* son," I repeat. "He's sleeping. Next. Door."

Fifty-Eight

Leonid

She freezes. Lips press tight.

I wait for the fight. The denial. Instead, her hands drop from my shoulders. Trembling.

"Look at me," I say.

"Leonid..." Her voice cracks. She won't meet my eyes.

She's trying to escape, but I don't let her. I grip her chin, forcing her head up, "Look at me, *Krasotka.*"

She doesn't move. Doesn't breathe. When she meets my eyes, they're empty.

" ... I don't know what I'm supposed to do now." A whisper escapes. Her brows draw together as if she's bracing for impact, her lips parting just enough for a shallow, uneven breath.

"You don't have to know." I say. I pull her closer, closing the small space between us, my hand still holding her chin.

"That's over. Let me take care of everything."

Her breath catches.

I hold her face, her eyes on mine. "You and Elijah are staying. I'm not gonna let you go."

Her eyebrows furrow with frustration, but no words come out. My grip on her tightens as I make my intentions clear: "He's my son."

Her lips quiver, her eyes glassy, and I feel her body tense under my grip. She's trying to summon the fight I know she has in her, but it's buried too deep right now.

"What am I supposed to say to that?" she whispers, "What do you expect me to do?"

I tilt my head, keeping my gaze locked on hers. "Say what you want. But you already know you're not leaving." My thumb grazes her jaw, a small movement that's more instinct than thought.

"You've spent years trying to keep him from me, Clara. Now, you'll spend the rest of your life making sure that never happens again."

Clara narrows her eyes, studying me like she's trying to decide whether to fight or fold.

She doesn't look scared, which is annoying. She should be—she's backed into a corner—but instead, she looks like she's trying to figure out if I'm bluffing.

"You're an asshole."

"Yes," I reply, deadpan.

Her lip quirks. "A tyrant."

"Obviously." My thumb brushes the edge of her jaw. Her skin is soft, warm, despite how tense she is. "Anything else?"

"Yeah," she says, tilting her head slightly, just enough to make me wonder if she's going to slap me or kiss me. "You're also incredibly full of yourself."

"I'm Russian," I say, like it explains everything. It kind of does.

She snorts. Nothing ladylike about it. A second later, she curses under her breath, one hand pressing to her side as the laugh makes her ribcage ache.

"You know," she says, her lips curving in a way that's half smile, half sneer, "I don't even know who you are."

"You're like... I don't know. Like Cinderella, maybe?"

I blink at her. "*Cinderella?*"

She shrugs, her hand brushing her ribs as she shifts uncomfortably. "Yeah, except with fewer glass slippers and more... *surprises.*"

My brow creases. "What do you mean by Cinderella?"

"I mean, I didn't even know who you were back then. How was I supposed to tell you about...?"

Her words trail off. I brush hair from her face, fingers grazing her cheek. "I'm not Cinderella. I'm your Prince Nightmare. The one you can't escape."

Her eyes find mine. Half-smirk. "Right. The big bad wolf in a fancy suit."

"Exactly." My hand slides to her jaw. "Big house. Deadly charm. And instead of a glass slipper..." The playfulness dies in my throat. "... I'll promise to burn everything they built. Make sure they know who sent them to hell."

The first tear falls before she can stop it, streaking down her cheek. She flinches, reaching up to swipe it away, but I catch her wrist, holding her hand still.

"Don't." My lips find her tear before it falls. She goes still under my touch. I kiss the corner of each eye, taking my time, letting her feel how gentle I can be.

When I pull back, her lips part.

She wants to speak... but I do not let her.

My mouth finds hers again. This time I don't claim—I ask. My lips brush hers, light as a whisper. She stills, breath catching. When her fingers drift up to my hair, they don't grab or pull. They explore, threading through, learning the texture.

I trace her bottom lip with my tongue, memorizing her taste. Her pulse jumps under my thumbs as I cup her neck. She sighs into my mouth, and I swallow the sound, wanting to keep it. Her body melts into me. No space left for secrets.

Her tongue meets mine, and we forget about revenge. About dead brothers and family empires. About all the reasons this can't work. Right now, there's just the way she trembles when I stroke her spine. The soft sound she makes when the kiss deepens, her tongue brushing against mine in a slow, deliberate motion that stokes the fire already burning in my veins.

Our lips move in sync, soft and eager, but there's an edge of desperation in the way she grips my hair, the way she tilts her head to give me more access. My hand slides up her back, steadying her as I shift the angle, claiming her deeper, tasting her fully.

The chair creaks beneath us, the leather warm against my ass as I hold her closer, deeper.

Her breath hitches as I nip at her bottom lip, just enough to make her gasp before soothing it with another kiss. Her fingers tighten in my hair, pulling me closer like she can't get enough, and I know I can't either.

When I finally pull back, just enough to let us breathe, her eyes flutter open, dazed and half-lidded, her lips swollen and glistening. I press my forehead against hers, catching my breath as my thumb brushes the curve of her waist.

"We'll make them pay," I murmur against her lips, my voice steady, my hand sliding lower to rest on the small of her back. "You and I."

I can see the strain in her eyes, the exhaustion she's trying to hide, but also something else—acceptance.

"You're done sitting here," I say, wrapping one arm around her back and sliding the other under her legs. She winces as I move her, her body stiffening for a moment, but she doesn't protest when I lift her from the chair. Her arms loop around my neck instinctively, her head resting briefly against my shoulder as I carry her across the room.

The skyline glimmers through the floor-to-ceiling window, casting soft light onto the wide bed with its rumpled black sheets. The city is alive beyond the glass, the faint hum of traffic below barely audible against the stillness of the room.

I lower her to the bed, mindful of her ribs. Her hair spreads across the pillows. She glances at the window before finding my eyes again. Silent understanding passes between us.

I settle beside her, pull her close. Her head tucks against my shoulder.

Then a small voice breaks the quiet.

"Mommy?"

Clara's head snaps to the doorway. I follow her gaze.

Elijah stands there, clutching his Pokémon toy in one hand, his blanket draped over his arm. His free hand rubs sleep from his eyes. His hair sticks up wild, small frame swallowed by the doorway.

"Baby, go back to bed," Clara whispers.

Elijah shuffles forward, the blanket dragging on the floor behind him. Sleep-heavy steps bring him to the bed. His eyes find mine before he curls in the space between us, one soft, sleepy sigh.

Clara draws him close, hiding her wince. One hand strokes his hair, the other stays near mine. Her eyes meet mine over our sleeping son.

I ease back, let his foot rest against me. The quiet fills with something new. Something whole.

My family. Here. Mine.

And I'll kill anyone who tries to take this away.

Fifty-Nine

Clara

It's a good thing this dangerously gorgeous man is my son's father, because watching the two of them play Jenga like it's an Olympic sport is doing weird things to my heart. And my brain. And fine, my ovaries.

The tower wobbles again as Elijah tackles another block, his tongue still poking out in concentration.

"If you stare any harder, the blocks might catch fire," Leonid says, and I have to bite back a smile at how he's leaning forward, completely invested in a children's game.

"I'm using my super powers," Elijah informs him seriously. "Like in that movie where the guy moves stuff with his mind."

"Telekinesis," Leonid supplies, then adds with perfect deadpan, "Though I should warn you, in Russia, we consider that cheating."

"Everything's cheating in Russia," Elijah says, mimicking Leonid's accent with surprising accuracy. "In Russia, breathing is cheating."

I almost choke on my water. Leonid's eyes meet mine, dancing with suppressed laughter.

"Who taught you to be so cheeky, *malysh*?"

"Mommy says I came this way. Factory settings."

This time Leonid does laugh, the sound rich and unexpected. My stomach does a little flip that I firmly ignore.

I shift in the chair, the plush cushions of this absurdly expensive armchair doing nothing to make me less squirmy. The chair, like everything in this ridiculous penthouse, screams Leonid Kuznetsov: sleek, bold, and entirely too much for me. Beyond the massive windows, the skyline stretches into jagged peaks, the sun sinking low and casting the snow-covered Alps in strokes of gold and pink. The view looks like it belongs on a postcard—or in the kind of retreat you'd use to disappear after staging a whole damn funeral for a spy's benefit.

We're still here, in the Alpine Aiguille Retreat. Leonid made sure to pull out all the stops, enough theatrics to convince anyone watching that someone—*anyone*—had died. The bloodstains, the black body bag being loaded into the chopper. It was a perfect performance. And for now, it's working. No one has come knocking. Yet.

"You're up," Elijah says, watching Leonid like he's the coolest person alive. There's no "*Papa*" yet, no grand declarations—just this small boy who thinks Leonid is good at Jenga, and Leonid acting like this is the most important mission of his life.

We agreed to take this slow. No sudden revelations, no big speeches. Just time—time for Leonid to figure out how to be in Elijah's life and for me to figure out what this new reality means.

Elijah grins, clearly oblivious to the silent conversation happening above his head. "You have to be really careful, or it'll all fall. And if it falls, you lose."

Leonid arches a brow at him, then reaches for the tower with deliberate precision. His hand hovers for a moment before he pulls a block free with a smooth, calculated movement. The tower wobbles, but it doesn't fall.

"Like that?" he asks.

Elijah claps his hands together, his face lighting up. "Yeah! Like that! You're really good at this."

"Practice," Leonid says, setting the block aside. "And patience."

I lean back in the chair, trying not to let the knot in my chest tighten too much. It's only *been three days* since everything unraveled. Three days since I learned the truth about Jake, Stephan, and the life I thought I knew.

It should feel like chaos. It does feel like chaos.

I should still be furious. Hurt. Mad as hell.

And I am. Somewhere deep inside, there's a version of me with fists clenched, ready to kill. But then there's this version of me—the one sitting in this obnoxiously comfortable chair, watching my son laugh with his father like it's always been this way.

It's not the life I would've chosen. But somehow, it's the life I've landed in.

"Oh, no!" The tower sways precariously as Elijah giggles. His small hands steady it, and I watch Leonid's fingers twitch like he wants to help but is forcing himself to let Elijah handle it.

"Tell me more Russia stories," Elijah demands, successfully extracting his block. "Did you have a pet bear?"

"No bears," Leonid says. "But I did have a very fierce hamster named Boris."

The mental image of little Leonid with a hamster is almost too much. I press my lips together, but he catches my expression anyway.

"Boris was very intimidating," he insists with mock gravity. "All the other hamsters feared him." His voice softens, taking on a different tone. "But he was lonely, and angry."

Something in the way Leonid says it makes my chest tight. I can picture it so clearly – a little boy in a huge mansion, with nothing but a hamster for company. The same loneliness that sometimes creeps into Leonid's eyes when he thinks no one's watching.

Elijah's bottom lip trembles slightly, his whole face crumpling the way only a 4-year-old's can when confronted with sadness. "That's not good," he whispers, abandoning his careful Jenga stance to scoot closer to Leonid.

Leonid reaches out, brushing back the dark curls that have fallen across Elijah's forehead. His fingers linger for a moment, and something about the gentleness in that gesture – this dangerous man touching our son with such care – makes heat pool in my stomach. It doesn't help that he looks unfairly attractive playing father, his usual sharp edges softened by the afternoon light.

"No, it wasn't good," Leonid agrees, his thumb brushing one last curl into place. "But then something magical happened. Boris realized he didn't have to be lonely anymore."

"Why?" Elijah asks, his caramel brown eyes – *his eyes* - wide with wonder as he stares up at Leonid. The sight of them together like this, mirror images in everything but eye color, makes my heart do complicated gymnastics in my chest.

"Boris actually had a very interesting love story," Leonid continues, eyes twinkling like he is about to turn a rock to gold. I shift in my chair, trying to find a position that doesn't make my ribs scream. Three days isn't long enough to forget what bullets feel like, even if they missed their mark.

"Like a princess story?" Elijah leans in, completely forgetting about the Jenga tower.

"Better. Boris met a beautiful hamster named Natasha at the pet store next door. Every night, he would escape his cage just to go visit her."

I scoff out a laugh. *More like Boris kidnapped her.* But there's something oddly compelling about watching Leonid spin our story into a hamster fairy tale.

The sleek phone Leonid gave me yesterday morning – "For emergencies," he'd said, though we both know it's more about keeping me informed – vibrates against my leg. Another update from Mitch, the encrypted message making my throat tight: Dad's office has become a graveyard of vodka bottles, while Stephan plays the role of grieving friend perfectly. Poisoning my father's mind with stories about how the brutal Russian mob boss murdered his only daughter. The perfect narrative to keep his own hands clean.

Getting played by Stephan. Again.

I can almost see Mitch's jaw clenching behind those ever-present sunglasses as he maintains his post, pretending not to notice how Stephan's making himself indispensable to my father. "I'll find Elijah," Stephan had promised Dad, his voice thick with fake concern. "Whatever it takes."

He'll fucking pay for everything. I clench my jaw.

"Did Boris have super powers too?"

Elijah asks, and I force myself back to the present, where my son is practically vibrating with excitement over a fictional hamster's love life.

"Of course. All Russian hamsters do. But his greatest power was persistence." Leonid's eyes meet mine over Elijah's head, and something in his gaze tells me we're not just talking about hamsters anymore. "He never gave up, even when everyone said it was impossible."

"Then what happened?"

"Well, one day, Boris and Natasha had a baby hamster. They named him Boris Junior, and he was the bravest little hamster in all of Moscow."

My chest tightens as Leonid's voice softens, telling our son a story that feels too close to home. A story about family and persistence and impossible odds.

"Was he as brave as you?" Elijah asks, and I nearly knock over my water glass.

Leonid's answer is careful, measured. "I think he was braver. Because being brave isn't about not being scared. It's about doing the right thing even when you are scared."

Like trusting the man who turned your world upside down. Like believing his plans will keep your family safe. Like watching him with your son and letting your heart hope, just a little.

"Mommy?" Elijah's voice pulls me from my thoughts. "Are you okay? You look funny."

"I'm fine, baby." The lie comes easily after three days of practice. "Just thinking about how Boris Junior probably had your smile."

Leonid's eyes catch mine across the space between us, and something in that look steals my breath. It's not just heat or want or even tenderness – it's understanding, bone-deep and terrifying. In that moment, the truth hits me like a physical blow: I love him. The realization makes my hands shake, because loving Leonid Kuznetsov might be the most dangerous thing I've ever done.

He winks at Elijah, giving me a chance to remember how to breathe. "Boris Junior liked Jenga too," he says smoothly. "But he was terrible at it. Kept knocking the tower over with his tiny hamster paws."

"That's silly," Elijah giggles, reaching for another block. "Hamsters can't play Jenga."

"You'd be surprised what determined Russian hamsters can do," Leonid says, and this time I hold his gaze, letting myself believe in impossible things.

The Jenga tower collapses. Elijah's laughter fills the room as he and Leonid gather the scattered blocks.

Two knocks.

I sit up straight, my ribs protesting the sudden movement. Maksim steps in, his usual swagger nowhere to be seen.

"*Pakhan.*" He gives me a quick wave, like we're neighbors bumping into each other at the grocery store. "He's here."

Sixty

Leonid

The mirror catches my reflection as I enter Vic's private meeting room, and for a second, I think I'm seeing double. But no - the neatly tied bleached-white hair in the reflection belongs to my brother, who's sprawled in one of Vic's insanely expensive leather chairs like he owns the place.

Blyat. Typical.

The room reeks of Vic's flair for wealth—gold-leaf ceilings, intricate tapestries, and a chandelier that could bankrupt most people just by being near it. A marble fireplace anchors one wall, its pristine white surface glowing faintly from dying embers. The windows stretch from the floor to the ceiling, casting harsh light that fails to soften the tension crackling in the air.

My eyes don't leave Ludis. Behind him, his shadow of a bodyguard looms in silence, his massive frame out of place against Vic's refined surroundings. The man's shoulders seem too broad for his tailored suit, and his hands flex subtly, like a predator waiting for the signal to strike.

By the door, Maksim leans casually against the frame, his arms crossed and his hand grazing his holster. He's loose but ready, his sharp eyes flicking between Ludis and me. Across the room, Vic sits behind his oversized mahogany desk.

He seems, calm. But I know, he is calculating, likely running odds on whether this room will still have a roof by the end of the meeting.

"No smoking in my office," Vic says mildly, his manicured fingers drumming once against the mahogany. His blue-gray eyes track the smoke curling around the gilded ceiling. "My artisans don't appreciate having to restore restore three-hundred-year-oldgold leaf because someone can't step outside for their nicotine fix."

Ludis's left eye twitches, a muscle in his jaw flexing before his lips curl to a smirk. He grins around his cigarette and takes one last drag before stubbing it out in what looks like an antique crystal ashtray. His eyes sweep the room—taking in the gold-leaf moldings, the priceless artwork, the subtle displays of old-world wealth—before landing on Vic with newfound interest.

Ludis shifts in his seat, one boot coming to rest on the edge of the table, the polished surface catching the scuffed sole. He gestures lazily toward Vic with two fingers. "So this is the famous Victor Montclair. I was starting to think my brother had made you up. Another one of his... personal assets he doesn't like to share."

"Unfortunately for everyone," I say, lowering myself into the chair across from Ludis, "this isn't about business."

The Glock at my back presses against the leather—a cold reminder that some conversations end in blood. I notice how his jacket pulls slightly on the left side. Armed, then. Of course he is.

Vic clears his throat, those calculating eyes missing nothing. "It's nice to meet you, Ludis. I've heard," he adjusts his watch, a tell I've learned to read like a warning bell, "quite a lot about you."

Ludis laughs, but his fingers tighten slightly around the crystal tumbler. "All terrible things, I hope. Though I have to wonder," his eyes shoot toward mine, "what's so important it couldn't wait for our usual death threats over the phone."

"So, let's cut to it," I say, ignoring how my stomach churns at the mention of phone calls. Three days of revelations sit like acid in my throat. "What do you know about Aleksei Sokolov?"

Ludis barks out a laugh. "Your father's loyal dog? Please tell me this isn't about territory disputes. I thought we'd moved past—"

"*Our* father's loyal dog," I correct him. "The same one who arranged our mother's murder."

The bear-like man behind Ludis shifts his weight, but my brother's face remains a mask of cold amusement. Only the slight pause before he raises his glass betrays any reaction.

"Now that's creative." He takes a deliberate sip. "Did you come up with that before or after you found your instant family?"

My knuckles go white against the armrest. Vic's tablet sits between us on the mahogany desk like a loaded weapon.

"Play it," I tell Vic, not taking my eyes off my brother. Part of me wants to look away—to not watch his face when he hears our mother's death discussed like a business transaction. But I force myself to watch, to memorize every micro-expression that crosses his features.

"If this is another one of your—" Ludis starts, his words dying in his throat as Aleksei's voice booms through the room, cutting off his bullshit excuses.

"Six-month-old twins," the recording plays. "Should've been an easy job."

The crystal tumbler in Ludis's hand trembles for a fraction of a second before his fingers tighten, knuckles bleaching white against the cut glass. His jaw works silently, that perpetual smirk slipping just enough to show something raw underneath.

"Who would've thought Sofiya had it in her?" Aleksei's recorded voice continues. "Diving in front of those bullets, using her own body as a shield."

Ludis's throat bobs. Once. Twice. The bear-like man takes a half-step forward, but freezes when Ludis raises his hand.

"Both *brats* survived because of that stupid *suka*." Stephan's laughter crackles through the speaker, and I watch my brother's face shift from disbelief to something darker, more dangerous.

The crystal tumbler shakes in Ludis's grip before he slams it down. He leans back, breathing hard through his nose. Each movement calculated, like he's solving a math problem that ends in bloodshed.

The silver lighter clicks. He lights another cigarette while Aleksei's voice fills the room with its poison. Vic doesn't bitch about his precious ceiling this time. His jaw works silently as he watches my brother, his fingers frozen on that fancy fucking watch.

Ludis's eyes close as smoke escapes his lips. Another voice joins in—Stephan's smooth bullshit mixing with Aleksei's gravel.

My gut twists hearing it again. The way they laugh about our mother's death like they're discussing the fucking weather. Like she didn't die choking on her own blood, protecting the sons they tried to kill. I want to put bullets in both of them. Make them count every second she suffered.

"Love makes men weak. *Pizdets*." Aleksei's recorded laughter scrapes through the room. "The fool wouldn't listen to me after he became a father. *Blyat*. He turned into a pussy. But convincing him to separate the twins? 'For their safety,' I said. The grieving father, so desperate to protect his remaining family, he'd do anything—even tear it apart."

The recording clicks off. In the silence, Ludis takes another drag, slow and deliberate like a man choosing his last meal. The bear behind him flexes his fingers, reading the room's tension like a weather report before a storm.

"Cute story." Ludis's voice comes out hoarse. He crushes the half-smoked cigarette next to its dead brother. "Really tugs at the heartstrings. Must've taken forever to edit."

Blyat. Of course the *mudak* doesn't believe it. I lean forward, my palms resting on my thighs. "You think I'd make this shit up?"

"I think—" He mirrors my position, close enough that I can smell the bourbon and smoke on his breath, "—that you're running out of ways to keep me from what's mine. First the brotherhood bullshit, now this fairytale about Mama being some kind of hero?"

"It's not a fucking fairytale." My fingers itch for my Glock. "These men killed our mother. Used our father's grief to tear us apart. And now—"

"Now what?" His laugh comes out sharp as broken glass. "We hug it out? Cry about our sad childhood? Maybe start a support group for abandoned little boys?"

The bear shifts again. Maksim's hand drifts toward his holster.

"They're planning to kill my son." The words taste like battery acid. "Your nephew."

Something flickers across Ludis's face—too fast to read. He reaches for the crystal decanter, pouring another two fingers of bourbon like we're discussing the weather. "Not my problem."

Red bleeds into the edges of my vision. Three days of watching Elijah build Jenga towers flash through my mind. Three days of seeing our mother's eyes in his face.

"*Blayt.* You stupid fuck." I'm on my feet before I realize I'm moving. "They killed our mother. They're coming for my family. And you're

MYA GREY

sitting there like some brain-dead gopnik pretending none of it matters?"

His glass hits the desk with a crack. "What matters," he stands, "is that you're losing your grip. On the Bratva. On reality. First, you find some whore and her bastard—"

The Glock appears in my hand the same moment his weapon clears leather. Behind us, the bear's massive frame tenses like a spring about to snap.

"Don't," I snap; I tighten my grip on the gun. "Don't fucking test me."

Ludis's eyes glitter with something wild. "Truth hurts, brat?"

The air cracks with safeties clicking off. Vic rises from his desk, but neither of us gives a fuck.

"The truth?" I spit out a laugh that tastes like copper. "You want truth, *suka*? Every time you got your ass kicked in that Siberian shithole? Every time you went hungry?" My finger kisses the trigger. "That was them. Every *pizdets* second of your pathetic life was their fucking game."

"*Blyat*." But his voice breaks on the curse. His gun hand shakes before steadying. "You're just like him. Like our father. Think you can control everything, manipulate everyone—"

"Papa died thinking he saved us." My jaw clenches so hard something cracks.

"Died believing he kept us apart to protect us. And you know what the real fucking joke is?" I lean in, close enough to see the pores in his skin. "Those *suki* want us to tear each other apart. Been playing us like fucking chess pieces since before we could walk. Because the second one of us kills the other," I bare my teeth in something that's not a smile, "they'll put a bullet in the survivor's head, just like they tried to do thirty-eight years ago."

A muscle jumps in his jaw. "And you care so much about my safety now, brat?"

"I care about—"

A phone cuts through the tension. Not mine. Not Vic's.

Ludis's face drains of color as he yanks out his phone. His eyes scan the screen, and for the first time since I've known this coldhearted *suka*, I see real fear.

"*Yob tvoyu mat*," he whispers. "*Nyet, nyet, nyet...*"

The bear lurches forward. "Boss—"

"They have Marina." Ludis's voice sounds like he's choking on glass. "Those *grizniy suki* have my daughter."

My Glock dips. "Your what?"

"They broke into her house in the Garden District. She's only 12, she's—" he is talking to the bear now.

The Glock hits Vic's expensive floor with a clatter. His face twists into something I recognize—the same look I had three days ago when I realized they were coming for Elijah.

"Her mother died in childbirth." His voice breaks. "She's all I—" He swallows. "Marina's all I have."

Sixty-One

Clara

The water beats against the fancy marble tiles—because heaven forbid Leonid should have anything normal in this place. Steam wraps around me like an expensive blanket, making my hair stick to my neck as I lean against the wall for support. My ribs scream at me with every breath, reminding me why taking a shower shouldn't feel like an Olympic event. Leave it to me to make something as simple as getting clean turn into a full-body workout. At least the hot water should help, though right now, it's doing absolutely nothing for the knots in my muscles except making me feel very sore.

"Come on," I mutter under my breath, wincing as I try to shrug out of my cardigan. The cashmere clings to my damp skin, the stubborn fabric refusing to budge. Every movement sends jolts of pain through my ribcage, and I have to bite my lip to keep from cursing loudly enough to wake Elijah in the next room.

"You'd think I'm wrestling a bear," I huff, gripping the edge of the counter for stability.

Thud.

The bedroom door clicks shut.

My heart stops.

"No, no, no," I whisper, frantically trying to cover myself with the cardigan I just managed to remove. The bathroom door is still partially open because, apparently, I've lost all survival instincts along with my ability to dress myself.

Heavy footsteps approach. "Clara?"

Leonid's deep voice sends a shiver down my spine that has nothing to do with being half-naked.

"Don't come in!" I yelp, pressing myself against the marble counter. "I'm... indisposed!"

A pause. "Are you hurt?"

"Only my dignity." I clutch the cardigan tighter. "I'll be fine, just... go away?"

The footsteps come closer. "You're in pain. I heard you from the hallway."

"That's just my natural charm showing through." My voice comes out higher than intended. "Really, I'm—"

The door swings open, and there he is—towering, bare-chested, and entirely too composed for someone barging into a bathroom uninvited. He's wearing nothing but black sweatpants riding low on his hips, his chest bare and still glistening with sweat from whatever violence he's been practicing.

My gaze darts up, but the damage is done. Heat rushes to my cheeks.

"What are you—?" I clutch at the cardigan like it's my last line of defense, backing up against the counter. "I told you not to come in!"

His eyes flick to the cardigan, the bruises peeking out from the disheveled fabric, and then back to my face. There's no smirk, no quip—just that unnerving intensity that makes my breath hitch.

"Move over," he says simply, stepping inside like it's his bathroom and not the scene of my impending mortification.

I gape at him, words failing me as he moves closer, the heat of him cutting through the steam. "Leonid—"

"Relax." He reaches out, his fingers brushing mine as he takes hold of the stubborn cardigan. His movements are maddeningly gentle, and before I can protest, he's slipping it off my shoulder with an ease that makes me want to scream. "You're hurt. Stop being stubborn."

"I wasn't—" The lie dies on my lips as his hand lingers, tracing the edge of a bruise just below my ribs. His jaw tightens, and for a moment, the calm mask slips, revealing something darker.

"You shouldn't be doing this alone," he murmurs, his voice low but firm. His thumb brushes against my skin.

"I didn't want to wake Elijah," I manage. "I've been taking care of myself for a long time."

"Turn around," he says quietly.

"I'd rather not," I squeak, holding the cardigan like a shield.

"Clara." His voice softens, but carries that edge of command that makes my knees weak. "Let me help you."

"The last time you 'helped' me, I ended up—" I stop mid-sentence, a grunt of pain escaping as I move too quickly. His scent hits me then—gunpowder and cedarwood, with something raw and masculine underneath that makes my toes curl. The combination of hot steam and his presence is doing dangerous things to my common sense.

His lips twitch. "That was different."

"Was it?"

"Yes." He steps closer, and I can feel the heat radiating from his body. "That was for punishment. This is for care."

Something in his tone makes my heart flutter. I stay frozen as he gently takes the cardigan from my trembling fingers and sets it aside. His calloused hands hover over my shoulders, not quite touching.

"May I?"

The vulnerability in that question undoes me. I nod, not trusting my voice.

I sigh, letting my walls come down. The stubborn, independent part of me that always needs to be in control gives way to something softer, something that wants to trust in the tenderness of his touch. For once, I let myself be taken care of.

His fingers trace the edge of my bra strap with devastating gentleness. "Breathe, *solnishko.*"

I hadn't realized I was holding my breath. When I exhale, some of the tension leaves my body. His large hands grip my shoulders, turning me to face the mirror. The movement is gentle but deliberate, and my breath catches again at the sight of us reflected in the steamy glass—my small frame dwarfed by his towering presence behind me.

His hands move with practiced ease, unhooking the clasp I'd been fighting with.

"You've had practice with this," I murmur, trying to mask my nervousness with sarcasm.

Instead of smirking or making a suggestive comment, he simply says, "I've had practice taking care of wounds." His fingers ghost over a particularly dark bruise on my side. "And the people who matter to me."

The words hang in the steamy air between us, heavy with meaning. I meet his eyes in the mirror again, seeing past the dangerous exterior to something deeper, something that makes my chest tight in a way that has nothing to do with my injuries.

"Leonid..." My voice cracks on his name.

His hand splays across my lower back, steadying me. "Let me take care of you, Clara. Just for tonight."

I lean back against him, letting his warmth seep into my skin. But there's tension in his frame that wasn't there before, a rigidity to his shoulders that speaks of carefully controlled anger. Something's wrong. The tenderness in his touch doesn't match the storm I can see brewing behind his eyes.

"Who...?" I hesitate, then turn to face him fully. "Who's here?"

His jaw tightens, and for a moment, I think he won't answer. Then his fingers brush my cheek.

"Ludis."

"Ludis, your brother?"

"Yes. I thought he should know about the... truth." The defeat in his voice makes my chest ache.

"What's wrong?"

"He's angry. Full of hate. And now..." His voice catches. "His daughter Marina was taken."

"Daughter?" The word comes out as a whisper.

"Long story," he says, tension radiating through every line of his body.

I turn in his arms, ignoring the twinge in my ribs. My hands find his face, thumbs brushing along his jawline.

"Listen to me," I whisper, pressing a gentle kiss to the corner of his mouth. "He's your brother. Your blood. And trust me..." My voice catches as Jake's face flashes through my mind. "If I had a chance to see my brother again, even if he hated me, I'd move heaven and earth to make it right."

Something breaks in his expression. His mouth finds mine, tender at first, then hungry. His fingers find the drawstring of my silk pants, tugging until they pool at my feet.

His mouth hovers just above mine, his breath hot against my lips. "The things you do to me, *solnishko*," he growls, his voice rough with need. "Making me want to forget about everything except how perfect you feel in my arms."

I reach up to touch his face, but he catches my wrist, pressing a kiss to my palm that makes my knees weak. His other hand slides down my bare back, pulling me closer until there's nothing between us.

"Ludis can wait," he murmurs against my skin. "Right now, I need to show you exactly what you mean to me."

Sixty-Two

Clara

The last thing I register before his mouth claims mine is the dangerous gleam in his eyes - the look of a man who's about to make me forget my own name.

I gasp into his mouth, my breath quickening as his hands trail hungrily over my curves. My fingers find his abs, tracing them as his rock-hard cock strains against his sweatpants, begging for my touch. He reaches behind me, his arm a warm, possessive band around my waist, the door's lock clicking shut with a muted finality.

I tease his neck with my lips, my tongue tracing the rapid beat of his pulse.

"Clara," he rumbles, his voice a low, primal sound that sends a shiver of anticipation through me. His cock twitches in my grasp, straining against his pants. He pulls them off, revealing his length, full and hard, in my hand.

My fingers tangle in the soft curls at his base, his warm skin sending sparks of pleasure up my arm. I caress him slowly, my strokes teasing, my breath warm against his throbbing cock.

"Fuck, you're so wet, so ready for me." he grunts, his fingers sliding against my wetness, teasing my slick folds.

He circles my clit with a tenderness that makes my knees weak, my breath hitching as I gasp his name.

"Leonid," I moan, my hands gripping the counter for support. "Don't stop."

His fingers pick up speed, driving me wild, my body arching in a silent plea for more. I gasp and shudder.

His mouth claims mine, his kiss hungry and demanding, every touch a testament to his need. My body melts into his, every resistance fading as my core clenches around his fingers, each thrust driving me closer to the edge.

"Shh," he whispers against my skin, his finger fucking me deeper, his thumb finding my clit and circling in a relentless rhythm. "Don't want to wake the kid, *devochka*."

My orgasm crashes over me, a tidal wave of heat and pleasure, my walls clenching around his fingers as I shudder in his embrace. Pain and pleasure mingle as my teeth dig into his shoulder, my body straining to remain silent.

He spins me around, the mirror reflecting our tangled bodies, the steam of our passion clouding our vision. I catch a glimpse of him, his eyes dark and wild, his body tense with need. *God,* he looks ready to devour me, his eyes hot and hungry. I can practically feel the heat coming off him as he reaches for my hips with one hand, guiding me back towards him. With his other hand, he strokes his rock-hard cock, lining it up with my soaked entrance. As he gently pushes inside me, I moan softly, feeling every inch of him filling me up and stretching me out. He groans in response, enjoying the tightness and wetness of my body as he sinks deeper inside me.

My breath quickens as he slides deeper into me, my body arched back and quivering. The feel of him inside me is like a drug, addictive and heady, and I crave more. I push my hips back to meet his thrusts, feeling the veins of his cock pulse against my walls, his cockhead pressing against my sweet spot over and over.

"Fuck, Clara," he growls, the pace of his thrusts picking up as he buries himself to the hilt. The friction between us is electric, my body buzzing with pleasure as we move together.

Leonid's voice is gruff with desire, but his hands are gentle as they grip my hips.

"*Devochka* are you okay? This isn't hurting you?"

I press my lips together, nodding, and shaking my head wordlessly as he continues to move inside me. Every thrust is a careful symphony, his cock gliding against my slick walls with a delicious friction. It's almost like he's trying to protect me, to be as gentle as possible.

Every stroke of his cock sends a wave of pleasure and pain through my body, I try to stay quiet, biting my lip to stifle the moans that threaten to erupt from my throat.

In the mirror, Leonid watches me, his eyes filled with a mix of desire.

He groans, grinding his hips against mine as his hand slips between my thighs. His thumb circles my clit, teasing out another wave of pleasure. "Fuck, Clara. You're such a good girl, *devochka.*"

His breath is warm against my neck, his words making me throb around him. My body was on fire with every thrust, building towards an explosive climax. But I had to stay quiet, stifling my moans as I felt him fill me up and pulsate against my walls.

Leonid's thrusts grow faster, rougher, but he's controlling, his breaths become ragged, his grip on my hips tightening as he edges closer to his climax. I meet his intense gaze in the mirror, our eyes locked as we both approach climax.

"Yes...oh god..." I whisper, desperately trying to contain my moans and gasps, feeling my body begin to contract around him, he lets out a low, primal groan, his body shuddering as he explodes deep inside me.

"Feeling better?" I trace my finger along Leonid's jawline, feeling the slight tension there. He's been quiet since we got out of the shower, both of us wrapped in thick white robes, lying on his ridiculous bed that could fit half the Swiss guard.

Through the skylights, stars glitter against the backdrop of Alpine peaks. The dim bedside lamp casts shadows across his face, highlighting the sharp angles that somehow seem softer now.

He catches my hand, pressing a kiss to my palm. "Yes, *devushka*."

"Really? Because that vein in your forehead is doing the thing again." I prop myself up on one elbow, studying him. Water droplets still cling to his chest where the robe gapes open.

"The thing?"

"The 'I'm carrying the weight of the entire Russian underworld but pretending I'm fine' thing."

He snorts, but his fingers find my hip, thumb brushing over the spot where he knows my bruises are healing. "How are your ribs?"

"Deflecting much?" But I soften, seeing the genuine concern in his eyes. "They're okay. Better after the hot shower."

His hand slides up to my waist, steady and warm through the fluffy robe. "Good."

I chew my lip, gathering courage. "Can I ask you something?"

"Always."

"Why aren't you angry with me? About Elijah?" The question that's been burning inside me finally escapes. His chest rises and falls under my palm, and I feel the slight hitch in his breathing.

He says nothing for a few seconds. Beneath my palm, his chest rises and falls slowly, as if he's keeping something locked down. His muscles flex under my touch, then go still, like he's fighting for control.

I start to pull back, but his hand catches my chin, tilting my face up to his.

His eyes are impossible to ignore in the soft lamplight, their intensity unnerving and magnetic all at once. His irises shift slightly, back and forth like he's searching for something in me he doesn't want to admit. They're darker than Elijah's but also framed by lashes so absurdly long and perfect that it's downright unfair.

His thumb brushes my bottom lip, and I stop breathing altogether. For a second, I wonder what he's about to say—but instead, his other hand flicks my forehead.

"Hey!" I jerk back, scowling. "What was that for?"

His lips twitch. "For thinking too much." His voice drops lower, rougher. "Because you didn't know. And because you gave him everything I couldn't."

"But if I had—"

"Stop, *devushka*. You protected him. Kept him safe." His hand slides to cup my cheek, and this time, when his eyes meet mine, they're fierce with conviction. "Made him happy. You're a good mother, Clara."

His words sink into me, and something cracks. The weight I've been carrying, the constant need to prove I'm enough—it all hits at once. Not because I need his validation. But hearing it from him, from Elijah's father...

Tears slip down my cheeks before I can stop them.

Fuck.

"Are you okay, *devushka*?" His thumb catches a tear.

I flinch, the confession burning in my throat. "I..." The words feel like glass. "I almost aborted him when I found out I was pregnant."

His hand slides from my chin to cradle the back of my head, fingers threading through my hair. He stays quiet, waiting.

"Stephan, he..." More tears fall, like a dam breaking. Years of pain, betrayal, and guilt pouring out. "He even offered to take me to the clinic. Said it would be easier."

"I know, *devushka*." His fingers still in my hair. His other hand grips the edge of his robe, knuckles white. Surface-calm, but I feel the tension radiating through him, see the muscle jumping in his jaw.

A sob escapes me, but it burns into rage. Stephan. The man who killed Jake. Who manipulated my father. Who tried to—

Leonid's lips brush mine, barely a touch at first. Then his hand cups the back of my head, fingers tangling in my damp hair. He kisses my tears, one by one, working his way across my cheek until he reaches my mouth again. This time, when our lips meet, there's nothing gentle about it. His other arm wraps around my waist, pulling me closer until I'm pressed against the solid warmth of his chest.

He kisses me deep and thorough, like he's memorizing every detail, like he's trying to say everything he can't put into words. I feel it in how his breath catches when I kiss him back, in the way his hand tightens in my hair, in how he slows down just to press his lips to the corner of my mouth, gentle again.

When we break apart, he keeps me close, his forehead resting against mine. His thumb traces my bottom lip, and I feel the slight tremor in his touch.

"Clara Caldwell," he says, voice rough and low. "Let me take care of everything."

I pull back, narrowing my eyes. "Everything meaning what, exactly?"

"Meaning you stay here. Safe. With Elijah." His hand slides down to my neck, thumb tracing my pulse point.

"While you go after Stephan alone?" I push up on my elbows. "Like hell."

His hand drops from my neck. He sits up, shoulders rigid, staring out at the Swiss peaks through the skylight. "This isn't a negotiation."

"You're right. It's not." I meet his gaze, unflinching. "Because Jake was my brother. And I've been hunting his killer for fourteen years. You don't get to fucking bench me now."

Sixty-Three

Leonid

Two days later

P*izda, she is so fucking beautiful.*

The moment Clara steps into the room, she has the attention of every breathing person here—not that she notices, or maybe she does and just doesn't care. She stands there with her arms crossed, back straight, chin tipped up just enough to challenge the entire damn world. And me.

Mostly me.

"This is ridiculous!" she snaps, yanking off the stupid flight attendant cap and tossing it onto my desk. The thing bounces once before sliding off onto the floor, and I catch Maksim biting his lip to keep from laughing.

I don't answer right away. I'm too busy watching the way the navy-blue airline uniform hugs every inch of her, the skirt hitting just above her knees. It shouldn't work. It's borderline absurd. But Maksim, the prick, knew exactly what he was doing when he suggested it.

I lean back in my leather chair. My gaze catches the hem of her skirt, trails up to where her fingers grip the edge of my desk. When I reach her face, her eyes lock with mine. Her right eyebrow inches up. The corner of her mouth twitches.

Neither of us blinks.

The clock on my wall ticks. "You insisted on coming back with us," I remind her.

"And this—" she motions down at herself, the tight blue airline skirt clinging to her hips—"this is your idea of laying low? I look like a rejected extra from a B-rated spy movie."

Maksim snickers from his spot leaning against the wall, arms crossed casually over his chest. "You're welcome."

Her glare swings to me. Eyes blazing.

I can't help but grin. *Angry Clara looks damn fine.*

"You said you wanted a disguise. The uniform does the job. Nobody suspected a thing." I answer.

"*Nobody* suspected a thing because the fucking jet is yours, Leonid. So is the bloody private airport," Clara fires back, glaring at me.

Maksim shrugs, all nonchalance. "You'll never know—enemy eyes could be anywhere." He gestures vaguely around the room, as if Aleksei himself might pop out from behind the vault door.

Clara narrows her eyes. "You're impossible."

"No," Maksim says, his grin widening, "I'm thorough."

"Enough," I let out a heavy sigh, my breath exiting through pursed lips.

Mudak Maksim is enjoying this too much, and Clara's pacing like a caged tiger isn't helping my patience. "You made it back. That's what matters."

She stops mid-step, spinning to face me. "What's the plan?" she demands, cocking her hip as she folds her arms across her chest.

I exhale slowly, leaning back "The plan is for you to stay out of it."

She rolls my eyes, "Unless you plan to chain me up."

Maksim coughs, covering his mouth with his hand. His shoulders shake with barely-contained laughter as he moves toward the chair in front of my desk and drops into it.

I don't bother with a glare; he wouldn't take it seriously anyway. Instead, I focus on Clara. "Think about Elijah," I tell her, "He needs at least one parent alive."

She presses her lips into a hard line, her shoulders tensing. For a second, I think I've gotten through to her, but then she takes a step forward and waves me off like I've just suggested she sit down and knit. "Elijah's fine," she says, pacing now. "He's got Pam, he's practically a snow bunny already, and he made me promise to let him show me his ski tricks when we get back."

"Relax. We'll be fine. They'll be too busy looking the other way to notice."

Blyat. This woman could argue with a brick and still think she's winning.

I exhale sharply, dragging a hand down my face before glancing over at Maksim. He's leaning back in his chair, arms crossed, watching the exchange like it's the best entertainment he's had all week. His grin widens when our eyes meet, and he gives me a little shrug, like – *Pretty sure she's carrying your balls around like marbles.*

If I didn't need him alive, I'd shoot him.

My phone buzzes on the desk, breaking the tension. I glance at the screen—a message from Viktor. Another update about Elijah attempting the bunny slope. The boy's determination mirrors his mother's. *Stubbornness must be genetic.*

"*Moya upryamaya devochka,*" I mutter, my stubborn girl.

Maksim snorts. "You're getting soft, boss."

"Shut up before I skin you alive you, *mudak*," I snap in Russian.

Maksim raises his hands in mock surrender, but the grin stays firmly in place. "Relax, boss. Just saying. She's already proven herself."

Maksim unfolds himself from his chair, stretching. "I think we could all use a drink after that flight." He doesn't wait for my response, just heads to the cabinet where I keep the good whiskey.

Clara pushes back from the desk. "Why don't you trust me, Leonid?"

"Because—"

"You've got that look," Maksim cuts me off, walking back from my cabinet and completely ignoring my death glare. He sets three crystal tumblers on my desk, followed by my private reserve—the one I specifically told him to leave alone. His eyes fix on Clara. "The one that says you're about to do something stupid."

"No one asked for your opinion." Clara doesn't move from her spot at my desk, but her fingers tighten on the wood edge.

The right corner of his mouth twitches up, just enough.

Something clicks. Twelve years of watching this bastard plan hits means I know exactly what that twitch means.

"You should drink," he says, pouring three fingers in each glass. He slides one toward Clara first. "Long flight, longer night ahead." He downs his own in one go, then refills it immediately.

Clara ignores her glass, laser-focused on me.

"Tell me the plan."

Maksim sets the bottle directly in front of her. The crystal stopper catches the light, throwing fractals across my desk. His next words make my jaw clench. "Come on, boss. This isn't her first mission. She'll be fine."

"Shut the fuck, Maksim," I bark.

Clara tilts her face toward Maksim, then back to me, her arms folded tight across her chest. She's waiting, daring me to deny her.

Maksim tips his glass back, draining it in one go. He makes a show of savoring it, dragging his tongue across his teeth. "Stephan won't know what hit him. In, out, clean job." The glass hits my desk with a sharp click. "*Bozhe moy,* that's smooth. Almost worth getting shot for."

Clara finally reaches for the glass, her fingers wrapping around it. Her eyes stay on me as she brings it to her lips and takes a sip. Maksim's grin widens slightly, but something about it sets my teeth on edge.

She puts the glass back on the desk and opens her mouth to speak, but her eyelids flutter once, then twice. Her hand drifts to the edge of the desk, gripping it tightly for balance as her legs start to give.

"Maksim," I growl, standing so fast my chair scrapes against the floor.

Clara sways, her body going limp before I catch her. Her breathing is steady, her face soft, almost peaceful.

"She'll thank me later," Maksim says, pouring himself another drink, completely unbothered.

"*Blyat*, Maksim," I hiss, my voice low and dangerous. "If this back-fires, you're a dead man."

He shrugs, lifting his glass in a mock toast. "You can't kill me if it works."

Sixty-Four

Leonid

Two hours later

The first raindrops hit my windshield as the convoy rolls to a stop. Behind us, three identical black SUVs form a barrier between my car and the treeline. Only a fool wouldn't have men positioned among those ancient oaks.

"Twenty of ours spread through the trees," Maksim murmurs from the driver's seat, his fingers tapping against the steering wheel. "Another fifteen by the mausoleums. We have better angles if this goes south."

I adjust my cufflinks—gold. The weight feels right. "And the ground team?"

"Twenty-eight scattered among the mourners." His lips quirk. "Though I doubt anyone's actually mourning. Half these people probably wanted to kill her themselves."

My laugh comes out harder than intended. Clara would appreciate that—knowing her enemies showed up to weep crocodile tears over her empty casket.

"*Suka*'s getting desperate." I check my Glock, the familiar weight settling something in my chest. "All his failed attempts to get to her, and he thinks an empty box will fix his fuck up? Amateur."

Maksim's reflection grins in the rearview. "Maybe he's hoping the audience makes you behave."

"When have I ever?" The leather seat creaks as I lean forward. "How many of his men showed up for the circus?"

"Twelve by the gate. Another eight trying to blend in with the civilians." He drums his fingers on the wheel. "Want us to thin the crowd a bit? Dmitry's boys are getting bored."

The memory of Clara's fury before she collapsed makes my jaw clench. Maksim's little improvisation with the sedative... Part of me wants to put a bullet in him for that stunt. But another part—the part that's seen too many coffins that weren't empty—whispers maybe he had the right idea. Chaining her up starts to sound reasonable when the alternative is watching Stephan put her in the ground for real.

"She's going to kill us both when she wakes up," Maksim says, like he's commenting on the weather. "Probably start with your balls. I'm guessing she'll save me for dessert."

I glance at him, debating whether to dignify that with a response. The memory of Clara's fury—those blue eyes cutting like a storm before she collapsed—flares to life. My jaw tightens, and I look back out the window. The rain streaks the glass, softening the shapes of the mourners gathered ahead.

"She's not risking her life here," I say finally, the words low and even. "That's what matters."

Maksim snorts. "Touching. Almost romantic. Should I get you flowers to hand her when she wakes up? Maybe a card that says, 'Sorry I didn't stop the sedative.'"

The urge to break his nose flashes hot, but I push it down. The now is what matters. The rain falls heavier, turning the cemetery into a tableau of umbrellas and wet grass. A flash of lightning forks across the horizon, pulling my attention back to the task at hand.

"No civilian casualties," I tell Maksim, tucking the phone away. "But his security? Consider it a graduation present for the new recruits."

Maksim's grin turns feral. "Been a while since The Raven had a proper bloodbath. The boys will be thrilled."

Through the tinted windows, I watch the cemetery sprawl out like a chessboard. Ancient oaks loom over marble headstones, their shadows stretching long across the wet grass. Historic mausoleums dot the grounds, their weathered stone offering perfect cover for anyone planning to start a war at a funeral. The mourners cluster near a fresh grave, black umbrellas blooming like deadly flowers. At the center, a mahogany casket draped in white lilies sits ready for its performance.

"Stephan really went all out," Maksim says, nodding toward the string quartet huddled under a nearby tent. "The flowers alone must have cost—"

"Lilies," I cut him off. "I'm sure that's not her favorite." I study the flowers draped across the casket, wondering what she actually prefers. Roses would be too obvious for someone like Clara. Maybe something with thorns, or those blue flowers that can kill if you're not careful. The kind of beauty that demands respect.

The door handle digs into my palm as I step out into the rain. Water beads on my suit jacket—Italian wool, chosen for the way it conceals my shoulder holster. Clara would probably have an opinion about it. She seems to have opinions about everything else.

The crowd parts as I approach, whispers following in my wake. Some clutch their purses closer. Others reach for concealed weapons.

A woman in Chanel sobs into a handkerchief—probably one of Stephan's plants. The performance would be amusing if it didn't make my trigger finger itch.

Maksim gives a signal to Dmitry, who's leading the the rest of the men; they fan out, slipping into the crowd, behind trees. Weapons visible.

I fix my eyes on Stephan. He's still playing his part by the casket, handkerchief dabbing at dry eyes. The sight of him standing near Clara's portrait makes me see red.

My shoes sink slightly in the wet grass with each step. The distance between us shrinks—fifteen feet, ten, five.

Close enough now to see the slight tremor in his hand as he adjusts his tie.

Close enough to notice how his security detail tenses, hands hovering near concealed weapons.

Maksim is at my side, black umbrella tilted to shield us both, though the cold drizzle pricks my face anyway.

But the *ublyudok* doesn't see me yet; he's too busy holding court, shaking hands and murmuring platitudes like he's a goddamn politician.

I recognize every face he greets—casino owners who launder our competition's money, dock workers who conveniently forget to check certain containers, cops who know when to look the other way. All here to see which way the power will shift. A funeral's just another networking event when you're swimming with sharks.

Maksim steps closer. "Half of these people are his," he mutters. His eyes scan the crowd, cataloging faces. "The other half are here for the free wine."

A smirk pulls at the corner of my mouth, brief and humorless. The wind shifts, carrying the scent of rain-soaked earth and cut flowers. The priest drones on about eternal rest.

But the whispers around the crowd swell, a ripple of unease spreading through the air. I step forward, letting my men fan out subtly behind me. Maksim's hand signals to Dmitry's crew near the mausoleums, their presence blending into the shadows but unmistakable to anyone paying attention.

Stephan's gaze finally lands on me. His eyes narrow, the faintest flicker of recognition sparking there as the pieces click into place. His handkerchief freezes mid-motion, no longer dabbing at eyes that were never wet. The silence stretches a second too long. He spots Maksim next, and then Dmitry's men stationed among the tombstones. The truth hits him like a hammer.

The game has shifted.

With a steady hand, he folds the handkerchief neatly and slips it into the inside pocket of his jacket.

As his hand lingers, his fingers graze the cool steel of the gun hidden beneath the fabric. A fleeting touch, more instinct than necessity, but enough to ground him. He smooths the lapel of his jacket, exhaling quietly before clearing his throat,

"I didn't expect to see you here." He clear his throat, "*Leonid Kuznetsov.*"

"Of course you didn't." My lips twitch.

"Why would I miss the chance to pay my respects?"

His jaw shifts, a faint muscle jumping as he keeps his composure. He lets his gaze flick over my men, then back to me, his eyes narrowing. "Come to disrupt a funeral?" His voice dips lower, "Even for the Kuznetsov Bratva, this is a particularly tasteless stunt."

I stop beside Clara's portrait. The rain beads on the glass, distorting her smile.

"Tasteless?" I glance at him, my tone as casual as if we were discussing the weather. "You'd know all about that, wouldn't you, Stephan?"

Stephan doesn't move back. Instead, he straightens, his posture tightening as two of his men edge closer.

The rain picks up, drumming against the umbrellas, soaking into leather and fabric alike. I take another step toward the casket, narrowing the distance between us. Up close, I see how Stephan's performance works—the controlled presence, the way he plays the role of protector so convincingly. It's the same act that let him manipulate Clara for years, wrapping her in a web of lies while pretending to be the steady hand she needed.

Suka blyad. He's good, I'll give him that.

"Bold of you to host," I say, stepping closer, my hands sliding casually into my pockets. The rain patters against my shoulders, soaking through the wool of my jacket, but I don't move to adjust it. I hold his gaze instead, watching the flicker of calculation cross his face as he braces himself for whatever comes next.

"Considering it's your fault she almost ended up in one for real."

He's catching up.

I smirk. "I'm here to make sure it's you we bury today."

He recovers quickly, his head tilting just slightly, a subtle signal. His eyes flick to the left, then back to me. A message. An order.

I glance at the edges of the crowd as some of the mourners begin to peel away, their murmurs rising above the patter of rain. They've seen enough. They know when to clear out before blood spills. I let them leave. The fewer distractions, the better.

Stephan clears his throat, his hands brushing over his lapels with exaggerated calm, like he's already moved on. But I see the tension in his jaw, the barely-there tremor in his fingers. He's rattled, even if he's too arrogant to show it outright.

"You think you're clever?" he finally says, his voice dropping low, almost a growl. "Playing your little games while—"

The movement behind Maksim catches my eye. One of Stephan's men, thinking he's subtle.

I don't answer Stephan. Couldn't be bothered. Words won't end this.

My Glock clears leather in a single motion. The shot cracks the air before his man has time to react. The bullet tears through his throat, and he collapses, gurgling, blood spilling onto the wet grass. The crowd freezes for a beat, then erupts into mayhem—screams, umbrellas dropping, people scrambling for cover.

Time to shut this bastard down.

I swing my aim back to Stephan, but he's already moving. His hand dives into his jacket, pulling out a sleek pistol. His men surge forward to shield him, but they're too late. My reflexes take over as I pivot to the side, avoiding his first shot by inches. The crack of his gunfire echoes across the cemetery, shattering a marble angel near my shoulder.

My second shot finds him just above the knee, and he drops with a guttural curse, one hand gripping the slick, rain-soaked headstone for balance. Blood pours from the wound, painting the stone in violent streaks. He looks up at me, raw fury twisting his face.

"Fucking shoot them!" he bellows, his voice hoarse with pain. His men respond instantly, drawing weapons and firing as Maksim's voice cuts through the chaos.

"Get down!" Maksim barks, his Glock already spitting bullets. His grin is feral, adrenaline-fueled, as he ducks behind a tombstone and returns fire. Dmitry's men descend from the treeline, their movements calculated and precise, tearing through Stephan's security with ruthless efficiency.

Bullets ricochet off the statues and mausoleums, the cemetery erupting into a battlefield. I crouch behind the shattered angel, my breath steady as I reload. Rain mixes with the acrid tang of gunpowder, and I hear the distant bark of Dmitry's orders over the bedlam.

Stephan drags himself up, his face pale but his movements frantic. His eyes dart between me and his men, calculating his odds. *Coward.* His bloody hand catches the collar of one of his men, yanking him into position. The shield flails, panic etched across his face as Stephan shoves him forward to block my line of sight.

"Really?" I mutter, rising from cover and firing again. The shield jerks violently as the bullet rips through his side, dropping him instantly. Stephan stumbles toward a waiting SUV, his remaining security closing ranks around him.

The tires screech as they pull him into the car, the vehicle lurching through the mud and scattering mourners in its wake.

Maksim appears at my side, his Glock still raised, his breathing measured despite the carnage around us. "Want me to chase him down?"

I lower my weapon, watching the taillights fade into the distance. "No," I say, Ludis has got this."

Sixty-Five

Clara

*S*on of a goddamn motherfucking cocksucking piece of shit! A string of curses forms in my head before my eyes even open.

My skull feels like someone hammered nails into it and left them there to rattle around for fun. My mouth tastes like I licked the inside of a vodka bottle—because of course Maksim couldn't just let me have a normal fucking day without drugging me like I'm some unruly pet.

The lavender-woodsy scent hits next, wrapping around me like a smug reminder of where I am. *Leonid's house.* The stupid spa-like blend he probably thinks is calming only pisses me off more. My fingers twitch against the silky sheets, my nails curling into them as my brain catches up to the last thing I remember: the tight airline uniform, Maksim's stupid smirk, and that drink—

That fucking drink.

I swear, when I see him again, I'll cut his balls off with a butter knife. Slowly.

I crack my eyes open, the dim light from the bedside lamp sharpening the edges of the room I've come to recognize. Cream-colored walls, flawless hardwood floors, designer everything. Of course, there's a glass of water on the nightstand—like that'll erase what they did. Next to it, a folded note catches my eye.

I grab it, unfolding the paper with a flick of my wrist, already bracing myself for the bullshit.

"Be a good girl. It's for your own good."

My blood pressure spikes so hard I think I see stars.

"Good girl?" I hiss, crumpling the note into a ball. "What a mother-humping, ball-slapping, dick-toothed clusterfuck."

The uniform clings to me like a second skin, making every movement a reminder of Maksim's little plan. I shove the sheet off, sit up, and chug the water in one go, if only to clear the acid bubbling up my throat.

The water helps, but my throat still feels like I swallowed sand. I snatch my phone. 3:47 AM. Six missed calls from Pam about Elijah's skiing adventures and one text with a video I'll watch when the screen stops trying to stab my retinas.

I hit Leonid's number and bring it to my ear. The line rings once. Twice. Then it goes straight to voicemail.

I grind my teeth and call again. Same thing.

"Coward," I mutter, my thumb already hovering over the voicemail button. Fine. If he won't answer, he'll hear me, anyway.

"Listen here, you arrogant bastard," I snarl after the beep. "When I get my hands on you—and I will—I'm going to take that fancy watch of yours and shove it so far up your ass, you'll be telling time with your teeth. And Maksim?" I laugh. "Hope he's written his will. Actually, no. I hope he hasn't. I want his koi fish to inherit everything just to spite him after I'm done."

I hang up and toss the phone onto the bed—or I try to. It bounces once, then lands on the edge, wobbling precariously before settling, mocking me. My anger flares hotter. My fingers twitch.

I grab the phone again, hitting Leonid's number with a little too much force. The rings stretch out, dragging my patience until it finally dumps me into voicemail again.

When the tone beeps, I tighten my grip on the phone, letting the words fall into the silence like a challenge.

"Leonid Kuznetsov, I swear to God, if you don't pick up this phone, I will personally find you and make you regret every decision you've ever made. Drugging me? Keeping me out of this? Who the fuck do you think you are? You'd better pray Maksim is faster than me because when I'm done with him, you're next. And that *note*—'Be a good girl'? What am I, a dog? Watch your back, Leonid. That's all I'm saying."

I end the call with a jab at the screen and fling the phone onto the bed. *Fuck.* This time, it bounces once, twice, then skitters off the edge, landing with a sharp thud on the polished hardwood floor. It slides toward the door just as it swings open.

Kayla steps over it without missing a beat, balancing a silver tray that smells like heaven. The faint clink of a glass against the plate breaks the tense silence as she nudges the door closed with her foot. Her sharp, knowing eyes take in the scene—me, still in the ridiculous uniform, standing by the bed with my hands clenched like I'm ready to strangle someone.

"*Señorita* Clara." She lowers the tray onto the small table by the window. The faintest twitch pulls at the corners of her mouth before she schools her expression. "You missed dinner."

"Kayla," I say, tugging at the hem of the skirt where it's climbed halfway up my thigh. The damn thing feels like it's welded to my skin. "You didn't have to bring me anything." I glance at the clock and sigh. "It's late. You should get some rest."

Kayla doesn't so much as flinch at the suggestion. Instead, she shakes her head with a knowing smile, her hands smoothing her apron like it's a reflex.

"Late? *Señorita*, this is nothing." Her tone is calm, almost amused. "I've worked for *Señor* Leonid long enough to know what real late looks like."

She pauses, giving me a pointed once-over that lands squarely on the ridiculous uniform. "And I've definitely seen worse."

I huff a small laugh despite myself, gesturing down at the uniform. "You mean worse than this? Hard to believe."

Kayla steps closer, her smile faint but genuine. "This?" She raises an eyebrow and waves at the tight blue fabric. "This is... memorable. But I've seen *Señor* Maksim attempt to cook. That was worse."

I snort, the sound unexpected even to me. "I'll bet. Let me guess—he thinks vodka's a seasoning?"

Her shoulders shake with quiet laughter as she moves behind me. "Among other things. Now, hold still, please."

"Wait—" I start, but Kayla's already reaching for the zipper, and before I can protest further, the uniform loosens around me. The sudden relief makes me sigh.

"This is too tight," she mutters, shaking her head like the fabric personally offended her.

"I know," I say through clenched teeth.

Kayla's eyes crinkle at the edges, but she doesn't comment. Instead, she steps back and gestures toward the mirror. "There. Better, no?"

I glance at my reflection and groan. My hair's a mess—half falling loose, half plastered to my face. My makeup's a smudged disaster, and I look like I've gone three rounds with a wind tunnel.

"Fantastic," I mutter.

Kayla doesn't react, just pats my arm lightly. "Shower, *Señorita*. You'll feel better."

"Is Leonid back yet?" I ask, more out of habit than hope.

Kayla shakes her head, turning toward the wardrobe to pull out something far less constricting. "No, *Señorita*. But he left instructions. Shower. Eat." She glances at me with a sly look. "He said you'd argue."

"Did he now?" I mutter, crossing my arms.

Kayla steps closer, gently but firmly guiding me toward the bathroom. "And *Señor* Dmitry is waiting in the car."

I pause mid-step, narrowing my eyes. "In the car? At this hour?"

Kayla doesn't look at me, instead smoothing invisible wrinkles in the plush robe she's hung on the door. "*Señor*Leonid said you're to join them."

"To join them for what?"

Her movements still for the briefest moment before she turns back to me, her face calm but unreadable. "For the farewell."

"Farewell?" The word sticks in my throat, my mind racing.

Sixty-Six

Leonid

Blood drips steadily against concrete, each drop echoing in the basement's silence. Stephan hangs upside down, zip ties cutting into his ankles. His designer suit jacket lies shredded on the floor, soaking up the growing puddle beneath him.

Dim light flickers from a single bare bulb overhead, casting their twisted shadows against the cold, damp walls. The bricks here are old, stained with stories I don't need to hear to know they ended badly. Ludis keeps his torture room meticulously efficient. He's a madman, but his methods are disturbingly effective—and today, they're mine to use.

Aleksei whimpers from the metal chair to my left. Most of his nails are gone, leaving raw, mangled stubs. His left ear dangles by a thread of cartilage, the rest somewhere on the floor behind me.

Ludis stands by the workbench, wiping his blade with slow, practiced strokes. The steel gleams under the harsh light as he inspects the edge.

"Leonid..." Aleksei croaks, his voice cracking like brittle glass. "Please..."

I crouch, eye-level with him now. The desperation in his eyes flickers when I get close.

Aleksei's remaining fingers scrabble against the chair's arms. "We can fix this. I can—"

"Can what?" I lean close enough to smell his fear. "Bring our mother back?"

Aleksei's eyes widen, tears streaming down his face as his nose runs uncontrollably. His mangled hands tremble, blood dripping onto the floor. I lift his chin with two fingers, forcing him to meet my eyes. "My father trusted you like a brother."

For a moment, there's silence, broken only by Aleksei's ragged breathing.

And with that, I slam his head back against the chair. Hard. The sickening crack echoes in the room, and Aleksei slumps, barely conscious.

I straighten and turn to Ludis. My twin. My blood. Years of hatred simmer beneath the surface, fed by lies and manipulation. I've imagined this confrontation a thousand times, but now that we're here, the bitterness feels insurmountable.

I glance at Aleksei's limp form, then back to Ludis. "He's all yours."

"Twelve years." Ludis's voice comes out flat. Dead. "Twelve years I kept her safe, hidden." His fingers flex around the pliers. "And you thought what? That I wouldn't tear the world apart to find her?"

Aleksei pisses himself. The stench mingles with his blood and fear.

"Please," he sobs, "I didn't know. Stephan said—"

"This is your fault, you sniveling little coward," Stephan growls, his words slurring slightly from the swelling in his jaw.

Aleksei shakes his head frantically, tears mixing with the blood streaking his face. "I didn't—I didn't plan anything! I swear! Leonid, please..." His voice cracks as he looks at me, his swollen eyes pleading. "You know me! You—"

I crouch in front of him, close enough that he can see the disdain on my face. "I knew you, Aleksei. And then you sold me out."

His mouth opens, but no sound comes. He knows there's no convincing me, no explanation that will stop what's coming. But he tries, anyway.

"Leonid, please! I—I didn't mean for it to go this far! Stephan... Stephan made me do it! He planned everything!"

"Shut the fuck up, you spineless cunt!" Stephan thrashes against his restraints, face contorting. "This is your fault. You're fucking useless!"

A faint smirk tugs at the corner of my lips as I stand up, ignoring Aleksei entirely, and walk toward Stephan.

"You almost had us fooled." I circle Stephan slowly, letting my boots click against the concrete.

Stephan spits blood, missing my shoes by inches. His face has purpled from hanging, but his eyes still burn. "Fuck you, Kuznetsov."

"The thing is—" I pause behind Stephan, my eyes tracing the crude state flag tattooed across his shoulder blades. My fists tighten, but I keep my voice even. "Your plan had flair. Kill Jake Caldwell, pin it on me. Brilliant, really—keep the Kuznetsovs tangled in bullshit rumors, then send Clara after me, hoping we'd tear each other apart."

I flex my jaw, the muscle twitching as I drag in a breath sharp enough to cut. The urge to crush his throat in my bare hands burns like fire, every muscle in my body coiled to strike. My fingers curl, nails digging into my palms until they threaten to draw blood. I yank back my coat sleeve with a jerk, baring my wrist like it's the prelude to an execution.

"But instead, here you are," I snarl.

"I'm sick of listening to your sorry ass blabber on like some brain-dead dipshit with a cocksucking mouth. Just do it, you spineless fuck-knuckle." Stephan's spit splatters his own face, pooling at his temple as he dangles helplessly.

Ludis moves faster than the blood dripping from the ceiling. His blade flashes silver under the fluorescent lights as he seizes Stephan's face with one hand.

"*Ty dolbanyy ublyudok.* You fucking bastard." The knife traces a line down Stephan's chest, leaving crimson beads in its wake. "Still running that mouth?"

"AHHHHHHH!!" Stephan's scream tears through the air, raw and primal, like the agonized wail of a dying animal. Aleksei's sobs escalate as the blade plunges between Stephan's ribs. Not deep enough to kill, just enough to make him dance. Stephan's body jerks against the restraints, muscles spasming as Ludis twists the knife.

"Remember what you said about our mother?" Steel parts flesh with surgical precision. Blood mists across Ludis's face as he works. "How she was just some stupid *suka*?" Another cut, deeper this time. "Dying to protect her worthless sons?"

"Ludis." My hand finds his shoulder. Not to comfort—to control. Stephan's wheezing breaths fill the silence between heartbeats. "Not yet." I lean closer, letting Stephan see the promise in my eyes. "Death's too easy for what they've done."

The blade stops just below Stephan's heart. "Thirty-eight years." Ludis leans in close enough for Stephan to see his own reflection in dead eyes. "That's how long you and this piece of shit played us. Used her death like it was nothing."

His knife traces patterns in exposed muscle.

"What's wrong? No more clever words?" Ludis's knife finds another spot, digging deeper. "Maybe I should give you matching ears, *da*?"

"Fuck you, cunt," Stephan hisses through blood-stained teeth. His body swings like a grotesque pendulum from the force of his struggles, zip ties cutting deeper into his ankles. Blood runs down his face, drips from his hair, pools beneath him in an ever-widening circle.

His next insult drowns in a gurgle as the movement sends fresh waves of agony through his mutilated chest. The fluorescent lights cast shadows across the mess Ludis has made of him—strips of flesh hanging loose, crimson muscle exposed beneath. Still, his eyes burn with hatred, even as his face purples from being upside down too long.

"Tsk, tsk, tsk, tsk, tsk." Maksim clicks his tongue and leans back against the wall, arms folded. "Patience, Stephan. Not everyone's as eager to meet their end as you are." His eyes flick to the hallway as a faint thud of boots echoes closer.

Three sharp knocks echo through the basement. Boris's massive frame fills the doorway, nodding once before stepping aside. The hinges creak, cold air rushing in.

"What... the... fuck... is this?"

Clara strides in wearing one of my old black Henley shirts, stolen from my closet—sleeves pushed up to her elbows, too big on her frame. She's paired it with the first things she probably found: dark jeans and trainers. Her hair's yanked back in a hasty braid, loose strands framing a face that promises murder.

"Stephan..." she whispers.

Clara's shoes leave wet marks on the concrete as she takes in the scene. Her throat works, swallowing hard. The sight of Stephan—her second father, her protector—hanging like slaughtered meat hits her harder than she expected. I see it in the way her fingers curl against her thighs, in how her chest barely moves with each breath.

My muscles coil, ready to move between them, but Clara needs this. Needs to see the monster beneath Stephan's mask. Still, my hand twitches toward my holster when she steps closer to him.

"Finally." Maksim pushes off the wall. "We've been waiting."

Metal wheels creak behind her. Mitch appears, hulking and silent, his large hands gripping the back of Maxwell Caldwell's wheelchair. The old man's hollow eyes widen, taking in the carnage. His hands grip the armrests so tightly that his knuckles blanch, trembling as sobriety collides head-on with the brutal reality in front of him.

He looks like a man forced to confront every ghost he'd spent years drowning in a bottle to forget.

Stephan's thrashing stops mid-swing. "Cla-Clara?" Blood sprays from his lips, painting his chin crimson. His next words drown in wet coughing that splatters red across the floor. More seeps through his shredded shirt where Ludis carved his message.

"Well," Maksim drawls, drawing his weapon. "Looks like the rest of the family's here."

Sixty-Seven

Clara

The basement air hits my lungs like ice. Blood and metal and darkness.

The Henley I'm wearing—Leonid's scent still clinging to the fabric—feels too big, too warm. Everything narrows to Stephan hanging there, pieces of him dripping onto concrete.

Sixteen years old. His office. "You're family." The knife he gave me that birthday digs into my hip, its pearl handle cold against my skin. The same hands that taught me to drive, that braided my hair, now twist uselessly above zip ties.

My feet move without permission. One step. Another. Each splash of my shoes through puddles of his blood echoes wrong.

Dad's wheelchair creaks behind me. The sound pulls my spine straight—muscle memory from years of his drunken disapproval. But it's the sobriety in his voice that cuts deeper.

"Cla- Clara?" Stephan coughs, spraying red. His eyes find mine, and for a second, I'm 15 again. Ice cream at the pier. Learning to shoot in his private range. Every father-daughter moment twisted into a knife he planned to bury in my back.

Each step brings me closer to the stranger wearing Stephan's face. It's a mess of purple and red, but those eyes—the ones I thought held kindness—they're the same. Just empty now. No mask left to hide behind.

"Fucking... bitch." The words bubble through blood. "Should've died with... your brother." His lips pull back from red-stained teeth. "Too stubborn. Just like Jake. Never knowing when to give up."

I stop. Something hot runs down my cheek. My hands shake as his words keep coming, a poison I can't unhear.

"Your fault." His chin drops to his chest, words slurring together. "All your fault. Wouldn't just... fucking... die. Had to keep digging. Had to keep pushing." A wet laugh. "Should've put a bullet in you right after Jake."

My fingers trace the knife scar on my forearm—his first lesson in self-defense. "Always be ready," he'd said. Now I understand why. He'd been preparing me for this moment, teaching me how to kill while planning my death.

"What... is going on?" Dad's voice breaks through the basement's silence.

I look over my shoulder, catching Mitch's gaze. His jaw tightens—the same expression he wore at Jake's funeral. When I look down, Dad's bloodshot eyes are clear for the first time in fourteen years. The bourbon haze is gone, replaced by something worse: understanding.

His hands shake as he takes in the scene—Stephan hanging like meat, blood dripping onto concrete, Leonid standing in shadows. Recognition hits him like a physical blow. His spine straightens in the wheelchair, muscles remembering the man he used to be.

"You..." Dad's trembling finger points at Leonid. Spittle flies from his lips as he lurches forward. "You killed Jake, you bas-bastard. My son. My only son!" The words slur together, muscle memory from a decade and a half of whiskey.

Leonid doesn't move. Doesn't blink. Just watches with that predator's stillness that makes my skin prickle.

"Boss, you're wrong." Mitch's voice carries the weight of five bullet holes and fourteen years of guilt. He tilts his head, drawing Dad's attention like he used to do when Jake and I were kids. "It wasn't Leonid." His eyebrows draw together, the scar above his left one pulling tight. "You've been lied to." His eyes flick to Ludis. "We all have."

"Play it." Ludis's command cuts through the air.

The recorder clicks. Static crackles. Then Stephan's voice fills the basement, and my lungs forget how to work.

"Jake had to die. He was too loyal, too soft. He'd ruin everything."

My knife handle bites into my palm. When did I grab it?

"Maxwell? That weak drunk? He's too busy drowning in his bottles to notice anything."

Dad's face crumples. Tears cut tracks through years of alcoholic bloat.

"I stood right in front of Clara at Jake's funeral, and she never even suspected."

The pearl handle warms against my skin—Stephan's sixteenth birthday gift. His voice keeps playing, but blood rushes in my ears, drowning out everything except the memory of him straightening my black dress at the funeral, wiping my tears with his monogrammed handkerchief.

"No..." Dad's whisper scrapes raw. "No. Jake... my boy..." His fingers dig into the wheelchair's arms until the metal creaks.

Stephan's laugh sprays blood across the concrete. "Oh, come on, Max." His words gurgle wet through torn flesh. "You really think you were a father? Jake was weak, just like you. Someone had to take control, and it sure as hell wasn't going to be you."

The pearl knife slips from my numb fingers. It hits the floor with a sound like breaking glass.

Something snaps inside my chest. My lungs burn. Can't breathe. Can't think. Tears blur everything except Stephan's bleeding face.

Leonid's boots scrape concrete. "Clara—"

I slam into him, fingers clawing for his shoulder holster. The Glock comes free before he can grab my wrist. The grip is cold. Familiar. Stephan taught me how to shoot with one just like it.

The first bullet takes out his right knee. His body jerks like a puppet, curses dissolving into wet choking sounds.

The second one explodes through his left thigh. Blood sprays.

The third shot punches into his shoulder. The recoil travels up my arm, but I barely feel it.

"Do it, bitch." Blood bubbles between Stephan's teeth. "Finish it."

The Glock shakes in my hands. Fourteen years of lies stare back at me through one swollen eye.

Metal scrapes behind me. Dad's grunt of effort. His feet hit the floor.

"Dad—"

He stands on trembling legs, gripping Mitch's Colt .45 in both hands. Fourteen years of bourbon weakness vanish as the barrel finds Stephan's mouth.

"Go to—" Stephan starts.

The Colt roars. The back of Stephan's head paints the wall red.

Sixty-Eight

Leonid

Two weeks later

The scotch burns going down. Two weeks. Fourteen fucking days of silence from the room upstairs.

"Still brooding, boss?" Maksim sprawls in the leather chair across from my desk, boots propped up on mahogany like he owns the place. "Or is this your new thing now? The whole dark and mysterious act?"

I don't bother looking up from the security feed. Third floor, east wing. Clara's door hasn't moved in six hours.

"*Blyat.*" Maksim's chair creaks as he leans forward. "You know what your problem is? You're thinking too much. Should've seen your face when Aleksei started screaming. The moment Ludis pulled out that skinning knife—" He whistles low. "Heart attack did us a favor, really. Saved on cleanup."

The crystal tumbler cracks in my grip. "*Zatknis.*"

"What? Too soon?" He grins, all teeth. "Come on, boss. Two weeks of watching you pace like a kicked puppy. It's painful. Even Golubka's stressed—tried to eat my favorite boots yesterday."

"Your boots were already garbage."

"They were Italian leather!"

"They were knockoffs." I set the cracked glass down. "And my python has better taste."

Maksim clutches his chest. "You wound me. Also, she's getting fat. Maybe ease up on the comfort rats?"

The security feed flickers. Movement. Clara's door opening a crack, then closing. My shoulders tighten.

"Ah." Maksim's voice shifts. "Still not eating?"

"Kayla leaves food. It disappears." Sometimes. When Elijah visits with drawings of him and that damn snake.

"Better than week one." His boots drop to the floor with a thud. "Remember when she threw that vase at your head? Good aim for someone running on grief and rage."

I trace the scar on my temple. "You found that funny."

"Found it hilarious. Also found it interesting." He pauses, studying me with unusual intensity. "You let her."

"What?"

"The vase. You saw it coming. Could've dodged." His eyes narrow. "But you didn't."

I reach for the scotch again, but Maksim's next words freeze my hand in mid-air.

"*Blyat*, never knew you had this side to you, boss." His voice carries an edge of wonder. "The great *Pakhan*, taking ceramic to the face because he thinks he deserves it."

"One more word—"

"What? You'll feed me to Golubka?" He snorts. "She likes me better, anyway. I don't make her fat."

The urge to punch his smirking face wars with the truth in his words. The same truth I've been drowning in scotch for two weeks.

Clara's sobs echo through the walls at night. Maxwell's words before he left—"Take care of her. Please."—hang like smoke in every room. The weight of Stephan's lies crushes what's left of her world while I sit here, uselessly watching security feeds.

"You did what needed doing." Maksim's hand lands on my shoulder, startling me. His usual sarcasm gone. "Truth's like surgery, boss. Hurts like hell, but infection's worse."

"When did you get wise, *mudak*?"

"Please." He rolls his eyes. "I've always been wise. You just never listen." He squeezes once, then steps back. "Now, about those knockoff boots..."

"Out."

"Fine, fine. But, boss?" He pauses at the door. "Maybe try talking to her instead of watching cameras all day? Just a thought."

The door clicks shut behind him. On screen, Clara's room stays dark and silent.

Maksim's words echo in my head. *Talk to her.*

As if it's that fucking simple.

As if I didn't force her to watch her father figure bleed out in my brother's torture room. As if I didn't destroy every last piece of her world in one night.

I open a drawer on my right. The black velvet box sits where it has for years, since I found it in Papa's safe after his death. Inside, the emerald catching light like it does in every photo of her—deep green against pale fingers, three carats set in vintage platinum. The only piece of my mother I have left.

In the photos, she's always smiling. Young, beautiful, wearing this ring like it was made for her. Papa said she chose it because it reminded her of the Siberian forests she left behind. Said she wanted her sons to give it to someone as fierce as she was.

I trace the box's edge. For years, I never understood why Papa kept it. Now, all I see are Clara's fingers, delicate but strong enough to pull a trigger. To swing a pipe at her enemies. To draw pictures with Elijah.

To teach *our* son how to be brave.

Blyat. I rake a hand across my stubble.Since when did I start thinking of us as a—?

I slam the drawer shut.

I reach for my phone instead. Need to check on Elijah. But before I can pull up Dmitry's number, my phone buzzes.

Dmitry's text shows Elijah beaming at the camera, cotton candy bigger than his head, brown eyes bright with sugar rush. Behind him, carnival lights blur against the gray December sky. Another photo loads—my son hanging off the merry-go-round horse, Dmitry's hand steady on his back.

> **Having fun, boss. Kid wants a stuffed snake. Says Golubka needs a friend.**

Cold rain pelts the windows, typical New Orleans winter. The grounds turn slick and dark while I sit here, watching an empty fucking doorway like some lovesick teenager. Three screens over, Clara's curtains shift. A pale hand pulls them shut against the dreary light.

One month. Christmas decorations mock me from every store window in the city. Maksim's already hung mistletoe in every doorway like the insufferable piece of shit he is.

I down the rest of my scotch, fingers hovering over the phone. "Tell the little terror no more sugar. What does he want for dinner? And Dmitry—if that snake is bigger than Golubka, you're feeding it."

Movement on the security feed catches my eye. Clara's door opens. My face inches closer to the screen, like some teenage security guard on his first night shift.

A ghostly figure emerges—Clara, wrapped in what looks like every blanket from her bed. Her hair's a wild mess, dark circles under her eyes, but she's moving. Actually moving.

Suka. Where the hell is she going?

My breath catches as she turns left. Then right. Then—

Blyat. She's heading straight for my office.

The scotch glass slips from my fingers.In thirty seconds, she'll be at that door.

Thud, thud, thud.

I don't get a chance to answer before the door swings open. Clara stands there, drowning in blankets, rings beneath her eyes making her look like an angry ghost.

She takes three steps forward, and my body tenses automatically—remembering the vase, the paperweight, that bronze statue from last week. My ribs still ache from the crystal ashtray she launched at me four days ago.

But her hands stay buried in the folds of fabric. Her eyes, red-rimmed but clear, bore into mine like she's searching for something. The blanket slips from one shoulder, revealing my missing black hoodie.

"We..." Her voice cracks from disuse. She swallows, chin lifting. "*I have to visit Jake.*"

Sixty-Nine

Leonid

The Bentley Continental GT motorcycle roars beneath us an hour later, and I'm questioning every life choice that led to this moment. Miles on Louisiana backroads in November, watching the last of the fall colors blur past us. *Suka*. The things I do for this woman.

Clara's arms tighten around my waist as I tilt us to a forty-degree angle, swerving past some *mudak* in a pickup who slammed his brakes without warning.

"*Pizda*!" I curse, the bike growling beneath me as we swerve past its bulk with inches to spare. But I can't help loving the feeling—her body molded against my back like she belongs there. Which isn't helping my concentration. *At all. Blyat.* The leather of my jacket creaks as she presses closer, seeking warmth, and my internal temperature spikes despite the bitter wind hitting my face.

"You could have taken the Range Rover," I mutter, knowing she can't hear me over the engine. But she'd insisted on the bike.

"It's faster," she'd said, those ice-blue eyes challenging me to argue. "And harder to follow." As if anyone would dare tail the *Pakhan* of the Kuznetsov Bratva.

The sun beats down on the empty road ahead. *Blyat*. No security detail, no shadows watching our backs—just us.

My phone vibrates. Ludis, probably.

Still can't believe we're actually working together now. That crazy *mudak's* proving useful—his web of informants running deeper than anyone suspected. Three of Stephan's old contacts were found this week alone. *Suka*. Hate to admit it, but my brother's sick methods get the job done.

The wind tears past us, loud and relentless, like the road itself is trying to peel everything unnecessary away. At this speed, there's no noise but the engine's growl and the howl of the wind. The handlebars vibrate under my grip as the motorbike surges forward, and for a moment, I let myself enjoy it. The freedom. The raw, unrestrained power. The way the open road stretches out ahead, nothing but asphalt and possibility.

In the side mirror, Clara's helmet catches the sun—a stark black curve resting against my shoulder. I can't see her eyes through the visor, but the way her fingers tighten in my jacket tells me enough. She's not just holding on—she's leaning in. Trusting me. It's a weight and a privilege, both too heavy and too light all at once. My gaze shifts to the small GPS screen on the dashboard.

The glowing line cuts through the map, the destination marked with a pin that feels more like a reminder than a waypoint.

Two more hours to Cypress Haven, the private cemetery nestled in the heart of Vermilion Parish. Old money land, where Louisiana's finest rest beneath ancient oaks draped in Spanish moss. Jake Caldwell's final resting place, far from the tourist-packed graveyards of New Orleans.

A sign for Abbeville passes in a blur. Small towns give way to sprawling sugarcane fields, dormant for winter. The morning fog lifts to reveal a sky so blue it burns. The November sun beats down, but at this speed, the wind still carries a bite that reminds me winter's coming. Not Siberian cold—I almost laugh at what my grandmother would say about Americans calling this "cold"—but enough to make me grateful for every place Clara's body presses against mine.

Blyat. Something's happening in my stomach. It's weird and unsettling, like I've just eaten bad caviar. Except this doesn't feel like poison—it feels... *light? Fluttery? Chyert.* If this is what people mean by butterflies, I'm throwing my masculinity into the nearest ditch.

The sun hangs low over Cypress Haven, spilling amber light across the still water. The lake stretches out before us, smooth as glass, broken only by the occasional ripple where a fish breaches.

The air smells of pine and wet earth, with a faint metallic tang that comes from the iron-rich soil. The trees around us are ancient, their gnarled branches twisting toward the evening sky like they've witnessed a thousand secrets.

I kill the bike's engine.

The sudden silence feels like a physical weight, broken only by the whisper of wind through ancient oaks. Clara's arms loosen from my waist, but she doesn't move away immediately. I feel her exhale against my back, a sound so fragile it makes my chest ache.

The gravel crunches beneath our boots as we dismount. I take a step toward the wrought-iron gate that marks the entrance to the cemetery, but Clara hesitates, standing beside the bike.

She's wearing a simple black turtleneck underneath, fitted enough for the ride but warm against the November chill. Her riding pants and boots complete the sleek silhouette as she stands frozen, eyes fixed on the family plot ahead.

"It's peaceful," I say, though the words feel inadequate. I don't expect a response, her gaze slipping past me to the headstones hidden among the trees.

The Caldwell family has money, but there's no ostentatious display here—just a simple plot of land edged by cedar trees and sloping gently down to the lake. I glance at her again, and when she finally starts moving, I fall into step beside her.

The tomb is near the water, a modest white stone set into the earth. Jake Caldwell. His name is etched in clean, bold letters, with his birth and death dates beneath. No flowery epitaph. A bronze photo frame embedded into the stone, holding an image of a man with a sharp jawline and an easy smile. His resemblance to Clara is undeniable. Same eyes. Same fire.

Clara drops to her knees before the stone. Her fingers trace each letter of his name with reverence, shoulders hunched against some invisible weight. I stay back, giving her this moment. Leaves scatter around the base of the tomb, a layer of earth dulling the white marble.

"It's dirty," she whispers, voice cracking.

Without a word, I kneel beside her. We work in silence, clearing away nature's attempts to reclaim the stone. The lake laps quietly behind us, marking time with each gentle wave.

"Thank you," she murmurs eventually, her voice so quiet I almost miss it.

I nod, still crouched, my fingers scraping against the rough edges of the stone. "It's nothing."

She stops, her hands resting on her thighs, and stares at the photo. Her lips press into a thin line, but her eyes betray her. The grief, the guilt—it's all there, simmering just beneath the surface.

"I hated the wrong person," she whispers, so faint I have to lean closer to catch it. "For so long... I blamed you. I blamed all of you." Her fingers clench into fists. "I thought... I thought if I hated you enough, I could stop missing him."

I swallow hard, the weight of her words settling like a stone in my chest. "Clara..."

She shakes her head, cutting me off. "I was wrong. I know that now. And I'm sorry. I'm so sorry, Jake." Her voice cracks, and she presses a hand to her mouth as the tears come. "It wasn't him. Leonid didn't do it. It was Stephan. It was always Stephan."

Her sobs are soft at first, but they build, and I can't take it anymore.

I move beside her, wrapping an arm around her shoulders. She stiffens for a moment, then crumbles, turning into me as the dam breaks. Her hands clutch at my jacket, and I hold her, my chin resting on top of her head.

"I'm sorry," I whisper into her hair. "For hurting you. For not stopping it sooner. For all of it." I pull her closer. "

"Shhh... *moya dorogaya*," I murmur softly, My dear. My everything.

Her fingers tighten on me, but she doesn't pull away. Her tears soak through my jacket, and I don't care. I'll take it all—her grief, her anger, her pain—if it means I can give her even a fraction of peace."He's not your killer. He's the father of your nephew."

Clara shifts slightly, pulling away just enough to face the grave again. Her voice cracks as she speaks, her words trembling in the still air. "Elijah has your smile, Jake," she says, her fingers brushing the edge of the stone. "Did you know that? The same deep dimple you had.

The one that made everyone think you weren't carrying the weight of the world."

She laughs bitterly, her breath hitching. "But you were, weren't you? You always were. And I didn't see it. I didn't see any of it. I hated all the wrong people." Her voice wavers, and she presses her palm flat against the marble. "I'm sorry. I'm so sorry, Jake."

My heart constricts at the mention of our son. At everything we lost to Stephan's lies. Everything we might still have.

I reach for her, my hands gentle as I turn her to face me fully. My thumb brushes a stray tear from her cheek, and for a moment, the world shrinks to just this—just us.

Clara pulls back slightly, tear-streaked face lifting to mine. The last light paints her skin gold, catches in her eyes like fire. The words escape before I can cage them:

"I love you, Clara Caldwell. Marry me."

Seventy

Clara

J ust act normal. Just act normal. *Just. Act. Normal.*

The garage door hums closed behind us, the sound echoing off gleaming black epoxy floors that reflect our distorted images like dark mirrors. My hands shake slightly as I fumble with my helmet strap.

Why won't it—Ugh.

The clasp is stuck, because of course it is, and I'm probably turning purple trying to—

"Let me." Leonid's voice rumbles close to my ear, and suddenly his hands are there, warm and steady against my neck. I freeze.

He loves me. He *loves* me.

He wants to marry me. *Marry me?* Is that even real?

Because that's insane. Absurd. Completely unhinged.

His fingers brush my skin as he works the clasp free, and I'm hyper-aware of every point of contact. Of his chest barely inches from mine. Of the way he smells like leather and wind and *him*.

The helmet comes loose, and I stumble back a step. My hair tumbles free, probably a mess, and I try to smooth it with trembling fingers. *Get it together, Clara.*

"Thank you," I manage, my voice embarrassingly breathy.

I sound like a teenager.

I *feel* like a teenager, all racing pulse and butterflies, which is ridiculous because I'm a grown woman and a mother and—

"Clara."

I realize I've been staring at the Ferrari 812 Superfast as if its matte red finish holds the secrets of the universe. Leonid hasn't moved. He's watching me with those chocolate eyes, intensity rolling off him in waves. My knees feel weak.

Traitors.

"You're thinking too loud," he says softly.

A laugh bubbles up, slightly hysterical. "Well, someone just dropped quite a bomb on me back there, so excuse me if I'm a little—" I wave my hands vaguely, nearly dropping my helmet.

He catches it easily, setting it on a nearby workbench without taking his eyes off me. The garage lights catch the planes of his face, throwing shadows that make him look carved from marble. It's unfair how beautiful he is. Unfair how his simple black t-shirt stretches across shoulders that could carry the weight of empires. Unfair how he's looking at me like—

"Like what?" His voice is rough.

Oh God, I said that out loud.

"I meant it," he says, taking a step closer. "Every word."

My back hits cool metal—the Bentley we just rode. I hadn't even realized I was retreating. Leonid stops, leaving space between us, but his presence fills every molecule of air.

"You can't just—" I swallow hard. "You can't just say things like that and expect me to function normally."

A smile tugs at his mouth, something soft and dangerous all at once. "Since when have we ever been normal?"

"That's not—" I press my palms against the car behind me, seeking anchor. "Fourteen years, Leonid. Fourteen years of thinking—and now everything's different, and you're looking at me like *that* and saying these things, and I can't *think* when you—"

He moves then, one hand bracing against the metal behind me, the other coming up to cup my face. "Then don't think."

His thumb traces my bottom lip, and my breath hitches. "Elijah—"

"Will have everything we didn't," he promises, his voice fierce with conviction. My fucking heart stops.

"A father who's present. A mother who isn't alone. A family that's whole." His forehead touches mine. "Let me give that to both of you."

God. Help. Me.

The tears come without warning, but before I can brush them away, his lips find mine. The kiss is gentle at first, a question more than a demand. But then I make a sound I'll deny later, my hands fisting in his shirt, and everything ignites. He kisses like he fights—all-consuming intensity and deadly precision. His hand slides into my hair, tilting my head back, deepening the angle until I'm gasping against his mouth.

When we break apart, we're both breathing hard. His eyes have gone dark, pupils blown wide, and I can feel his heart hammering where my palm rests against his chest.

"*Ya lyublyu tebya,*" he murmurs against my temple. "My fierce, beautiful Clara."

I let out a watery laugh, hiding my face against his neck. "I'm a mess."

"You're perfect." His arms tighten around me. "And you still haven't answered my question."

I pull back just enough to meet his gaze, seeing everything I feel reflected there—hope, fear, love so intense it burns.

"Yes," I whisper. "Yes, to all of it."

His smile—God, I want to spend forever making him smile like that.

Unable to resist any longer, I tug him back down, my fingers threading through his hair as our lips meet again. This kiss is different—hungry, desperate. His hands span my waist, pressing me harder against the Bentley's cool surface as he deepens the kiss. A sound escapes my throat, half gasp, half moan, and I feel his responding growl vibrate through his chest.

His mouth trails fire down my neck, and my head falls back, giving him better access.

"*Solnishka*," he murmurs against my skin, the Russian endearment making me shiver. His hands roam possessively, leaving trails of heat everywhere they touch.

"Leonid," I breathe, dizzy with want. The garage spins around us, the polished cars mere blurs in my peripheral vision. Nothing exists but this—his solid warmth pressing me into the car, his hands mapping my curves like he's memorizing every inch, his mouth reclaiming territory too long denied.

The last coherent thought I have is that the security cameras are probably getting quite a show before Leonid's lips find that sensitive spot behind my ear, and thinking becomes impossible.

His mouth claims mine again, hungrier this time, my fingers twisting through his dark hair as I pull him closer. The cool metal of the Bentley presses against my back, a stark contrast to the heat of his body against mine. His hands hold my waist, tightening as I gasp into the kiss.

"*Ty prekrasna*," he growls against my lips. One of his hands slides up my spine, tangling in my hair as he deepens the kiss. The other grips my hip, pulling me flush against him until there's no space left between us.

My hands explore the broad planes of his chest, feeling the powerful muscles flex beneath his shirt. When his mouth trails fire down my neck, I arch into him, a breathy moan escaping my throat. He responds by pressing me harder against the bike, his teeth grazing my pulse point.

"We should," I gasp as his lips find that sensitive spot behind my ear, "take this somewhere more private."

He pulls back just enough to meet my gaze, his eyes dark with desire. Without warning, he lifts me into his arms. "Your wish is my command, Mrs. Soon-to-be Kuznetsov."

Seventy-One

Clara

A week before Christmas

"You try to poison Lyonya; he deserves it sometimes. But now? You take care of each other. That's what family does."

Galina's weathered hands move with surprising grace, weaving the last sprig of baby's breath into my hair, her deft fingers threading it into the loose braid that cascades down my shoulder.

"What?" My thoughts, which had been circling like panicked birds, zoom back to the present.

She steps back, surveying her work with a critical eye.

"There. Beautiful. Like Russian snow princess."

I glance at the mirror. A gilded masterpiece, the antique frame gleaming faintly in the morning light spilling through the floor-to-ceiling windows. And there I am, staring back at myself, looking... like a bride.

A bride.

It hits me like an avalanche. I'm getting married today. To Leonid Kuznetsov. A man I never imagined standing next to at an altar, especially not now, just a week before Christmas.

I said yes.

He proposed to me in front of Jake's tomb.

The memory flashes vividly: His eyes were a burnished brown, like the sweet earth after a long summer rain that locked on mine, his words raw and trembling with something I hadn't dared believe until that moment.

"I love you, Clara Caldwell. Marry me."

And now here I am, in a bridal suite perched high in the Swiss Alps, preparing to marry a man who terrifies and fascinates me in equal measure. A man who has broken me, remade me, and somehow, despite all the chaos, made me believe in love again.

"You are thinking too much." Galina's voice snaps me out of my spiral. She leans down, her sharp gray eyes peering into mine through the mirror. "You'll wrinkle your pretty face. Lyonya will think you changed your mind."

I let out a shaky laugh. "Maybe I have."

Galina tuts and gently smacks my arm. "None of that. You love him. He loves you. Even if he's a big idiot sometimes." She picks up a pearl-encrusted hairpin and slides it into my braid. "Men are like *borscht*—messy, but worth the effort if you do it right."

The room around me feels like a dream. The soft crackle of the stone fireplace mixes with the faint hum of voices outside the door—Kayla, Elijah, and who knows who else. The scent of pine and lavender lingers in the air, grounding me amidst the chaos in my head.

"You don't understand," I whisper.

Galina pauses, her hands hovering near my hair. She meets my eyes in the mirror, her gaze softening. "I understand more than you think, *dorogaya*."

The words hang between us, weighted with truths neither of us needs to say.

"Do you think Jake would—" My voice cracks, and I have to swallow hard before finishing. "Do you think he'd think I look beautiful?"

Galina's hands settle on my shoulders, her grip firm but comforting.

"Jake would say you look like the queen of the world. And if Lyonya ever forgets that, Jake would haunt him."

A laugh bubbles out of me, mixing with a fresh wave of tears.

Galina brushes them away with the corner of her apron, clucking softly. "No crying. You'll ruin my masterpiece." She fusses with the edge of my braid one last time before stepping back. "Now, stand up and look at yourself properly."

I do as she says, smoothing down the lace of my dress as I rise. The gown is breathtaking—long-sleeved with intricate embroidery that catches the light, a perfect balance of elegance and simplicity. The fitted bodice gives way to a flowing skirt that pools around my feet like a cloud.

For the first time, I see it.

I look like a bride.

I look like someone who's survived, who's dared to hope, who's standing on the edge of something terrifying and wonderful all at once.

"You're ready," Galina declares.

I swallow the lump in my throat, my eyes drifting down to the ring on my finger. Leonid had slipped it on so confidently that night, as if it had always belonged there. The emerald glints faintly in the soft glow of the firelight, the diamonds catching the light with a subtle brilliance. I twist it absently, marveling at how something so beautiful, so intricate, could feel so heavy. Not in weight, but in meaning.

"My mother's," he'd said, his voice low, reverent. His fingers had lingered over mine for just a moment longer than necessary, his gaze steady and unguarded. "She'd love you. She always wanted someone who wasn't afraid of me. Someone strong enough to hold her place. You'd make her proud."

I'd nearly laughed—his mother would be proud of *me*? But the way he said it, with such quiet certainty, broke something open inside me. Tears had stung my eyes, unwelcome and unbidden, because I'd never had a mother to make proud. My own had died the day I was born, leaving behind only my father's bitterness and a hollow space in my chest I'd never been able to fill.

I press my thumb to the cool metal, feeling the slight snugness of the band around my finger. It fits perfectly, as though it had been waiting all these years for this moment, for me. A part of me hates how much that thought lingers, how it feels like something inside me wants to believe it.

A faint sound pulls me out of my thoughts.

Footsteps echo faintly outside the door. Then, three soft knocks. I barely manage to exhale before the door creaks open, and Kayla steps in.

She's dressed beautifully, but simply—a deep wine-red wool dress, warm and practical against the snowy chill outside. A soft cashmere shawl wraps around her shoulders, and her dark hair is pinned back in a sleek, no-nonsense bun. Her ever-present calm feels grounding in the chaos of my emotions.

Her eyes sweep over me with quiet approval before she speaks.

"*Señorita* Clara," she says, her voice soft but clear, touched by her lilting accent. "You look... *hermosa*. Truly."

"Thank you, Kayla," I whisper. The way her gaze lingers on me makes my heart ache in a way I'm not prepared for. Like how a mother might have looked at me, proud and loving. It's not the kind of look

I grew up knowing, and the unfamiliar warmth in it makes my chest feel tight.

Galina steps into view behind me, her sharp gray eyes catching the subtle tremble in my hands.

"None of that," she chides, her voice firm but fond as she places a steadying hand on my shoulder. "*Nyet, nyet*, no crying now."

I tilt my head back, blinking furiously to stop the tears from falling, my hands fanning my face in a desperate attempt at composure.

"Not crying," I insist, though my voice betrays me. "Just... blinking. A lot."

Kayla steps closer, her calm presence grounding me as she holds out a bouquet wrapped in ivory satin ribbon. It's breathtaking—ivory roses nestled against white ranunculus, their soft petals framed by sprigs of silver-gray eucalyptus and delicate accents of blue thistle. The arrangement feels both delicate and strong, like a perfect reflection of this moment.

"For you, *Señorita*," Kayla says. "You deserve to be happy."

I glance back at the mirror, taking in the reflection one last time. The gown flows around me like liquid light, its lace embroidery catching the soft glow of the fire. The veil drapes perfectly, and the bouquet feels steady in my hands.

For a moment, I let myself imagine Jake standing behind me, his teasing voice cutting through the quiet.

You look like a million bucks, bug.

I smile at the thought, the ache of missing him mingling with the strange peace settling over me.

Galina gives me a small nudge toward the door, her hands firm but kind. "Time to go, *moya lyubov*."

Kayla doesn't leave. She stands by the door, waiting with quiet patience as I take one last deep breath. My heart races, but it's steadier now, the weight of the bouquet grounding me.

I nod to my reflection, determination flickering in my chest. "I'm ready."

Seventy-Two

Leonid

"*Blayt*. Stop fucking fidgeting," Ludis growls. "You're making me dizzy."

"*Idi nahui*," I mutter, but my fingers still their restless tapping against my thigh. The golden Alexander McQueen cufflinks catch the late afternoon light, reminding me of the way Clara's eyes gleam when she's plotting my murder.

"The mighty *Pakhan*," Maksim snickers from my other side, his midnight blue Tom Ford perfectly tailored to his broad frame. "Terrified of a tiny American woman."

"I will shoot you both. Right here." The threat would carry more weight if my voice didn't crack slightly. A blast of Alpine wind cuts through the heated terrace, making the thousands of fairy lights above us dance. Through the glass panels, the Matterhorn looms like a silent guardian, its snow-capped peak painted gold by the setting sun.

"Seriously, boss, you look like you're about to puke," Maksim mutters from my left, his breath fogging in the cold.

"I'll hold the bucket," Ludis adds from my right, smirking. The gold band he's holding glints mockingly under the fairy lights as he flips it between his fingers—*my* wedding band for the ring exchange later. He's wearing a deep forest-green coat trimmed with a fur collar that makes him look like a Bond villain. Of course, he pulls it off. The bastard always does.

My focus shifts back, pulled unbidden to the far end of the aisle. The spot where Clara is supposed to walk out.

Instead, there's a flash of motion, small and lively. *Elijah.*

He's wearing a mini version of my suit—black, tailored, with a deep red boutonnière pinned to his lapel. His shoes gleam like he's polished them himself. He's clutching a basket, tiny fists gripping the handles like it's the most important job in the world.

My heart swells. It's not the nerves this time. It's...him. My son. The most handsome flower boy I've ever seen.

Next to him, Marina stands tall. At twelve, my niece's long legs and striking presence make her impossible to ignore. She's wrapped in a winter-white dress, fur-lined at the collar and sleeves, paired with boots meant for stomping through snowdrifts. Elijah says something to her, and whatever it is makes her laugh so hard she has to grab his shoulder for balance.

"She's taller than half your men," I mutter to Ludis.

"Her mother—" he stops. That smirk vanishes in a blink like a switch has been flipped. His eyes dart, unfocused for a moment, his jaw clenched tight as if he's holding back a thousand memories. Then, in a heartbeat, he coughs—a single bark, raw and rough—and his face slides back into the mask of the boss. Whatever window opened, he slams it shut so fast it's almost like it never cracked.

I glance at him, arching a brow. "Never thought I'd hear you admit she didn't get it all from you."

"She's got my brains," he says, straight-faced.

I laugh, shaking my head. Who would've guessed? Ludis Kuznetsov, the cold, calculated son of a bitch I've spent years fighting, turns out to be a sentimental bastard. Brains and beauty—he's practically bragging about his daughter like a proud dad at a school recital.

The heater hums louder as the chill creeps in, but no one complains. The wedding is small, intimate—a world away from the grand affairs we're used to. That's the point. Fewer eyes, fewer risks. Just the people who matter.

Victor Montclair sits near the front, his wife Juliette tucked against his side like she belongs there. One of his hands rests on her back, his fingers brushing the fur collar of her coat. The other holds his daughter's hand—a casual grip, like it's second nature. Alix leans toward him, her head tipped slightly as she whispers something to her brother. Mathis huffs in response, clutching the notebook in his lap a little tighter, but Victor's calm doesn't waver. He adjusts Mathis's scarf with steady hands, murmuring something low that makes the boy nod, his shoulders easing.

It's not a display. Victor isn't performing for anyone. It's just him, effortlessly keeping his family anchored, as though no empire or enemy could ever pull them apart.

I swallow hard, my throat tightening against the sharp air. The wind cuts through the terrace heaters, biting, but it's not the cold that gets to me. It's the way Victor moves—how he leans toward Juliette when she murmurs something, the faint smile tugging at his lips, the way his hand lingers on her shoulder for a moment too long. His son looks up at him like he's unshakable. His daughter, tall and confident, holds his hand like she's never doubted it'll be there.

It hits me in a way I didn't expect. I, Leonid Kuznetsov, am going to be a husband. A *husband*. And—God help me—it's something I never thought I'd want. Not until now. Not until Clara.

The thought sneaks in, uninvited but impossible to ignore. Could I have this? Could I *be* this? A husband. A father. The kind who isn't just feared but trusted. Needed.

For the first time in my life, the idea of losing something scares me more than anything I've ever taken.

I drag my gaze from Victor and his perfect, unshakeable family and scan the terrace, hoping the distraction will steady the unrelenting pounding in my chest. It doesn't.

Maxwell Caldwell sits off to the side in a wheelchair, his once hard and bitter gaze now softened by something heavier—regret. His hands rest lightly on the blanket covering his lap, no longer clutching his ever-present flask. Instead, they tremble slightly, unsteady but unburdened, as if the truth he's learned has stripped away years of anger he can no longer afford to carry.

Mitch stands behind him, steadying the wheelchair with a calm patience that feels out of place in the towering man's imposing frame. For all his bulk and scars, Mitch moves carefully, almost gently, as though he understands the weight Maxwell is trying to bear. When Maxwell glances toward the aisle, there's no resentment in his expression—only a quiet ache and a flicker of determination.

Behind him, Mitch pushes the wheelchair with surprising gentleness for someone of his size. Ludis's hulking underboss, towering even over Dmitry, doesn't need to loom to command attention. Yet there's an ease in the way Mitch handles Maxwell now, as if he understands that this fragile man has already fought his toughest battles—against himself.

And then there's Mysh—*Mouse*. The irony of that nickname still gets me. A walking mountain of a man, with shoulders that could double as a fortress wall, pacing near the musicians as if one of the violinists might be carrying a bomb. His fur-lined coat flares with every heavy step, making him look like a pissed-off grizzly rather than the rodent his name suggests. Even the choir sneaks wary glances at him, though Mysh seems oblivious, too focused on keeping an eye on Ludis and me.

Dmitry stands farther back, by the choir, dressed in a sharp black coat but somehow managing to look like he'd rather be anywhere else. I catch his eyes as he scans the terrace. He gives a small nod, the silent *all clear* that eases some of the tension coiled in my spine.

Kayla flits around the edge of the crowd, adjusting details that don't need adjusting—fluffing ribbons, repositioning candles, and whispering orders to Galina and Ivan, who shuffle nervously, trying to keep up.

The choir hums softly as they tune up, their voices blending with the faint plucking of strings from the musicians. The soft sounds swirl through the terrace, mingling with the crackling of the fire pits and the occasional gust of icy wind. The fairy lights strung above us sway with each breeze, throwing golden flecks across the glass panels framing the Matterhorn.

I flex my fingers, restless, and glance down at the band Ludis is still flipping between his fingers like a damn coin.

"Are you done with that?"

He grins, tossing the ring into the air and catching it without breaking stride. "Not yet."

The urge to punch him in the face grows stronger by the second, but I resist. Barely. Instead, I glance toward the aisle, the place where Clara will walk out. The thought makes my pulse spike, and I shift in my seat, trying to focus on anything but that.

It doesn't work.

The live choir begins singing, their voices rising in perfect harmony with the strings. The melody cuts through the icy air, rich and vibrant, making the crowd fall silent. The faint murmurs fade, replaced by the music and the distant crunch of snow under someone's boots.

I flick my gaze upward—and there she is.

Clara.

My heart stops.

She stands at the far end of the aisle, wrapped in white and shimmering faintly in the light. Her shoulders are bare beneath a soft fur stole, her dark hair pinned up to reveal her neck. The dress is simple, elegant, clinging to her like it was made for her alone. The gold embroidery at the hem glints faintly as she takes her first step forward.

Her eyes find mine, and suddenly, the cold is gone. The wind, the choir, the crowd—everything fades until there's only her.

God help me, I've never wanted anything more.

My wife. Mrs. Kuznetsov.

Epilogue

Leonid

A Kuznetsov Christmas

The smell of turkey hits me the moment I step into the kitchen. One week since our wedding in the Alps, and my house looks like Christmas threw up everywhere. Tinsel, lights, and enough decorations to make the Rockefeller Center jealous. Never thought I'd see the day when the Kuznetsov mansion would look like a Hallmark movie set.

"*Bozhe moy,*" Maksim groans from his perch on the counter, watching Dmitry baste what has to be the biggest turkey I've ever seen. "This is so... American. Next thing you know, we'll be singing carols and wearing matching sweaters."

"We are wearing matching sweaters," I point out, tugging at the red monstrosity Clara insisted on. "And you're still here because...?"

"Where else would I go?" He grins, swiping a cookie from the cooling rack. "Besides, someone needs to document the mighty *Pakhan's* first American Christmas."

Clara whirls around, flour dusting her cheek, brandishing a wooden spoon. "Touch another cookie, and you'll be celebrating New Year's in the hospital."

"Such violence," Maksim clutches his chest dramatically. "And here I thought Kayla was the scary one. Speaking of—"

"She's in California with her family," Clara cuts him off, her expression softening slightly. "Everyone deserves to be home for Christmas."

Home.

The word hits differently now. A week ago, this place was just a house. Secure. Fortified. Functional. Now there are stockings hanging from the fireplace, each hand-picked by Elijah. Even Pavel the peacock has a tiny one.

A piercing screech from outside makes Maksim jump, nearly dropping his stolen cookie.

"Pavel!" Elijah's voice carries from the garden. "Papa! Papa, come quick!"

Papa.

My heart still stops every time he says it. Started three days ago, over breakfast. I'd been checking security reports on my phone when he'd simply said, "Papa, can you pass the syrup?" Like he hadn't just demolished every wall I'd ever built. I'd had to leave the room, blame it on an urgent call.

Because Leonid fucking Kuznetsov doesn't cry over a word.

I find him pressed against the garden doors, nose leaving smudges on the glass. "The turkey must have been Pavel's friend," he says solemnly, eyes wide with concern. "He sounds so sad."

Something in my chest cracks open.

I scoop him up, settling him on my hip with practiced ease now. "Want to know a secret, *malish*?" I press a kiss to his curls. "Pavel's not sad. He's excited. He's never had so many people to show off for at Christmas."

"Really?" He pulls back, studying my face with that intense focus he gets sometimes. Pure Clara.

"Really." I catch my wife's reflection in the glass, watching us. Her eyes are suspiciously bright, but before I can comment, she blinks rapidly and turns back to her baking.

"Marina!" Elijah suddenly squirms in my arms, pointing outside where my niece is leading our resident giant around the garden. "Uncle Mysh, what's on your head?"

Mysh—all six-foot-eight of lethal muscle—adjusts his reindeer antlers with dignity. "Your cousin is very persuasive," he rumbles, while Marina beams up at him.

"Papa, can I go show Marina the new swing?" Elijah asks, already wiggling to get down.

I set Elijah down, watching him race out to his cousin. Ludis steps aside to let the children pass, his hand automatically steadying Marina as she bounds past. The softness in his expression as he watches her is still jarring to see on my twin's face.

"You're going soft, boss," Maksim murmurs next to me, but there's no bite in it. He's watching the children too, something wistful in his expression.

"Says the man who spent three hours setting up the Christmas tree because 'it had to be perfect for the little prince,'" I reply drily.

Maksim snorts, his gaze still lingering on the kids. "Someone had to step in. You'd have just thrown lights on it and called it done."

Before I can retort, a loud *clang* echoes from the kitchen. The unmistakable crash of pans hitting the floor.

"Sounds like your queen is calling," he teases, deftly pivoting the conversation away from himself.

In the kitchen, Clara stands at the center, sleeves rolled up, with Dmitry at her side, the two of them a surprisingly synchronized team.

"No, Galina," Clara says, her tone calm but firm as she intercepts the older woman with a ladle mid-step. "I've got it under control. Why don't you check on the table instead?"

Galina hesitates, clearly wanting to protest, but Clara's faint smile softens the command. "Trust me," she adds quietly. "We'll be fine."

Galina relents, backing away with a faint grumble, and Dmitry smirks as he balances a massive tray of ingredients on one arm.

"You run a tight ship," he remarks, glancing at Clara as he adjusts a cutting board.

"Someone has to," she replies, brushing flour off her hands. Her eyes flick briefly toward the doorway, where Maksim and I linger, before she calls out, "If you're going to hover, make yourselves useful—or leave."

Maksim nudges me, already retreating with a mock salute. "Told you. Line of fire."

I don't move right away.

I stand by the door frame, looking at My *zhyeh-NA*. my *wife*.

She's beautiful, I watch her as she blows a strand of her hair from her face, smudging her cheek with a streak of flour as she pushes a tray toward Dmitry.

The kitchen light catches on the faint pink flush at her temples, the way her lips press together in concentration as she shifts her focus to the stovetop.

She's perfect. Even in the chaos, she looks... radiant.

She glances up suddenly, and her blue eyes lock with mine. Her expression softens, a smile tugging at her lips. It's quick, almost shy, but enough to make me weak on my fucking knee.

I can't help the smile tugging at my own lips as Elijah's voice cuts through the moment. "Papa! Grandpa is here! And he's got me a *big* present!"

Elijah barrels toward me, grabbing my hand and pulling with all the determination his little body can muster. "Come on! You have to see!"

He drags me into the dining room, where Maxwell Caldwell stands with Mitch at his side. Maxwell looks smaller now, the weight of years etched into his hunched shoulders, but there's something steady in the way he holds himself.

I stop in front of him, meeting his wary eyes. For a moment, neither of us moves, the space between us thick with unspoken words. Then, slowly, I step forward and wrap an arm around him in a firm hug.

Maxwell stiffens, caught off guard, but after a beat, I feel his body soften. He hesitates, then lifts his hand and pats my shoulder—a small but deliberate gesture. Forgiveness. Acceptance.

Elijah bounces on his heels beside us, oblivious to the gravity of the moment. "Papa, look! Grandpa brought me *this!*" He hoists a brightly wrapped box, his excitement breaking the tension like a warm breeze.

In the background, Galina fusses over the place settings, her hands adjusting already-perfect linens while Ivan lingers near the door, his sharp gaze scanning the room.

I glance around, taking it all in. The long table stretches beneath crystal chandeliers, their soft light casting a golden glow over evergreen centerpieces and polished silverware. It's strange, seeing them all here. Together.

Family. The word still feels foreign on my tongue, but tonight, it feels just right.

Later, after too much food and several bottles of wine, Maxwell
clears his throat. The conversation dies down, and something in his
expression makes me reach for Clara's hand under the table.

"I've never been good at this," he starts, his voice rough. "Being a
father. Making the right choices. But Clara—" He looks at my wife,
and I feel her grip tighten. "You've always had an Onyx Heart. Strong.
Unbreakable. Even when I wasn't there to see it."

Clara's breath hitches, and I pull her closer, feeling her tremble
against my side. Around us, our mismatched family—Russian and
American, blood and chosen—sits in understanding silence.

"To the Onyx Heart," Ludis raises his glass, and for once, there's no
trace of sarcasm in his voice.

"To *seem-YA,* family." I add, and I mean it.

The End

Hooked on Mafia heat? I've got you covered.

Dive into *Silken Chains*, Book 1 of the *Morozov Bratva Series*—a story
guaranteed to grip you from the very first page. Don't miss your next
obsession!

Grab it now for just 99¢ or read free with Kindle Unlimited.

https://mybook.to/nUn59te

Grab it now for just 99¢ or read free with Kindle Unlimited.

https://mybook.to/nUn59te

After the Chaos: A Kuznetsov Bratva Bonus

Extended Epilogue

Read Bonus Epilogue for an exclusive glimpse three years into the future!

https://dl.bookfunnel.com/y1xqk6g6vt

(Hint: A Christmas morning that starts naughty, with Clara's growing belly and Leonid's hands everywhere—before the chaos of presents and family takes over!)

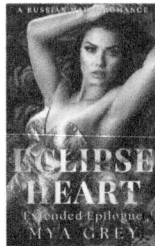

Your Review

Hey Lovers,

If you've finished *Eclipse Heart* (Book 2 of the *Kuznetsov Bratva Series*), I'd love to hear how it made you feel.

Did my story make you laugh, cry, swoon, or stay up way too late promising "just one more chapter"? If so, we have a small request that will make our hearts as warm as a fresh cup of coffee (or as thrilling as a dramatic plot twist):

I'm so curious to know which parts stuck with you the most!

Leave a review! AMAZON

https://www.amazon.com/product-review/B0DLNN58QT

P.s: Your words—whether they're a simple "loved it" or a passionate breakdown of your favorite moments—mean the world. They not only help others find this book but also give us authors the happy tears we live for (and maybe fuel for that next epic love scene).

XOXO,

Mya

—⊖✦⊖—

Want more steamy mafia romance?
Follow my author page to stay in the loop!

AMAZON

https://amzn.to/2YzmH3U

GOODREADS

https://www.goodreads.com/book/show/53192966-a-billionaire-s-fi

rst-love

BOOKBUB

https://www.bookbub.com/authors/mya-grey-c6b5463a-f6c8-49e7

-a0ea-1ce28f496f76

Let's keep the conversation going! Follow me on social media for more

fun and engaging content.

FACEBOOK

https://www.facebook.com/author.myagrey/

YOUTUBE

https://youtu.be/XEQ1ZAJSwGs

TIKTOK

https://www.tiktok.com/@myagreywriteslove?is_from_webapp=1

&sender_device=pc

.

Printed in Great Britain
by Amazon